THE
NIGHT
IT
ENDED

KATIE GARNER

mira

Recycling programs
for this product may
not exist in your area.

ISBN-13: 978-0-7783-3445-3

The Night It Ended

For questions and comments about the quality of this book, please contact us at
CustomerService@Harlequin.com.

Mira
22 Adelaide St. West, 41st Floor
Toronto, Ontario M5H 4E3, Canada
BookClubbish.com

Printed in U.S.A.

Praise for *The Night It Ended*

"*The Night It Ended* is a dark gothic murder investigation at a mysterious school for troubled girls, but don't judge, don't assume, don't try to figure it out—just let Garner's masterful sleight of hand carry you away through the gasp-worthy twists and turns. Do not miss this!"

—Hank Phillippi Ryan, *USA TODAY* bestselling author of *The House Guest*

"A gorgeously atmospheric dark academic thriller set at a snowy boarding school so vividly rendered you can practically feel the frost freezing your blood. Garner centers female rage in the most delicious and page-turning of ways, plunging readers into a world where women's machinations, conspiracies, anger, and even violence rule all."

—Ashley Winstead, author of *The Last Housewife*

"*The Night It Ended* is dark, twisted, and utterly compelling. You won't know who or what to believe and the creepy location will have you looking over your shoulder more than once. One heck of a debut with an ending that left me speechless."

—Hannah Mary McKinnon, internationally bestselling author of *Never Coming Home*

"Disarmingly sensory, with plot twists that are sure to give readers whiplash, Garner has done a phenomenal job of giving us just enough information to think we know where the story is going, only to pull the rug out from under us—over and over again. A nail-bitingly spectacular debut!"

—Amanda Jayatissa, author of *You're Invited*

"Compulsively readable. Brilliant use of the unreliable narrator. I enjoyed the police interviews interwoven with the present-day mystery. It kept me on my toes. And that last plot twist...amazing. I did not see it coming."

—Amber Garza, author of *When I Was You*

"Katie Garner's debut novel is a chilly, twisty ride—think dark academia meets Gillian Flynn. *The Night It Ended* is both a brooding Gothic mystery set at a boarding school for wayward girls and a jittery domestic thriller and just when you think you've got a handle on the story, Garner pulls the rug out from under you. I couldn't put it down."

—Halley Sutton, author of *The Lady Upstairs*

For Graham

THE NIGHT IT ENDED

THE YEAR BEFORE

FILE NAME: JPN00.012.00030923.mp3

[00:00:00]

INT: Are you ready to begin? Remember, I'm on your side to try to get to the bottom of this. I want to prove you're innocent in all this, okay?

RES: [inaudible] I understand.

INT: … Great. So, uh, I'm going to ask you simple, easy questions. Just take your time. We'll go nice and easy.

RES: Okay.

INT: First, uh, please state your name.

RES: My name is [redacted].

INT: And I'm [redacted], working on behalf of the [redacted] Police Department. Please remember, no matter what we discuss, that I am on your side. Okay?

RES: Okay.

INT: So, let's get started. Today is Monday, December 13, 2021. The time is 0-4-0-3-P-M. Okay, um, [redacted], let's start from the beginning. Let's start with how you met [redacted].

RES: How I met him?

[00:01:35]

INT: Yes, just walk me through. When did you meet? How?

RES: [inaudible] We met about…maybe, six months ago.

INT: And what was your relationship, when you first met [redacted], before it progressed?

RES: We—he was…my husband is an attorney. Um, he works a lot. We were happy.

INT: [redacted], this works best if you're honest with me. Okay? Look at me, hey, I need you to be honest with me. I know it's painful. I know. I do. But you have to trust me. You have to promise me you will be honest and you will trust me.

RES: Okay. Yeah. I'll be honest. I promise.

Friday, December 16

1

I'm speeding home when the phone rings, persistent and angry, demanding to be heard. I know I should answer it, even though I want nothing more than to throw it out the window. I could let the call slide into voice mail, delete it, never hear the voice on the other side.

But I can't.

I jerk to the side of the icy road to a chorus of blaring horns, dig the phone out from the cavernous tote bag resting on the passenger seat beside me. The phone is sleek and black, brand-new—opposite of the cracked, chunky white one I'm used to shoving in my back pocket.

A sweet little chime and the ringing ends.

1 new voice mail.

Quickly, I glance in the side mirror. Car exhaust melts away into the morning winter sky. Nothing is behind me, nothing but air. I exhale a deep sigh of relief, press the phone to my ear.

"H-hi, this message is for Dr. Madeline Pine—"

A siren wails in the distance. The phone slips through my fingers, lands mutely in my lap. A knot swells in my throat. I glance in the side mirror again, feel my heart pound, each breath shrinking to tiny gasps. The sirens near. An emergency vehicle speeds past.

It's only an ambulance.

My body wilts. I take a deep breath. *In. Out.* The knot in my throat loosens.

I hate the person I've become. I've never been this nervous, this afraid, anxiety and fear clinging to my every move. I wish I could escape—step into someone else's life, if only for a moment.

Just twelve short months ago everything was different. *I* was different. Any other December, I would've been home, prepping for the holidays, shopping online for last-minute deals on things none of us needed. My husband, Dave, would be staying too late at work, his dinner wrapped in a blanket of aluminum foil, kept warm on the stove. My teenage daughter, Izzi, would be upstairs in her room, scrolling noiselessly through her phone, feet kicked up on the bed behind her.

The house would've hummed with the steady softness of disjointed home life, but instead here I am, lurched to the side of the road, the air frigid in the tiny cabin of my car, listening to a voice mail I never thought I'd hear.

I replay the message:

"H-hi, this message is for Dr. Madeline Pine. If you get this, I'm Matthew Reyes, a private investigator working on behalf of a family. Listen, I was hoping you could please call me back at this number, I—I'd really appreciate it. We have a sixteen-year-old female who died on school property. The police believe it's an accident, but the mother hired me to be sure. The girl was found at the bottom of a hill. No witnesses.

I thought you might be able to help—given your expertise. Please call me back. Thanks."

I repeat his words in my head. *The girl was found at the bottom of a hill*—I can picture it, picture her. She's there, fallen sideways, her body splashed across the woodland floor. Moss and stones, skin and blood, leaves and twigs. I don't know her, but I don't have to. I already feel as if she were mine.

The man who left the voice mail, Matthew Reyes, has a voice both gravelly and weary, and I know what he wants the moment he mentions the school. Police often believe they can demand anything they want and get it immediately—even psychological evaluations—but it takes time to gain trust from strangers, and even more time to tease out the truth. Especially from teenage girls.

I start weighing my options. I'm not sure I'm capable of this, of anything. Especially after last year…especially after what just happened in that too-hot office during this morning's disastrous therapy session.

My face flushes at the memory of the woman who'd been sitting cross-legged in front of me. Her beautiful face. Her pink silk shirt blurring out of focus. Her condescending tone—as though the therapy sessions weren't all for her benefit to begin with.

That's what I have to remind myself. That's what I have to hold on to. They're for *her*. Not me. *I'm* the one who's fine. I should be taking comfort in that, taking comfort in the fact that I never have to see her beautiful face again, never have to be reminded of—

It's over. I didn't have a choice before. Now I do. I have lots of choices. An avalanche of choices. My life before today was preprogrammed for me. Not anymore. I fixed it.

Tears slip down my cheeks. I bite them back, strangle the

phone in my lap, squeeze it so tight I wonder how it fails to snap in two. *Choices. Possibilities.*

My mind whirls as I punch the gas, merge into traffic, race home. I run inside, slam the door, bolt the lock. Gazing around my gloom-infested house, I shrivel back as wind blows branches of a nearby tree, scraping the side of the house like fingernails.

Peering at the bulging paper bag of prescriptions on the kitchen island, my eyes prick with tears. My glasses fog. I take them off, rub the lenses clean on my turtleneck.

After so many months, the pills should be working. I should stop taking them altogether. Just throw them all in the toilet, flush them down, watch them whirl around the porcelain bowl.

I think of words my daughter, Izzi, said to me: *Mom, please just stop.*

Stop.

I don't know the person I've become, too empty, too full, all at once. I need to change. I want to be different. Every day, I think of ways I can be. It can still happen. I'm free now. I have choices now, possibilities. Maybe it's never too late to change everything. Maybe I just need to escape.

Besides, wiggle room is all it takes for a snake to get out of its skin.

The phone rings again. I snuff the urge to hurl it across the room before glancing at the screen. It's the same number as before. The same number as the voice mail. I hold my breath and answer.

"Hello?"

"Hello—is this Dr. Madeline Pine?"

"Um—yes. It is." My heart thuds. "Who's this?"

A sigh of relief, deep and heavy, into the phone. "This is private investigator Matthew Reyes. Thank you so much for answering, Dr. Pine. I—I know it's a chaotic time of year and you're probably busy with family but...would you be able to make a trip up to Iron Hill?"

"I—I don't know where that is."

"It's about two hours north of Poughkeepsie. Upstate New York."

"Right, okay." *Far. Very far.* Too far for my ailing car to make it. I know I should just buy a new one, but I can't. My husband Dave always said the color perfectly matched my eyes. Now I can't even remember the last time we looked at each other.

"So, are you busy this weekend?" Reyes asks, then pauses. "I mean, you're sure you don't mind ditching your family right before the holidays?"

"When you put it that way, it sounds horrible." *Awkward laugh.* "But, um, my husband and daughter aren't home now, anyway—they've gone away to visit my in-laws."

"You have no idea how grateful I'd be if you could make it," he says, sounding hopeful. I don't know what he looks like, but I can imagine him smiling. "I mean, I've been calling around to different psychologists all day, and—well, it should only be for a couple of days. You'd definitely be back by Christmas, *the latest.*"

I wince, feel a surge of sorrow. I'm too embarrassed to admit that Dave and Izzi have no intention of spending the holidays with me this year. It's what I deserve after what I did.

"I'm sorry," I say, "please refresh my memory. Have we ever met? You said you're a private investigator hired by the victim's—er, the deceased's—family?"

"Yes, I mean, we haven't met, but I read about the work you did on the Strum case last year. I believe one of the victims was around the same age as our current victim. And I pulled up your book online—*Dark Side: A Psychological Portrait of the*

Criminal Female Mind. You specialize in women. Just so happens the case is at an all-girls boarding school."

My stomach clenches. *Focus. Deep breath*. I shift my gaze to the calendar hanging in the kitchen. I don't even know why I bother to keep one anymore. I have the same schedule now, week in, week out. Before, the month of December would've been filled with holiday office parties, Izzi's end-of-year school activities, Dave's plans for winter break, which I'd always beg him to change.

I glance up. Friday, December 16. This morning's therapy session slashes across my mind again. I see her face. Blank, empty. Her lips begin to curl around a word. I see myself in the reflection of her eyes. I'm close. Closer. I swallow hard.

"The, um, the students don't go home for the holidays?" I ask, slumping down to the floor.

"Winter break is Saturday, the tenth to New Year's. A few students stayed behind." Reyes pauses. "The students who either couldn't travel for various reasons or chose not to go home."

I lean the back of my head against the wall.

Reyes continues. "The school is asking me to wrap up my investigation before students and staff return January 2."

"Okay..."

He senses my discomfort, keeps talking. "Please. *Please* say yes. You mentioned you have a daughter. How would you feel if it were her?" he asks. "If she was found dead, you'd want closure, right? To be sure everything was done by the book and no stone was left unturned."

My stomach flips. "Of course I would."

"So, please. Please say you'll help."

I think of my daughter, Izzi, the lengths I'd go to if she was found at the bottom of a hill. Even if it was an accident, I'd want to know why. I'd want to know how she got there.

If she was alone. Afraid. Or if someone else was responsible. I'd want to know. I'd find them, I'd—

"I don't know if I can do this," I confess.

I shut my eyes, see *her* face again, legs crossed, sitting prim in that too-hot office, the heat blasting, the furniture too big for the tiny space. I tug at the neck of my sweater, suddenly tight, see my reflection in her eyes—close, so close.

No. Stop. I suck up a big breath, blow it all out.

"I don't know if you're aware, but after that case last year—" My voice cracks.

"The Strum case?" A note of curiosity in Reyes's question.

"Yeah. Since then, things have been difficult. I ended up taking some time off—"

"I—I wasn't aware. I'm sorry."

"It's fine. It just—it makes cases like this difficult."

"Oh—"

"But before I say yes or no, can you give me an overview? What, exactly, I'll be doing when I get there? I want to be sure I know what I'm stepping into."

Reyes lets out a breath. "Yeah—yes, of course," he says, a hint of desperation in his voice. "Well, it happened at a private, all-girls boarding school called Shadow Hunt Hall. They have a very small student body on a very large campus. It's densely wooded and incredibly isolated. It's one of those 'back-to-nature, no technology on campus' sort of places. The girls are mostly... I guess the best word for it is—troubled?"

"Isn't that the best kind of girl?"

"Uh, here," he says, ignoring my attempt at a joke. "I'll send you some info."

I glance at the screen, see he's texted a link to the school's website. I tap it open, swipe down the page. The school is ancient. Giant and stone, with iron gates and actual turrets, like a possessed fairy-tale castle. The curriculum looks interesting.

Definitely nontraditional. It's all music and arts and dance. I skim the mission statement:

We believe in a holistic, individual approach to learning and rehabilitation, focusing on a curriculum centered on nature, group trust, and a healthy mind-body connection.

Code words for no junk food or internet.

Reyes waits patiently on the other end as I peruse the site. I click on the Tuition & Financial Aid page and flinch. A single term is more than twice the down payment we put on the house.

"You there? Dr. Pine?"

I lick my lips. "I'm here."

He pauses. "I'm having trouble getting any of the students to even talk to me," he admits. "That's why I need you."

I think of Izzi, chewing on her fingernails, avoiding eye contact when I ask how her day went. Ever since she started high school it's been all one-word answers—*good, fine*—before she'd bound upstairs, not to be seen again until dinner.

So I can't imagine how the girls at this boarding school would react to a male private investigator showing up out of nowhere, prodding them with questions right after their classmate died. No doubt they'd recoil, want nothing to do with him.

"Okay... I'll help you," I whisper.

I have choices. An avalanche of choices. I'm free.

Finally, it's time to escape.

"Just one more question, then I'm all yours," I say.

"Sure, you can ask me anything."

"You mentioned in your voice mail how the police believe the girl's death was an accident."

"Right."

"Do you have any reason to believe her death *wasn't* an accident? You said her mother isn't so sure—do you agree with her?"

Reyes pauses. In the background, a car engine starts. "Let's just say there are some things that don't add up. I'll explain more when you get here, but there is something I should make you aware of…" He trails off.

"What?"

"The school has been locked down for the remainder of winter break. No one in. No one out."

"Except you," I say.

"Except me."

"Security is a good thing when you believe there might have been a murder," I say.

"I never said it was a murder."

I hesitate, gulp, crawl up from the floor.

"Right, sorry."

Reyes pauses. I can practically hear his mind working. "Don't be," he says quietly. "Because I think you're right."

"What?"

"I can't explain it all now, but something happened here," he says. "Something awful. And if this student *was* murdered— her killer is still inside the school."

2

The tracks bend, pushing me forward through the mountains, snow burning white, sky steeped a mean blue. The flash of a garden. A whip of slick black road. Gray curtains zoom by, a blur of tangled trees. I've never been this far north. It's unknown, uncharted, new and terrifying, and all I can think about is how big a mistake I might've made.

I had a feeling I'd end up on the train. The tires on my car have been bald for months. Not the best situation to be in during the dead of winter when you have to trudge up an icy mountain in the middle of nowhere. I wasn't even going to attempt it.

Car maintenance is always something Dave does. He has a little notepad on his phone where he jots down oil changes and mileage and when he needs to change to the winter tires. I never kept up with it. He's extraordinarily proficient in daily minutiae, and I can never fill his shoes. My mind is preoccupied with other things.

If I had to do it all over again, I wouldn't choose to leave the week before a major holiday. The train is packed full of people on their way to visit relatives, their voices hushed as they gossip about demanding bosses and other people's marriages. Shopping bags bursting with presents swell into the aisle, wrapping paper crunching like broken glass.

I lean against the icy window, sweater slipping off my shoulder, eyeglasses tumbling down my nose. I shut my eyes, hoping the train can lull me to sleep, but a knock into my shoulder has them popping back open. A boy hovers beside me, a pout adorning his chubby face.

His mom places a hand on the top of his head, mouths a quick *I'm sorry*, as I bend down to pick up his fallen superhero toy.

"What do you tell the nice lady?" the mom prompts.

"Thank you, nice lady."

"You're welcome," I mumble, handing him the toy. The mom gives me a wobbly smile.

Reaching into my tote bag, I pull out my crumpled paper bag of prescriptions. Also inside are my wallet, phone, a stack of old case files to brush up on so I can hopefully feel less inept. Nestled at the bottom beside a broken pair of sunglasses is a sleek, silver, very expensive voice recorder.

I line up my orange pill bottles like little soldiers on the flimsy flip-down tray and take my midday doses, swallow them down with water, chase it with a stale protein bar. Not even chocolate can cover the bitter aftertaste lingering on my tongue, thick and acrid.

The little boy's mom leans over in her seat across the aisle, gives the orange bottles a sideways sneer. I pop open another, throw back a pill, give a polite nod after I choke it down. She raises a disapproving eyebrow, leans back in her seat.

At home, after I hung up with Reyes, I searched for train

times. I'd be lonely sitting in the house all weekend, anyway. Normally Dave would be reading files for a new case, stubbornly forgoing any vacation time for the holidays. Izzi would probably be slouched over the kitchen table on her iPad watching makeup tutorials.

So I packed a few things, just enough for the weekend. I have a daily rotation of five tops and three pants, plus one pair of basic black boots. Dull brown hair scraped back in a messy bun. Silver watch Dave had gifted me on my thirtieth birthday. Platinum wedding band. Square black glasses. No makeup. I look fine. I am fine. Carve me out of an old silent film, all black and gray and white.

The train jerks, slamming my shoulder into the window ledge. Outside, the backs of small houses have broken away to dead, snowy fields. I stare through the foggy glass, let myself drift away.

I want, so badly, to help Reyes and the victim's family. I do. But I'm not sure I can do this. The past year has broken me in every possible way a person can be broken. What if I'm not ready? What if I can't pretend all the pieces are glued back together?

The train jolts around a corner, lurching me sideways. I check the news on my chunky white phone, see no recent headlines or messages or alerts. I sigh in relief, toss it into the tote bag, pull out the sleek black phone. Sliding off a paper clip from an old patient file, I uncoil it, jam it into the tiny hole on the side. The SIM card tray pops out. I grab the tiny chip with my fingertips, place it on my tongue for safekeeping, like a strip of acid.

It's too late to turn back now. My stop is quickly approaching. Reyes will be waiting. I swirl the SIM card around my mouth in thought, clack it against my teeth.

A blast of cold air hits me. I shiver, reach for the sweater that had slipped off my shoulders, tie it tight around my neck. A pinch on my throat. I lift a hand, glance down, see a faint trail of blood smeared across my fingertips.

I turn away, feel my stomach heave from the sight. I tug the sweater off. Hidden in the folds of wool is a stockpile of tiny glass shards. I laugh quietly to myself. Glass in my sweater. I'm not surprised. No matter how hard I try, somehow, the mess I am on the inside shows up on the outside.

I steal a blurry glance at myself in the window as I blot the cut on my neck with a tissue. Showing up to a fancy private boarding school bleeding all over myself was not the good impression I was hoping for.

Sliding the SIM card off my tongue, I flick it beneath my train seat, feel the weight of a thousand worlds lift off my shoulders. It's gone now. Gone forever. Waiting to be swept up, taken away, a tiny piece of litter soon to disappear into the ether, like a gum wrapper or a leaf.

Taking a final look at the sleek black phone resting in my hand, I jam it into the tiny space where the wall meets my seat and exhale, relieved I can now pretend it never existed. I don't need it. Not anymore. I have my old, trusty white phone, scratched and chunky. I don't need to be upgraded. I'm fine the way I am. I like my old phone. It has history, imperfections. It may not be new and sleek and perfect. But it's mine. It's me.

I glance back at my reflection in the window. *History. Imperfections.* It's what makes a face, isn't it? Still, maybe I should rethink the no-makeup *fuck-it* look I've had since my thirty-third birthday. Maybe I should start trying, just a little. I look tired. Exhausted. I look like the human definition of a grudge.

I slide off my glasses, lean closer. My eyes have aged into swollen jailbird eyes, bloodshot and bulging. I imagine myself framed by prison bars, unpolished tobacco-stained fingers curling around the iron. Downturned mouth and downturned eyes—dark and dead that never seem to sparkle.

The train shudders.

I'm giving myself until New Year's Eve. Less than three weeks from now. Just a little more time to see if I can redeem myself. Make amends. Help someone else. Be someone else. Stitch my life back together. Maybe answering that phone call wasn't a mistake. Maybe this is my chance.

Only thirty minutes left before my stop—the stop that will take me to a place I've never been. My pulse quickens. I swipe sweaty palms on my pants, stare out of the window, try to relax, breathe, but I can't keep my eyes focused.

I think of Dave. Of Izzi. How at Christmas one year they made the entire dinner themselves, wanting to give me the day off. They'd made the best apple pie I'd ever tasted. Swirls of melted butter and cinnamon floated through the house. Warm apples melded with the flaky crust. Ever since then, it'd become our family favorite. When Izzi had a bad day at school, apple pie. When Dave lost a case, apple pie.

Feeling blue, sunshine? he'd ask, slicing me off a piece.

Then Izzi grew up. She wanted to lose weight. I told her she didn't see how beautiful she was. She said how wrong I was. Sometimes when my daughter looked at me, I wondered if she hated me. It wasn't until later that I found out she actually did.

Dave stopped having dinner with us. I'd wait for him to come home, look out through the tiny window above the kitchen sink, stare at the empty driveway. I knew he was tremendously busy. Most people are. But work wasn't the only reason he'd stayed away.

I turn away from the window.

Twenty minutes. I tilt my head, shut my eyes. Rest my forehead against the icy glass, pull my long gray coat tight across my chest. A heartbeat passes, and I wake to see the train has stopped, and I'm the only person left onboard.

I shove everything back into the tote bag and rush down the aisle to meet Reyes. With no idea what he looks like, I scan the faces outside, look for people who may fit the profile of a private investigator—maybe fifties, brooding, a pair of polished shoes, sharp part in the side of their grayed, combed hair.

No one on the platform fits the description I'm searching for. There's a woman crouching to tie a child's shoe. An elderly man walking away, picking at the edge of his nose. A teenage boy rushing by, earbuds in his ears, eyes on his phone.

And then, I spot him. He waits on the edge of the platform, hands deep in his pockets, dark eyes trained on me as I reach the open doorway.

It's him. It has to be. He fits the profile perfectly—combed hair, dark and shining in the afternoon sun. Heavy wool overcoat. Polished leather shoes. The only thing I guessed incorrectly was his age. My gaze meets his. He looks up, grins. Cute. Handsome. That, I wasn't expecting.

As I descend the stairs to meet him, my mind flashes to a little dream I just had. A dog was *barking barking barking*. I walked into my kitchen, nearly slipping in a lake-size pool of blood.

3

"Dr. Madeline Pine?"

"Detective Matthew Reyes?"

He adjusts his glasses, round and black with lenses almost as thick as mine. "Thanks for coming all this way," he says, taking my luggage. The wheels roll stubbornly across the gravel parking lot as we walk toward his dark SUV. "Are you hungry?" he asks, slamming the back hatch closed. "We can stop at a... I think I passed a truck stop on the way down."

I shake my head, climb into the passenger seat. "No, thanks. I just want to get to the school, Detective Reyes."

He lets out a short laugh. "Please, call me Matt."

Secretly, I study him when he turns away. He's around my age and wears a heavy black peacoat and plaid scarf, evergreen and chocolate, matching his combed-back brown hair, sprigs of gray sprouting near his temples. A hint of dark stubble on his face and circles under his eyes that match my own tell me he's had more than a few sleepless nights. He looks like he'd smell of pipe tobacco and mulled cider, but really all I smell is mouthwash and stale coffee.

Something about him assuages my uneasiness. I lean a little deeper into the leather seat. Matt's eyes flicker in my direction as he starts the engine. I look away.

"Let me tell you a little about Shadow Hunt Hall," he begins, merging onto a two-lane highway. "The main building is very old. I think it's listed with the state on the national register of historic places. There's a stone wall surrounding the property. One main gated entrance."

"And the girl—she was found within the school walls on campus? Or was she in the surrounding area?"

Matt shakes his head. "Oh, no. She was found on campus. But by campus I mean three hundred acres of dense, mature forest. It's one of the school's selling points," he adds. "More space for outdoor activities. Hiking, camping, group trust exercises. I think the website even refers to the school as 'an island in the woods.'"

I don't know why, but the thought terrifies me. To be alone, lost in the woods, knowing there are walls around you, yet still being unable to find safety…

Matt peers at me over the top of his glasses. "You know, not too many people around here are as qualified as you. I read all about you."

My head snaps toward him.

"Uh, I mean, I read all about that case you had last year," Matt says quietly. "That was really something." I shift in the seat, suddenly uncomfortable. "And from what I read, you specialize in violent women—"

"*No,*" I staunchly correct him, feeling the need to defend myself. "I'm just a criminal psychiatrist with a focus on the, uh, female mind. Mostly, I work with police, that's all. I'm not anything special."

"I find that hard to believe," he says thoughtfully. "And I've been a private investigator for eight years, worked with a lot of your kind."

I shake my head. "Thanks?"

"Why specialize in women?" he asks.

I shrug. "It's what I know best."

Matt laughs. "That makes one of us." His dark eyes fall to the wide, silver wedding band on his finger. He drops his hand from the steering wheel.

"And what about you?" I ask when the car fills with silence. "Why did you take this case?"

He shrugs. "It's hard to say no to a mother calling you in tears from across the country, desperate to know why her daughter was found dead in the middle of the woods, on a secure campus, alone, wearing nothing but her pajamas."

I gulp. "Why was she only wearing pajamas outside in the woods when it's so cold?"

He lifts his dark eyebrows. "That's a part of what I meant when I said some things just don't add up."

"And you said she died on December…"

"Preliminary autopsy states it was late on December 10, the first day of winter break." He nods his head toward the back seat. "On the floor in the back is a bag with some files and printed news articles. You should read some on the way to get a feel for the case."

My heart drops. "Will I be on the news?" Panic rises in my throat.

"What? No, no, nothing like that. This isn't like your case last year with the Strum murders," Matt says. He takes a sip of water from an aluminum canteen, swishes it around his mouth. "I'm guessing you were bombarded with reporters last year with that case." Glancing at me, his brows lower. "I'm—I'm sorry, Dr. Pine," he says calmly, reading my stoic reaction. "I won't mention that case anymore. I can see it really bothered you."

I clear my throat, toss him an unsteady grin. "It's fine, really," I lie and quickly unbuckle my seat belt to turn around and grab the bulky canvas bag wedged behind my seat. It's heavy, jammed full of papers. I drop it on the floor near my feet, fish around inside.

"When we get to the school I can show you more evidence I was given by the local police who initially worked the case," Matt says. "Earlier, on the phone, you asked why I needed your help." His voice deepens, tone turning somber. "I need your help because... I don't know what happened. Because of the snow, there's not a lot of physical evidence. And we're still waiting on the final autopsy results."

"So instead of evidence, you need witnesses. You need leads..."

He nods. "I've only been trained in interrogation—and that's not something I think will get teenage girls to open up about Charley."

I clear my throat. "Charley?" I ask. "That's the victim's name?"

Matt nods, exhales a deep breath. "Charlotte Ridley. Goes by Charley," he says, glancing at me. "She and her family are from Las Vegas."

"It must be hard to have your daughter all the way across the country," I say.

Matt raises his eyebrows. "I can't imagine," he muses. "But her mother believed this school was the best place for her. Charley was having issues at her old high school. Issues with bullying. It's why her mother called me."

"Does she think the problems from Charley's old school have followed her here? That she was still being bullied?"

Matt licks his lips, tilts his head. "She—she just wants to know the truth. What happened to her daughter. You understand."

"Of course," I whisper. "Even if my daughter's death was an accident, I'd still want to know why."

Matt nods slowly to himself, turns the wheel as the road curls around a steep mountainside. "Me too," he says. "It's why I took the case when she called. I couldn't say no."

I shift sideways. Through the windows, hills roll into mountains. The autumn leaves have mostly fallen up here, making way for the bare branches of winter, all except a few stragglers who refuse to let go.

"So you need *me* to get the students to open up...to dig into their brains and pass off any findings about Charley to you."

"Yes," he admits. "You may not agree with me, but..." Matt's elbow brushes against my knee as he retrieves something from the glove compartment.

He tugs out a folder, passes it to me.

"This is what the police uncovered at the scene." He chews on his bottom lip. "It's a little hard to see. You don't have to look if you don't want to."

I reach forward. He releases his grip. The first picture is of the woods surrounding the school. It's nighttime, the trees dark, the middle of the shot blanched by the stark light of the camera flash.

I flip to the next picture. It's a small deer trail cut through overgrown brush, tamped down, broken twigs where animals have passed through. The glow from the camera lights only a few feet ahead, leaving the sides of the trail settled in darkness.

Next is a tree. A giant, twisting tree, crooked and bent, the arms wrestling with their own weight, bowing down to

THE NIGHT IT ENDED

the snow-dusted forest floor. In the dark, it looks eerie, like a movie prop, a tree constructed of foam, painted to resemble stone.

I blink.

The camera flash had oversaturated the picture, flooding the image with bright white light. I flip to the next one.

Behind the tree, a hillside breaks away, tumbling down the mountainside as if the world ended. Below, along the craggy hillside, there's nothing but dead brush, tall grass coated with a faint breath of snowflakes, the occasional sapling desperate to grow roots.

Matt studies me as I flip to the next photo.

And stare.

And stare.

It's a girl—Charley—her head down, chin-length, mouse-brown hair tousled across her sideways face, leaves caught in the knotty strands. She'd fallen, rolled down the hillside, bits of dried leaves and dirt embedded in her pajamas, made of nothing more than a layer of thin cotton. Her lips are blue. Her skin is gray. Light snow laces in her hair. On her forehead, beneath the layers of her wispy hair, a red abrasion peeks through the strands.

"What's this?" I ask Matt, holding up the photo of Charley's face.

Matt inhales a deep breath. "The preliminary autopsy concluded it was blunt force trauma," he explains. "Conclusion was she fell down the hillside and hit her head on a rock. Because of the holidays, it'll be a few more days before I get the final autopsy."

Tears prick my eyes. She was alone. Alone and afraid and bleeding in the snow before her injury from the fall had overtaken her. I shut my eyes. Charley's face fills my head. If this were my daughter, I'd want to disappear. I'd want to crawl into the earth and disappear.

I look out of the window. The sepia fields from the train have grown into bare, rocky mountains. The sky has darkened to a solid gray overcast, obscuring any tinge of sun.

"So," I say, my gaze sweeping over the white-blotted hills, "you need me to interview the students. One by one."

"That's right," Matt says. "See if anyone saw Charley that night. Maybe someone knows something."

"Or maybe she was just out there alone and got lost," I say softly.

"It's possible," Matt whispers to himself, shaking his head slowly. "People go for a walk. They trip. They fall. It's no one's fault. But Charley wasn't wearing any shoes, Dr. Pine. She was wearing a white tank top and pajama bottoms outside alone at night in December. None of that fits with any rational possibility."

I fall silent. There has to be an explanation. I just can't see it yet.

"So she was outside. Alone. The temperature was freezing. No shoes, wearing only her pajamas," I say, mostly for myself to help remember the facts of the case. "It was cold—snowing. You know, I remember hearing how sometimes, in the later stages of hypothermia, the afflicted removes their own clothing. They truly believe they're hot when really they're freezing to death."

Matt tilts his head. "That's a good theory," he admits, stealing a glance at me. "But then where are Charley's clothes? Where are her shoes?" Frustration fills his voice. "Why weren't they ever found? She was barefoot, yet her feet showed no signs of bruising or damage of any kind. They were clean. It's almost as if she—" He stops himself, shakes his head clear.

The evergreen forests grow denser. My ears pop as the lone highway curls up another mountain. "So what's your theory?" I ask.

"My theory?" he says. "My theory is whatever the truth is. Wherever the evidence leads me, that's what I'll believe. All I want is the truth, either way."

"Either way?"

"If it really was an accident…or if it *was* something else." Matt pauses, peers at me sideways. "You know, you look different from your picture."

The SUV lurches sideways. I grip the side of the seat.

"Picture?"

"From your book. From the author photo. Maybe it's the glasses."

"I—I thought you didn't know what I looked like," I mumble. "I guess I just assumed." I let out an awkward laugh. My hands start to sweat.

I can practically feel his stare burning the side of my face.

He laughs. "Come on, relax," Matt says, turning away. "I wasn't stalking you or anything, I swear."

"It's fine…it's just—I look a little different because they wanted me all dolled up for the author photo. There was a lot of airbrushing," I confess with a shrug, embarrassed. "It never felt like the real me. Plus, it was years ago…things change. People change."

The woman in that author photo does resemble me—slightly. We could be sisters. One, rich, chic, taken care of. The other, a mismatched, lumpy frump. She's a better version of me. A younger version. Sleeker. She's the version you're proud of, the version you wouldn't mind seeing naked. You know everything would be right where it should be.

But it's not me. Not anymore. *She's* the million-dollar version of me, and I'm—I'm the discounted version. The woman you pass on the street and never see. The woman who hasn't slept a solid night since before she got pregnant. *She's* dazzling and perfect and has everything, and I'm...a nobody.

"Yeah. I know the feeling." Matt sighs. "But I think you look better in person. I like this new hair better. Longer, darker. And without all that makeup and stuff, you look younger, even."

He's lying, but still, I feel myself blush and turn to look out of the window. The car settles into silence.

"Uh, so...how many girls are at the school during break?" I ask, changing the subject.

Matt clears his throat, seemingly relieved I switched the topic back to the case.

"Normally when the school is in session, there's about sixty-two girls who live on campus. But with the winter break, they're down to four."

"Okay," I mumble. "Four. I—I can do that," I say, my nerves already humming with the possibility of making a mistake.

I'm rusty. I'm more than rusty. I'm inadequate. I couldn't even keep my shit together this morning during my session with—it doesn't matter. I'm delusional if I think I can handle four teenage girls.

I imagine Izzi hearing this new development. She'd laugh, roll her eyes at me. I can hear her now: *Seriously, Mom? Why are you even doing this?*

"You'll be great," Matt says, breaking me out of my trance. "Just remember, focus on Charley. Who she was friends with. If anyone disliked her. If anyone saw anything out of the usual the month or so leading up to her death."

I clear my throat, push away my thoughts. "Right. Got it."

Matt rubs the back of his neck. "By the way, I'm really sorry to keep you away from your husband and kid right before the holidays. Hopefully they didn't take it too hard."

"No, they're fine with it," I say. "Maybe some time away is a good thing. They're, um, both kind of mad at me right now. I did something—thoughtless."

"Oh yeah?"

I look down at Charley's file resting open in my lap. "Yeah. It can be—family can be hard…" I trail off, my gaze catching on his wedding band. "How long have you been married?" I ask when he doesn't reply.

He shakes his head. "I'm not," he says. "Divorced. Three years ago."

"I'm sorry," I whisper. "Do you ever think about getting remarried?"

Matt grips the steering wheel tight, glances again at his wedding band. "Nope. Never."

"Never?"

"Have you ever been cheated on?" he asks.

I turn away, stare out of the window. After a moment, I say, "Yes."

He tips his head. "Then you should know."

I don't reply.

He turns off the quiet song playing on the radio. "Almost there."

Matt pulls onto a narrow, dusty lane. Rolling hills stretch out ahead before mutating into the sharp curves of a mountain, thickly coated with dense, emerald pines. Ahead is a towering, ornate iron gate, looping spirals across the top, like a crown. Wind clangs the iron gates open against a stone wall that stretches forever in both directions.

The forest expands onward as we crawl up the never-ending lane, carving deeper and deeper into the woods. Giant, sagging arms of weeping firs scrape along my window.

I look out of the windshield. Up ahead, there's a break in the trees. Pale sunlight paints the air a silvery haze and through it, a giant structure rises from the stony mountaintop. The haze echoes across endless windows, each pane glittering like the sharp tip of a blade catching in moonlight.

Dread pours itself inside me. We're here.

Too late to turn back now.

THE YEAR BEFORE

FILE NAME: JPN00.012.00030923.mp3

INT: Okay, good. Great. And I'll tell you right up front, anything you tell me now can only help you in the future, okay? It can help with arraignment, if need be.

RES: Arraignment? I did nothing wrong.

INT: Well...that—that's up to me to determine.

RES: [inaudible] him, I don't know.

INT: Please, can you speak a little louder. Clearer, please, into the voice recorder.

RES: Fine.

[00:02:54]

INT: Now, when did you and [redacted] first meet.

RES: Five, six months ago. I had come home from work. My daughter was home alone. She was busy practicing her music up in her room. My husband had left her.

INT: Did he often leave her alone?

RES: Yes.

INT: And what happened when you came home?

RES: She was, um, crying. She was in tears and I just—she was upset.

INT: What was she upset about?

RES: Her father was always working. He's an attorney, like I said. He works odd hours, he works a lot.

INT: Why was your daughter upset?

RES: My husband had left. He left her, and she told me he left after he got a call from a woman.

INT: A woman? Maybe, a coworker?

RES: My daughter alluded to how she didn't think that was the case.

INT: Okay, so, um, your husband left your daughter alone to meet a woman?

RES: Yes.

[00:03:33]

INT: And what happened next?

RES: She was crying. Mostly, she was upset at me because I was at work, too, like her father. She said I should've been home with her. That she was always left alone. I felt horrible. I'd completely forgotten I'd promised to take her shopping for new clothes for school. It made her upset.

INT: And you forgot, because you were at work?

RES: Yes. I'm a [redacted] at [redacted].

INT: And this was in the evening, when you came home to find your daughter crying?

RES: Yes. I'm sorry…can I please have some water?

INT: Of course…

RES: Thank you. Yes, she was upset. The dog was in her lap—she fed him, she never forgot. Oh god…

INT: It's okay. Just walk me through nice and slow.

RES: The next morning, I took her shopping. My husband was, uh, still gone.

INT: After he never came home that night, did you try to contact him? [inaudible] Try not to shake your head or nod. Please verbally state—

RES: No.

INT: And what happened when you were out shopping?

[00:05:01]

RES: That's the first time I met [redacted].

4

The brakes squeal in the cold.

"Ready?" Matt asks, turning off the engine.

I step out of the SUV, freezing wind instantly biting my cheeks. Winter up here is a different kind of cold, the kind that feels like a thousand tiny knives stabbing you all over your body.

Matt tugs my luggage out of the back. The wheels thump across the cobblestones as he walks toward an arched carriage tunnel cut in the center of the building. Soon, he disappears into the shadows.

I tuck my tote bag under an arm, seize a breath. I'm used to tweed sofas and polite, two-ply tissues centered on a coffee table. Four beige walls of a tiny, too-hot room. Coming up here—this isolated, this far from home—has already set my teeth on edge.

I gaze up at the sky, trying to focus on anything but my

own writhing thoughts. A thin crescent moon hovers over the forest, though it's barely sunset. I focus on it as I take my first step forward, breathe in a lungful of chilly, pine-scented air.

The main school building looms around me, not exceedingly tall but surprisingly long. It doesn't look like any school I've ever seen. Like an old, haunted mansion, it's imposing but has clearly fallen into disrepair, left to rot beneath the winter sky.

Shaped like a giant letter *H*, it's made of heavy gray stone, moss eaten and damp. Arched windows dot down never-ending walls, the glass a shimmering white, reflecting the dreary sky. A dozen stone chimneys sprout from the dark mansard roof, like tombstones.

I step closer to the carriage tunnel. In the disappearing sunlight, Matt waits for me to follow, the handle of my luggage twisting in his hand. He pulls open a heavy wooden door tucked into an alcove, steps aside for me to enter first.

Inside is an empty, abandoned lobby, and our footsteps echo across ancient marble floors. I half expected the lobby to be spacious and grand, but it's low-ceilinged and stone, the walls made of giant slabs of smooth, creamy marble.

The air is dark and every time I take a breath I inhale a different scent: a waft of fruity perfume mixed with mildew, fresh pine and old stone, damp and cloying, like a tomb.

Ahead is a spiraling staircase carved from white stone. Two hallways split off the staircase, shooting in different directions, left and right.

A solitary door slams in the distance.

"Mrs. Hawke?" Matt calls out, voice bouncing off the stone. He releases the handle of my luggage, wipes a sweaty palm across the front of his coat. "The headmistress is named Emilia Hawke," he says quietly. "She's been here about two years."

A girl with wavy brown hair and round, owlish glasses steps

around a corner to steal a glance at us before disappearing up the spiral staircase.

"Wait, can you please—" Matt attempts to get the girl's attention. Too late. He grumbles.

"Maybe she's going to get someone."

"Maybe."

We stand together in silence, listening for any trace of footsteps. Minutes pass before we speak again.

"Two years, huh?" I inquire, raising an eyebrow.

"What?"

"The headmistress. You said she's only been here two years. She's still somewhat new. Might feel like she has a lot to prove."

"She might…" He trails off.

We exchange glances. In the distance, movement, shuffling. Whispers. Matt raises his chin, the muscles in his jaw working. I tense, clasp the straps of my tote bag tight.

The girl with the round, owlish glasses has returned. Only this time, she's not alone.

"Good afternoon, Detective Reyes." A smooth voice echoes from across the lobby.

I turn to see a woman hovering near the staircase. Surrounding her is a small flock of students huddled against each other, their hair uncombed and wispy, bitter expressions painted on their smooth, pouting faces.

At the mere sight of us, the group dismembers itself, scattering down the hallways like mice.

"*Ladies,*" Mrs. Hawke calls after them. Their sneakers squeak to a stop on the stone floor. "None of you are in trouble. Now come back here."

Only two of the girls return, sulking as they stand back beside Emilia. Together, they cross the lobby toward us.

"I hope you had an uneventful drive up," Mrs. Hawke says,

approaching us slowly, as if we're wild animals and she's unsure if we'll bite.

"We did, thanks. Uh, Mrs. Hawke, this is Dr. Madeline Pine, the criminal psychiatrist I was telling you about."

"Welcome to Shadow Hunt Hall, Dr. Pine," she says smoothly. Towering over me, she stretches out a thin hand, so thin, I can see her tendons working. I take it, give a gentle shake.

In her early fifties, she looks like someone peeled her out of *Southern Charm* magazine—take a whiff of her shiny blond hair and she'd smell of tulips and fresh-baked cookies. She steps away, carefully adjusts a bowed scarf tied tight around her fragile neck, perfectly matched to her silky white dress.

"Nice to meet you," I say, glancing at the girls flanking her sides.

On Mrs. Hawke's left is a short girl with puffy, mousebrown hair and round glasses half the size of her face. To her right is a tall, thin girl with long, even thinner braids and a downturned pout that rivals my sulky sixteen-year-old daughter's. She tosses a softball up and down in the air, catching it without looking, the ball hitting her palm—*slap slap slap.*

"These are two of the girls you'll be speaking with," Mrs. Hawke says, holding up a frail hand toward the bespectacled girl on her left. "Hannah, this is Dr. Madeline Pine. She'll be staying at the school for a few days along with Detective Reyes to learn a little more about Charley. She will be speaking privately with each of you, is that clear?" Mrs. Hawke turns to the tall, confident girl on her right. "Kiara, I expect you and the others will show nothing but respect and grace toward Dr. Pine while she's here. I want nothing but your best behavior when she speaks with you. Understood?"

The girl, Kiara, catches the softball one final time as she

glares at me behind long, thick lashes. "Yeah, fine, whatever," she mumbles.

Hannah, the short girl, steps forward, tucks her hands deep into her oversized hoodie's front pocket, plasters a wide grin on her face. "I'm more than happy to show you around, Dr. Pine," she says, her hazel eyes wide and unblinking behind her wire-rimmed glasses. "This school can get very confusing," she says with a laugh. "We wouldn't want you to get lost!"

Kiara snorts. "God, Hannah, back *off*," she warns, dark brown eyes flickering toward me. "Stop being such a teacher's pet for once in your life." She turns to Mrs. Hawke. "And how come it's always me and Hannah getting the lectures. What about Violet and Alice? They're here for break, too." Kiara scoffs and rolls her eyes, tosses her softball in the air.

Mrs. Hawke snaps a hand out, catches it midair. Kiara's pouty frown pops open. *"Enough,"* Mrs. Hawke says. "Both of you, upstairs. Now. And be sure to tell Violet and Alice precisely what I told you, nothing more, nothing less. Understood?"

Kiara exhales a deep breath as Mrs. Hawke tosses her the softball. She catches it with one hand, glances sharply at Hannah.

"Bye!" Hannah says, waving over a shoulder as she skips up the stairs behind Kiara.

Matt grabs my luggage. "Let me help you carry your bags—"

"Stop," Mrs. Hawke orders, holding up a hand. "I'll take it from here. Detective Reyes, you go do—whatever it is that you do. Dr. Pine, follow me. *I'll* show you where you'll be staying," she says primly, painted lips curling up at the edges.

Between her and the students I just met, I feel like a giant wave has crushed me and I don't know which way is the surface. "Thanks, Mrs. Hawke…" I manage to say, head spinning.

"You may call me Emilia."

I turn back to Matt before following her. "Your things," he says, holding out the luggage handle. "You have my number," he says. "And I have yours. I'm staying in one of the guesthouses on campus. Just follow the footpath through the woods. There are signs somewhere, I think."

"What, where—"

Emilia clears her throat impatiently. "She'll call you, Detective Reyes. Thanks for taking the time." She turns her attention to me, her expression pointed. I can imagine her running a 1930s orphanage; the woman has the glare of a nun and the posture of a midcentury housewife. "I'll show you your room, Dr. Pine."

I say goodbye to Matt and begin the climb up the spiraling staircase behind Emilia. Cobwebs cling to high corners, dust and gnats collecting in the gossamer webs. I tilt my head back. At the top of the stairwell is a giant glass dome. Moss and leaves gather around the perimeter, dulling the fading sunlight.

Emilia stops at the next level. Hallways shoot out around us, long and endless, one left, one right, one straight ahead, the end of each hall fading away into darkness. Everything looks identical—every hallway, every stone, every arched, wooden doorway, as if the school was purposefully designed to get people lost.

I try to shake away the feeling of unease but fail miserably. Something about this place…the cool, stone floors. The whistling cries the lead-paned windows make every time the icy wind blows. The scent of ancient, cold decay.

It doesn't remind me of any school I've ever seen.

It reminds me of a prison.

5

Passing a row of classrooms, I steal a peek inside one. It seems abandoned, the lights off, shades drawn. Long, wooden tables encircle the room, and dusty blackboards nudge up against the gray plastered walls. An engraved stone fireplace rests at the back of the room, wooden chairs clustered around it, obstructing its use.

"This way." Emilia's smooth voice echoes down the hall, and I rush to catch up.

As she guides me through the school, I can't help but feel alone; the building is surprisingly quiet, aside from the creaks and groans of an old, stubborn mansion. There are four teenage girls here, somewhere. But I'm not sure where they're hiding. If my daughter, Izzi, is any clue, they're probably sprawled out on their beds, feet kicked up behind them as they lie on their bellies binge-watching shows on their iPads.

Then I remember.

It's one of those "back-to-nature, no technology on campus" sort of places, Matt had said.

I clear my throat to try to get Emilia's attention, pick up my pace to walk beside her. "Emilia, I hear the girls aren't allowed to use—"

"Phones?" she asks, raising an eyebrow. "Or laptops. No electronic devices of any kind."

"So, no internet?"

"*Your* cell phone should work, of course," she says, turning away. "Possibly."

I look up, slide my glasses up my nose. Nestled high in a corner is an old security camera. I wrinkle my forehead. "But then why do you have cameras? Doesn't that defeat the whole 'no-tech' premise?"

Emilia laughs. "When you find yourself surrounded with troubled teenage girls, you need to be strict."

I think of Izzi's mood swings and fight the urge to roll my eyes. "I know how challenging teenagers can be."

Emilia stops short, turns toward me, whispers, "The students don't know the cameras don't work. That sort of security system would be a fortune to keep up," she says with a mild laugh. "They haven't worked in years. It's all smoke and mirrors."

"Oh."

She nods sagely, steps closer. "I don't know what Detective Reyes told you about Shadow Hunt Hall, but these are no ordinary girls. Many are here solely for rehabilitation. Some girls have faced abuse. Some have inflicted harm on themselves or others. It's our job to keep them safe. To get them on the right track. That does *not* include social media and watching television shows. We encourage therapeutic activities. Mentally challenging activities. Outdoor activities. The arts."

"I can't imagine how Charley's death has affected the students."

Emilia glances at me, her pale eyes sharp. "It was an accident. Weeks ago. And children are resilient. More resilient than we give them credit for."

"Detective Reyes said Charley was found December 11. That's only *one* week ago—"

She begins walking. "I've generously offered Detective Reyes a guesthouse to further his investigation," she says, ignoring me completely. "No one can accuse me of not doing everything that could have been done."

I squint at her. "You don't want him here, do you?"

Emilia slows her pace. "Incorrect. I want a full and *honest* account of Charley's accident, and I believe we already had that with our local police," she says. "Our school is built around nature. The outdoors. And above all, *safety* in nature and the outdoors. This is extremely damaging to our ability to give the students a curriculum that is beneficial to their rehabilitation. Not to mention our reputation..." She mutters under her breath.

"One of your students is dead," I say, trying to keep up with her steadfast pace. "I think the bigger question, pertaining to safety, is why a student was able to exit the school in the middle of the night—"

"There's all sorts of conspiracies about what happened," Emilia says. "But that poor girl most likely sleepwalked her way into the woods and fell to an untimely death. That's what the police said and so that's all there is to it."

"Sleepwalked? You don't think she could've just got lost?"

"Why would she be in the woods at night in her pajamas? She had to have been asleep," Emilia says with a light laugh, as if the mere mention of anything different is simply absurd.

"Her mother said she was bullied at her old high school. Maybe—"

Emilia stops. I nearly ram into her. She inhales a deep breath, whispers, "Do you hear that?"

"No…"

"It must be 4:30."

I listen closely, hear music notes flutter through the air. "Is that a violin?"

"Mm. One of the students practices every day before dinner," she says. "Just don't use the word *violin* to her when you meet. She's very sensitive about it. It's a *viola*."

"She's amazing," I say, listening close to the music.

"She likes to think so."

A voice behind us.

We spin around.

A girl stands alone in the hallway, slurping a mug of coffee. Her straight black hair swings down one side of her chest, glossy and thick, doll-like. She's extremely thin, so thin it doesn't look like there's even a person inside her clothes. Paint-smeared overalls, slathered in reds and greens and blues, fall off her bare, bony shoulders.

She steps closer, glares at Emilia beside me.

"Hello," she says, holding out a tiny hand to me. "I'm Violet." I almost flinch when she grins—her white braces have black rubber bands, an optical illusion that makes her smile look like a skeleton's.

I take her hand. Her skin is ice-cold, freezing. "Nice to meet—"

"Violet. Good of you to finally join us," Emilia says, cutting me off. "This is Dr. Madeline Pine, the psychiatrist I was telling you about."

"How interesting," Violet says, slurping her coffee again, green eyes peering at me over the rim of the mug, awaiting a reply. "Not every day we have *specialists* come to our little school, is it, Headmistress?"

Emilia ignores her, instead replies, "Dr. Pine will be meeting with each of you girls separately to discuss details about Charley. I expect nothing but honesty—"

Violet turns away.

Emilia snaps forward, grabs Violet's chin in her hand, jerks it toward her.

"*Honesty* and *compliance*," Emilia finishes.

My back straightens. If I caught an authority figure ever *touching* Izzi, I'd—I stop the thoughts from sprouting, inhale a deep, calming breath.

Violet smiles. Emilia drops her hand from Violet's chin.

Down the hall, the viola stops playing. A moment later, the door flings open. Violet turns to stare as a girl emerges into the hallway. I recognize her as the girl who disappeared down the hallway earlier before Emilia could introduce her, only now she holds a black instrument case in one hand, stacks of music sheets in the other. A gray hoodie is zipped up to her chin, hood pulled tight around her face, hair dyed a pale lavender frizzing out at the sides, falling past her shoulders.

Violet grins her skeleton grin. "Hey, Alice," she says, sickly sweet. "Nice of you to come out of your room and see the world for once in your life."

The girl—Alice—hesitates before slowly turning to glance down the hallway at us.

"Alice," Emilia calls. "Come here, please."

Violet rolls her eyes.

With her hands full, Alice tries to shut the door behind her, but the viola case catches on the doorframe.

"*Shit,*" she swears, as her folder filled with sheet music slips from her hand, dozens of papers fluttering to the ground.

Violet lets out a loud cackle before catching herself, her eyes flickering to Emilia. "Here, let me help you, Alice," she says, slinking over to her, lazily pinching a single piece of paper from off the floor.

Alice shoots Violet a look of warning—harsh and uncaring and cold. Violet grins, obviously delighted by Alice's slight hint of aggression, and picks up another piece.

Alice falls to the ground, sweeps the papers into a pile, hisses, "*Don't*. I can do it myself."

Violet ignores her warning and stands, holds out a hand to help her off the ground. Alice recoils, grabs her viola case from the floor.

"Just—stop," Alice says, swinging the case in front of her like a sword. "*Stop!* Leave me alone!" She rips the paper from Violet's hand and runs down the hall.

Violet delicately sips her coffee as Alice disappears down the shadowy stairwell.

Emilia sighs and walks away, ignoring Violet completely.

It's not until we've made it to the other end of the hall that I glance over a shoulder to see Violet is still standing in the center of the hall, staring back at us as we walk away.

Emilia doesn't speak again until she stops, pushes on a door. It creaks open on its hinges, like in an old horror film. Heavy curtains are drawn shut, stifling the room with darkness.

She enters, flicks on a light switch. Glass bulbs whine with electricity. Emilia crosses the room, pushes the curtains open. Rather than sunlight, the gray gloom of sunset seeps into the room. In the fading light, I'm reminded of an old Victorian hotel room. Spindly legged, antique tables clutter dusty corners. Beige floral wallpaper peels away at the edges. Five small hammered-glass windows peer out over the front of the school, down to the courtyard where Matt parked his SUV.

"Clean blankets are in the closet if you get cold," Emilia says, pointing to a narrow door. "Bathroom is over there." I turn to see another door. "Feel free to use the dresser, if you wish."

I release the handle of my luggage, drop my heavy tote bag on the bed—a wide canopy bed with no canopy, the quilt a frilly patchwork of pink and sage green. The scent of rose soap and old wood fills my nose.

Emilia watches me as I look around. "Dinner is at six. You're welcome to join us in the cafeteria. I'm sure the girls would be *delighted* to see you again."

I glance at her to see if she's being sarcastic, but her face is frozen, set in a flatlined glare.

"Thanks, sounds great..." I mumble to myself.

Emilia shuts the door on her way out. Stepping forward, I reach to lock it behind her, a subconscious attempt to try to keep her at bay. My fingers clasp around the cool brass door-knob. I look down. The door doesn't have a lock.

I stand alone in the room. My mind swarms with thoughts. Anxiety bloats inside me, fills me up, expands. One day, I'll pop. Infect everyone with a gush of rotten memories. I know when the time comes, it'll only take a pinprick.

I slump to the floor, press my back against the bed. Maybe I'm in way over my head. I'm not sure I can handle these girls, even though I lied to Emilia and said I could. I think of the four girls I just met—Kiara, Hannah, Violet, Alice. How each of them seem to be challenging in their own, dissimilar way.

What if I can't handle them? Handle this? Maybe I should leave tonight. I'm not sure I should be here.

I'm not sure what I'll do if they find out what I've done.

Saturday, December 17

6

I'm woken in the morning by three quick knocks on the door. I must've fallen asleep last night after Emilia left my room. My stomach rumbles as I kick the musty blankets off the bed, roll over to check the time on my phone. Barely seven in the morning.

I meant to have dinner in the cafeteria with the girls and Emilia as she'd mentioned, but I never know when sleep will overtake me. I've learned to welcome it after months of insomnia. The copious sleeping pills don't hurt, either.

Quickly, I swipe through the news and check for any new messages. No missed calls. No alerts. I exhale, slide my glasses on my face, glance in a full-length mirror next to the door. I'm still wearing the same wool turtleneck and black pants from yesterday, though my hair has exploded into a puff of brown knots. Feebly, I smooth it down, crack the door open, glance up at the camera near the ceiling in the hall.

Smoke and mirrors.

A tiny, rattled woman stands on the other side of the door in the empty hallway, frizzy sand-colored hair blowing away from her face like she's been standing in front of a fan.

"Good morning, good morning," she says in one hurried breath. "I'm Rosemarie, Emilia's school assistant." In her arms, she carries a silver platter crowded with all sorts of jars and cups and plates. I take the tray from her, slide it onto the unmade bed.

I look down at the breakfast splayed out on the tray. A brown banana, some kind of congealed porridge. Burned toast with chunky orange marmalade. A ceramic mug is half-filled with black tea, paired with a little plate of creamers.

"Wow," I say, scratching the back of my neck. "Thank you, you really didn't have to bring me—"

"No, no," Rosemarie says. "It's my pleasure. Emilia said you missed dinner and we both agreed you couldn't go hungry. It's not in our nature." She laughs, mouth open, displaying a row of tea-stained teeth.

I poke at the banana on the tray. Rosemarie watches me carefully, eyes wide, her thin lips still strangely parted. She isn't blinking behind her gold-rimmed glasses.

"Well, thanks again," I begin. "I should, um—"

"Emilia asked me to tell you a few things." She clenches her hands together, wrings them out.

"Okay—"

"Breakfast begins every morning at seven," she explains. "You're more than welcome to eat with the students downstairs, or you can ask me to bring a tray to your room." She holds out a stiff hand, gestures at the tray.

"Sounds good," I say, biting into a piece of burned toast. I nearly break a tooth. Rosemarie reads my face. "It—it's good," I lie. She can tell. Her unblinking eyes roll down to the floor in disappointment. "I'm so hungry it doesn't even matter." That's not a lie.

Rosemarie nods stiffly, pushes her golden glasses up her long nose.

"Have you worked here long?" I ask.

"About five years. I help Emilia with anything—anything she needs done. I do some cleaning, but I've been in the kitchen, too. Chef's gone."

"Right," I say. "Gone for the break." Rosemarie nods again.

"Do you have children?" she asks, still standing in front of me as I sit at the edge of the bed, picking at the bowl of white mystery mush.

My eyebrows furrow from the question. "Uh, yes, one. A daughter, Izzi. Her full name's Isabella, but we call her Izzi. Her seventeenth birthday is coming up soon."

Rosemarie nods. Her teeth part as she grins a flat smile, lips incapable of curling up at the edges, like some sort of wooden doll.

"Do you have kids?" I ask awkwardly, as I shovel in a spoonful of mush. It's not bad. It doesn't taste like anything, at all.

Rosemarie shakes her head. "No, no. The students are my children," she says. "But what happened to our Charley..." She trails off, grimaces. "So sad. We miss her every day."

I drop the spoon, pick at my cuticles, stare at the portrait of a young girl hanging on the wall behind Rosemarie's tiny shoulder. The girl's eyes are textured, made of swirling green paint so thick I could reach out and feel the layers. I blink and the girl morphs into Izzi. She smiles.

Suddenly, my head spins. I'm dizzy. I want to lie down, take my morning pills. Anxiety steeps into my bloodstream. I try my best to hide it, grab hold of my kneecap, gnash my teeth together. I turn away, sip on the tea, try to hide the sudden flash of heat crawling up my cheeks.

"Well, I know you need to begin your work." Rosemarie's voice snaps me back to reality. I blink again. My vision clears. Izzi is gone. "I can show you, if you'd like."

"Show me?"

Rosemarie nods. "Yes—oh! I almost forgot." She reaches behind her, lifts up her shirt, pulls out a stack of files she had tucked into the back of her pants. Dropping them on the bed, she shrugs. "Emilia wanted me to bring those to you. She's busy this morning."

I glance at the stack of manila files on the mattress, the edges curled from living inside Rosemarie's pants. "Thanks... I'll take a look at them."

She rushes to leave.

"Wait—" I call after her.

She turns.

"Can you tell me anything you know about Charley? What she was like? What she was interested in?"

Rosemarie clasps her hands together, seemingly delighted to be asked her opinion. I get the impression that's not something Emilia bothers with much.

"She was a sweet girl," she says. "Minded her own business. She only had a couple of close friends, but...but that night— when Charley ran away—I had the day off. I just always think, what if I had been there? I could've been outside, maybe. I could've seen her and—and stopped her from running away, somehow. But I wasn't here."

I shake my head. "What happened is *not* your fault, Rosemarie."

Her face collapses, and for the first time, in the rising morning light, her skin displays a road map of fine lines, brown splotches, years of worry for the students—her "children."

She sighs, swipes at her thin lips with a trembling hand. "I hope you're right."

"You said Charley ran away," I note. "Why do you say that? What would she be running away from?"

Rosemarie blinks rapidly, drops her gaze, thinks deeply about her words. "No, I—I don't want to say anything. Please, I don't know anything."

"Do you know if anyone disliked Charley?"

"Not that I know. Charley was well-liked."

I say nothing further.

Rosemarie's shoulders relax. "Please, I'm just an assistant. I'm in the kitchen. I know what to help with…with the laundry and organizing the employee schedules and—"

"Can you tell me about the employees?" If there are any workers staying on campus during winter break, I should speak with them, see if they were at the school when Charley went missing.

Rosemarie keeps her eyes on the silver tray beside me. I try asking her a different way. "Do you know how many employees stayed on campus for break?"

Rosemarie nods slowly. "Yes, okay, there's me," she says with a hesitant grin. "But like I said, I was not working that night. And then of course there's Emilia. And Mr. Edwards, and then the younger Mr. Edwards—"

"Who?"

"Blake and Jeremy Edwards. Blake is Jeremy's father," she clarifies. "They live on campus, in the little cottage on the hill. They're the only two workers living on campus at the moment. Well, I do and Emilia does, but we stay in the employee wing upstairs."

"Were they living here a week ago?"

Rosemarie's hazel eyes trace my face, her lips parting when she understands my question. "No, no. They'd never do anything. They're…nice," she says, breathless. "Blake is our maintenance man, cleaning the forest trails, clearing trees and stumps and mowing, shoveling. Heavy work. Jeremy is more like our janitor."

"He works *inside* the school?"

Rosemarie nods. "Yes. Jeremy is our little light bulb fixer. He unclogs toilets, fixes leaky sinks. Old building, old pipes." She laughs. It sounds like a choke.

"Does—"

"Let me show you where you'll be working," Rosemarie says, cutting me off. "I—I should get back to the kitchen."

I can't argue with that. I don't want to get her in trouble. She's done nothing but be kind to me. Rosemarie waits in the hall for a few minutes so I can get ready. I rush around the room like a tornado, spritzing myself with body spray so I don't smell, swallowing my morning pills so I don't get off schedule. Tossing on a clean gray turtleneck, I slide on my boots and lump everything in my giant tote bag, sling it over a lopsided shoulder.

The room spins the faster I move. I gulp water from my bottle and glance back to the portrait of the girl on the wall. When she doesn't move this time, I know it's okay to leave.

I open the door. Rosemarie stands in the hall, unmoving. Wordlessly, I follow her through the hallway, down the spiral stairwell to the main floor. We turn right at the bottom, into a dark wood-paneled hall that shoots straight ahead. At the very end are double doors, stained-glass windows at the top that let in the pale morning sunlight.

"This way," Rosemarie says.

Rounding a corner, I follow her through an archway, opening into a large library. Dusty and dark, bookshelves span gloomy wood-paneled walls. Velvet sofas cluster into little sitting nooks. Bronze sconces with little caps of green glass glow feebly in the dark air.

As I look closer, the residue of time and neglect nudges

through. The bookshelves are swathed with cobwebs. The ceilings have stains from water damage, brown spots where rain has devoured the once-fine coffering. The scent of a derelict antique store fills my nose.

"Thank you…" I say, turning around.

Rosemarie has disappeared. But I'm not alone.

THE YEAR BEFORE

FILE NAME: JPN00.012.00030923.mp3

INT: And how did you meet [redacted] when you were out with your daughter?

RES: She went into a store in the mall. I—I, uh, had a headache. I went to sit on a bench and he approached me.

INT: He approached you?

RES: Yes.

INT: And what did he say?

RES: Just, um, hi…small talk. He mentioned he had a son about [redacted] age.

INT: And what did you think of him?

RES: He was…he seemed nice. He was handsome. He gave me his phone number. I had planned to throw it away.

INT: But you didn't?

RES: No.

INT: And then what happened?

RES: [inaudible] daughter and I went home. My husband was still not home.

[00:06:17]

INT: And when did you realize [redacted] was a police officer?

RES: When I looked at what he'd given me.

INT: At the mall?

RES: Yes. He'd given me his card.

INT: And what did it say?

RES: It said his name and his title.

INT: … And that he was a police officer?

RES: Yes. I ignored it for a long time. I never wanted to call him.

INT: What prompted you to call [redacted]?

RES: [inaudible] home after work one day and walked in to see my husband and my daughter speaking quietly. They stopped when I came in.

INT: And what were they talking about?

RES: … I still don't know.

INT: Can you take a guess?

RES: At the time, I… I believed he was planning on taking my daughter from me.

INT: And why did you feel your husband would do that?

[00:07:47]

RES: I believed—at the time—he was going to leave me and take her with him, that he'd divorce me and try to get custody of her.

INT: You believed he was cheating?

RES: Yes.

INT: And—and what happened when you walked in on them talking?

RES: Nothing. I took the dog outside in the backyard. I think I stayed out there a while, thinking.

INT: And what happened next?

RES: The dog almost went through a hole in the back of the fence. I called him away so he wouldn't go through. Then I, uh, went inside to ask my husband to please fix the hole so the dog wouldn't get out.

INT: And so you went inside with the dog?

RES: Yes.

INT: Then what did you do?

RES: I went inside and my husband was on a work call.

INT: What time of the day was this?

RES: This was the evening. He works long hours. So I reminded myself to ask him in the morning, and I went upstairs to say good-night to [redacted].

INT: And then what happened?

RES: I tucked her into bed. I remember asking her if she was happy.

[00:08:34]

INT: Because at this time, you believed she wanted to live with your husband?

RES: For a brief time I… I believed he was going to move in with another woman and take my baby with him.

INT: And how did your daughter reply?

RES: Reply…?

INT: When you asked her if she was happy.

RES: She said she was trying. She was trying to be happy.

INT: And how did that make you feel?

RES: [inaudible] know.

INT: Please speak louder, closer to the—

RES: I don't know. Awful. Like an awful mother. An awful wife.

INT: Then you went to bed?

RES: Yes, the dog sleeps in her bed, and I kissed her and the dog good-night and went to bed.

INT: And then what happened?

RES: … I heard my husband downstairs. I, um, I went to talk to him. He was off the phone. I just wanted to ask him to fix the hole in the fence.

INT: How did he respond?

[00:10:09]

RES: I never got to ask him.

INT: Why is that?

RES: I tried to rectify things. I tried to tell him how much I love him…

INT: It's okay, take your time.

RES: … I told him how much I love him and [redacted] and then I tried [inaudible] and hug him and he moved away. We had a huge fight about work and a million other things. I don't know where it, um, went wrong.

INT: How does this make you feel?

RES: How would it make you feel?

INT: It would make me feel very upset if my partner and I had a fight, of course.

RES: It wasn't just a fight. He said how we should see other people.

INT: Um…uh…and how did you reply?

RES: I said I didn't want to, that I wanted to make it work with him. He's my husband. We have a daughter. This is my life. This is what I chose for my life…

INT: And then what happened, um, after your husband said you should both see other people?

RES: I thought about it. I thought about everything, about us, a lot. I realized the fight kind of just solidified what I already knew.

INT: And what was that?

RES: That he was already having an affair.

INT: So what did you do?

RES: A few days later, I called [redacted].

INT: And until this point, you had no contact with him?

RES: No.

INT: Not since you met at the mall?

RES: Right. No contact. Not until I called him.

[00:12:17]

7

Violet, the paint-splattered girl from the hallway, sits on a sofa near the library's roaring fireplace, which is carved intricately from stone and stretches up to the water-stained ceiling. Calmly, she crosses her legs as she stares at me.

A dog begins to bark outside, the sound muffled through the thick stone walls. I turn away. Still, it keeps *barking barking barking*. I look at Violet to see if she notices, but she only sits there, staring.

"Did you hear that?" I ask. She answers with a slow shake of her head. "I—I thought I heard a dog barking."

She pinches her lips together, holds back a grin. "It could've been a stray," she offers. "I've never seen one, but it's not impossible."

"Maybe..." I inch closer toward a small window cut between bookshelves and peer outside. The barking stops.

I turn around. Violet has materialized behind me, a hand

on her hip. "Should we get started?" she asks. "I was ordered to be honest when answering your questions. And I will be, I promise." Violet grins, flashing her skeletal black-and-white braces.

I grab the strap of my tote bag, squeeze it in a fist, nervous. I can't do this. I can't talk to a stranger, find ways to pluck information from their head. That's not me...not anymore. I'm incapable of it now. Helpless and hopeless and completely in over my head.

Violet seems to sense my discomfort, walks in front of me back to the sofa. Paintbrushes are stabbed in every one of her pockets, like she's a human pincushion. A violent slash of white paint stretches across her ribs.

"Do you paint?" I inquire, wanting to kick myself immediately for stating the obvious.

Violet nods enthusiastically. "I began selling portraits when I was eight," she says proudly. Every so often, she slurs some S-words—a braces side effect. She moves closer to me, her strong patchouli perfume stinging my eyes. "My mom kind of exploited me to pay the bills. But I didn't care. I loved it anyway."

We sit on opposing sofas. Violet crosses her skinny legs, stares at me with wide, emerald eyes. She's the reason I'm here, I remind myself. Violet and the three other students who'd stayed behind for winter break. They're the only link back to Charley, back to last week when Charley was still alive.

I think of what I'd asked Matt yesterday: *So you need me to get the students to open up...to dig into their brains and pass off any findings about Charley to you.*

Yes, he'd said.

This is it. This is why I'm here. Why I'd hopped on a train. Why I rode in Matt's SUV for another two hours to get here. My goal, our goal, is to find the truth behind Charley's death.

If she got lost and it was an accident, so be it. As long as that is the truth, then that is what we tell Charley's grieving mother.

All I want is the truth. And it begins with the girl sitting across from me, staring at me as if awaiting an answer to an unspoken question. It begins with Violet.

I clear my throat, hold up a shaky hand, signal for her to please give me a moment. Digging into the bowels of my tote bag, I pull out the files Rosemarie had brought to me this morning, along with my bottle of water. Floating at the bottom of the bag is a sleek silver voice recorder. I center it on the coffee table between us.

"Just, uh, one second, please," I say nervously.

Violet's eyes widen. She sighs. I can practically feel her annoyance rippling off of her. I steal a deep breath, slide out the file with her name written neatly on the edge.

KALASHNIKOV, VIOLET

DOB: 12/27/06 Ithaca, NY

-*Enrolled fall/20—Conduct & impulsive behavior focus*
-*Excels at artwork (e.g. drawing, painting)*
-*Visual & kinesthetic learner*
-*Prefers outdoor activities*
*** *ALLERGIES: Shellfish, penicillin*

Then, a short list of the medications she's on—the usual cocktail for depression and anxiety:

Lexapro (20mg/x1 daily)
Xanax (as needed, 0.5mg/x2 daily)
Seroquel (200mg 100mg/x1 daily)
* *Dr. on call: Rubenstein, Jane V./p: (516) 352-1147 6382*

I read it again. An entire section has been blocked out, erased.

Redacted.

I glance up at Violet. Her eyes bore a hole through me. I slap the file closed.

"I'm sorry," I say apologetically. "I haven't had a chance to look at your file yet."

She shrugs. I slide my glasses up my nose, cross my legs, try to stop my knee from bouncing. In my lap I have a notebook, two pens (just in case), and a bottle of water. Mirroring Violet's contented posture, I lean back a little deeper into the cushions, prop my arm up on a pillow.

"Thanks for coming, Violet. If I'd known you'd be here so early, I'd—"

"It's fine," she says, cutting me off. "The headmistress told me during breakfast. I didn't know this," she stops, waves a hand between us like she's conjuring a spell, "was going on until, like, two seconds ago, anyway." She smiles her skeleton smile and says nothing further as she tucks a knee under her thigh, back straight, face motionless, like a mannequin.

Deep breaths. Take your time. Go slow. You can do this.

"So, Violet, tell me a little about yourself." I reach over, switch on the button to begin recording.

She fidgets with a loose string on the cushion, looking tense, so I move on to something I'd preplanned in the long car ride up: a little opening about myself to make the students feel at ease.

I tell Violet how I have a daughter around her age, Izzi, and about Izzi's likes and dislikes: how she hates bananas and is afraid of heights. How she loves autumn leaves and strawberry smoothies and naps on hot summer days. Violet nods enthusiastically when I name-drop some movies we'd watched together.

Violet pauses, asks, "Have you been a shrink long?"

I glance over a shoulder to where her gaze seems to have settled. If the trajectory is correct, she's staring out of a stained-glass window framing a copse of bare willow trees.

"Yeah, kind of," I say, turning away from the window. "I've been in this profession about, um, ten years."

Violet's vivid green eyes have now moved to the fireplace, scanning the stone mantel, looking at a bronze clock perched in the center, no doubt checking the time. The clock ticks louder in the empty silence. I glance at the voice recorder, wonder if Violet notices my uneasiness. If she does, she's not showing it.

"Do you like your job?" Violet asks, biting the corner of a cherry-painted lip, bouncing her tiny knee up and down.

"I do."

"Do you like it here?"

I try not to hesitate. Too late. "It—it's interesting. I love the building," I say, too cheery, emphasizing the point by looking up and around, marveling at the coffered ceiling, the artwork on display—*ah-ha*—the perfect segue. "Do you like any of the paintings in this room?" I ask, pointing my pen toward the wall near the archway.

Violet instead stares absently into the fireplace, at the flames licking the ashen stones. "Meh," she says, gives a little shrug. "What do you think about The Rule?" she begins, not taking the bait.

I narrow my eyes at her, try to figure out what she means.

"You know...no tech? No phones or internet?" Violet prompts when I stare back, silent. "Everyone hates it. I mean, we only get wi-fi under supervision anyway, but now during break there's like no one even here to watch us, so the wi-fi access is totally gone," she laments. "I mean, yeah, I get that this place only exists to punish us, but I don't know why *I* have to be punished for the mistakes other girls have made, you know?"

I take off my glasses, rub my eyes. "I—I think it's—" Sliding my glasses back on, my throat tightens. "It's what's best for you at this point in time. Your parents thought it was the right thing to do to enroll you here, so I have to agree with their judgment."

Violet smirks, moves to sit at the edge of the sofa. "Even though you have no idea *what* I've done to be trapped here. Or even *who* my mother is."

It's not a question. I lean forward, tap my pen on the notepad. Violet's eyes follow the motion. I stop, sit back, try to relax. She changes the subject as if reading my thoughts.

"You can ask me, you know. About Charley. It's okay," she says. "I know that's why you're here. You're helping out that guy, right? That weird detective guy who's staying out in the woods."

I breathe out a laugh, ignore her question. "Okay, h-how

does the loss of Charley make you feel?" I ask, not letting go of this opportunity. I ready my pen. Check to see the recorder is still taping.

Violet stays silent.

"I'm listening," I nudge. "You can talk about anything. You can tell me anything."

"It makes me feel…"

"Go on."

"I feel sorry for her, of course. I really miss her," Violet says, her high-pitched voice pinching up at the end. "She was such a good person. The best." She stops, laughs softly to herself. "We were roommates a couple years ago, my first semester here. She always borrowed my plaid scarf. Then I'd find it later somewhere else in the school. It always smelled like her, you know? Like her perfume."

I nod, nod some more. When she doesn't speak again, I uncross my legs, show her I'm listening, relaxed, here for her. Trustworthy.

I study her, study her movements. She's at times slow and deliberate, but her eyes move quick, constantly on alert. An engrained method of self-protection. Sometimes, people reveal their true selves when they think no one else is looking. I've learned to pay attention.

Violet remains silent. Flames from the fireplace flicker in her eyes, a miniature reflection.

I tap my pen against my notepad again, stop before she notices. My heart races. I wish I could unspool her mind, squeeze out the insides.

"I wonder if anyone spoke with Charley the day she disappeared," I say to myself, hoping Violet will jump in. "Maybe, if someone did, her family can get a better idea of what was in Charley's mind that night she went into the woods."

THE NIGHT IT ENDED

Violet bites her bottom lip, a subconscious signal people tend to do when they want to hold words inside.

"You can tell me," I purr. "Nothing you say here leaves this room." *Lie.* She says nothing. "Do you know if Charley was bullied?" I ask. "Her mother claims she was bullied at her old high school."

Violet doesn't take the bait. Instead, she tilts her head. "I didn't talk to Charley that day," she begins, "but I saw something."

I lean forward. "What did you see?"

She inhales a gulp of air. "I mean, I didn't see anything that day, but I saw something when she was my roommate." She looks up at me, hesitant, as if unsure she should disclose this new, top-secret information.

"It's okay," I pry, "you can tell me."

She leans forward. "Two years ago, when I first came here, I saw her—sleepwalk."

"Sleepwalk?"

Violet nods. "Yeah. She'd get up, walk around. Once, I followed her," she says, voice growing low and soft. "She walked down the hallway into the bathroom. And I watched her, standing there, staring at herself in the mirror. I was, like, freaked out. I didn't know what to do. She just stood there, staring. Eventually I got tired of watching her so I went back to bed."

"And then what happened?"

She shrugs. "I don't know. She was in bed the next morning so I guess she came back." Violet pauses, wipes her mouth with the back of a hand. "But I've been thinking. What if she sleepwalked *that* night?"

"Into the woods?"

"It's possible, isn't it?"

I lean back, scribble in my notepad, *Violet claims Charley sleepwalked.*

I look up at her. She's already looking at me, eyes unblinking, searching mine.

"I'll be right there!" Kiara's voice calls from the hallway.

Violet flips her head around, exhales. "That's my cue," she says, standing to leave. "Your next victim is here." Slowly, her lips part open against her black-and-white braces, grinning her skeleton grin.

"Thanks for coming. See you soon, Violet." I bend over, switch off the voice recorder, release a massive sigh.

When she leaves, I take a moment to stand, stretch, head over to an antique wooden desk beneath the stained-glass window to covertly glance at Emilia's student files before Kiara arrives. But she's already here, I realize, when the floor creaks behind me. Emilia must be shuffling them all in today, one after the next, so she can get me out of here ASAP. Fine with me.

"Have a seat, Kiara. I'll be right there."

I drop the files on the desk, smooth my hair back in a bun, ready myself for another session.

But when I turn around, no one is there.

8

My gaze fixates on the squeaky spot on the floor, eyes gone dry.

My throat tightens. One interview session and already it feels like the walls of the library are closing in. I shiver. There's something *off* about this place. Something wrong.

I take a deep breath. The musty scent of old books punches the back of my throat. Fresh air. I just need fresh air. To breathe it in, smell the earth. That's all.

"You okay?"

I jump, startled, spin around to see Kiara standing in the archway behind me.

"Yeah, sorry about that," I mumble, paste on a fragile smile. "Are you ready to—"

"*Actually...*" Kiara says, "I have to run, but I'll be back, I swear, it's just—now isn't a good time."

"Oh, okay—"

"I only wanted to tell you. I didn't want to leave you high and dry."

"Thanks, that's very kind of you," I say as Kiara rushes out of the room.

My shoulders slump. I exhale, fight the urge to steal a nap before another student arrives. Instead, I grab my bag off the sofa, shove everything back into it—water bottle, voice recorder, notepad, pens—and exit the library. I dash down the dark hallway toward the double doors at the end of the hall. Hiding up in a corner is an old wall-mounted camera.

The students don't know the cameras don't work, Emilia had said. *They haven't worked in years.*

I look over a shoulder to be sure no one's watching, and when I know I'm alone, I burst through the doors, the December cold instantly nipping at my cheeks. The campus is entirely empty, the only sound the wind lashing in my ears.

Glancing behind me, I realize I must be at the back of the school. The rear of the building looms high above me, the myriad of windows reflecting the white winter sky, like eyes. Ahead is a small clearing and overgrown lane leading to twin, stone guard towers, ancient and forgotten.

My teeth begin to clatter as I walk around the side of the school toward the front courtyard, the forest looming all around me. Though it's the dead of winter, dense evergreens glow bright green, their long arms outstretched, covered with the faintest breath of midmorning snow.

My heartbeat slows. I need to breathe, need to think, even though I'm only wearing a sweater and my hands have already turned to ice. Ever since the moment I woke up I feel like I've been in a battle. With Rosemarie waking me and then Violet waiting for me, knowing I was fully unprepared, to swearing I wasn't alone in the library when I was… I feel completely inept. Maybe I shouldn't have come up here. Maybe I shouldn't have told Matt I would.

I just wanted to escape.

After I've walked the length of the building, the front courtyard finally comes into view. My feet are ice, and I tuck my hands into my armpits, attempt to keep them warm. Matt's SUV is still the only car parked in the cobbled drive. Seeing his car makes my anxiety ease slightly. Just knowing he's still on campus is a relief, even though I don't know where the guesthouse Emilia provided for him is.

I escape the courtyard and head down a gentle hill toward a grassy ridge at the edge of the forest. Nestled between a pair of pines is a little bench, and I sit, dropping my heavy tote bag on the needle-covered ground. Facing the dense woods, I stare into the shadows. The evergreens are so thick I can hardly see ten feet in the distance.

What made Charley come out here alone that night? It was cold, Matt had said. Freezing, maybe around the same temperature it is now. I roll up the sleeves of my sweater, leave my hands exposed, and pull down the turtleneck, exposing my throat.

Charley was wearing pajamas, lightweight and flimsy. She had no coat. No shoes. Just a minute sitting outside with my skin exposed is making my entire body shiver uncontrollably. I give up, tuck my cheeks down into the turtleneck, tug my sleeves over my frozen hands.

I don't know how she managed to make it as far as she did into the woods. I wouldn't last fifty feet. She was later found over a mile from the main school building. How did she make it that far—barefoot?

Maybe Violet was right. Maybe Charley *was* sleepwalking. That would explain it, certainly. She was asleep. When sleeping, the human mind often isn't aware of outside elements—

sound, temperature, touch, smell—as we are when we're awake. There have been people who've slept through earthquakes and fire alarms, babies screaming, sinkholes engulfing their home.

Or… Charley experienced something far worse.

What if Charley *did* sleepwalk into the woods. But not far, at all. Just ten feet deep into the woods ahead of me is where my vision ends. Ten feet of visibility. In the dead of night, who knows how much Charley could see ahead of her. What if she woke up? What if the school was right there, right through the trees, yet she couldn't see it? What if she got lost, trying desperately to find her way back in the dark?

She'd be terrified.

My gut aches with the thought. I want to help Matt give Charley's mother the truth behind her daughter's death. As a mother, I'd want to know *why*. If it was my daughter—if it was Izzi—that's all I'd want. If I couldn't have my daughter back, the truth is all that would matter.

And so, knowing my flaws, knowing I'm inadequate, in this moment, as my breath fogs into the icy air, I decide to stay.

A sudden *bang* behind me.

Bang.

Bang.

Constant and steady, the sound travels through the icy air. I turn around, sling my tote bag over my shoulder, cross my arms to keep the heat in. I bite my bottom lip, try to stop my jaw from clacking. It doesn't work.

I follow the sound, walking back up the gentle hill toward the front courtyard. In the distance on the other side is a little stone cottage; sprouts of smoke escape a pair of chimneys. The sound continues, *bang bang bang.*

I narrow my eyes, push my glasses up my nose. Outside on the side of the cottage is a man. I walk further up the hill, cross the courtyard toward him.

The man wears a bright orange vest, the kind hunters wear. He's chopping wood, I realize, as he lifts an axe high over his head, slams it down onto a log. Wood splinters in two, cleaves in half, falls to the ground.

I approach him, clearing my throat on the way. Suddenly, he stops, looks up, watches as I stand at the edge of the courtyard, body shivering from the cold.

If this is the man Rosemarie had mentioned, he lived and worked on campus when Charley—

"And who might you be?" he calls out.

I step closer, wonder how he's not shivering like me. Aside from his orange vest, he wears nothing but dusty blue jeans and a snug flannel shirt, the buttons down his chest aching to pop open. His face is harsh and mostly shielded by an unkempt black beard, the only visible part the finely lined skin surrounding his sunken, dark eyes.

"My name's, uh—Dr. Madeline Pine," I say, remembering what Rosemarie had told me earlier this morning: *They live on campus, in the little cottage on the hill.* But I can't remember their names.

"Why are you outside," he asks. "Women should stay indoors in the winter."

My jaw drops, closes, begins clattering again. "What's your name?" I ask, crossing my arms tight across my chest.

The man scoffs, takes another slice at a log, the wood splitting in two.

"Blake," he mumbles.

"What?"

"Blake Edwards." He glowers at me suspiciously, raises the axe ever so slightly. "Why? Who's asking?"

Footsteps.

"Dad—Dad, I—"

A teenage boy rounds the corner of the cottage, a red chain saw held in his fist.

Blake spins around, yells, "What did I teach you about sneaking up on people using tools?"

"You said—"

"I said *never* do that, didn't I?"

The boy places the chain saw by his feet. "Yeah." He shrugs, eyes trained on the ground. "But I thought this would make it easier."

Blake sneers at the boy, shakes his head. The boy's eyes flicker toward me, embarrassed, ashamed.

I gulp, begin to turn around so I can get the hell out of here. I was planning on talking with him a little, to see if he knew anything at all about Charley, but that plan is out the window.

"Who are you?"

I turn around.

The boy steps forward, shoulders slumped. "Are you here with that police guy?" he asks meekly. "Detective Reyes?"

Blake drops the axe, turns to glare at the back of the boy's head. He walks like a seesaw, swaying back and forth, edging closer.

I bunch my sweater in my fists. "Uh, yeah. Yeah, you can say that," I say. "My name's Madeline. What's yours?"

He glances back at Blake before answering, "Jeremy."

Jeremy. Blake's son. I remember what Rosemarie had said now. Jeremy works inside the school. The *little light bulb fixer*, she'd called him. He looks like his father, though underneath his overstuffed camouflage coat I can tell he's at least fifty pounds lighter. A swollen black eye throbs purple above his cheekbone; his face is peppered with facial hair and the throes of teenage acne. Dyed black hair sags straight to his jaw, auburn roots creating the illusion his scalp is on fire.

"Are you here about Charley?" Jeremy asks.

I nod.

"Do they know anything more? Do they know what happened?"

I step closer, try to make eye contact. The boy lowers his head, looks away.

"How old are you, Jeremy?" I ask, guessing he's older than he looks.

"Eighteen."

I offer a grin. "Uh, well, we're working on it," I say. "I only arrived yesterday, so it's still early."

"I found her," Jeremy says morosely. "Out there...in the woods." He lifts an arm, throws a hand back to scratch the top of his head. The angle of his elbow juts through his coat, sharp, bony.

Blake shakes his head. "Jeremy—"

"Far from everything."

"*Shut up—*"

"I called 911," Jeremy continues.

My eyes widen.

Blake notices my reaction, steps forward, grabs Jeremy by the back of his neck.

"I said *shut up!*" His fingers pinch into Jeremy's neck and the boy squeals, shoulders tensing for protection.

"Okay, stop, stop! *Please!*"

Blake releases his son.

Jeremy's eyes glaze with tears. "I—I didn't do anything!" he cries before sprinting away, disappearing back behind the cottage.

Blake glances at me before grabbing his axe, seesaws closer toward me.

"Anything else?" he says, the handle twisting in his fists.

"I—I have to go, I have to meet someone," I say, not knowing or caring who, so long as I can escape him.

I keep my eyes on Blake as I slowly back away. When I feel I'm far enough, I turn around and run across the courtyard back to the safety of the school.

9

Pulling open the main door of the school, I'm hit by a blast of icy wind as I step into the carriage tunnel.

Whispers.

Kiara and Alice approach from the other end, nothing but shadows until they near the dim light of a chandelier dangling overhead. Their eyes flicker toward me, then turn straight ahead, tragic and unconnected, tethered to nothing.

I can't take my eyes off of them, even after they've disappeared.

"Hey—"

I spin around, breath catching in my throat, mouth open, ready to scream. "*Shit*—you scared the hell out of me."

Matt holds up his hands, apologetic. "I'm sorry, I tried calling your phone but it never went through, so I figured I'd come get you."

Shit. I'd almost forgotten. I'd traded phones, got rid of the sleek black phone on the train, swapped it for the chunky white one now burrowed deep in my tote bag.

"Let me give you a new number to try. Sorry." I laugh weakly, embarrassed, somehow.

Seen.

He steps closer as I tell him the number for the white phone. A smile grows across his face as he taps his fingers across his screen. "And *this* number works?"

"Normally, yeah. But up here in the middle of nowhere, who knows," I admit.

Matt gives a laugh. "That's true," he says, breath fogging into the cold air.

I tilt my head. "What did you mean when you said you'd, 'come get me'? Did I forget we were supposed to meet today?"

"Yeah, remember when we spoke on the drive up yesterday...?" He trails off, searching my eyes for any hint of remembrance. When I don't chime in, he continues, "I mentioned how when we got to the school I'd show you evidence initially gathered by police."

"Oh, right," I say, smoothing my frazzled hair back into a low bun. "Sorry, I forgot." *I've been preoccupied with strange school assistants, students, and maintenance men with axes*, I think but don't say.

"Follow me," Matt says.

He leads me across the wide courtyard, kicking through a faint dusting of snow that hides, unmelted, in every shadow. Still without a coat and freezing, I shove my hands into my pockets, curl them into fists.

Matt notices.

"Here," he says, shrugging off his heavy peacoat. "Take it."

"No, no, I'm okay."

"Take it. Please," he says, adjusting his glasses. "I'm hot."

I roll my eyes, take his coat, drape it over my shoulders.

Warmth envelopes me. The lining is quilted maroon corduroy and smells of old clove cigarettes.

Matt gently places his hand on my back, guides me down a narrow pathway stretching deep into the woods, down a gentle hill. Shadows of cottages and woodsheds hiding between copses of evergreens overtake the dappled sunlight bleeding through the pines.

Matt's boot crunches a twig in half. He glances at me sideways, holds out an arm. "May I introduce you to my humble abode?"

Up ahead is a small stone cottage, lights on inside glowing the windows bright. A little painted slab of slate nailed near the door reads: *Guesthouse II-Shadow Hunt Hall.*

Matt unlocks the door, tosses the keys on a table beside the stairs. It's modest, beautiful yet simple, with wide wood-plank floors, like an eighteenth-century barn. Every inch of plaster is covered with bucolic paintings of forests and streams. Toward the back is an all-white kitchen, a tiny wooden table for four in the center.

I follow Matt into the kitchen, the countertops and table completely littered with files, photographs, loose papers, and an open, empty gun box.

"Some of the work I've done so far," Matt says, waving a hand around the room. "Not much yet. I've only been on the case a few days."

"I'd say for a one-man crusade, you've done quite a lot," I admit, flipping open a manila folder to sneak a peek inside. "Do you have a copy of the preliminary autopsy?"

Matt nods, walks toward the kitchen table, excavates a laptop buried beneath layers of paperwork. Glancing at me, he types in the password.

"Why's Emilia allowing you to stay on campus, anyway?"

I ask, as Matt pulls up Charley's autopsy report. "And why aren't you staying in the main building?"

He bites his lower lip, clicks open a file. "I've been getting the impression she doesn't want me on campus," he says. "Let alone in the main building. But I'm comfortable out here. And I'd rather not risk the students being around my weapon."

"Fair enough."

"And I'm sure Emilia has her reasons for allowing me to stay here," he says. "I'd bet at the top of the list is her wanting to save face with the parents. It would look bad if she didn't cooperate with a request from the mother of a deceased student. Accident or not, Charley's death did occur on school property."

I nod. "True. The school could face some nasty publicity, too," I say. "I mean, think of how bad it would look if Emilia didn't allow the police to investigate the death of one of her students. It would look like she was trying to hide something, right?"

"Absolutely," he says. "It could open the school up to a lawsuit, if not a lot of bad press. All right, here we go." Matt scrolls through the opened file. "Dr. Pine—"

"Madeline."

"Madeline," he says. "Before you see these photos—you should sit down."

Suddenly burning hot, I shrug his peacoat off my shoulders, yank down my turtleneck to get some air. Matt notices the tiny scabs on my neck from where I'd cut myself on the train. He eyes it for a second, chooses to ignore it. Nothing more than a mere surface wound.

"The final autopsy report won't be done for several more days," he says as he begins to click through the file.

At the top of the page is Charley's biographical information: name, date of birth, height, weight. Below that is a new section titled, *Type of Death* with the word, *Accident* circled in thick black ink. Drawn underneath is a simplistic outline of the female body—head, torso, legs, arms. Black ink litters the drawing, highlighting the numerous injuries Charley had endured.

Matt points to the screen. "Charley had head wounds," he explains, the reflection of the screen mirrored in his glasses. "The medical examiner claims they were caused by her tripping and hitting her head on a rock."

"When she fell down the hill."

He nods, points to another part of the drawing. "She also had internal bleeding, which they claim is from the fall." I gulp. He continues. "She had defensive wounds on her hands and forearms."

I lean back in the chair. "Let me guess," I say. "From falling down the hill."

Matt grins slyly. "Her pajamas were torn—possibly from the fall—but also could've been from the woods. Maybe catching on bark or twigs."

I lean forward, point to a tiny mark noted at the top of Charley's skull. "What's this?"

"Charley was found next to a rock in the woods," Matt says, clicking to the next page in the report. "The police believe she fell on it. Her blood was found on it. No fingerprints, though." Matt stops, hesitates.

"What are you thinking?"

Scratching stubble on his chin, he says, "To be perfectly honest…no one would ever really be able to tell the difference between if she fell on it or was beaten with it."

I recoil from the thought. "Beaten with it? As in, blunt force trauma?"

Matt nods sagely. "That's one part of the puzzle."

I let out a deep breath. "Whatever happened, that's a hell of a beating," I say. "All of that trauma. I can't imagine how afraid she was. Whether she died from tumbling down a hill or—"

"If something *else* happened to her," Matt adds softly.

The kitchen falls into silence.

After a moment, he asks, "Do you want to see more photos?"

I shake my head. "I've seen enough."

He nods in understanding. "I think you can understand now why Charley's mother wants answers," he says.

I lower my head, not wanting to give my opinion. I'm not here for an opinion. I'm here for the truth, whatever that may be.

Matt continues, "Charley's mother believes something's not right with the autopsy. And no matter what, she deserves the truth."

"She does," I say. But deep down I have a feeling that the truth won't be so easy to come by.

Cases like Charley's have a tendency to close with no satisfying answers for the family. Cases like Charley's have a habit of lingering in online message boards, where amateur sleuths will discuss their visits to the wooded hill where Charley was found, and try to decipher leaked autopsy notes and interviews with the students.

Cases like Charley's tend to go unsolved.

Matt closes out of the report, leans back in his chair. "I know you haven't been at the school long, but have you learned anything?" he asks. "Anything from Emilia or from the students? Anything at all?"

I bite my lip, reach into my bag I'd dropped on the floor next to me. Flipping open my notepad, I read Matt the few lines of notes I'd managed to take this morning at the school.

"A student named Violet claims Charley sleepwalked in the past," I say, clearing my throat.

Matt nods, jots down a note for himself on a yellow legal pad. "Sleepwalking," he says flatly to himself. "Interesting. Okay, what's next?"

"Um, Rosemarie, Emilia's school assistant—"

"Met her," Matt says. "She claims she was at home the day Charley disappeared."

I narrow my eyes. "Funny, she told me she lives on campus and was off that day."

"So if she had the day off and lives on campus…" Matt trails off.

"She *was* on campus, regardless of if she was working or not." He presses his lips together. As he scribbles down another note, I continue, "Anyway, she says she thinks Charley was running away from something." I shrug. "I don't know. That makes sense, I guess."

Matt keeps writing in his notepad in handwriting that's less private investigator and more surgeon; I'd never be able to make sense of his words.

"Running away." He stops, drops his pen. "Running from what? Did she say?" I shake my head. Matt exhales in frustration.

"Oh," I begin. "I also ran into some colorful characters. One had an axe."

Matt's dark eyebrows rise. "I have an idea who it is, and if it's not him, I'd be surprised."

"Blake?"

He groans. "So you were lucky enough to have your very own meet and greet with the infamous Blake." Matt looks up at me. "The guy hates me. Wants me gone. I swear, he thinks this entire campus is *his* property."

"His son, Jeremy, was interesting, too."

Matt's eyes narrow. "And *I* am interested to hear what you have to say about him."

"He seems… I don't know…" I trail off, thinking of his dyed black hair and swollen black eye. "Sad? He said he's the one who found Charley's body."

Matt sighs, nods. "Jeremy found her, called 911. Didn't do anything after that, just waited for the police to arrive."

I imagine the scene: an early winter morning, fresh snowfall painting the woods with a ghostly haze. Jeremy, alone with Charley's body, staying with her until the sound of sirens screamed through the trees.

"What the hell was he doing out there?" I ask.

"He stated he was, 'out for a walk.'"

"Do you believe him?"

He laughs under his breath "I'm not sure what I believe," he says. "Not yet, anyway. I've done this long enough to know *anyone* is capable of anything."

"Have you spoken to them yet?" I ask. "About Charley?"

"Believe me, I've tried. But Blake—he's, uh—difficult. It's a shame…he fits my profile nicely. Single, early forties, physically capable. Appears to be socially isolated—aside from his son. He had the means and the opportunity. I just can't figure out the motive."

"Means, motive, and opportunity," I mutter to myself. "The three pillars of murder."

We discuss the case for the rest of the afternoon. Before I know it, the entire day has flown by. By the end, Matt has touched every piece of paperwork he has. I glance out of the window, see the forest outside has grown dark.

"Stay for dinner," he offers with a smile. "I think I have a spare frozen pot pie."

I smile back. "Sounds tempting, but I have to get going." I scoop my tote bag off the floor as Matt grabs his peacoat, drapes it over my shoulders. "No, really, I'm fine—"

He ignores my protest. "Don't go yet. I have a present for

you." He dashes into the other room, returns a moment later, arms bursting with a stack of files. I groan. "For you," he says, passing them to me. "Some copies of preliminary notes I compiled this morning. I made a set for you."

"Thanks," I mumble, flipping through the pages. Glossy crime scene photos are paper-clipped haphazardly to some edges. I avoid letting my eyes linger.

"I don't think I have to remind you to keep them away from the girls," Matt says. "We can't have them seeing what happened to their classmate. Christ, can you imagine?"

I shake my head, glance at my new stack of files, wrap them tight in my arms. One piece sticks out on the side. I drag it out, lay it flat on top. "What's this?"

Matt peers over to see. "Article from this morning's paper. Nothing new in there, just general info on what happened. But I have to warn you," he begins, nodding at the stack of files. "Don't spend too much time reading through, okay?"

"Yeah, I get it," I say. "Time is of the essence."

He lowers his head. "No, it's not that. It's just—promise me you won't stare too long. Stare too long and it becomes a whole different animal. It becomes personal."

I clear my throat, look away from the news article. For some strange reason, I can't help but think that's precisely what's already happened to him.

I swallow down his warning. "I promise."

"Please, let me walk you back."

"I'm fine," I say, plastering on a smile. "Really."

"At least take this," he says, passing me a flashlight once I step outside. "We'll talk soon, okay?" He closes the door behind me. I catch him peeking through the window curtains.

Stepping into the darkness, I press the stack of papers close to my chest. Cold flutters over me. But it's not from the winter winds.

If Charley's death was an accident, why did she have defensive wounds on the palms of her hands? How were her feet bare with no scratches on the soles? No dirt embedded between her exposed toes?

I can't help but think—was Charley's death really an accident?

Or murder?

Either way, if someone else was responsible for her death, I want them to suffer.

Matt's warning flickers through my head: *Promise me you won't stare too long.*

I push his warning away. Because for me, it was always personal, right from the start. From the moment he called, I felt like I knew Charley, as if she were my own. As I'd listened to his voice mail, a single thought kept puncturing my mind:

What if she was Izzi?

From now on, there's only one way I can continue. I have to assume until proven otherwise that Charley's death was *not* an accident. That something else, something still unknown, happened. Questioning the unquestionable is the only way to learn the truth.

And I will learn the truth.

Before I realize it, I've reached the school. Pulling open the front door, I remember something Matt had said earlier. It shoots through my mind like a comet, so fast and fleeting it nearly disappears.

Anyone is capable of anything.

10

Going up the stairs to my bedroom, I tilt my head back, stare into the glass dome high above. Moonlight swells into the stairwell, throwing my shadow against the stones. Everything looks different in the dark, more solemn, formal, like a funeral home.

The doors lining the hall to my room are closed, the regular inhabitants away for winter break. One has faint light coming from a crack near the floor from one of the girls staying up late. I think it's engrained in teenage girls. Sometimes, Izzi would hide under her covers, watching hour-long conspiracy videos about fast-food restaurants and hidden messages in movies. I'd hear her laughing at two in the morning sometimes before I'd have to get up and tell her to go to sleep.

But sometimes I was the bad influence. We'd binge-watched an entire season of *The Vampire Diaries* once, snuggled up together on the sofa by the stairs. The living room was dark.

I'd made homemade pizza and we ate until we got sick. We stayed up so late Izzi slept through her alarm clock the next morning and missed the bus. I was already at work. When I came home, she shouted at me, blamed me until she fled the room in tears. We never stayed up late together again.

Mom, please just stop.

I creak the door open, shuffle into the bathroom. A claw-foot tub rests down a deep cubbyhole, an intricately tiled archway surrounding it. Placing the files Matt had given me beside the bathtub, I peel off my watch and shoes and grab a bar of soap from the linen closet. I untangle my coat, my pants, my disheveled hair. My glasses slide down my nose, lopsided. I feel like a knotted-up necklace. The old pipes sing as I turn on the hot water and plug up the drain, let it run until water creeps to the top.

I need a million things right now. My evening prescriptions, food, a bath, sleep. As the steaming tub slowly fills, I pop open a bottle, tuck a few pills beneath my tongue. Cupping a hand beneath the faucet, I watch the water pour through my fingers, then fill my palms, bring them up to swallow down the mouthful of pills.

Slowly, I step into the bath. The hot water melts away the frigid winds and macabre pictures. Matt's files rest beside me, balanced on a little wooden stool I'd dragged in from the bedroom. On it is a protein bar, my medications, an emergency pack of cigarettes I keep hidden in the lining of my luggage.

I haven't smoked one yet. I'm slightly terrified of the fire alarm going off. But if I ever get to *that point*, I know they're there. I know it's unhealthy. At least I don't drink, anymore.

I sink deeper into the water. My head dances to imagining Charley's weeping mother at home in Nevada, planning her daughter's funeral, tear-soaked tissues fluttering around her like fallen birds. The courage and strength it must've taken to find a private investigator, to call him, to tell him about the case. To relive it all. My gut aches. It would've broken me. I would have broken.

My skin squeaks along the bottom of the tub as I reach for something to read. Carefully, I pluck a printed online article from the pile and bring it into the tub with me.

IRON HILL, NY—A 16-year-old student at Shadow Hunt Hall, a private, all-girls boarding school, was found dead in a heavily wooded area inside school grounds early Sunday morning, according to Iron Hill police.

The teen from Las Vegas, NV, was missing overnight and into the morning before being found by a staff member who lives on campus.

Police told reporters they were called to the scene near Star Point Lane around 7:45 a.m. The preliminary autopsy shows no signs of foul play. Paramedics pronounced her dead at the scene.

Police indicated that it appeared the student was sleepwalking in the woods on campus before accidentally falling into a ravine. Iron Hill Police Chief Joseph Ackerman commented, "My heart goes out to the family. What a sad way to lose a child."

The teenage girl's identity has not been released, pending contact with the family.

Charley's face flashes in my head. It'd just snowed before the initial crime scene photographs were taken, leaving her body encased in a faint, snow-coated film. My throat tightens with a stab of nausea.

I read the article again. Sleepwalking? The police on the scene believed she was out there alone, with no shoes on, not even a coat...

I grind my teeth, drop the papers on the floor, and sit up in the tub, sending water sloshing over the sides.

Stepping out of the bath, I wrap a towel around my waist, plop down naked on a footstool matched to a makeup vanity tucked in a corner. Hanging above it is a mirror, a cherub with outstretched arms carved into the frame.

I turn sideways toward the window, look out into nothingness—the field and courtyard in front of the school nothing but a gaping, black hole yawning into the night.

As I stare at my reflection, a hundred thoughts bounce through my head.

How did Charley really die? Did she get lost in the woods at night, somehow end up falling into a ravine? I've heard of people waking in the middle of the night on camping and rock-climbing trips. They lose their sense of direction on their way to relieve themselves in the woods or in rocky mountains and tragically fall to their deaths. But is that what happened to Charley? Could it be that simple?

The simplest answer is often the truth.

I begin unknotting my tangled hair. The steam from the bath has fogged the window. I wipe a hand through the condensation, stare out into the night.

A dark figure lurks in the courtyard below, their body nothing but a shadow. I wonder who on campus it could be. The girls—Violet, Alice, Kiara, and Hannah—should be in their rooms for the night. Rosemarie and Emilia wouldn't go out this late in the cold. Matt should be in the guest cottage where I'd just left him. He'd mentioned working late on Charley's case, then heading to the police station early to check the status of the final autopsy report. That leaves only two people it could be. Blake and Jeremy.

The moment their names enter my mind, the dark figure turns. The shadow shrinks, takes the form of a girl. I sharpen my eyes in the darkness. Her face blurs into focus beneath a slice of moonlight. She looks up, looks at me, eyes trained directly on my window.

I stare back, frozen and numb with a creeping chill. Even from up here, I know exactly who she is. Her thin frame. Her purple hair and heart-shaped face. It's the girl I'd seen in the hallway, the girl playing the viola. Alice.

I move away from the window, wrench the curtains closed.

From down in the courtyard, was it possible Alice saw me naked? What could someone really see from that distance? My cheeks flush with embarrassment. But there are more important questions. Why was Alice outside alone at night? Where was she going? If I get dressed and go after her, I can't know for sure where she'd gone. I could be out there all night chasing a ghost.

I toss my hairbrush onto the vanity, resigned to learn the answers in the morning, and turn off the lights on my way to bed. Sitting on the edge, I can't keep a phrase from Charley's news article out of my head: *My heart goes out to the family. What a sad way to lose a child.*

Is there a happy way to lose a child? No matter what, you lose them. They're gone. No matter how, when, or why, they're out of your life, forever. You'll never see them again. Hug them again. Hear their laugh…

My chest tightens. I think of Izzi. All I want is to tell her I love her. To say I'm sorry. To beg forgiveness. I miss her—miss her father. I'll admit it. I miss him. Just forgive me. I made a mistake. I knew it then. I know it now. But I can't go back. No one can. No one can fix what has happened, especially me.

But it's okay. It's fine, really. I can punish myself. It's all I have left. Punishment. I'll keep punishing myself until I earn their forgiveness. Maybe if I try hard enough, if I can just do something good, help someone else, Dave and Izzi will forgive me. It can start here. At this school. With these girls.

With Charley.

I close my eyes and fall into bed, tears running down my cheeks. My head lands on the pillow. *Thunk.* A splitting pain shoots through my head, down my neck. I see stars, rub the back of my head. Pain hammers in my skull.

What was that? My head didn't land on a pillow. It wasn't soft. Well, it was, but beneath it, under it—

Jolting up, I turn on the bedside lamp, grab the pillow, throw it across the room.

Resting on the mattress is a brick.

I stare at it until my eyes go dry.

I'm afraid to touch it. To move it. It can't be real. It can't…

Why is there a brick under my pillow? Who put it there? I've only been at the school two days. Had I already done something to someone that had angered them? Did I say something wrong?

My head spins. Pain oozes around the sides of my head like vise-grip headphones. More tears spill down my face. The muscles in my forehead begin to hurt from crying. I wipe away the tears, massage the back of my neck, wish I'd brought my other painkillers with me instead of just my usual cocktail.

The rest of the night, my head pulses with pain. I sit on the cold floor with the lights on, the brick still resting on the mattress and my eyes wide open.

Sunday, December 18

11

A restless night.

My body is heavy when my alarm goes off. The floor is cold and hard. My neck pops. It smells like apple pie in my room. I lift my head, breathe in the melted butter and sugar, savor every second.

Dave's voice: *Feeling blue, sunshine?*

My throat begins to clench. I drop my head back onto the floor. I can't swallow, can't breathe. The sudden flood of anxiety is thick, choking, growing barbed roots inside my lungs. I inhale a deep breath, let it out slow, remember how to find control. But sometimes, nothing can stop it once it starts.

My back aches as I stand from the floor. I twist my body back and forth, wring myself out like a wet towel, try to make my spine crack. Stepping onto a footstool, I reach to remove the batteries from the smoke detector, and crack open a heavy, lead-paned window. Focusing on pushing the anxiety away,

I light a cigarette, inhale as deep as I can, cough out a lungful of smoke.

The tightness in my throat begins to ease. I breathe in, out, steady and rhythmically, like a heartbeat.

Slowly, the anxiety begins to wane.

I've been told depression is living in the past. Anxiety is living in the future.

For me, it's both. All the time.

I click on a lamp, take a bite from a stale protein bar. Uncapping my prescriptions, I toss the white tops across the nightstand. Never take pills on an empty stomach, I always remind myself. Even a tiny bite of food helps stop acid from burning away your insides.

I grab my phone, press it to my ear as I walk into the bathroom, listen to a voice mail Dave had left me:

Hey, just wanted to call and say hi. I hope things are going okay at work. Izzi is fine. She's upstairs now. She told me she wants to talk to you about something, so maybe when you come home, keep that in mind. Okay, talk to you soon… Love you.

I drop the cigarette into the toilet, listen to the sad little sizzle it makes as it hits the water. An inescapable chill washes over me. A feeling like I'm not alone.

I shake my head clear, turn to unzip my luggage to unfold a fresh shirt. Today is a new day. The cafeteria is starting breakfast soon, I realize, glancing at my watch. Almost seven. I can sit with the girls, observe them a little, see them in their natural habitat before I begin my interviews for the rest of the day. Maybe I can even get Alice alone, ask her what she was doing last night when I saw her outside in the courtyard.

As I'm about to get dressed, a soft knock sounds at the door. I rush to throw something on, hesitantly crack it open. Emilia stands on the other side, a heavy silver tray balancing in her hands.

"Good morning."

"Good morning," I grimly mirror back.

Her face opens into a smile. "You didn't come down to eat," she says, slightly annoyed.

I double-check my watch. Breakfast in the cafeteria began one minute ago. I open the door wider. She comes in, heels clacking on the wooden floor. She glances around quickly, like I'm hiding something. I stare at the back of her head.

Emilia slides the silver tray onto the bed, sits, pats the spot next to her. "Food's a little cold, but it's just some fruit and toast. I gave you mine. I have to watch the carbs," she says, patting her slim, belted waist.

I scan the tray. On a little glass plate are a few pieces of burned toast and a ramekin of orange marmalade. Beside it is a white bowl filled with overripe peaches in a clear sauce, maraschino cherries floating on the top like buoys. Next to that is a porcelain mug of black tea and a crystal goblet filled with water.

"Thanks, but I was going to go down to have breakfast with the students," I say, subtly refusing to take a seat beside her. "I smelled apple pie when I woke up and was hoping to grab a slice."

Emilia lets out a laugh. "We never have apple pie here, Dr. Pine," she says warily, crossing her legs. "The girls aren't allowed to have sugar until after dinner. Nothing sweeter than fruit during the day. It's part of our mission statement. Whole bodies, whole minds."

She peers at me, catches the confusion painted across my face. She knows something's wrong. Thankfully, she chooses to ignore it.

"Okay, never mind…" I trail off. "Actually, I'm glad you're here. I have to show you something."

"As headmistress of this school," Emilia begins, "I wanted to apologize if I've not been as welcoming as I could've been."

I ignore her, circle the bed, walk toward the brick hidden beneath my pillow.

She has to know what happened last night. I could've seriously hurt myself. If I fell onto the pillow just a little harder, who knows what could've happened. And who would even do that? Who would think to place a brick beneath a stranger's pillow?

I grab the pillow in a fist. "Emilia, I have to show you something."

Her eyebrows swerve together. "What is it?"

I exhale, grip the pillow tighter. "Last night when I went to bed, I felt something—hard—under my pillow."

Emilia cocks her head, birdlike.

"When I lifted it up, I found…a brick."

Her eyes ignite. "I'm sorry, you found a what?"

"Someone put a brick under my pillow." I grab the pillow, lift it up, watch her face fall. Slowly, her eyes lift to meet mine. Confusion clouds her expression.

I glance down at the mattress.

The brick is gone.

"I—I don't understand," Emilia whispers. She says nothing more. She doesn't have to.

My insides tremble from embarrassment, from frustration, from confusion. I drop the pillow on the bed, stumble backward toward the door. I don't understand. It was there. Last night. I saw it. When I went to bed, I saw it. I turned on the lights. I slept on the floor. How can it be gone? I was alone last night. No one was here, no one but me. Right?

"Dr. Pine, are you okay?"

I nod, watch as her eyes fall to my nightstand, to where my

army of orange bottles litter the tabletop. She looks back up at me. My spine straightens.

"I—I have to go," I say.

Rushing across the room, I battle back the tears. I know I'm not imagining things. It was there. The brick was there, under my pillow, only last night. It was there and—

Emilia stands, tries to stop me as I push by.

"I need to know what just happened," she says brusquely, examining me.

I don't answer. Instead, I stuff my feet into my boots, loop a scarf around my neck, jam my phone and laptop into my tote bag.

"I have to talk to the girls. I still have a lot of work to do."

She sighs, flustered. "You can't make a claim like that and expect me not to worry."

"Let's just forget it," I say, feeling the first nudge of a blistering headache. "I must have, I don't know, had a dream about it. Confused reality and fantasy. It happens to people all the time."

Emilia studies me. "You dream about bricks under your pillow?"

"When you're in my line of work." I shrug, force a laugh. "A dream about a brick is actually a relief."

Still, she studies me. After a moment, her posture relaxes. "I guess that's true," Emilia says, reclaiming her spot on the bed. "Of course, being a criminal psychiatrist must be very taxing to the psyche," she says, throwing another glance at my orange prescription bottles. "Besides, I have my own confession," she begins. "I came up here because I wanted to talk to you a little bit about your role in this investigation." Emilia stares at me, unblinking, awaiting my answer.

"Sure, I—"

"Because I want you to know," she says, cutting me off.

"I take this job very seriously. I rearranged my entire life to take this position—" She cuts herself off. I narrow my eyes at her. Emilia steals a deep breath, clasps her hands together. "My husband—*ex*-husband—didn't want me coming here. It was...a struggle. In the end, it was for the best. For everyone."

I stare at her. Somehow, I can't shake the feeling that there's something else going on.

"We're not on speaking terms," Emilia confesses.

"We're not really either," I mutter. "My family and I..."

Emilia looks at me knowingly. Chills flutter down my arms to my fingertips.

"Anyway," she says, her back going straight. "What's happened, happened. There's no going back now. My point is—I only have one interest, Dr. Pine. My only interest here is to protect these girls. And in order for me to do that... I think you and Detective Reyes should leave the school grounds as soon as possible."

"What?"

"I know he had plans to stay for the remainder of winter break."

"He did," I say, "and I highly doubt Detective Reyes is going anywhere without knowing what, exactly, happened to Charley. And neither am I."

Emilia taps a fingertip against her berry-painted lips, deep in thought. She stands to pace the room again. "I was afraid you'd say that," she says. "I don't know if you've been watching the news, but a Nor'easter is headed this way."

I sigh. "The news always tries to scare everyone. I'm sure it won't be that bad."

Her mouth pops open. "You also don't live up here. We're on top of a mountain. In the middle of three hundred acres. If we get even ten inches of snow—"

"*Ten* inches?"

Emilia laughs bitterly. "Ten inches means we're stranded. The back roads surrounding the school are always the last to be cleared. Plus, we have to plow the drive, the footpaths, salt the entrances, and that can take days, since it's only Blake and his son who know how to work the equipment."

"Just how much snow is predicted?"

"The storm due this week is going to be at least twenty inches."

I shake my head in disbelief. "I doubt we'd be *stranded*…"

"If you don't leave soon, you're stuck here. *At least* until after Christmas."

I stare blankly at her. "You don't want us here, do you?" I ask flatly.

Emilia's lips pinch up a little at the edges. "You have me all wrong," she whispers. "I think Charley's death was an unfortunate accident. And it's a waste of your and Detective Reyes's time to be here investigating something that was an *accident*."

I shake my head. "Wouldn't you want to know if it was your daughter?"

Emilia huffs. "I don't *have* a daughter," she snaps. I flinch away. "Even if I did. Your presence only gives Charley's mother false hope."

"What if you're wrong?"

Emilia shrugs, heads toward the door. "Oh, and about the storm?" she says, ignoring me completely. "Don't say I didn't warn you." She moves to leave, turns back around. "And tell Detective Reyes, though I'm sure he must already be aware." She twists the doorknob open. "Your next student will be waiting for you in the library at eight."

Emilia leaves the room, closing the door behind her. My shoulders droop. Immediately, I check the weather on my phone. Emilia was telling the truth. The screen ignites with dire warnings and red alerts about the incoming storm.

My head pounds. I fall onto the bed, imagine Dave coming home after a long day at work. How he'd always hang his coat in the hall closet, take off his shoes, pet the dog, give me a hug. It was a routine I looked forward to.

Feeling blue, sunshine? he'd ask.

No, Dave.

I can't help but lie to him, even now, even in my head.

No, Dave. I'm not blue. I'm beyond blue.

I think of Izzi, think of her beautiful face, how she laughs with her entire body whenever Dave makes a corny joke. How my wonderful little girl has the biggest heart and always seems to share. I held her in my arms and rocked her to sleep in front of the fireplace, singing softly to her, smoothing her fine baby hair away from her pink cherub lips.

Last year, we went on a family vacation to my in-laws'. I'd subscribed to a music service for the car so we could listen to literally any song we wanted. I wanted to count road signs and laugh and joke and talk about what kind of house we'd build if we could build any house at all.

Izzi got in the car, jammed earphones in her ears, never spoke a word. I tried to talk to her, but she refused. Dave ignored me, too. Three hours later, when we arrived at my in-laws', I learned they'd had a fight when I was outside packing the car.

Izzi had found pictures of another woman on my husband's phone. She didn't have the heart to tell me.

Her voice sounds in my head: *Mom, please just stop.*

Okay, Izzi, I'll stop. I promise.

I sit up from the bed, begin to clear away the tray of cold food Emilia had brought. My stomach grumbles. I tear off a piece of burned toast, nearly chip a tooth. As I lift the plate to scoop the contents into the trash, a serrated edge slices hard against my palm.

I drop the plate, wince, see the side of the glass plate is chipped, a sharp, exposed ridge now covered in my blood.

I cry out, fling the plate into the trash can, rush into the bathroom. Running my hand under hot water, I watch waves of pink beat against the sides of the porcelain sink. With no bandages, I keep a washcloth pressed to the cut until I can ask Emilia or Rosemarie for one.

I fall back into bed. My mind buzzes. Izzi's face flashes in my head. She's standing in the kitchen. She smiles when she sees it's me coming down the stairs.

Mom, please just stop.

I can't, Izzi. I'm sorry.

A tear falls, cold and wet, onto the mattress. I leave it there, feel its chilly trail inch down my cheek. It's something small to hold on to, just for today.

12

Wind howls against the windows of the library as my next student, Hannah Bouchard, wrestles to get comfortable. At first glance, when we briefly met in the lobby, she seemed bubbly and helpful. Now she seems reserved and cautious. She doesn't know what to make of me. She doesn't know how to feel about my presence at the school.

The voice recorder rests on a coffee table between us. Hannah changes positions, tucks one leg under the other, slouches against the armrest. She pushes her round, owlish glasses up her nose, thick lenses making her eyes comically large. Paired with her small, thin mouth, she reminds me of an alien. Long, wavy brown hair gathers in the hood of her blue hoodie, the NASA symbol emblazoned on the front.

I'm unsure how to begin the conversation, and she can sense it. Uneasiness lingers in the air, hovers there, like smoke. We sit in silence as I study how she moves, fiddling with the corner of a pillow she'd tucked under her arm, her shoulders hunched, her posture poor.

The timer ticks on the voice recorder.

I curl the washcloth tight in my hand, wound stinging. I wince from the pain.

Hannah rolls up the sleeve of her hoodie, begins to fiddle with a large bandage taped near her elbow.

Perfect—a way to puncture the silence. "Are you okay? Did you get hurt?" I ask, tapping a finger on my elbow.

"I—I was helping in the kitchen," Hannah answers, her expression twisting, a sudden sign of tension. "With the—uh, dishes. Sometimes, I help when it's break or something like that—you know, when there's not that many people working. I like to help out. But I'm fine. It's nothing, really," she rambles. "What about you?" She nods toward the white washcloth clenched in my fist.

I offer a faint smile, lean forward. "Just, um, cut it on a piece of glass," I say. "So, Hannah," I begin, "tell me a little about yourself."

Hannah's eyes flicker for a split second. She catches herself, gulps, lifts her eyes to look at me. "About myself?" she asks, voice small.

I nod. "Maybe start with why you're at the school during winter break?"

She sighs. "Because my parents suck?" she says, laughing a little. "They wanted me to come home and milk *cows* for charity."

I don't know what I was expecting, but it wasn't that.

She continues, balls up the sleeves of her NASA hoodie in her fists. "The past few years they've gotten really into things like health and food and stuff. I thought they were weird when they didn't want me standing too close to the microwave, but then it like, morphed into something else."

My palm starts to sweat from clutching my pen too tight. I blink. Drop the pen. "Is that why they enrolled you here?" I ask, remembering the mission statement I'd read on the school website: *We believe in a holistic, individual approach to learning and rehabilitation, focusing on a curriculum centered on nature, group trust, and a healthy mind-body connection.*

I also remember the school's massive tuition fees, room and board, and extracurricular fees… You'd have to be extremely wealthy to even think of sending your daughter here. Ironic, since the school seems to have gone back to basics, forgoing opulent splurges that could warrant the steep price tag.

For a moment, I wonder where all the money goes. It definitely doesn't seem to go toward food or security or technology. I shiver, wish I had a heated blanket. It doesn't go into heating this giant place, either.

I wonder if Izzi would like it here. Would she hike in the spring? Paint the mountain views? Or would she rebel, retreat into herself, reject the school's mission statement? Resent her phone being taken away, despise being isolated and remote. I wish I knew. Sometimes, I feel like I've failed. I don't even know my own daughter. Not anymore.

Hannah narrows her eyes at me, lowers her head. The gesture reminds me of what Izzi would do whenever she got into trouble. Suddenly Matt's words enter my mind: *The girls are mostly, I guess the best word for it is—troubled?*

I curse myself for not reading Hannah's file before meeting her in the library. After Emilia left my room this morning, I found it hard to focus on anything else. It's a miracle I'd actually managed to drag myself here on time.

I chastise myself, look up, see Hannah is still watching me. Her wide eyes focus on me behind her thick glasses, as if she'd just heard every word spoken inside my head.

"They sent me here," she says slowly, "because they hate me—they wanted me gone."

"I—I'm sure they only want what's best for you—"

"No," she says sharply. "It's not that."

I stay silent, watch her, wait for her to speak in her own time.

Slowly, she drags her gaze to mine. "What were your parents like?"

"Mine?"

She nods.

I lift my eyebrows, a little stunned by her question. "Well, I never really knew my dad," I confess. "And my mom, uh, died fifteen years ago, when I was only a few years older than you."

Hannah's plain face crumples. "I'm sorry," she mutters. "But I bet she didn't believe that wi-fi scrambles your brain and tap water has microchips in it."

I fight to hold back a laugh. Seeing my struggle, Hannah's shoulders relax. She smiles. After a heartbeat, she leans closer, pinches her thin lips together. Her eyes widen, innocent and honest.

I look away. Restraining eye contact alleviates pressure to speak, making people feel more at ease, more open. More apt to spill secrets.

"I know why you're really here."

I tilt my head, curious. "What do you mean?"

"Well, Headmistress says it's because of Charley. But there has to be something more to it."

"I'm not going to lie to you," I say. "I *am* here because of Charley's death, at her mother's request." Hannah gives a bitter expression: *See, I knew it.* "But there's nothing more to it. I only want to talk to you girls to hear if there's anything more to the story."

Her eyes narrow. "I didn't know there *was* a story."

My hands go cold. "There's always a story," I whisper. "Even if it's one you've never heard."

Hannah nods, swallows hard.

I remove my glasses, rub a hand over my face. "Can I start with a couple of questions?" I ask, sliding my glasses back on.

Again, Hannah pushes up her sleeve, itches the bandage on her arm. "Well, okay, but I'm not in trouble or anything, right?"

"Of course not. Why?"

Hannah shrugs. "Just asking." She grins, tucks one leg under the other, leans back. "Dr. Madeline Pine..." she ponders. "I've met lots of you. My parents, well, my mom, *loves* to send me to therapists. I think it makes her feel less bad for going to so many herself."

I lift a hand, chew my cuticles. "Do you know why she sees a therapist?"

Hannah's face lights up with laugher. "Oh god, for everything!" she says. "She was a shopaholic once. Then an overeater. It's what happens when someone has too much time and money. They get *obsessed* with things."

I switch to a new finger, think about how much that's true. Once, when Dave won a big case, he got really into fishing. He'd never expressed any interest in fish or water or boats before, so when he started coming home with expensive fishing rods and elaborate vests and jackets, Izzi and I couldn't help but laugh. He spent thousands on fishing gear and went on a charter boat once.

I bite a cuticle too short, hit a nerve, force myself to lower my hand. Hannah watches me as she slowly braids her long brown hair, lets it slip through her fingers.

"Let's shift focus," I say, tucking my hand under my leg to stop myself from gnawing. "Let's talk about Charley. Did you know her well?"

Hannah groans, rolls her eyes. "That's all anyone ever wants to talk about anymore," she says. "Fine. Yes, I knew her well. We were all friends. It's a small school."

"Do you know if Charley was ever bullied at school?"

"What? No."

I nod, glance at the voice recorder. The red, digital numbers still tick by. Matt claimed Charley had been bullied at her old school, causing her mother to relocate her here. Maybe the bullying had stopped. Maybe it didn't. Maybe Hannah *is* lying…

But then again, why would she? Hannah has nothing to gain by lying.

Right?

I shake my head, lift my gaze back to Hannah, remember what Emilia had said about Charley: *That poor girl most likely sleepwalked her way into the woods and fell to an untimely death.*

"Hannah," I begin, clearing my throat, "have you ever seen Charley sleepwalking?"

Her face knots. "No. Why?"

I make a note in my notepad: *Charley bullied & sleepwalking— Hannah says NO*

Swiftly, I move to my next question, one that's been living inside my head ever since Rosemarie had mentioned it yesterday morning in my room.

"Do you think Charley had a reason why she'd want to run away? Or maybe just to sneak out somewhere at night?"

A quick memory of seeing Alice walking alone in the courtyard last night flickers in my head. If Alice managed to slip outside, then others could, too. And if someone could get out, someone could get in…

I look up, see Hannah staring at me, unblinking.

"No?" she whispers to herself, bulging eyes fixated on my

face. She snaps out of her trance, nudges her silver-rimmed glasses up her nose. "I mean, yes. Maybe."

I curl the edges of my notepad between my fingers. "Can you tell me?"

She looks at me, suddenly apprehensive. "I—I don't know," she says. "I don't want to be a tattletale."

I lean closer, elbows on my knees. "Listen, Hannah. What-ever you say to me here, stays here, okay? You wouldn't be a tattletale." *Lie.* "I'm only here for you, just to listen." *Lie.* "I promise you, I'd never tell anyone else." *Lie lie lie.*

Hannah glances over her shoulder, checks to see we're still alone in the library. "If you promise not to say anything to anyone…" she says, awaiting my reply.

"Yes, of course," I mumble.

She sighs, checks over her shoulder again. "Maybe you're right," she whispers. "Maybe Charley *was* running away."

13

Hannah leans back, crosses her legs, pulls her thick hair back into a ponytail. It's a small sign she's feeling more comfortable, that she's opening up. It's a good thing. A great thing.

"What makes you say that?" I ask. "Why would Charley want to run away?"

"Well, no one really dates anyone here, you know? Some girls have people back home they're allowed to write a letter to once a week, but that's it," she explains. "And no one knew Charley was with—" She stops, licks her lips, reaches into the pocket of her hoodie, pulls out a tube of ChapStick. "Well," she says, smacking her lips together. "We know *now*."

"Charley was in a relationship with someone?" I ask. "Someone on campus?"

Hannah nods.

My eyes widen. I write furiously in my notepad, pen nearly tearing through the paper.

"Can I ask who?"

Hannah swirls her tongue, sucks the ChapStick off her lips, whispers, "Alice."

Charley dating—Alice.

I picture the quiet girl with lavender hair from the hallway, her folder of sheet music and viola crashing to the floor. A flicker of her face creeps into my mind again—her head, turning quick over a shoulder, eyes pinpointed on my bedroom window as she trampled through the snow-dewed courtyard.

I wish I had studied the student files Rosemarie had given me. I kick myself for not being better prepared. Maybe I shouldn't have come here. Maybe I can't do this—

Hannah nods. I force my mind to still.

I lift my head to look at her. "Did something...*bad* happen between Charley and Alice?"

Hannah looks toward the hallway, shrugs. "I don't know," she whispers. "But I *saw* her."

I drop my pen.

"Who?"

"That night—that night I think I saw Alice running into the woods."

My body goes cold.

"The night Charley disappeared?"

She nods. "Sometimes, I can't sleep at night. I like astronomy, stargazing, things like that," she says proudly. "But we're not allowed outside after lights out..." Hannah trails off, dejected.

"So you snuck out to stargaze?"

Hannah shakes her head, her body caving in on itself. "No—not that night. That night was different," she whispers to herself, eyes blurring on a spot behind my shoulder. "That night I was woken up."

I gulp, lean forward. "I'm not sure I follow you, Hannah."

Her body visibly deflates. "Can you tell me *why* that night was different? What made you go outside that night for a reason other than stargazing?"

Hannah rolls her eyes. "It was nothing *that* different," she says quickly, sensing I may have taken it out of context. My shoulders slump.

"Can you walk me through that night?" I ask softly. "Maybe start back at what woke you?"

Hannah slowly shakes her head. "I have to go back further than that."

I nod. "Okay. Okay, anything you'd like to say, I'm listening."

She inhales. "Alice and Charley thought no one knew their secret hiding spot out in the woods. But everyone knew, just like everyone knew they were dating, thanks to—"

She stops.

I glance at the voice recorder. The numbers march by.

I take a sip of water, drink half the bottle. Hannah reapplies her ChapStick, promptly sucks it off her lips.

"Let me, uh, get this right, okay?" I ask. "I want to get this right. So you—everyone—knows Charley was dating a girl on campus, Alice, who is also here during winter break, along with you, Charley—"

I pause. Hannah picks it up, finishes my sentence. "Me, Charley, Alice, Violet, and Kiara. Five of us. Well...*four*, now."

"Yes, thank you," I say, slightly embarrassed. My head suddenly feels like it's in a vise grip. I can practically feel my mental clarity dissipating. I unfurl my fingers, peek under the washcloth, see a mahogany Rorschach blood blot in the shape of a gun.

Hannah nods, tucks her hands beneath her legs.

"So...you saw Alice outside in the woods heading toward

a spot where she and Charley used to meet—the same night
Charley disappeared."

"Yes…" she says meekly.

"Do you believe Alice was going into the woods to meet
with Charley?"

Hannah shrugs. "I—I have no idea, Dr. Pine. All I know is
I went downstairs and saw Alice running to their secret spot
in the woods. I don't know anything else."

I tap my pen on my chin in thought. "What made you go
downstairs?"

"What?"

I adjust my glasses, see a trickle of sweat has formed at Hannah's hairline. Nervously, she wipes it away with the sleeve
of her NASA hoodie.

"I—I don't—"

"You mentioned how sometimes you wake up at night to
sneak out to stargaze and—"

"*Please* don't tell anyone that. I could get in trouble," Hannah interrupts.

"I promise you, I won't," I say, holding up a hand. "But
did you ever see anything else out of the ordinary any other
time you were stargazing? Did you ever see Charley outside
at night? Or Alice?"

"Maybe, like, once or twice. I—I see pretty well at night."

"But that night was different—something woke you up."

Hannah nods slowly, as if in a trance. "Yeah. I heard something."

"What did you hear?"

Her chest rises and falls, like she's just run up three flights
of stairs. "I heard—a scream." She bites her lip, looks down
at her lap.

"An—and…" I trail off, losing my concentration. I bounce

my knee, completely thrown off guard. I grip the washcloth tight in my fist.

"At first, I thought I heard something. So I woke up and went into the hall to use the bathroom," Hannah explains. "But then I heard a scream. I worked up the courage to go downstairs. I wanted to see what happened. I—I mean, I wanted to see if someone was hurt. I wanted to *help* them," she says quietly. "If it was me, I'd want someone to come and help me."

For some reason, her words make my stomach clench.

"Who screamed?" I ask.

"No one. No one was even there," she says, puckering her chapped lips. "But I saw something on the floor. Outside of the library. I… I think it was *blood*."

Her words hit my ears like a punch. I look away, astonished, stunned. I stop bouncing my knee. Our heads flip toward the hall.

I shift on the sofa, tap my pen incessantly before realizing it's a sign of anxiety. I stop, drop the pen in my lap. "So you wake up, go into the hall to use the bathroom. You hear someone scream. You go downstairs, but no one is there. And you see blood on the floor."

"Yeah. Then I looked outside and saw Alice running into the woods."

"Then what?"

"Nothing," Hannah says. "I went back to bed. In the morning, I woke up early to go see if the blood was still there. I—I was going to tell the headmistress."

"And was it?"

She shakes her head. "No. It was gone."

"Gone."

"I—I didn't imagine it." Hannah's shoulders slump. "I know I didn't!"

"No, I'm sure you didn't," I assure her, though in my heart, I know what she'd seen that night could've been anything. Spilled tea. Someone could've dropped soup or paint. Maybe someone vomited. I'd bet anything Rosemarie saw it in the morning and cleaned it before breakfast so the girls wouldn't slip.

"When you saw what you believed to be blood," I say, "why didn't you tell someone? The headmistress? Rosemarie?"

"I—I—" Hannah stammers. "I don't know."

"What if someone *was* hurt?"

"I guess I—"

"If *I* saw blood on the floor, I'd tell someone…" I say, keep going, keep prodding, trying to throw her off guard, off balance, try to get her to confess anything she might be holding back.

But she doesn't. She looks right at my face, resolute, tears boiling in her eyes.

"I just didn't!" Hannah bursts out, chest heaving. "I didn't…" Her voice goes soft. "When I saw it, it didn't even cross my mind to tell anyone. And *that's* the problem! Why didn't I think to? What's wrong with me? What kind of person *am I*?"

I stare back at her. Tears break free, trickle down her full cheeks.

"It's okay," I mutter, feeling guilty. "I understand."

"I'm sorry," she says to herself. Slowly, she removes her glasses, wipes them clean on her hoodie. "I'm sorry I can't help you more."

I glance at the golden clock ticking on the fireplace mantel. I didn't realize we've been speaking for almost an hour. "You did help, Hannah. You did."

We say our goodbyes. I scribble what she'd stated as fast as I can in my notepad and turn off the voice recorder. Still, a part of me can't help but think the girls are offering up anything they can, their minds imagining things that aren't truly real:

Violet seeing Charley sleepwalking.

Hannah seeing blood in the hallway.

Hannah seeing Alice running into the woods.

Mysterious screams when no one is there...

But it's not over yet. I still have two more girls left to speak with. Kiara and Alice—Charley's girlfriend. And, according to Hannah, quite possibly the last person in the world to see Charley alive.

I shiver. Look over my shoulder. Make sure I'm still alone. I let out a long sigh, lean my head back against the sofa, stare up at the coffered ceiling.

What if it wasn't spilled tea or dropped paint? What if Hannah really did see blood in the hallway the same night Charley disappeared? What if the blood was Charley's? If Hannah is telling the truth, then that can only mean one thing.

Charley didn't die in the woods.

Charley died inside the school.

THE YEAR BEFORE

FILE NAME: JPN00.012.00030923.mp3

INT: When was the first time you met with [redacted]?

RES: … We had our first date the night after I called him.

INT: Just a few days after you had a fight with your husband?

RES: Don't look at me like that.

INT: … I—I apologize, um, I'm not…

RES: Please… Don't judge me. Not now.

INT: I'm here to help you, [redacted]. I'm on your side. With all of this. I'm only here for you. You have to trust me.

RES: I trust no one, not anymore.

INT: …[inaudible] we'll make this right, we'll get this sorted out. This is just a formality, okay? You understand. With situations like this, we have to walk through this.

RES: I know. I know.

INT: Okay, please, remember I'm—I'm on your side. Through all of this. Okay?

RES: Yes. Okay..

INT: So you met with [redacted] and was this on a weekend?

RES: No, it was a Monday. My husband was at work. [redacted] was staying over at her friend's house after school. They were going to study together then have a pizza night.

INT: And what did you do?

[00:13:42]

RES: Uh—we went to dinner.

INT: And then you came home?

RES: No.

INT: Please, [redacted]. This is best if you tell me the truth of what happened...take your time, please, we don't need to rush, but this has to happen...this has to be done while it's still fresh—

RES: I know that. I just...

INT: I know, believe me, I can't even understand what you must be going through, and when this is all over, I'll help you, whatever you need—here are some tissues. [redacted], please, let me help you. We'll get this all worked out. I'm on your side.

RES: I know you are.

INT: We need to do this now, okay? Let's finish, then

you can…if you need to go stay at a friend's house, wherever you're staying—I'll even take you, okay?

RES: Yes, okay.

INT: Okay…so you and [redacted] went on a dinner date. Then you did not go home, correct?

RES: Correct. We went to a hotel.

INT: Which hotel?

RES: I don't know. A local one.

INT: And then what happened?

RES: My husband and I…we—we didn't…

INT: It's okay, you can tell me.

RES: We hadn't—we hadn't had sex in months. He—I swear he was having an affair.

INT: And did you and [redacted] have sex that night?

RES: … Yes.

[00:14:59]

INT: And then you kept seeing him?

RES: Um, yes.

INT: When was the next time you met him?

RES: I met him a few times a week, sometimes more. We found a way.

INT: And your husband, did he ever know?

RES: No.

INT: You're sure?

RES: Yes.

INT: He never suspected anything, anything like that?

RES: No...no, he was always at work. He wasn't really home that much during the day. Um, he saw me and [redacted] mostly on the weekends at this point.

INT: So you and [redacted] met a few times per week for the past five, six months, you said, right?

RES: Right. Almost six.

INT: And how far did your relationship progress?

RES: We were serious. It—it got serious.

INT: How serious?

RES: It was—it was very serious. It was fast. Things got really intense very quickly. I don't think I was prepared for it.

INT: And what were your feelings about your relationship with [redacted] at this time?

RES: It was great. We had a great time together. He understood me. He was kind. It was…very stress free.
It came very easily with him.

INT: And then toward the end, what happened?

RES: … I don't know how to answer that.

INT: How did your relationship end?

[00:16:25]

RES: It lasted… I didn't know how long it could've lasted.
I knew it had to end, we both did…then one night,
when I wasn't supposed to see him, he came to my
work.

INT: And what happened?

RES: He brought me a huge bouquet of flowers.

INT: [redacted] showed up at your work with flowers.
And did anyone see him?

RES: No, I don't think so. It was getting dark out early
at this point.

INT: And what did you do?

RES: He brought me, um, flowers—big, bright, yellow
flowers. I told him yellow was for friendship. He
said that yellow flowers also meant, "I'm sorry."

INT: Did he have anything to be sorry for at this point?

RES: No. No... I don't think so. I don't remember.

INT: And then what happened, after he gave you the flowers outside your work?

RES: Um...we went to a hotel.

INT: The same hotel?

RES: We always went to the same two hotels.

INT: And you had, um, sex?

RES: No. No, not that night.

INT: What happened? It's okay...it's just me and you. You're just telling me, you can tell me, okay?

RES: [inaudible]...that night...that night I—I saw who he was.

INT: Who he was?

RES: Yes. I saw who he really was. That was the first time.

14

After Hannah leaves, I press Play on the recorder. It lurches forward, stops, plays.

Static. Shuffling.

Hannah's voice fills the library.

…then I heard a scream. I worked up the courage to go downstairs—

I click it off, toss it in my bag, pull out the files Rosemarie had brought to my room yesterday morning. I'd read Violet's, so I tug out the remaining three files: Hannah Bouchard, Kiara Cole, and Alice Bitar.

I flip open Hannah's, see she's from Wisconsin. Her father is listed as a business owner, her mother, a homemaker. It must be the cleanest file I've ever seen. No misconduct noted, no reprimands. She's the perfect student.

Flipping it closed, I slide out the next file—Alice's. Out of nowhere, a bubble of anxiety seeps into my throat. I gulp it down, push the worry away. Anxiety is steadily becoming the only feeling I understand. It has tentacles, strong as a fist, wraps around you, holds you tight. It won't let go unless you let it. But I was always afraid of being alone.

My hand aches. The wound has scabbed over, gluing the cotton washcloth to my skin. Gently, I tug it off, toss the bloody washcloth into my tote bag along with the files.

Standing to go see Matt to fill him in, I hear a meek, "Hello?"

Alice stands in the archway behind me, a small, black instrument case clenched in her fist.

"Can I come in?" she whispers, her shoulders curled forward protectively. "The headmistress sent me. She said I have to talk to you."

I stand from the sofa, walk to greet her, stop halfway when she recoils into herself.

"I'm, uh, Dr. Madeline Pine," I say. "And you're Alice, right?"

"Yeah."

Alice hesitates before entering the library on tiptoes—timid, hesitant. Her hair is faded lavender, long enough to spill over one shoulder. A black beret sits sideways on her head. Her tee-shirt is pale gray and knotted at her waist. An oversized, fuzzy pink cardigan drapes down to her bony knees.

Sitting back down on the sofa, I grab the recorder out of my bag, turn it on, motion for her to take a seat across from me. I ready my pen and notepad, greedy for details.

"Thanks for coming, Alice," I begin. "It's nice to officially meet you."

I can't help but examine her. Now that I have the chance to see her closer, she feels so—*familiar.* She sits at the edge of the chair, body almost hovering midair. Gently, she places her viola case on the rug beside her.

"Are you having a good day so far?" I ask. It's a bland, benign question. But it's better than the ones I really want to ask: *Is Hannah right? Were you really in the woods the night Charley disappeared? Did it have something to do with where you were going last night?*

Alice looks at me with big, pale blue eyes, the light from the lamp beside her glowing tiny dots of white in the centers, like a cartoon. I remember her from the hallway on Friday. How she'd dropped her viola and sheet music. How Violet sneered as she'd watched her struggle to pick them up. Something had happened between the two girls, but I don't know what.

"I... I guess so," Alice mumbles in a tiny, high-pitched voice. "If you can call waking up and doing the same shit over and over a good day."

The sleeve of her fuzzy cardigan slips down her tiny wrist as she lifts her hand, tucks a strand of purple hair behind an ear. I firmly press my lips together as I catch a gathering of thin lines across the underside of her wrist, delicate and cross-hatched.

A memory fills my mind. Izzi in the bathroom. She'd wanted a special razor to trim her long, thick hair. Using a razor thins out the heavy layers, she'd explained, excitedly showing me a YouTube tutorial. I told her she looked beautiful, that her thick hair had come from her grandmother and was a trait many women would kill for.

Izzi in the bathroom. The doorknob turning in my palm. Crosshatched scars, thin, pale, my failure as a mother reflected in every line.

Mom, please just stop.

I narrow my eyes at Alice, force myself to focus, lean in a little closer. "What—*shit*—do you normally do on a good day?" *Pen at the ready.*

She sighs, glances down at her viola case. *Yes, it's still there.* "You know, wake up, wash my face, have tea, sit alone, play more. Same shit," she says, lifting a leg to lean against the arm-rest, her bony knee popping through a hole in her leggings.

I can tell she's having difficulty opening up, so I start with the same warm-up I'd used with Violet: a short spiel about Izzi, what she did in her free time, her favorite movies. Things maybe they can relate to, clasp onto, open up about.

Alice doesn't bite. Instead, her eyes begin to glaze over.

I glance at the voice recorder and run through my list of questions I'd written out on my notepad as I unscrew my bottle of water. Losing my grip, I almost drop the bottle, and water tips out, spills across the ink, turning my words into an oozing watercolor landscape. *Shit.*

Head turned sideways, Alice secretly studies me, one eye peek-ing out between strands of hair. *Shit shit shit.* I had questions—I had things to ask, important things, things Matt had wanted me to ask, things Hannah, Emilia and Violet had told me, and—

"Are you okay?" Alice asks.

I look up, heart racing. Why am I so goddamn nervous? Why can't I do this fucking job? What's wrong with me?

"Uh, yeah. Yes. Thank you, Alice," I say, my voice ach-ing with embarrassment. "I just… I need one second. Is that okay?"

Slowly, she nods.

I look down, exhale, force myself to concentrate.

Hannah had mentioned Alice was Charley's girlfriend. That she'd seen Alice running into the woods the night Charley disappeared, just as I had seen Alice outside last night in the courtyard. Do I confront Alice about that? Do I go for the jugular? Or do I dip a toe in, go slow?

If Alice had anything to do with Charley's death, I can learn a lot from how she handles being confronted. Or she could just get up and walk out. That's the last thing I want.

Alice fidgets, inches toward her viola case to grab it and go.

Shit. I can't lose her. My pulse quickens. I bite my lip, quickly yank her file back out of my tote bag. Alice's eyes widen, watching my every move.

> *BITAR, ALICE*
> *DOB: 07/04/05 Alpine, NJ*
> *Unnamed father, deceased / Jennifer, mother*
> ** No known family history (?)*
> *-Enrolled Sep/20, expulsion—Oppositional defiant disorder (Mar/20 diagnosis)*
> ****REQUIRES monitoring due to previous self-harm****
> *-Excels at string instruments-learns via auditory methods*
> **** ALLERGIES: None known (?)*
> ~~*No known medications*~~*-mother claims homeopathic methods preferable* <u>*CORRECTION: Albuterol as needed to control asthma flares*</u>
> ** Dr. on call: Mallory, Josephine/p:* <u>*Need updated contact info*</u>

I slap the file shut. I want to give Alice a fair shot. No pre-conceived notions. No games.

And then, I realize who she reminds me of. Why she feels so familiar. I see it the moment she begins sucking on a long strand of lavender hair. Alice could be Izzi's twin.

Alice's hair initially threw me off, but they both have the same big, round eyes and pointed chin. The same heart-shaped face and widow's peak. My heart pounds. I push the thoughts away, force myself to break my stranglehold stare.

The silence has bubbled to a level where it can't be sustained. It's now or never. I steal a deep breath, decide to jump straight in.

"Alice, how did you know Charley?" The moment I finish the sentence, I want to smack myself in the face. Of course she'll say she knew Charley from school. God, what was I thinking?

Alice stares at me. Suddenly, I feel anxious. I tap my pen against my notepad, fully aware yet unable to stop.

"Are you sure you're okay?" Alice asks again, her blue eyes flickering to my tapping pen.

"Oh. Yeah, sorry." I force myself to relinquish it, drop it in my lap, begin to bite my cuticles instead.

"You don't have to be nervous," she says. "I'm nervous, too."

I let out a deep breath. "Thanks, that's kind of you. Let's agree neither of us should be nervous," I say, and I mean it.

Alice offers a lazy smile. But still, she doesn't answer the question. She either didn't understand and is just ignoring it— or she's purposefully dodging. Either way, it puts me on alert. I decide to go slow before I go headfirst.

I start again with a new approach. "Let's begin with a little about me, then we can talk a little about you, okay?"

Alice nods.

I gulp, feel my heart thudding. Memories of the past swell inside my head. This time, I can't push them away. I tell Alice things I haven't thought about in years. How my parents divorced when I was four. How my dad moved away to Montana right after, started a second family, forgot my entire existence. How when I saw him for the last time eight years ago, he didn't look the same. He was never the person I thought he was. The man I'd thought I knew only lived inside my memories.

Alice laughs softly. I want to stop digging up all these ancient memories, but for the first time, ever so slightly, she inches in.

I keep going, not wanting to drop this thread between us. The words fall out, faster now, moving on to my mom, how she'd died when I was in college. How Dave and I had our daughter, Izzi, when we were twenty-one and living in a studio apartment. How finally, with the help of my mom's life insurance, we were able to finish school, get settled, live a normal life—all thanks to my mom's death.

"Good for you," Alice says numbly.

I blink, unsure if I've said too much. Too late. I clear my throat. "My point is—life doesn't end here, at this school. Life keeps going, whether we like it or not. You'll graduate before you even know it. You can do *so* much—" I stop myself. I forgot, just for a moment, who I'm speaking to.

She's not Izzi, I remind myself.

Alice parts her lips to speak. "I—I haven't seen my dad in eight years, either." Glistening tears glaze her wide eyes. "He, uh, died when I was eight. Cancer."

"I'm sorry…"

She shrugs. "*Life keeps going, whether we like it or not. But I'd prefer it not.*"

My stomach wrings with sadness. Alice seems to look at the world with a certain bitterness a girl so young should never possess. I'm drawn to her immediately.

I uncross my legs, lean in. For once, I've stopped chewing the inside of my cheek.

It's time I try again. Different this time. More relaxed. Instead of going for the jugular, I'll drain it out of her, one drop at a time.

15

Inhaling a breath, I wrangle Alice's blue eyes with mine. "I've heard many things about you," I begin, attempting to thaw her, make her malleable. "I know you were close with Charley." Her eyes shift away, drop down to her lap. I keep going. "You may have been the closest person to her at this school. I know losing her must be difficult for you."

Alice shrugs, chews her bottom lip. Her gaze has fallen into an unblinking trance. I follow her line of sight to see she's looking at my phone resting on the sofa beside me, staring at it as if it's the Holy Grail.

Remembering what both Violet and Emilia had mentioned earlier, I ask Alice the same question I'd asked Hannah. "Do you know if Charley ever sleepwalked?"

Alice doesn't break her trance on my phone. "No, I don't think so."

"Are you sure?"

She nods. "I—I was her roommate," she whispers. "Before…"

I inhale a short breath, swiftly move to a different question.

"What was your relationship with Charley?" I ask, already knowing the answer.

"Charley, she—" Alice stops herself, whips her eyes to me. "I—I mean," she stammers, shifts uncomfortably. "We were dating. We broke up. Happens every day."

I nod sympathetically. But inside, I'm on high alert. "Okay, I understand," I say, voice soft. "Can you walk me through what, exactly, happened between you and Charley?" I ask, the pen lax in my hand. I've forgotten all about taking notes. Fuck the notes.

"Charley was my best friend. My only friend. She was so smart. So much smarter than me. She didn't care what people thought. Last year, she cut off her hair and people still liked her. She could dress like she wanted and people still liked her." Alice stops, pouts, her face twisting in a mournful knot. "I miss her…" she cries. "I miss her all the time. At first, when she broke up with me, I didn't believe her. Then she got mad. I'm not sure she ever even loved me, you know? And I—I keep making the same mistakes," she gasps, "and I can't get out of it. I keep choosing the wrong people."

"How did you feel after Charley did that to you?"

She doesn't answer.

I push my glasses up my nose, realize my hand is shaking. I breathe out, bite my lip when the cut on my palm begins to pulse. "Why don't you tell me," I begin, fighting like hell to keep my voice steady, "and you'll see I understand." I gulp down the knot in my throat, a pang of heartbreak intruding.

"I felt…*alone*. I—I still love Charley," she whispers. "No matter what she did to me, I can never hate her. Ever. She's my soul mate."

"If it's okay with you," I say softly, "would you mind if I ask why you and Charley broke up?"

Alice shakes her head, gazes down at her lap, dejected. After a moment, she looks up at me, sniffles. "We were roommates," she says, staring at the voice recorder on the table between us. "We tried to keep it a secret. No one is allowed to date on campus. Plus, we didn't want to be split up."

"Split up—because you were roommates?"

Alice nods, wipes her eyes with her pinky finger. "Then one day, we were. We were forced into separate rooms. And later, Charley broke up with me. She said someone who knew about us told the headmistress. The headmistress called her mom and her mom threatened to pull her out of school, buy her a plane ticket to come home during break because she wasn't *focused* enough."

A worried look etches across my face. I've never been a single mom, but my mother was. I know firsthand how hard it is. Maybe Charley's mom didn't know the full story. Maybe she thought she was only trying her best, as best she could from half a world away.

I keep the thoughts inside, say nothing. Alice reads my expression. Her eyes narrow, probably trying to figure out what I'm thinking. Tears slide down her cheeks, fall onto her shirt, darkening the gray cotton in drops that resemble a constellation.

"Moving to a new school was the *last* thing Charley wanted," she says. "She'd just come here, made a home here."

I nod in understanding. "Change is never easy."

Alice stares at the floor, whispers to herself, "Of course... it's only when Charley's *finally* happy...only then does someone tell the headmistress about us and fucks everything up." She stops, looks up at me. "But that's why *you're* here, right? To make sure things go back to normal?"

My spine straightens. Blood rushes out of my head, as if I've seen a ghost. To anyone else, I'd lie. But I can't lie to her. I can't lie to a girl sobbing her body dry, drowning in grief.

Someone has to start telling the truth. It should start with me.

I bite my lip, say, "No, Alice. Nothing can make things go back to normal. I'm sorry."

Alice chokes air back into her lungs, like she's stealing her final breath before plunging into the sea. "Then *why* are you here?"

I gulp down the anchor lodged in my throat. "I'm here because… Charley's mother wants to know what really happened to her daughter."

She looks away—worried? Relieved?

Terrified.

She exhales the gulp of air, rubs her eyes dry with the palms of her hands.

I clear my throat, hope Alice doesn't tell the others what I'd just told her. But I know it's delusional to hope that. This is teenage catnip.

"Do you know who told the headmistress about your relationship with Charley?"

Alice gulps, pushes her eyebrows together deep in thought. "Yeah."

"Can you tell me their name?"

Alice doesn't hesitate. "It was Violet."

I clench my teeth, scribble her name in my notepad so hard the pen tears the paper in two.

Violet.

Violet was the one who'd found out about Charley and Alice's relationship. She'd told the headmistress, resulting in Charley and Alice being separated to different rooms, and a phone call made to their parents. Charley's mother threatened to pull her out of school, said she wasn't focused enough, told her she was buying her a plane ticket home. Charley, in turn, broke up with Alice—anything to avoid switching schools again. And then...

A buzzing begins in the tips of my fingers—my body's way of warning me to stay on schedule with my medications. I should get back to my room soon, before the anxiety grips me like a fist.

"Alice, when was the last time you saw Charley?" I ask, remembering Hannah had mentioned seeing Alice outside the night Charley disappeared.

Alice's face flatlines. She sniffles. Sneers. "I—I don't know," she mutters. "Probably when she broke up with me."

I spin the pen in my fingers. "And when was that?"

Slowly, she scans the room, as if searching for a way out. "I guess...a few days before she—"

I nod, watch her, assess her reaction. She's still, frozen, watching me watch her. Gently, she grazes her fingertips across the thin, cross-hatched scars beneath the sleeve of her sweater. I offer her a grim smile, remembering what I'd just read in her file:

REQUIRES monitoring due to previous self-harm

Either Hannah is lying about seeing Alice run into the woods toward their secret meeting place the night Charley died.

Or Alice is.

"Can—can I go?" she asks. "I think lunch is about to start. The headmistress takes a tally if you're late."

I nod, click off the recorder. "Just one more question before you leave, please, Alice."

She freezes midrise from the chair, body hovering. She looks at me warily, sits back down.

I lean forward, tap my chin with a finger. "Last night, I

saw you in the courtyard," I say. Her eyes alight, yet she says nothing. "How did you get out of the school?"

"What do you mean?"

I repeat some of the first words Matt had ever spoken to me. "The school is supposed to be locked down for the remainder of winter break," I say. "No one in. No one out."

Alice rolls her eyes, turns away. *"Locked down,"* she repeats. "Yeah. Some lockdown. They don't even know where all the exits are, let alone have time to check them every night."

I peer at her, lean back in the sofa. "So you left last night. Do you mind telling me where you went?"

She shrugs, bends down, grabs her viola case. "Just out." Standing, she flutters away like a moth.

The library settles into silence. The fire begins to shrink into ashes as the clock on the mantel *ticktocks ticktocks*. The lanterns flicker on, wood-scented air glowing soft gold.

Now alone, my mind races as I try to conjure up a connection to something, anything. I repeat Alice's name over and over in my head, as if casting a spell. I think about Charley. Think about how afraid she must've been. How it must've felt to be alone, lost in the cold dark woods. Think of all the things that led to that night.

Doubt creeps in. The doors of my mind slam shut.

No matter what, I can't deny Alice is in the middle of things, a circle drawn around her. A bull's-eye.

I want to believe Alice. I want to trust her, more than anything.

But I can't.

16

I stand and stretch, amble around the library, breathe in the spicy scent of burning logs in the fireplace. On the mantel, there's a small bouquet of dried flowers in a vase. The crisp golden petals have mostly fallen, leaving the stems bald. I drag a finger through dust clinging to the endless bookshelves, swipe the powder off my fingertips.

Turning back to the desk, I check the time on my phone. Izzi is my wallpaper. It's a picture of her smiling in the kitchen on her first day of high school. She'd carefully chosen her outfit the night before, so nervous, but ended up wearing leggings and a raincoat.

We'd gone shopping for new clothes, a mother-daughter date, and I was looking forward to spending time with her before the mundane routine of a new school year began. Izzi tried on countless pairs of jeans, and I waited, held her lem-

onade, until finally she opened the changing room door, tears
welling in her eyes.

She said none of the jeans looked right. She'd gained weight
in her hips, as many young women do. I said it was perfectly
normal. She'd always be beautiful, no matter what.

*Try a different size, Iz. I know you'll find a pair that looks amaz-
ing.*

But size wasn't the issue, I realized too late.

Mom, please just stop.

We left the store, silent, and she quickly walked ahead of
me, all the way outside, until we reached the parking garage.
I heard her stomach rumbling in the car on the way home,
offered to stop at our favorite place to grab some lunch.

Just stop.

I made it worse. Everything I did made it worse. I was losing her.

Soon, she'd be gone.

The screen goes black. I click it on again.

A text message from Matt pops up, the notification erasing
Izzi's smiling face in the background. I click it open.

Hey, are you free to stop by for lunch?

I pause, think of the car ride home. Think of what I'd said
to Izzi. I could've worded it differently. I could've done a lot
of things differently. Now it's too late.

Footsteps.

I click off the phone, glance over my shoulder. Violet stands
in the archway. In her arms, she clutches a book. Hesitant, she
steps inside, slides the book facedown on a table.

"I was hoping no one was in here..." she says. "I just wanted
to leave this for you on your desk."

I walk over, lift up the book, look back at her.

"I've finished it," Violet says with a shrug. "Your book."

The cover is bloodred—the color the publisher had chosen for *Dark Side: A Psychological Portrait of the Criminal Female Mind.*

I press it to my chest, give it a tiny hug. It feels like home. Comfort.

"By the way," Violet says. "Kiara asked me to tell you she's busy and can't come to your session today. She said try her tomorrow."

"Oh, okay," I say, perfectly professional and hiding any hint of irritation. "Please tell her I need to speak with her tomorrow, okay?"

Violet nods absently.

"Hey, Violet?"

She lifts her gaze from the back of the book. "What?"

I shift my stance, chew on my lower lip, think of my wording. "Do you know who told the headmistress about Charley and Alice's relationship?"

Her emerald eyes narrow.

"Who found out they were dating and caused them to be split apart?" I clarify, act as if I don't already know the answer I'm searching for.

Violet breathes out a tiny laugh. "I don't have to tell you anything," she whispers, lifting a shoulder. "Besides, I'm not a rat. I'm not going to rat someone out." Her dark eyebrows stitch together as she plants her fists on her tiny hips.

"Fair enough," I say, pretending to give her the cold shoulder, a method I use all the time with Izzi to showcase my disinterest. As if I could ever be disinterested in either my own daughter or the brooding girl standing before me now.

I circle my back toward her, text Matt back a quick: **Sounds good.**

When I turn around, Violet is staring at me. "You know, I

learned some interesting things," she says, eyes glued on the bloodred book in my arm.

"Oh, yeah?" I ask hesitantly. "Like what?"

She jams her hands in her pockets, stretches out her shoulders. "Nothing in particular," she says. "But at least now I'm ready for next year's Psych 101 course they make us all take. They told me to read any three books on psychology that I find interesting to prepare."

"Good for you, Violet. I'm proud you followed that advice."

She smirks, taps her finger on her chin. "You know what? I guess I did learn *one* thing."

I tilt my head, feel a smile stretch across my face. "What?"

Her green eyes pierce through me. Coldly, she whispers, "I learned I'm not the only one with secrets."

I stiffen. Her lips twitch in a little grin as she pivots around on the tip of a toe, leaves me standing alone, speechless, numb. Realization oozes through me. The blood drains from my face. I should've remembered what was hidden in these pages.

The book slips through my fingers and falls to the floor.

THE YEAR BEFORE

FILE NAME: JPN00.012.00030923.mp3

INT: When did this occur, how long ago?

[00:18:07]

RES: Um, around a month ago.

INT: That's when you say you saw who he really was.

RES: Yes. That was the first time.

INT: So walk me through what happened that made you realize this.

RES: He brought me flowers and drove to the hotel... I'm sorry, it's cold in here. Can I have a blanket or something? Do you have like, a, blanket—oh... thank you.

INT: No problem. You were saying you went to the hotel?

RES: Yes, [inaudible] hotel, and we went upstairs. We were—we were kissing. He wanted to... I mean, we—we were about to—

INT: Have sex.

RES: ... Yes. Right. We were about to when my phone rang. And normally I'd ignore it. Normally— well...normally I would have it on vibrate, then only answer if it was [redacted], uh, in case of an emergency or if something happened at school.

INT: Right, of course.

RES: So when my phone rang and it was [redacted], I was surprised because he never called me. Not anymore. Not in a while—so I answered.

INT: So you stopped kissing [redacted] and answered your husband's phone call?

RES: Yes.

INT: Then what happened?

RES: Then I answered and that was the first time [redacted] told me he—that he…he had, uh, cancer.

INT: Your husband told you he had cancer—he called and told you he—that he had cancer over the phone?

RES: Yes. He told me over the phone.

INT: Uh, when you were—you were with—

RES: Yes, I was with my lover, [redacted], in a hotel.

INT: About to—

[00:20:21]

RES: Yes, jesus, we were about to have sex.

INT: Okay, okay. I'm just clarifying. And so what did your husband say to you, um, when he called?

RES: He was blunt. To the point. He, uh, said he's been going to chemo, that he was having chemo done and…he never told me.

INT: And he told you this over the phone?

RES: Over the phone. And when I answered, you know—I had no idea.

INT: Right, of course.

RES: And…it was just—it was a shock. And when I hung up with him…uh, sorry, I—

INT: It's okay. Hey, hey listen to me, [redacted]. You did nothing, wrong, okay? Listen, hey, it's okay. This will all be okay.

RES: No—it won't…it can't—

INT: Yes. Yes, it will. Here—

RES: Thank you. Thanks. God, I'm—

INT: It's okay. I'm here.

RES: He was having fucking chemo. I mean, jesus, how was I supposed to know? I had—no, I should've known, he's my husband! Oh god…

INT: [redacted], it will be okay. He should have told you. You're his wife, he should've told you.

RES: … No, I know.

INT: You did nothing wrong.

RES: No. I did everything wrong. Everything.

[00:21:58]

17

Matt sits at the kitchen table, hunched over his laptop. The entire downstairs of the guesthouse is littered with paperwork, photographs, and manila files, dry coffee rings staining the paper.

His dark brows knit in concentration. Every time I glance at him, I wonder if he's found something new. Something to stitch the evidence together, make it whole.

Glancing at my watch, I see it's almost three, and while he'd invited me over for lunch, we haven't had a crumb of food. I stand from my chair, open the freezer. Inside is a stash of iced-over frozen dinners and vacuum-sealed bags of raw meat. Grabbing two mystery dinners, I toss them both in the microwave, cook them to hell.

Matt had given me cotton gauze to wrap around the wound on my palm. As I wait for the microwave to finish, I pry the edge up, try to steal a peek beneath. Healing. Slowly. I then quickly check my local news on my phone, see if there's anything new, anything I need to be aware of.

I breathe out. Nothing but a three-car pileup from an overnight ice storm.

That reminds me.

"Emilia said there's a pretty bad storm coming," I say, watching the timer on the microwave. Already, Matt is too focused on his work to hear. I smirk. "I killed my husband. He wouldn't drive me to the movies, so I poisoned his spaghetti."

Matt shakes his head, drops his pen, spins around. "There are other ways of getting my attention," he says, grinning, staring up at me over the rim of his glasses. I laugh.

The microwave beeps. Lunch is served.

I pass Matt the melted, nondescript microwave dinner, sit down next to him. Too quickly, he brings it to his mouth, burns his tongue. "*Ouch*—shit," he cries, dropping the fork. "So, you said a storm is coming?"

I nod. "Emilia said. It sounds like she wants us both gone before it hits."

Matt blows on his food to cool it, steam feathering into the air, fogging his glasses. "I bet she does," he grumbles. "Well, I did hear we're supposed to get a nasty Nor'easter, but there's a tractor here with a sizable plow. We should be able to make our escape in that if it gets too bad."

I imagine Matt and I confined in the tiny cab of a tractor, my luggage strapped to the back gathering fifty inches of snow as we slip down a mountain of ice.

"Don't worry," he says, as if reading my mind. "We won't be trapped here. I promise. So tell me—how's it going with the students?"

I drop my fork, take a sip of water. The faces of the three girls I'd spoken with so far flash in my head: unflappable Violet, chatty Hannah, lamblike Alice.

"Going okay," I say. "Only one student left—Kiara." I think of the first time I'd met her in the lobby when I'd arrived at the school. How she'd tossed a softball in the air. How confident and self-assured she'd seemed. How much I wanted to pick apart her brain.

"Decent progress so far," Matt says.

I shrug.

He takes another mouthful, looks at me thoughtfully as he chews. "Please tell me...tell me anything you've learned from them. Tell me you got *something*." Concern clouds his eyes.

My heart thuds. "Um, okay," I begin, stretching to reach for my notepad. "Let's go in order. First, I met with a girl named Violet." I flip to the first page.

Matt nods, pulls over his laptop, scoots his microwave dinner out of the way.

I rub my forehead, drop the notepad. "Violet found out Charley was dating someone on campus and told the headmistress."

His eyes widen. "Whoa, whoa. Charley was in a relationship with someone at school?"

I nod.

His hands fly across his keyboard. "Who was she dating?"

"Another student who stayed behind for winter break. Alice Bitar."

Matt swallows hard. "And—"

"Alice is lying, Matt."

"Lying?" he asks. "Lying about what?"

I sigh, grab my notepad again. "Well, I *think* she's lying. Either she's lying or Hannah is," I mumble under my breath. "I—I have to talk to them more, I have to—"

"Dr. Pine."

"Madeline."

"Madeline," he says, leaning back in the chair. "It's okay. Relax. Let's talk things through."

I tell him everything. How Charley and Alice were trying to keep their relationship a secret. How Violet had told Emilia they were together. How Emilia then called Charley's mom and made them split into separate rooms. How Charley broke up with Alice, shattered her heart, only to later be found dead, discarded at the bottom of a hill.

"I don't know what to believe, Matt. I just have a feeling some of the girls aren't being honest with me. They all seem to be lying about something."

"What do you mean?"

I exhale, lean back. "I don't know," I whisper. "Every time I think I've learned something new, when I verify it, it all falls apart."

Matt's shoulders slump. He slides off his glasses, tosses them on a pile of papers. "I know the feeling."

I pause, watch as he rubs his tired eyes, pinches the bridge of his nose. "I know you do," I answer and flip through my notepad, past the pages where my water had spilled and turned my notes into an abstract watercolor, toward the back to see if there are any forgotten notes.

"Shit."

Matt glances up. He looks completely different without his glasses. Younger, but more exhausted at the same time. The dark circles under his eyes have nowhere to hide. Redness encroaches in his brown eyes, turning them bloodshot.

"What?" he whispers, slides his glasses back on. "You remember something? Something that can help?"

I look at him wearily. "I—I don't know…" I trail off, remembering something else Hannah had said.

Matt lets me stew a moment before asking, "What are you thinking?"

I think about Hannah. What she'd said. How she'd woken up that night, heard a scream. Working up the courage to see who it was, she got out of bed, went downstairs. No one was there. But that is when she claimed she'd seen Alice outside in the woods.

I look at Matt. He inches closer. "One of the girls told me she heard a scream."

I press down on the gauze, hold my thumb on the pink inflamed skin beneath, feel the cut rip open under the cotton. I hold back a gasp of pain.

Matt's dark eyes follow the motion. I stop, try to relax, shake out my hands.

He pinches his lips into a flat line. "When?"

"The night Charley disappeared. The night she died."

Matt's dark eyes ignite. "What—what else?" he says, scrambling to type notes on his laptop.

I inhale a deep breath. "The student, Hannah, said she'd heard a scream and followed it downstairs. When she got there, she saw another student, Alice, outside near the woods."

"How did she manage to see that far in the distance?" he asks.

I shrug. "Through a window."

"In the dark? In the middle of the night?"

I stop. Sigh. "That's for you to decipher. I'm just telling you what I've learned," I say. Matt tilts his head, nods in agreement. I continue. "Hannah then claimed she saw blood on the floor by the library entrance. When she went back to check in the morning, the blood was gone."

Matt's body goes rigid. Slowly, he drags his eyes to mine. "What if *she's* lying too?" he says, breaking his gaze, looking down to the table. "What if she's fucking with you? With *us*?"

My shoulders slump. "I don't know," I confess. "What if everyone's wrong—the police, the autopsy? What if Charley *didn't* die in the woods. What if Charley died inside the school?"

"For Christ's sake, I hope not. That would mean Charley's body was carried to the woods and staged to mimic an accident."

"Who would do that?"

Matt shakes his head. "If you're right and it *was* Charley's blood the student saw on the floor, then it may be too late for this whole investigation."

"Why?"

Matt sighs. "It means I may have missed my chance to gather crucial evidence inside the school—at the original crime scene. Whatever evidence was left behind is compromised now."

"But wouldn't that leave us in the same place, anyway? We still don't have much evidence from the spot in the woods where we *know* she was found."

Matt shrugs. "Yes, but the police never even looked inside the school. If what you're saying is true—if a student really did see *blood* on the floor—the police should've searched for evidence in the building, too, not just in the woods." Matt groans, angry from the realization of a missed chance. "What if the police knew there was blood found outside of the library? They would've looked for other evidence—more blood, fingerprints, signs of a struggle. It would have changed *everything*."

"But they didn't know. No one did. Not until now," I mutter.

"No…not until now."

I drain the rest of my glass, clear our plates. Outside, the sun has begun to set, the falling light blanketing the woods with a deep purple shadow.

"I have to get going," I say, grabbing my coat off the back of the chair. "Before it gets any darker."

"I'll walk you back. You shouldn't go out there alone, not anymore."

"What? Of course I can."

He chews his bottom lip, deep in thought. "You shouldn't. It's not safe out there, not until we know more. It's just not." Matt sighs, drops his head.

I listen to the sounds of the night. The refrigerator whirs. Wind blows against the windows. An owl hoots outside. Matt taps his fingertips on the table.

Suddenly, the cottage falls silent. The whirring stops. The wind dies. The owl quiets.

And then, like thunder, a bang at the door.

THE YEAR BEFORE

FILE NAME: JPN00.012.00030923.mp3

INT: Um, and then, then after you hung up—well…let's back up. So did your husband call you specifically that day just to tell you about his cancer diagnosis?

RES: … No…no, he needed me to come home. [redacted] had come home early from school because she was sick. The school nurse never even called me, I would've—I would've left, you know? I would've gone home right then, I wouldn't have stayed.

INT: And the school didn't call you, they called your husband?

RES: … Yes. They called him and he called me to come home. He needed me to come home to watch [redacted] because he had to go get—get chemo. He thought I was at work and called at work first and they—I think they had to have told him I wasn't there.

INT: And then he called you?

RES: Right. He needed me to come home and watch [redacted]. He said she'd caught some kind of stomach bug, one of those twenty-four-hour ones. She was fine in the morning before school.

INT: So then you left the hotel?

RES: Well, yeah, I hung up with him, fucking destroyed,

livid—just—feeling so many things, not knowing what to do—I felt so lost. I was in a hotel with a man who wasn't my husband—who wasn't my sick husband—and…and so I left, I just got dressed and left.

INT: What did you tell [redacted]…when you went to leave?

RES: He asked what happened, if everything was okay. I said it was.

INT: [inaudible] you lied to him.

RES: Yes, I lied. What was I going to say? My husband just told me he has cancer over the phone? I—I'm not sure I even processed it at that point.

INT: I understand. Then you went to leave?

[00:24:13]

RES: Yeah, I went to leave and [redacted]—he…he freaked out, and I had never seen him like that. It scared me.

INT: Of course. Did he say anything to you? When you went to leave?

RES: Yeah. When I said it was my husband and I had to go, he stopped me from leaving. He, uh, he put his hand on the door, then—then he started, um, telling me about his, his, uh, ex-wife.

INT: You mean [redacted].

RES: … Yeah, [redacted]. He'd never mentioned her, ever. I mean, I knew he was divorced, but he never really wanted to talk about her.

INT: And what did he say about her?

RES: He said—that…[redacted] left him two years ago because he had anger issues. He said he didn't have anger issues, and that he wishes he never met [redacted]…that he wishes he could go back in time and meet me instead. That if he did, his life would've been different.

INT: Did he say what kind of anger issues?

RES: No. No, this was the first time he'd ever mentioned it. It was the first time I'd ever seen that side of him. He'd never been like that, he'd never—he never would've stopped me from leaving anywhere.

INT: But he did this time.

RES: Yeah, he did this time. And I was kind of afraid. I was more confused—I wasn't really thinking after [redacted] called. I wasn't thinking clear.

INT: No, I don't think I would, either, if he called and told me that…

RES: … No, right. I wasn't. It was like my head just fogged up, everything was blurry. And you know, at first when he called, I thought he was going to say he wanted a divorce. That he was about to admit to me that he had been cheating on me this entire time. But instead he told me something even worse than that. And—and he was… My husband didn't tell me he was sick. That he was going to the doctor all this time… I just—

INT: It's okay.

[00:26:42]

RES: … I just…

INT: Deep breaths. Take your time. Go slow.

RES: I'm sorry. I just, I can't believe I even thought like that, looking back. Then I hung up the phone and looked at the naked man waiting for me in bed, and I just—my god, it hit me how horrible I was. My god—how fucking horrible I was…

INT: We've all made mistakes, [redacted]. You're human.

RES: I'm human. Yeah. Sometimes, I'm not sure.

18

I freeze, stuck staring at the front door as the banging echoes through the small cabin.

Matt's head snaps up, his expression confused. "No one is supposed to be here," he says softly, reaching for the gun resting on the chair beside him. Slowly, he moves out from behind the table. "Who's there?" he shouts, tiptoeing to the door, gun held low near his hips.

I hold in a breath.

Bang bang bang.

"I'm not opening until you tell me who's there!"

Silence.

Then, "It's me. Blake."

Matt glances at me over a shoulder as he reaches for the door. *Relax*, he mouths when he sees me staring, a concerned look etched across my face.

But I can't relax.

Not with him. Not with Blake. Not after a couple of days ago when I'd first met him. How he'd tossed his axe over a shoulder, sauntered toward me, a menacing grin biting across his sunken, black-bearded face. How I'd backed away, cautious, shivering. How still, he stared.

The door whips open. Blake seesaws into the front room, boots muddied, face red. His son, Jeremy, follows in close behind him, a mere shadow in his father's raging footsteps.

Freezing air fills the house. Matt closes and locks the door behind them, slips his gun back into the holster.

"What are you doing here, Blake?" Matt asks, crossing his arms. "You can't just barge in. You have to call—"

"Yeah, yeah," Blake says, lashing a hand in the air. He scratches dirty fingernails through his thick beard, stomps into the kitchen, stops right next to me. His eyes circle the room, grazing the endless papers littered across the table, the laptop with case files wide open.

"Listen to me—I came to say one thing," Blake says. "What's my business is my own damn business."

Matt enters the kitchen, stands beside Jeremy, leans his shoulder against the wall. Jeremy inches away from him, tucks his arms close to his chest, keeps his eyes glued to the floor.

"What are you talking about, Blake?"

"I ran into the chief of police in town," he begins, pinching open a manila folder to steal a peek inside. His dark eyes circle a photograph of Charley. "He says he hasn't a damn clue why someone like you'd be up in my woods, my school. You're treading on dangerous ground, Mr. Private Eye. Chief said you being up here won't bring any closure." He drops the folder closed, glares at Matt with a look so ruthless my mouth falls open. "Closure's what we *all* need."

"It's not any of his business. Or *yours*." The words spill from me. Immediately, I wish I could suck them back up.

Blake comes toward me. I tense. His hip grazes my arm and he turns, lowers his head, speaks deep into my ear.

"It *is* my business. That poor girl's death was an *accident*. My son may have found her…but it doesn't matter. That doesn't mean either of us did anything wrong!" His voice is so loud my eardrums vibrate.

"Blake, you—"

Blake cuts Matt off. "Don't you *dare* start sniffing around us, around our home, when we didn't do a goddamn thing to that poor girl. She was—she was just…wrong place, wrong time, okay? That's it, that's the end of it. If the chief says that's all there is to it, I believe him. Leave my son alone. Leave *me* alone. I know you're going to try to blame it on me—you have no one else to blame it on but *me*!"

Matt holds up his hands. "Now you listen a min—"

"No, I won't listen. I *refuse* to listen!" Blake's gaze lands on me. I sit up straight, keep my eyes focused on him even though I want to run. "Stay out of it. I swear to god—I know you want to pin this on us. But my boy is innocent—*I* am *innocent*!"

"Blake—no one," Matt says, obviously fighting to stay calm, attempting to wrangle Blake's eyes with his. "*No one* is pinning anything on anyone. Okay? You hear me? All I'm doing—all *we're* doing here—is trying to bring closure to the victim's family." Matt stops when Blake turns his head away. "Isn't that what you said matters? Closure?"

Blake remains silent.

I look at Jeremy. He stands wearily in the corner, skinny arms wrapped tight around his chest. All he's wearing is a pair of gray sweatpants and a torn Iron Maiden tee-shirt. No coat. No shoes. Just dirty white socks, his big toe poking through a hole in the top. The black eye I'd noticed the other day is beginning to heal, the swelling nearly gone. Only now it's turned a vomit-colored shade of mustard.

He must feel me staring at him because he turns to look at me. His lips are wet and shiny, and he tucks his arms closer into his armpits, tries to stay warm. Tossing his head to the side, he flops his dyed black hair away from his tired eyes.

"Dad," he says quietly, voice cracking. "Dad, stop. Let's go."

Blake turns, looks down to the boy gazing up behind him. Slowly, he lifts a hand, acts as if he'll backhand his son right here, right now. Jeremy flinches, looks down, looks away.

"Jeremy never even knew that girl," Blake says, glaring at Jeremy. "Isn't that right? You never knew her—what's her name?" he says, snapping his fingers to conjure her name. "Charley."

Jeremy shakes his head, eyes flickering at Matt.

Suddenly, Blake's hand snaps forward, smacks the back of Jeremy's head.

"Speak up!"

Jeremy gulps, his eyes glazing with tears. "No! No—I—I never even met Charley." He hangs his head. "I—I was told not to talk to any of the students."

Matt tenses yet remains still.

I narrow my eyes at Blake. How dare he. How dare he come in here, scream at us, threaten us—threaten his son. For all we know, the only thing Jeremy is guilty of is finding Charley's body and calling the police. But we have a responsibility to investigate everyone.

I think of Blake's words. His voice. How he'd grabbed Jeremy by the scruff of his neck, a rabid animal plucking a newborn rabbit by its throat.

I found her, Jeremy said. *Out there...in the woods...*

Somehow, I need to get Jeremy alone, without Blake. If anyone knows more, it's him. Maybe he saw something else when he was out there. Maybe he heard something. Matt said the police barely even questioned Jeremy. Why would they once they determined there was no crime? Just a lost girl dead in the middle of the woods.

"Listen, Blake," Matt says calmly. "We're not trying to pin anything on you—or your boy. We just want what is fair and right under the law. Isn't that what you want, too?"

Blake remains silent. "They told me," he begins with a knowing smile. He stops, squares his shoulders at Matt. "Yeah—Chief told me all about your tactics." His eyes graze past Matt's shoulder, center on me as he speaks. "He said you'd try to find a culprit—a suspect—someone to take the fall, take the blame. I know you're going to start digging. You haven't found shit since you've been up here and now you brought *this one* up here," he says, tilting his chin at me, "rounding up everyone, questioning them, getting inside their heads." As he says it, he taps his temple, laughs to himself. "You are *not* doing that shit to me. I'm *not* going to let that happen. Mark my words."

Blake spins on a heel, grabs his son by his spindly arm on the way. Jeremy winces, tries to stop himself from being tugged away, wriggles under his father's grip. Blake holds him tight. Jeremy cries out. Blake tries to open the door. But it's locked.

Matt slowly walks toward him, unlocks the door. *"Get out."*

Blake grins and stomps out of the house. Jeremy glances back at us, expression withering. Blake tugs him outside. Jeremy stumbles behind.

Matt slams the door behind them, locks both locks.

"Matt," I say, voice shaking. "What the hell was that?"

He drags his eyes to me, presses his back against the door, slumps to the floor. "Promise me you'll stay away from him. He's dangerous. Him and his son."

I hesitate, say nothing.

"*Promise* me, Madeline."

But I can't hear him. My mind has wandered… I can't stop

thinking about Blake. How he stood over me, close, the heat emitting from his body, his warmth crawling underneath my skin. The axe held over his head. His stare, so cold it made my hands tremble.

I think of his face. Standing there. Looking at me. Staring. I think of him just now, leering at the open manila file on the table. At the glossy photograph of the crime scene in the woods. At the picture of Charley lying in the dead, snowy brush, hand up near her face, frozen.

Blake had stared at the picture of Charley, and I stared at him. His expression relaxed. Awareness and clarity filled his eyes. For a split second, I watched as he gulped down his sorrow, his remorse.

His guilt.

And all I could think was, he doesn't seem shocked. He doesn't even seem surprised. He's staring at a picture of a dead teenage girl, lips blue, eyes glazed open. It's a shocking, terrible image for anyone to see, even an abusive, coldhearted man like Blake.

It was almost as if he'd seen it before.

Monday, December 19

19

I open my eyes to darkness.

Wind blows against the windows, rattling the wooden frames. I'm groggy, sick, skin clammy, slicked with an ice-cold sweat. I don't want to get up. Don't want to move. My hand rests unbandaged near my face, palm up on the mattress. I thumb over the wound, caress the sharp, dead skin.

I had a dream. A dream I've never had. Just a few seconds long. Long enough to wake me. Long enough to snap my eyes open and make me want to go home.

Izzi sat on the kitchen counter, legs dangling, the sound of coffee brewing. She sipped a glass of orange juice, leaned her head back against the cabinets. She looked down at me. Took another sip, her fawn-colored eyes hovering over the rim.

"Mommy," she whispered into the glass, her sweet voice amplified, a megaphone. She never called me mommy. "Today, can I please dig a hole in the backyard to feed daddy?"

I snap up, run to the toilet to throw up. With no food in my stomach, all that comes out is pale yellow foam. I flush it down, rinse my mouth, splash cold water on my face.

What the fuck am I doing here? Why am I doing this? Why don't I go home?

Last night, Matt and I stayed up late, until we were both too tired to read, our eyes going bleary, minds limp. He walked me back to the school beneath the dark and starry sky, held my hand as I climbed the icy trail. The hallways were cloaked with shadows as I dragged myself up to my room.

I grabbed the crystal goblet, left over from the tray of food Emilia had brought me yesterday morning, balanced it precariously on the doorknob. It's an old trick I'd seen in some Lifetime movie, where a woman thought she was being stalked by her killer ex-boyfriend. Turns out, she was right. The sound of breaking glass woke her in the dead of night when he was trying to break in while she was sleeping. The sound of breaking glass had saved her life.

I curse softly under my breath knowing my room doesn't have a lock on the door. If someone came into my room at night and stole the brick from under my pillow, they could come back again. Only next time, I'd know.

I peek around the corner. The crystal goblet is still on the doorknob. I exhale a sigh of relief, stare into the bathroom mirror above the sink, stare until my face doubles, stare until my eyes go dry and my skin turns cold.

Vomiting. Muscle spasms. Soon, it'll be headaches. Nausea. I know what's causing this queasiness. I should know better. I should know to stick to a strict schedule. This happened because I let it happen. I'd forgotten not one but two doses of my medications yesterday. No wonder I'm feeling the side effects.

A sound in the hallway.

I peek to see the door still closed, walk into the bedroom, press my ear to the wood.

Silence.

A crash. Down the hall, from the girls' rooms. Footsteps. Voices.

I remove the goblet, crack the door open, poke my head into the hall. Above me, the broken camera high in the corner glares back.

The voices stop.

"Hello?" I whisper into the darkness.

I'm alone.

I close the door tight. Push my back against the wall. Everything seeps into my head, melds together until my knees shake.

Hannah. A scream. Blood in the hallway.

Seeing Blake. Seeing him stare. Feeling his touch, his warmth, how my skin buzzed from his heat.

The brick under my pillow. The gush of heat spreading across the back of my head. How it vanished the next morning.

I have to try to relax. But I can't.

Still listening for sounds in the hallway, I begin my morning routine: comb my hair, put on a bra, brush my teeth until my gums start to bleed. There are only two protein bars left in my luggage, so I begin to ration, pray my pills won't knot my stomach. My insides already feel hollow, mouth dry, hands trembling.

Flipping open the top of my luggage, I start to pull out a clean shirt when I notice something strange. Clean clothes I keep folded on the right side. Dirty, unfolded on the left. But inside now is nothing but a tangle of unfolded clothes, some still with the tags on turned inside out.

This isn't right. I wouldn't do this. I have a system, a method. I zip the luggage shut and slowly back away like I'm defusing a bomb.

Chills flutter over me, the feeling like I'm being watched, as I unplug my phone, grab my black scarf and bulging tote bag. When I turn toward the door, something else out of place catches my eye.

Standing upright in a corner behind the bed is a silver baseball bat. I chew my bottom lip, decide it had to have been hiding there the entire time. I just hadn't noticed it until now.

I shake my head clear, fish around my tote bag for my medications. I pick it up, shake to hear the rattling sound.

No sound. No bottles.

Flipping the bag upside down, I spill the contents onto the bed. Frantic, I search through what poured out. But they're not here. Gone. *Poof.*

I try to think about the last time I'd taken them. It was yesterday morning before I'd gone to the library and met with Hannah. I should've taken them midday, too, but had forgotten. I'd been so busy with Hannah and Alice and Matt, wondering what really happened to Charley. If what Hannah had said about the blood in the hallway was true. How someone had watched blood pool at their feet...the blood turning dark red, thick, black...a lake. I could step in, fall through the earth, disappear...

I shake my head clear. Focus. *Focus.*

If I've lost them—if they're gone. I sit at the edge of the bed, jittery, bounce both knees up and down. *Keep it together.* Think. *Where'd you last put them?*

In my bag, I answer myself. *I always keep them in my bag.*

I lunge for the tote bag again, check all the pockets, feel inside the cotton lining. *Nothing.* I move to my luggage, pick it apart, unzip the zippers, check all the areas I didn't even know the luggage had. *Okay. Just think.*

I light an emergency cigarette, inhale too deep. The smoke

burns my lungs. I gag, pain ricocheting up my throat, cough so hard my larynx moves sideways.

The bathroom. I run to the door, push it open. Drop the cigarette into the toilet, *pssssssttt.* Check the tiny linen closet. Check the table near the tub. Check every place a piece of lint could ever reach. Then I calmly walk toward the bed, pick up my phone, search: *pharmacy iron hill, ny.*

Somewhere has to be open. Matt could drive me—*no.* Not Matt. I don't want anyone to know my personal business, my medications, the reasoning behind them. *Shit.* I'll walk—no, I can't, three hundred acres surround me. An island in the woods.

I'm trapped here, a prisoner. My mind spins. I can't make it stop—then I see them, sitting on a little shelf near the door. I run for the bottles, grab them, clutch them to my chest like precious orange gems, gulp the pills down.

They slide down my throat, press against my spine. *Cough, gag,* run to the bathroom, stick my head beneath the faucet. Cold water plummets into my mouth, stinging my gums, my teeth, my tongue.

I gasp, slow my heartbeat, stop hyperventilating. *Everything will be okay.* I peer into the bedroom, glance at the spot where the bottles stood neatly next to one another, lined up perfectly, labels facing forward.

I wouldn't have done that. It couldn't have been me. Why would I have put them there? I would never have put them there…would I?

Falling into bed, I pull the covers around my face, turn on my side, grip the blankets so tight my fists shake. Footsteps shuffle outside my bedroom door. I grind my teeth, throw a comforting glance toward the metal baseball bat leaning in the corner. Safety, protection.

But it's gone. The bat is gone.

Someone has been inside my room. I know this now. I'm not imagining things. They must've come in when I was in the bathroom. The bat was there before. Now, it's gone. My medications were moved. My clothes were unfolded in my luggage. Then I remember. I'd hung the glass goblet Emilia had left behind in my room on the doorknob last night. I don't understand. I don't—

I press my eyes tight, so tight I hear the muscles straining. I open my eyes in the darkness under the blankets, a secret, underground world. I have to think of other things. Something else. Anything else.

I think of Dave. Think of how I caught him on the phone with another woman. It was always another. Work. Izzi. Clients. *Her.*

Never me.

He answered it right there, right in front of me as we sat on the couch watching TV. He went in the kitchen, paced around. I kept flicking my eyes over to him, seeing if he'd come sit with me, but he never did. Right in front of me, he just stood there, pacing, talking, looking at the floor, a gentle smile playing on his lips.

When he hung up, I asked casually, *Who was that?* I expected him to shrug it off, say it was a work call. But he didn't.

Lynn, he said. Just like that. *Lynn*. No explanation, no nothing. Not even, *Lynn—from work*. Nothing, as if I should know who the hell this other woman was. He moved to sit next to me on the couch and took my hand, made me feel like I was being paranoid, jealous, possessive. But I was just a wife who wanted to know why *Lynn* was calling my husband at night.

The next week, Dave and I went out to dinner, trying to revive whatever was missing, like we could order linguine and clams and a good relationship could somehow be shoehorned into our empty, hollow one.

A song came on in the restaurant. Dave looked up, sighed, said, *I can picture Lynn singing this.*

A headache sprouted. I hated hearing the shape of her name leaving my husband's lips. I hated how she was on his mind in that moment. What did I have to do to get him to think of *my* name when a pretty voice sang and not hers? Where had I gone wrong?

At home that night, I sat alone in the bathroom, crumpled up in a ball, knees tucked to my chest. I stared across the room toward the long mirror hanging on the back of the door. My hair was rumpled. The black eyeliner I'd so carefully drawn had smudged into dark circles under my eyes. *Who am I fooling?* I'd thought. *I know I'll be alone in the end.*

I peer down at my simple, platinum wedding band, spin it around, push the memory away. I wish I'd stolen *Dark Side* after Violet returned the book to the library. I'd read through those pages so many times—maybe there's something in there, some secret knowledge I've long since forgotten. I make a mental note to steal it from the library.

My dark world under the blankets begins to glow soft gray as the sun creeps over the forest-lined horizon, a light mist clinging to the tops of dark trees. Even the sun looks happy today, bright orange and stinging. Emilia must be wrong. There's no sign of rain, let alone a winter storm.

After a few minutes, I push the blankets off. Look outside. Suddenly, clouds weigh down the sky, erasing any sunlight. Alice's viola faintly plays from down the hall as I force myself out of bed. I hesitate.

Little red smears of blood splatter across the white bedsheets, an abstract painting. Seeing the blood makes the cut on my hand pulse, alive, like it's grown its own heart.

I look at my hand. My wound from the broken plate Emilia had brought me now looks as fresh as if I'd just cut it. It's swollen and red, the wound reopened, burning if I so much as brush it against my tank top.

Carefully, I peel off my clothes, turn on the faucet, start a hot bath to clean the disobedient wound. The soothing sound of Alice's viola drifts down the hallway, curling under the crack of my door, like smoke.

Some part of me can't wait to leave this place. I only have one more student to speak with. Then, maybe, I can leave. But another part wants to bolt my feet to the floor, become a permanent part of the school, something innocuous, maybe, like a plant.

The water is boiling when I step into the bathtub. I dunk my wounded hand under the water, wince as it's scalded clean. I've laid out my medications on the stool beside me, take one after the other with an old bottle of water, absorb their metallic, bitter taste. Then take a few more. One more of this. One more of that, like a chef peppering sauce. A dash of this, a smidge of that.

I've never doubled up my doses before. I know I probably shouldn't. But there's something about this place, these girls—I just need to make it through the next few days. Then I'll go back to my normal dosage. I will. I promise.

Mind in a daze, I linger in the bath, long after the water has cooled. The room is nighttime dark, dense storm clouds putting down roots overhead. I plunge my head underwater, come up slow, test to see if I can hold my breath.

The water edges out all sound, a buffer muting my thoughts, my regrets. My memories. Sometimes, I come up for air right away, unable to hold my breath. But those few magical times I'm able to stay under, my mind goes free, left to see things clearly, unmoored of the strangles of my past.

But not today.

I surge out of the water, gasp for a breath, hook my elbows over the sides of the tub like anchors.

I've been lying to myself. To others.

I don't *just* have panic attacks and anxiety. Yes, I have those. But I had something else last year, too. The medical term is a "psychotic depression," a type of major depressive episode with the bonus of nasty hallucinations.

I call it a nervous breakdown.

My stomach plunges at the thought of someone inside this school being in this room, poking around my things, seeing my medications. I feel invaded. Naked. And what would they think when they saw them? A psychiatrist who needed to see a psychiatrist? It's borderline hilarity, even to me. A never-ending cycle of going to get refills at the pharmacy, white paper baggie in my hand, swinging it back to the car like a schoolgirl's lunchbox.

The bags always bulged: a cocktail of antidepressants, antianxiety, and sleeping pills, of course. Then there were the early days of antipsychotics. My body didn't react well to those.

Months later, I quit them altogether, feeling like my blood was buzzing and alive and radioactive with an endless drip of pharmaceuticals pumping through my heart like toxic green ooze, pulsing through my brain. Poison.

If I'd gone to a blood drive, I imagined the bag filling with glow-in-the-dark slime. The nurse would give a silent gasp, stop herself, remember what she's been taught in her required empathy courses. She'd glance at me, kindly say, *It happens. We're well aware of people like you.* Then she'd turn around, drop my bag of green blood in the toxic materials bin.

There are some images I wish I could unsee. One above others. My stomach knots itself tight just thinking about it. I force it away, tuck it deep inside. The memory is a locket.

It's always there, a chain around my neck. But I don't have to open it. I know what rests inside. Some things don't have to be remembered.

Filling my lungs with air, I dunk my head under the water again. In the soundless hum, I remind myself of three things:

1) I am competent.
2) I can do this job.
3) I remember everything—I just don't want to.

20

Three quick knocks.

From inside the tub, I see the edge of the door. I didn't replace the crystal goblet on the doorknob before I walked away. I stare, make sure it doesn't open.

"Who is it?" I listen close, hear gurgles, a muffled voice.

"Emilia."

I sigh, slink out of the bathtub, water dripping across the tiled floor. I look in a mirror to fix myself. Look away quick.

"Emilia?" I ask once more to be sure it's her and not some unhinged impersonator sneaking into my bedroom at night, moving my prescriptions, putting bricks under my pillow, stealing the metal bat beside my bed.

Throwing a bathrobe around my shoulders, I tie it tight, pinch open the bedroom door.

"What are you doing here?"

She snakes in, face terse, heels clacking. Dressed head to

toe in black, a glittery silver scarf wraps around her thin neck, a bedazzled spider pin on her shoulder. She looks like a goth Christmas ornament.

"Good morning to you, too, Dr. Pine."

Plopping down on the bed, I begin to towel dry my hair. "Can you please move me to a room with a lock?"

Emilia glances at the door, shakes her head slowly. "None of the doors in the school have locks."

"Oh, great," I lament. "So what brings you here so early?"

She looks at me bitterly. "I've come to see if you've given any thought to what I told you yesterday."

I narrow my eyes at her as she hovers in front of the windows, stealing glances outside at the dark, rolling clouds.

"You want to know if I'm leaving before the storm," I begin. "No, I'm not. Not until I've finished speaking to the students. And neither is Detective Reyes."

Emilia leaves the windows, slowly crosses the room, heels tapping the floor like a pendulum.

"That's a shame…" she mutters to herself.

Brittle silence.

My stomach heaves. The double dose of pills I'd just taken is coming back to haunt me. Bile rises in the back of my throat. I gulp it down, keep my eyes on her, try to project confidence and keep my composure. On the inside, I'm decomposing.

Last night, Matt asked if I could speak to Emilia. If I could further question if she ever saw the students leave the school late at night. If she has, Matt will need to delve deeper into how much Emilia may have known regarding the security— or lack thereof—at the school. Did she know Hannah was sneaking out to stargaze? Did she know Alice and Charley snuck out to the woods to their secret place? I have to ask her. It's now or never.

I have to get it out quick before I vomit across the floor.

Emilia eyes me unsteadily, hesitant. I part my lips to speak, but the words won't leave my tongue.

"Dr. Pine," she says, "you look pale. Are you okay?"

I nod. "Yes—I'm fine."

She turns to leave.

"Wait—"

"What?"

My head spins. Dizzy, buoyant, the room a carousel.

I look up at Emilia. At her four eyes. Her two noses.

I gulp, grip the blanket in my fists, force myself to stay calm.

"I need to ask you..." I say. She studies me, her gaze unnerving. "Have you, uh, ever seen or heard of the girls leaving the school unattended? Particularly at night?"

She shrugs, breathes out through her teeth. "Of course not. I already told you, the students believe the security cameras are recording. I know for a fact they're a perfect deterrent to stop that sort of activity."

I focus on producing a follow-up question. It comes out too slow. Emilia gets antsy, her body wavering closer to the door.

"You're sure? You've never seen or heard anything?"

"As I've already told you, I've *never* allowed that sort of behavior and if you're trying to blame something on me—"

Slowly, swallowing down the burning knot in my throat, I circle the bed, kneel to the floor. I'd hidden the files on Charley's investigation Matt had given me under the bed. I need to show Emilia why I'm here. Why Matt is here. I need to show her what I've seen—the police photographs of Charley. How her mother deserves to know the truth.

I need her to see why we're doing this. Why it matters. I have to bend Emilia to our side. Even though she's not a mother and has a certain strong-willed strictness with her students, still, underneath her harshness, I know she cares about them. I know she doesn't want them dead.

Right?

I swipe a hand across the dusty floor. Feel the bare corners beside the bedposts. I fall on my hands, sweep my eyes back and forth under the bed, see Emilia's impatient heels standing on the other side.

I bolt up, blood gushing back to my head. I have to stay kneeling. I can't rise. I can't fall, *don't fall.* The walls turn wobbly. The bathroom is behind me. I can run. I can make it.

"What are you doing?" Emilia asks. "I have to speak to Rosemarie before breakfast. Are we done here?"

"You took them," I whisper.

"What?"

"The—the files. Charley's case files. You took them, didn't you?"

Emilia gasps. "I have no idea what you're saying. I don't even come into this room."

"I—I had them—"

Emilia laughs. Chills flicker through me.

"This is ridiculous," she says coldly. "Dr. Pine, you keep me here, ask me ridiculous questions and now you're blaming me because *you've* misplaced something?"

Bile creeps onto my tongue. I clench my jaw, press a hand over my lips, as if that'll keep it down.

Emilia stomps a hand on her hip, peers down at me, watches me, waits for me to give up. I'm a *doctor,* I could say to her. A criminal *psychiatrist.* I'm not some nobody from nowhere. I matter, I—

"It's *my* school. *My* home," she says. "*You* aren't helping. All I want is to help these girls—to do what's in their best interest—to be their advocate. To protect them and safeguard them, and that no longer includes *you.* You need to leave."

"No, I'm… I *am* helping."

"You *aren't.*"

"No, I—"

"You're sick, Dr. Pine. *Sick*. I know you're on medications."
I sway, grab the bedpost to keep steady. "I saw them—that
day on your nightstand. I took the liberty of researching those
prescription drugs." She begins circling me, prowling. She
wants to swallow me whole.

Slowly, I escape the bed, walk to the windows, crack one
open, gulp down the ice-thickened air.

"You're sick," she repeats. My head swims. "Delusional.
Otherwise, you wouldn't even have been prescribed these
medications."

I shake my head back and forth, neck creaking like an old
wooden door.

"I'm not—"

"This has got to stop. You can't keep doing this," Emilia
cries. "To me. To my school. To my students. They don't deserve this. Neither do I. Stop accusing me of things I did *not*
do. I did nothing wrong. *Nothing*. I've always done everything right. I've—"

"Where did you put the files, Emilia?" I say. "Just tell me,
and I won't keep asking—"

She stops. Moves closer. Slams the window closed. I slump
down, defeated, my insides detaching, floating around my
rib cage.

"We're done here."

She walks to the door.

"Wait—no," I cry, helpless, pathetic. "Come back."

Matt's words swim into my consciousness, bob in the murky
ocean of my brain.

Anyone is capable of anything.

I stare at her, at her perfect hair. Her perfect outfit. Perfect
facade. She's perfect and I'm...

"I want you and Detective Reyes gone by tomorrow morning," Emilia whispers, staring at the floor. "I'll give you twenty-four hours to settle things with the girls and pack." She lifts her head, looks right through me. "If you aren't gone by then, I'll have the chief of police personally escort you off the campus for trespassing."

21

Outside, the sun sets, filling the library with shadows.

I'd spent the day alone, thinking, listening to the crackling of the fireplace, paging through brittle pages of moldering books lining the wood-paneled walls. I've also been waiting. Waiting for the most elusive girl in the entire world, the final student I need to speak with—Kiara Cole.

Rosemarie entered the library around noon, kindly bringing with her a tray of tea and grilled cheese, the cheese unmelted and the bread stale, and noted that Kiara will be running a little late.

Three hours later, the tall, confident girl I'd met my first day at the school finally appears. But as soon as we sit down, my mind dulls, retreating back to what had happened earlier this morning.

I'd never seen Emilia like that. Spit rocketing from her mouth, eyes spasming, her entire body vibrating with anger.

She wants me gone. Wants *us* gone. When I texted Matt we had until tomorrow morning before she has both of us escorted off campus, he'd replied with a simple:

Shit.

Can she do that? I'd texted back.

Unfortunately, yes.

Matt and I are now officially on a major time crunch. With less than a day left, I have to finish my interviews with the girls, pass along all my notes and hypotheses to Matt, and somehow find the case files he'd given me that had been stolen from my room last night.

If a student stole them, they could be passed around, shared, photocopied. The only small mercy granted to me is that the students don't currently have access to phones or the internet to splash them across social media—or worse.

I know I didn't misplace those files. Inside was information about Matt's investigation, a photocopy of the preliminary autopsy, the police's official report, photographs of the crime scene...of Charley. They had to be stolen, taken by the same person who'd entered my room and placed a goddamn brick under my pillow my first night at the school.

I *know* someone took them, just as they'd taken the silver baseball bat leaning beside my bed. Just as they'd moved my medications. I know because it *wasn't* me.

"I once killed a cat—slaughtered it right on my dining room table."

I blink, look up.

"Now you're listening."

Kiara sits in the chair in front of me, spine straight. Crossing one long leg over the other, she adjusts her tight black top around her shoulders, brushes lint off her baggy cargo pants. Tall and ethereal, Kiara flicks her long, thin braids behind a shoulder.

I study her as she begins to pick apart the seam on the velvet chair. She didn't bring her softball with her today. A good thing. Less distractions.

Kiara's cheeks are full and round, though she's thin and athletic—a dichotomy, as are her patchy, sparse eyebrows, paired with long, lush lashes women would kill for. She appears so assured, so strong, her shoulders squared, not shying away from direct eye contact, like Alice or Hannah.

I close my eyes, set the thoughts aside. Reaching over, I switch on the voice recorder on the table between us. Numbers flash, brilliant red, electric.

I focus on Kiara, begin with my warm-up exercise.

"So, Kiara, tell me a little about yourself—"

"You should know I hate small talk," she says in a honeyed voice.

I close my mouth, tilt my head, try to read her. Swiftly, I mentally flip through her file. I'd read how she'd come to Shadow Hunt Hall from a private school in Oregon. How she'd been expelled.

COLE, KIARA
DOB: 09/12/05 Lake Oswego, Oregon
Dominique Cole, mother / Christopher Newsome, father
-Enrolled Spring/21, expulsion from previous private HS—
-Kinesthetic & auditory learner
-Fluent in English, Spanish & French
-Excels in sports, computers/technology
★ Prefers solo study—group projects not recommended

*** *ALLERGIES: Dogs, avoid nightshades e.g.: potatoes,*
tomatoes, eggplant, peppers,
* *Contact: Mother-work:* ~~844-836-8596~~ *844-684-3635*
Prescriptions:-Paxil-30mg, mornings with food
  -Ativan-1mg, x3 daily
  ~~*-Metformin, 500mg, once daily*~~
  * *x1 baby aspirin allowed daily*
* *Doctor on call: Weeds, Jennifer (Village Medical Center)—*
<u>*Update REQ*</u>.

"I understand," I begin, smiling, hinting to her I may secretly agree, trying to form a connection with some common ground. "So, you're a polyglot? I saw that in your file. What inspired you to learn so many languages?"

"Small talk," Kiara says. "Hate it."

I press my lips together, hold in a smile. I'll try one more time. If I fail, it's strike three. "Okay, why don't you tell me why you're here during winter break."

Kiara mirrors my movements, tilts her head to the side. "My mother didn't want me."

"Oh, that's not true," I say, leaning back.

She leans back, too, shrugs. "She wouldn't give me her credit card to buy a plane ticket."

I nod, nod more. Nod until my glasses become loose. I slide them back up. "So you stayed behind?" She stares at me, her expression blank, unamused.

Trying my best to warm her up, I ask, "Kiara, I know you hate small talk, but why don't you tell me what things you like. What classes or hobbies do you prefer? Do you like movies? Music?"

In my head, I've already lined up a fresh batch of movies Izzi and I had watched, ready to talk about them, get Kiara to let her guard down.

Kiara gazes down at her hands. Looking back up, she slides her long braids over a shoulder, mumbles, "I like sports."

Good, excellent. "What kind of sports?"

"What about you, did you play sports?"

"We're not here for me—"

"You seem like you wouldn't," she says, cutting me off.

"No? Why not?"

Kiara scrapes her dark eyes up and down the length of my body. From my boring black boots to my starched black pants. Then my white button-up shirt, gray wool sweater tossed over my shoulders, though it's slipped off one side. I adjust my glasses, straighten the silver watch on my wrist, suddenly self-conscious.

She breaks her gaze from me, sighs. "You're the smart type. Smart types don't play sports."

"Lots of types play sports," I rebut, keeping my eyes on her.

She shrugs again. "I played softball at my old high school."

"That's great—"

"But I got kicked off the team."

"How come?"

"I broke a girl's arm during practice."

"Oh," I say, breathless. "I'm sure it was an accident." *Please say it was an accident.*

Kiara locks her brown eyes on me. In the golden light from the lamp beside her, they glow, otherworldly, with a tinge of deep red, like marrow.

She shakes her head, cracks a piece of gum I didn't even know she had in her mouth.

I keep my eyes locked with hers, attempt to mimic her assertiveness. Right now, I'm unsure how fragile it is, if her wall can even be penetrated, at all.

"Do you want to talk more about that?"

"Nope."

"Do you miss playing softball?" I pry, trying to pull words from her.

"My mom said I wasn't allowed to play anymore."

"Why not? Because of *one* incident?" I play it down, show her I see her side.

Kiara rolls her eyes, shrugs. "Just no more sports."

"That seems a little harsh."

She laughs softly to herself, a delicate, high-pitched laugh. "Because it wasn't just *one* incident."

"Oh?"

"There was another one or two."

"Would you like to tell me about that?"

She shrugs again, one shoulder, nonchalant. "I made a threat. Told some girl I'd stab her one time for each year she was alive."

"Oh."

"I *didn't*, though," Kiara says firmly, staring deep into my eyes as if making sure I believe her.

I shift awkwardly on the sofa. "Why—" I pause, shake my head, start again. "Was she another girl on your softball team?"

"She was a bully," she says. "I hate bullies. Never liked them. Anyway, that's why my mom sent me here. Punishment. There's no sports here. No *nothing* here, nothing but boring art projects and nature walks and mindfulness sessions—but yes," she adds begrudgingly, dark eyes sweeping the room, "I miss softball."

I smile, hope she feels comfortable with me. It seems her mother had made the right decision. With no sports at Shadow Hunt Hall, there may be fewer reasons to flare Kiara's temper. It appears to be working. Her file is one of the thinnest of the bunch, second only to Hannah's.

"Can I ask you a blunt question, Kiara?" I ask, hoping a direct question doesn't instantly make her shut down. She nods, keeps her eyes on me. "How well did you know Charley?"

She blinks, stares, unwavering. *Shit.* I wait, hold my breath, wonder if she's closed herself off.

Kiara leans in, licks her lips. "Well enough," she whispers, voice brimming with concern.

"How well is that?" I ask.

"Well enough that I told her once that if I catch anyone messing with her, I'll break their motherfucking arm, too."

I can't help but smile. Finally, she smiles back.

The room holds in a breath, exhales. Kiara leans back, looks down, seems concerned. Her dark eyes light up, glowing with freshly conjured knowledge.

I hover my pen over my notepad, press the sharp nib to the paper. Prepare for the worst. Brace for impact.

"You know," Kiara says, "Charley wasn't a stupid girl. She'd never let herself get lost in the woods. Not like that."

I blink. "What do you think happened?" I ask, remembering I'd asked the other girls if they had any knowledge of Charley sleepwalking. Alice and Hannah both said no. Curious, I ask Kiara. "Do you think maybe Charley sleepwalked into the woods?"

She rolls her eyes, sighs, cracks her gum again. "I've known Charley for over a year. We're in every class together. She never mentioned sleepwalking," she says with certainty, her sparse eyebrows knitting together.

"What happened to her—in your opinion?"

Kiara shrugs. "I can only say what I saw happen—before."

"What happened before?"

A pause. Her mouth opens. "It's like…being in the outfield, and I can't see the ball through the sunlight. And it comes toward you, closer and closer, but you don't see it until it's right over you, and by then you're too late to catch it."

"Go on."

"That day," she whispers, "the last day I saw Charley. It… was different than other days."

"How?"

"There were just—things I noticed," she says, expression knotting. "Things like, overhearing a fight. Normally I'd just walk away but… I didn't. Not this time. This time was different."

"Who did you hear fighting?"

She licks her lips, leans closer, elbows on her knees. "Charley and Alice. But you know," she says, "I didn't hear a single word. I just remember a *feeling*."

I nod in understanding. Whatever Kiara heard that day had stuck with her. I wait for her to continue at her own pace. Her dark eyes fall to the floor, trace the lines of the threadbare Persian rug.

"What did you feel, Kiara?" I prompt.

"I felt—*sad*." She trails off in thought. "Sad for them, for both of them. Alice was *so* upset when Charley broke up with her. I knew Charley didn't want to do it, but she had no choice."

"Why not?"

Kiara shrugs. "I think it was her mother. Something about her mother wanting to pull her out of school. I knew that would be the last thing Charley would want. She already went through that shit."

I look up, see Kiara watching me closely.

"Something else on your mind?" I ask when I notice her proud and fearless demeanor has somehow shifted.

Kiara hesitates. "I just thought Charley was so smart…" She trails off. "I looked up to her, you know? She was one of the few girls here who I liked—who I *respected*. She didn't seem to take any shit from anyone."

I narrow my eyes. "What made your opinion of her change?"

Kiara shakes her head. "No, no. Nothing like that," she grumbles, leans back, folds her arms across her chest. Quickly, she leans forward again. "It's just—" she begins, bringing her eyes to mine. "I respected Charley. I liked her, everyone did. But she did something that always made me mad. She was so strong and so smart, but then she'd go off and do *stupid* shit that just left me confused why this girl would be *so* smart one second and then go off and do something dumb the next."

"What did she do?" I glance at the voice recorder. The red numbers tick by. The wound on my palm begins to itch beneath the bandage.

"Charley was a fixer," Kiara says, her eyes glued on mine. "She liked to fix broken people. She was like a moth to a flame—she couldn't help it, even if they ruined her. Even if they dragged her down with them, she couldn't stay away."

I drop my hand, the pen scratching an ugly black line across the notepad. "Why do you think that is?"

She inhales a deep breath. "She wanted to help people. To heal them. Their wounds became hers whether they wanted it or not. She told me the same shit happened at her old school, too, before she came here," Kiara says. "And then I heard that fight with her and Alice, yelling about someone, I couldn't hear who. And I just thought, *damn*. Charley probably loves that other person the most. They'll cause a fight between her and her girlfriend and make them cry and she'll still take their side, she'll still defend them over the person trying to help her, the person right there in front of her. *That's* what made her stupid. She gave the wrong people second chances."

A knot grows in my throat. I sip from my bottle of water, slide it onto the coffee table.

"This seems to really upset you," I whisper.

"Yeah it *does*," Kiara snaps, eyes shining with tears. "Why is it always the nice ones who get taken advantage of? Why can't bullies come at someone like me? Someone who can fight them off? Defend herself? Why's it always the ones who want nothing but to help people? *That's* what upsets me. First it was at her old school. Fine, okay, you leave. You come here. You do the same shit again. You meet Alice. You try to fix her. She's broken. We all know it. But then you don't stop. You need to do *more*. You need someone else to help. You find him—"

Kiara stops, looks up.

I hesitate. "When you say, *him*—who do you mean?"

Kiara doesn't reply.

I scratch the back of my neck, push up my glasses, study her. "Who do you mean by *'him,'* Kiara?"

"No one."

"Who? You can tell me," I say. "You can trust me."

I stare at her so long my vision doubles. When she doesn't speak again, I look away, blink my eyes clear, stare into the fireplace.

"If I tell you," she says hesitantly. "Will you promise not to let anyone know *I* was the one who told you?"

"I promise."

Kiara sighs. "Jeremy," she says and her shoulders slump, as if his name was the only thing holding her body together.

Jeremy.

Jeremy?

He'd claimed he'd never met Charley. He said it, just last night, right to my face, right to Matt's face in the guesthouse.

Blake's eyes. On fire. Vicious. Filled with hate.

Speak up!

Jeremy, slumped over, alone, afraid. Eyes glazed with tears.

No! No—I—I never even met Charley.

He said it, knowing it was a lie.

Was it possible? Could the same boy who'd found Charley's body have something to do with her death?

Before I realize it, my pen is scrawling over my notepad, so fast I can barely read my own handwriting.

"Can I go now?" Kiara asks.

I stop, blink, look up. "Of course. Thank you for coming."

She wrinkles her face, swings her legs off the chair, disappears in silence.

When she leaves, I let out a giant breath of air, try to slow my racing heart. I look back to the fireplace at the charred wood, the dusty ash, the blackened stones. Slowly, I glance at my notepad, see what I'd written.

My handwriting is sloppy, scrawled, barely coherent. But I'm able to sift a few words from the ashes.

Jeremy Charley Woods
Murder

22

I need to walk. Clear my head. Get away. Run away.

I run into the lobby, lungs aching to get outside, to inhale the cold, winter air. It's been another exhausting day. But now, I've finished. I've finally spoken to all four girls. Tomorrow morning, I'll talk to Matt. Share with him all I know. Depart on an early morning train. Disappear into nothingness. Gone forever.

Pushing the front door open, I step outside onto the cobblestone pathway. The sky is black and twisting. Wind blows fiercely in my ears, drowning out all other sounds with an angry *whoosh*.

I need to know.

I have to know.

It's a terrible idea to confront them by myself. And I did make a promise. I told Matt I'd stay away from Blake and Jeremy. But I can't. I need to know. I need to ask him to his face.

My shoes crunch through the frozen grass on my way to their house. I don't need to glance at the trail signs anymore. I know exactly where they live. I'd passed by it each time I'd taken the long walk through the woods to Matt's guesthouse.

It's a squatty old cottage, low-ceilinged and stone, with small lead glass windows and a black painted door—a skull with black teeth.

As I get closer, my hands begin to sweat, despite the freezing temperature. I think about what I'll say:

Jeremy, why did you lie?

How well did you really *know Charley?*

Did you follow her that night into the woods?

Is that how you found her body out in the middle of fucking nowhere?

Did you push her?

Hurt her?

Kill her?

Did you know that you would?

My eyes grow sharp in the darkness as I follow the too-dim footlights along the narrow path. When I near the cottage, one window on the first floor glows white from a light on inside.

As I step off the path, a twig snaps underfoot. I curl into a ball below the window. Slowly, I raise my head, peek inside. A TV plays the local news, the only light on inside the house. It ignites a snug living room, little tables, and stained beige couches circling the walls.

I edge closer to the windowsill. The news rolls into commercials. Still no sign of Blake or Jeremy. I keep my head low, study the guts of their house. An open beer can rests on a table. Blankets are strewn across the room. Piles of magazines on the coffee table.

Bang.

I jump back, slipping into thorny bushes. My arm flies out

to catch myself before falling backward. My bandaged hand bends sideways. I fall on my back, ankle cracking. A splitting pain explodes in the back of my head.

Shit.

Flurries of bats fly overhead. My heart thuds in my chest. I look up to see where the bang had come from. A loose shutter slaps against the side of the house, blown open by a gust of wind. I grab my bag off the ground, ankle sore, hand aching with stinging heat. I'm ready to run when something stops me.

In the flickering glow from the TV, something shiny catches my eye. It leans in a corner against the wall, staring at me, shining bright as spasming light flashes through the room, reflecting off the smooth silver.

It was missing. Missing—taken. Gone. It was beside my bed, then it wasn't. I know I saw it. I wasn't imagining it. I couldn't have...could I? I look again.

In the corner of their living room is my missing baseball bat.

I rush back to the school, unbuttoning my heavy coat on the way. I welcome the chill. It does well to stop me from sweating out of anger.

Now there's no doubt one of them have been inside my room. One of them, Blake or Jeremy, stole the metal bat. Moved my bottles of pills. Stole my case files. Hid a brick beneath my pillow.

But why?

A glance at my watch confirms it's nearly seven. Dinner should be soon, but I'll find something to eat later. Right now, I have to tell Matt. I have to tell him about the baseball bat.

A dog barks in the distance as I open the main door and step inside out of the cold. Even as I cross the lobby, the dog outside keeps *barking barking barking*. It follows me, relentless, echoing through the thick stone walls, creeping into my head.

Sitting on the staircase, I reach into my bag, pull out my

phone, chew my nails, stop only when I taste blood. My head spins. The room spins.

I call Matt. It rings once.

"Hello?" In the background, he types on his laptop.

"It's Madeline."

"Hi, what's up?"

"Can we meet? I have to talk to you."

A pause. "Yeah, sure. Now's a good time, if you want. I'll meet you halfway."

Escaping the school, I walk to meet Matt, following the narrow footpath back across the courtyard, through the woods. From a distance, Blake's cottage is dark save for a single porch light dangling above the black front door.

Gravel crunches in the distance. In the orb of white light from Matt's flashlight, he's a shadowy silhouette in the night. As he approaches, he lowers the light, careful not to blind me.

"Hey."

"Hey," I echo. His dark hair is brushed away from his face and even with his beard growing in, I can see his cold-bitten cheeks. "We have to talk." I whisper like I'm about to tell a secret. Maybe I am.

"What about? Did one of the girls tell you something?" I shake my head, glance down to my shoes.

They did. Kind of. But I can't focus on that now. He has to know. He has to know Blake or Jeremy has been lurking around inside the school, inside my room.

Matt lets out a heaving sigh, breath smelling of mouthwash. "What happened?" he asks, leading me down a forgotten footpath. I can't help but bristle at the sight of Blake and Jeremy's cottage through the trees ahead.

I tell Matt about the baseball bat—how it had been in my bedroom one day and then tonight, I saw it leaning against the wall in Blake's living room. I tell him about the moved prescription bottles. How the files he'd given me on Charley's case had vanished from my room. I tell him about the brick under my pillow.

Above all, I tell him what Kiara had told me. How Jeremy lied when he said he'd never met Charley. Charley *knew* Jeremy. They were friends, at least. If not more.

He listens dutifully as we walk, closer and closer toward the cottage, the flashlight bobbing up and down with each step. The untamed arms of fir trees grow out from the shadows of the woods, caressing my arm, my shoulder.

When I finish speaking, Matt stops, turns to face me. "All of this happened and you never told me."

"No…"

"You found a brick under your pillow—a *brick*—and you never told me?"

I shift, strangely embarrassed by the intense way he's looking at me. "I never told you because…it disappeared."

"It—what?"

"Can we please talk about something else?"

Thankfully, he nods, continues walking. "So your theory is that Jeremy knew Charley…" He trails off, rubs the back of his neck. "And that maybe Jeremy had something to do with this."

"It's the only thing that makes sense," I answer flatly.

"How would I prove this?" he asks himself.

"I don't know," I say. "That's your job. I'm only here to help."

The trees crowding the footpath fall away. Across the hilltop, a light fog has settled, dusting the wintery world in a faint, white haze.

Matt sighs. "How do you know the bat is at Blake's place?" I fight the urge to follow where his gaze has settled on Blake's cottage just ahead.

I say nothing, press my lips together.

"Did you break and enter?" he asks.

"No," I say quietly. "I just…"

"You what?" He stops again, looks at me.

"I did a little surveillance, that's all."

"Madeline…"

"Yeah, well, no one was there. I didn't see anyone," I rush to add. "The bat was in a corner—I couldn't help but see it." I throw my hands up in surrender.

"Hey," Matt interrupts. "You don't have to explain."

"I don't?" I tilt my head, curious. "So…you're fine with this? You're okay with one of them coming into my bedroom, stealing the bat, the case files—*your* case files—you think it's all in my *head*?" I back away, throat tightening.

"That's not what I'm saying."

"Then what *are* you saying?"

He stares at me in the dark, the flashlight clicking off, casting us into shadows.

"I'm saying, I know things like this can get hard, if you let it."

"Things like what?"

Matt sighs. "Being here, at a school like this, with people like this. Having to confront the details of a tragic case. It's not something everyone can do."

I circle around him in the cold, unable to stand still, adrenaline bubbling inside me. "You think I can't do this job?" My stomach churns.

I've known it all along, deep inside. It's entirely different hearing another person say aloud what's been hiding inside your own head.

He laughs softly, head swiveling as he watches me circle him. "Oh, I know you can. Maybe a little too well. Not every criminal psychiatrist hired to a case takes it upon themselves to conduct surveillance."

"Well, *I* do," I say caustically. "When I feel it calls for it."

"Maybe you were right about it," Matt whispers. "Just this time."

"I don't trust them," I say, staring at Blake and Jeremy's cottage through the thin fog that's settled on the hill.

Matt shakes his head. "I don't either."

In the faint glow from the footpath lanterns, I study his face. His worried expression. How his dark eyes flicker between me and the cottage. How his lips downturn disapprovingly whenever he looks away.

"You agree with me?" I ask. "You think Jeremy could be involved in Charley's death?"

"I don't think anything." Matt sighs. "Not yet. I can't. I have to keep all options open. For now."

"For now," I repeat as I glance around the darkness surrounding us.

The moon is a knife-sharp crescent peeking behind clouds steeped with a licorice shine. White fog puffs through Matt's lips as he studies me in the shadows.

Sound swells in the silence.

Matt grabs my arm, swings me around to stand behind him. A truck drives up the gravel lane, headlights aimed right at us, beams of light diffused by the fog. Matt clicks off his flashlight.

Too late. They already know we're here.

"What do we do now?"

Matt's back straightens. "Let's get this over with." He edges forward.

The doors slam shut. Crunching footsteps.

"Can I help you?" Blake shouts across the pathway. In the soft light from the porch, Blake's face is etched with shadows, white light focused like a pin in the reflection of his dark eyes.

Jeremy remains beside the truck, unmoving and silent in the safety of the darkness.

Matt drops his voice low. "Good evening, Mr. Edwards. Are you free to talk?"

Blake's eyes dance between us. Jeremy slinks out of the shadows, emerging into the light, back hunched, shoulders tensed. He scoops his black hair out from his eyes, lowers his head as he examines us.

Blake grunts. "Yeah. Yeah, sure. Come in."

Beside me, Matt's body relaxes. But I remain tense.

My blood feels electrified. I can't shake this feeling of knowing something true yet being unable to prove it. Jeremy *had* to have been involved in Charley's death. He'd lied about knowing her. He was the person who'd found her body. I want to scream. I'm so close, I can feel it. All I have to do is prove it. But how?

Blake glances at us over a shoulder as he unlocks the front door. I follow Matt toward the cottage, where Blake and Jeremy stand aside, allowing Matt and me to enter first.

The door creaks open. I step inside. The air smells of meat. Light from the TV flickers in the darkness, the sound muted. The low hum of the refrigerator whirs. Shuts off. The door slams shut behind us. The TV goes dark.

Silence encroaches.

A familiar feeling crawls through me.

Fear.

THE YEAR BEFORE

FILE NAME: JPN00.012.00030923.mp3

INT: Do you need to take a break?

RES: No...no, I'm fine. Let's keep going.

INT: Okay. And, uh, what happened then, when you went to leave the hotel?

RES: Well, I—I told [redacted] how my husband just called and told me he had cancer.

INT: You told him that? In the hotel?

RES: Yeah. At the time I felt like it was the only way he'd let me leave. I mean, my husband said we should see other people. He pushed me away. And I let myself be pushed. I did what he wanted. But to what end? So he could be with another woman? There's a woman out there, somewhere, who my husband wants to be with more than me. More than his wife. Do you know how that feels?

INT: Um, let's go back to, uh, to, uh—how did he react when you told him your husband had cancer?

RES: Not good. At first he seemed very genuine. Like, he, uh, he hugged me, said things would be okay. Then he tried to get me to stay. He tried to take off my clothes.

INT: When he saw you had just gotten dressed?

RES: I had just gotten dressed and I had my purse with me and I wanted to leave.

INT: What did you do?

RES: I told him I had to leave, I had to go—that my daughter was sick, and my husband was sick, and I had to go home.

INT: Did he let you leave then?

RES: … No—no, he, we had a fight. It was our first fight. He started saying things he'd never said before. It kind of—I don't know…it uh, made me very upset.

INT: What sort of things did he say?

RES: He said things like, "Leave him. Come be with me. We can be together. I will make you happy." Then I said I was sorry, we can't keep doing this, and that I was done.

INT: That you were done with—with your relationship with him?

RES: Right. I was done. I just—I had to be with my family. It was time to end things and be with my family.

[00:29:11]

INT: So once you told him that—that you wanted to break it off with him, did he let you leave then?

RES: [inaudible] yeah. He started crying and he sat down on the bed. I—normally I would have gone to him, but I didn't. I looked at him crying on the bed. And at this point, he was, uh, he was still—not wearing any clothes. And—and so I knew if I left now he couldn't follow me.

INT: So then you left the hotel?

RES: I left and I went home.

INT: And he didn't try again to stop you?

RES: No. I left. I remember hearing him—I heard him… he was crying. I heard him from down the hall. As I left. When I was walking. He was yelling, crying. I could still hear him.

INT: And do you remember what he was saying?

RES: … No. No, I don't remember. Nothing specific. Well…he did say, "Why are you going to make love to me and then go home to him?" And when he said that, it just crushed me. My god, it, uh, it—I don't think I really knew what I was doing until he said that.

INT: So you went home?

RES: Yeah. I planned to talk to [redacted] and [redacted] when I got home—when he got home. I knew I wasn't helping the situation. I was making things worse and, um, I didn't want to do that anymore to my family.

INT: And this was…about, you said, a month or so ago?

RES: Yeah. Maybe a month ago.

INT: So you broke off your relationship with [redacted] one month ago?

RES: Right.

INT: So when you went home, what happened?

RES: I went home and realized I couldn't lose my family. I couldn't believe my husband never told me how he was sick, what he's been going through. I could've helped—I don't know why he never told me. I mean, who does that? What did I do to make him not tell me?

INT: So did you go home right away?

RES: Well—I... I wanted to, then I wanted to buy [redacted] soup, something to make her feel better. All I wanted was to go home and try to fix everything. I just wanted to say I was sorry.

23

We hover in darkness until Blake enters the kitchen and flicks on the lights, keeping his sharp gaze on us. Jeremy slinks away, goes to sit in front of the TV. He unmutes it and voices flood into the silent house.

Matt walks into the kitchen behind Blake, shrugs off his coat. I don't follow. Instead, I wander into the living room after Jeremy. Quickly, my eyes scan the room. Corner to corner. Wall to wall.

The bat is gone.

The TV pauses, snapping me out of my trance. I lift my head, see Jeremy staring at me. He says nothing as I rush out of the room.

I plunk down in a chair beside Matt at Blake's kitchen table, my mind screeching through a thousand possibilities. Maybe the bat had fallen. Maybe it fell and rolled under a sofa. Maybe the angles of the room through the window refracted the light, made it seem like it was there when it wasn't. Maybe—

"Dr. Pine?"

I blink, see Matt looking at me.

Blake thrums his fingers on the tabletop. Stops. His eyes snap up. I turn, see Jeremy hovering over me. He moves to sit next to his father across the table from us. I study the kitchen, hoping to find the bat. I'm not imagining it. I saw it. It was there, it was right—

"Dr. Pine and I wanted to run through a few questions with you, if you don't mind," Matt begins. Blake nods, hides his hands beneath the table. "I know it's late, but anything you answer would be much appreciated."

"Go ahead," Blake says. "Get this over with."

"First, we—"

"Actually," I say, interrupting Matt. He turns to look at me, leans back in his chair. "Actually... I wanted to ask Jeremy a question first."

Jeremy looks at his father, turns back to me with a sneer. All I can think of is an imaginary scenario I'd created in my head. It repeats on an endless loop, over and over.

The knife-edged moon. Starlight seeping through the bare tree branches. Gentle snowfall.

Jeremy, no!

Jeremy Charley Woods.

Murder.

Knife-edged moon. Snow. A scream. A struggle.

"Jeremy..." I stop. My voice wobbles. My vision blurs. I pinch my eyelids shut, force away the screams inside my head. "Jeremy...how well did you know Charley Ridley?"

He pauses, eyes shifting to Blake, who nods. "Tell her."

"I—I never even saw her before," Jeremy mutters. "I already told you that."

I shift. Pivot.

"Do you do any work inside the school?" I ask, already knowing he does.

A nod.

"So you at least *see* the students."

His dark eyes flicker toward his father again. Afraid.

I narrow my eyes. *Knife-edged moon. Snow. Scream. Struggle.*

Matt shifts beside me. Soon, he'll jump in. Stop me. Take away my chance.

Blake tilts his head. "What are you getting at?" he snaps. "Why are you focusing on us? On my son?"

Matt holds up a hand. "Mr. Edwards, we—"

"This is a high school for *troubled girls.* If anyone's capable of something awful, it's one of them—*not* my son."

Matt sighs, glances at me, eyes sharp. He clenches his jaw, looks down at his hands knotted together on the table.

I exhale, decide to placate Blake, give him a reply, short and sweet, then swiftly move back to Jeremy. "We're doing all we can to be fair and equal to everyone. We're not asking your son anything that we aren't also asking the students."

Blake rolls his eyes.

I ignore him, focus back on Jeremy. Each passing second seems to make him more and more uncomfortable. Jeremy can't find a place to keep his hands. He can't keep his eyes off his father, can't cut that constant need of approval, to know what he's saying is right.

"There were only five—now four—girls who stayed at the school for winter break," I continue. "You're saying you don't know any of them, right, Jeremy?"

He locks his lips tight. Corkscrews them shut.

"Not even Hannah? Violet?"

Blake chokes out a grunt, crosses his arms again. "My boy isn't exactly known for being a ladies' man. If I didn't know where his stash of girly magazines was hidden, I'd think he wasn't even inclined that way," he says, laughing to himself. It bites the air, makes Matt lean forward, alert.

"Dad, *please* stop—" Jeremy drops his shoulders, turns away in embarrassment. "No—no, I don't know any of them."

"So how can you say you've never even seen Charley without already knowing what she looks like?"

"He's always looking down at his feet. Aren't you, Jeremy?" Blake says, grinning, though his eyes are frozen, stuck staring right at me. He knows something. He must.

Jeremy wrings his shoulders, sits upright. "Dad, stop—"

I gulp.

Blake lifts a shoulder. "I always tell him to look up when he walks. Look straight ahead. Watch your surroundings."

Blake's dark eyes travel back and forth across my face, down my neck, back up. I turn to see Matt's fingers clenching into a fist beneath the table.

"Dr. Pine," Matt begins, "can we talk outside for a second?"

Hotness crawls into the back of my throat, unannounced. I want my medications. I need to get out of here. Out of this house. I have to get home.

"I feel sick," I say, standing, the chair crying as it scrapes across the floor. "May I use your bathroom?"

Blake watches as I clutch my stomach, grab my bag, sling it over a shoulder.

"Upstairs. To the right," Blake says, unamused.

"Madeline—you okay?" Matt whispers to me.

I nod, rush past him, bolt to the stairs, drag myself to the top.

Shadows stretch ahead. Closed doors dot down a shrunken hall. I try the first one. It's the bathroom. I step in, run the water, make it sound like I'm inside, shut the door, try the next door down the hall.

It creaks open. I look over a shoulder, see no one has followed me yet. Inside, I quietly close it behind me. Jeremy's bedroom smells of dirty socks and body odor. What I'd imagine his room to smell like. Normal. A teenage boy's room.

I flick on the light. The room is messy, but only slightly—stained white tee-shirts and sweatpants drape over a computer chair. Empty water bottles rest crumpled on his nightstand beside a snake of charging cords. The carpet is freshly vacuumed with nothing out of place save for a plastic bin of random video-game controllers.

I near it. Something odd peeks up through the plastic, something wrong, out of place. Kneeling down, I push the controllers aside, tug it out from the bottom of the plastic bin.

It's a pink sweater, wrinkled and worn. I check the tag. Mohair and polyester, size small, from a store I've shopped at with Izzi to buy her new clothes for school.

Jeremy's small, but he's not this small.

I stop.

My fingers touch something rigid.

I tug it out, angle it up toward the ceiling light.

Across the front are stains of dried black blood.

Quickly, I fish around in my tote bag, try to pull out my phone to take a picture.

A voice behind me.

"Hello?"

I spin. Jeremy stands against the wall near the door, staring, eyes black as buttons.

I clench my teeth. There's no way I can talk my way out of this. The nausea returns, floods up my throat. It burns. I gulp it back, pinch my lips shut.

"Why are you in here?" he yelps, voice cracking. Behind him, he shuts the door. My heart thuds.

I lift my hand, drop the sweater. My mind blinks. Slowly,

I slide my hand into my tote bag, click on the voice recorder nestled at the bottom.

His eyes zigzag between me and my hand, disappeared into the bowels of the bag. I take it out, keep my eyes on him, make a move to grab the sweater off the carpet.

"That's nothing," he says, lunging across the room, making a swipe at it. I whip it away. "Give it back."

"Whose is this?"

He winces, terrified, and for a heartbeat I feel sorry for him. He recoils into himself, arms folding like a pretzel across his chest as he collapses at the edge of his bed.

"It—it's mine," he says with a worm-size amount of conviction. "Please—just don't tell anyone, okay? *Please* don't say anything. I—I had a nosebleed. That was all I could find."

Kneeling on the floor, I toss the blood-splattered sweater onto his bed. "Whose is it, Jeremy?"

He wriggles but keeps his gaze on me. The black ring around his eye has evolved into a swollen purple stain, worse than it was before. In the fluorescent light it appears to pulse.

His mouth falls open, tongue pressing the inside of his teeth. Slowly, he exhales, drops his head down.

"Please," he gags. "You don't know what he'll do to me."

"Your father?"

He nods.

"You can tell me," I say kindly. "I'm here at the school to help. Did you know that? I just want to help."

He eyes me for a heartbeat, deciding what he should say. Slowly, his shoulders relax. "What do you want?"

I tilt my head, uncross my arms, mold myself into someone he can trust. "The truth," I whisper. "How well did you know Charley?"

He shrugs again. "I…" he says quietly. "I would never hurt her."

"So you *did* know her."

He nods, stares at his hands, picks at his fingernails.

I gulp. "How well?" When he doesn't answer, I ask the same question a different way. "When you were in the school for work, did you—did you see Charley a lot?"

Jeremy doesn't answer. Doesn't move. Doesn't blink.

"I'll make you a deal." I stand from the carpet, take a step closer.

He gazes up at me from the edge of the bed. "*Please* don't tell anyone."

I shake my head. "I won't," I say. "Just answer one question."

He nods, defeated. His shoulders slump. For some reason, my heart feels heavy as I study him. His spit-shined lips tremble as he fights back a flood of tears. Even his fingers shake. He notices, shoves them between his thighs, curls his arms inward in protection.

I take a step closer. My shins tap the side of his bed. I watch his reaction at my sudden closeness. Still, he remains frozen. I go further, sit down beside him. Jeremy leans his head in my direction, keeps his eyes frozen on the floor.

A voice shouts from downstairs.

"*Dr. Pine?*"

Matt.

I ignore him.

"Jeremy," I say softly. "I'm not here to hurt you." He nods once. "I only want to know one thing. I promise you I will not tell your dad or the police or anyone about what I found, okay?"

"Okay."

"I just need the truth. Will you be honest with me?"

"Yes."

I lick my lips, clasp my hands together, show I'm focused

solely on him. "That night, when Charley died," I whisper, "did you see her?"

"Dr. Pine, can you come down?"

His eyebrows knit together. Confusion. He grows jittery, bounces his knees up and down. I try again.

"Did you follow her?"

His breathing escalates. He shifts away. "What, no—I—"

"Did you follow her into the woods?"

"No!"

I stop. The room cascades into silence.

His chest rises and falls, his breath quick. *"No..."* he exhales. "That's *not* what happened," he says, and for the first time, I hear his true voice. No fear. No hesitation. No intimidation. Just Jeremy. "I *always* walked up to that hill. It was my favorite spot whenever...whenever my dad... I went there sometimes just to clear my head. And when I went there that last time I—I found her. I found Charley. I told the police—I—"

"I know," I say. "I know you did."

"Charley and I were friends. She was my best friend. I'd *never* hurt her," he says quickly. "Her family is fucked up, too. Just like my dad. We were close. No one knew. If Mrs. Hawke found out, I'd be—my dad would—"

"Jeremy, come down here right now!"

Blake.

Jeremy's eyes meet mine. "Someone else was out there," he says. His knees stop bouncing.

"What are you saying?"

"Dr. Pine? I'm coming up!"

"One minute!" I shout back.

Jeremy licks his lips, gulps, silently weighs his options in his head. If I watch close enough, I can see his mind work, watch the gears click into place, see how he links his words together before he speaks.

He stands, angles himself directly in front of me. Straightforward. No lies. Honest.

"All I'm saying is, I was the one who called the police. That's it."

A knot in my throat.

His eyes go wide. Slowly, he shakes his head, as if coming to a sudden reckoning, stitching everything together in his mind.

"Don't you get it?" he asks. "Yes, I called the police. But my footprints weren't the only ones in the snow."

24

Windows knock against the walls, torn open by freezing wind. I rub my eyes awake, feel the bed around me. *Alone.* The room is dark. The wind howls.

I climb out of bed, lock the windows tight. It's freezing in the room now, so I tug a blanket off the bed, wrap it around my shoulders. A strange feeling settles around me in the darkness. A feeling of weight, of pressure.

I look at the door. The goblet I'd hung on the doorknob is gone.

My spine goes straight. I listen to the sounds of the room, but nothing but silence lives between the wind.

A storm is coming...

A sound thunders outside my door.

My body tenses. I shut my eyes, think of Izzi. Izzi making pancakes. She's in the kitchen, fighting with the oven.

We need a new one!

One day, Izzi…

I helped her. She made the batter. I made the coffee. The radio was on, playing hits from the aughts. I remember dancing with Dave to one.

Memories compound, disappear.

Izzi made a stack of pancakes six inches high and ate every one. With the butter melting in between each one and maple syrup drizzled on top, the three of us sat in the kitchen eating and laughing until our bellies swelled and our smiles hurt.

Izzi was never one to talk about feelings. But she did that day. We discussed school and her friends and how she felt left out a lot. I tried to give advice where I could. But to her I was old and out of touch and had no idea what I was talking about. But still, I tried. I tried and tried and tried until she got upset and grew angry.

I just wanted to know more. I wanted to get to know my own daughter. What kind of woman she was growing up to be. I pushed too far.

Twenty questions? Really, Mom?

I'm sorry—I'm just interested in your life, Iz.

Mom, please just stop.

I waited a month before asking if she wanted to make pancakes again. She didn't.

That was the first day I'd learned the depths of Izzi's pain. The first day I'd ever seen her scars. My beautiful little girl, scarred, angry, hurt, afraid. Alone. But she was never alone. She always had me. I just didn't show it. I followed her upstairs, up to her room. The door to the bathroom wasn't locked.

Izzi in the bathroom. The doorknob turning in my palm.

Blood—

I push the memory away, think of Izzi and Dave in the kitchen until the moon floats through the angry clouds, disappearing into the belly of the night sky. I think until I hear nothing and no one. Until my heartbeat is the only sound in the darkness.

Then, when I've managed to convince myself it's safe, I crack open the door. Quietly, I emerge into the hall, see no one is there.

I know I heard something. I didn't imagine it.

I couldn't have.

It was too real. I know I heard—

A scream.

A thought hits me like lightning: *Just like Hannah did.*

I open the door wider, step into the hall.

I know I heard it. It came from the stairwell. I run through the hallway, grip the blanket tight in my fists, run down the stairs. Slip, fall back, land on the blanket, keep moving, follow the scream downstairs.

"Who's there?" I ask the shadows.

Light flickers on the crimson wallpaper across from the library. I walk down the hall, hover beside the archway. Shuffling. Movement. Someone is inside.

I seize a deep breath and step into the room.

It's a black hole, the fireplace the only light source. Shadows twitch across the dusty bookshelves. Cold air bites my cheeks. A girl sits on the floor, staring into the fire, watching the flames lash against ashen stones. The floorboards creak under my footsteps.

The girl whips around.

"Violet?"

"Dr. Madeline…"

I clutch the blanket tight around my shoulders. Something about Violet's gaze makes me feel uneasy. "Are you okay?" I ask. Slowly, I approach her, the blanket swishing behind me. "Did you hear a scream?" I sit on the edge of the sofa by the fire.

Imperceptibly, she tightens her arms, recoils away. "No, why?"

"Nothing. Never mind."

"I can't sleep," she says. "You?"

The clock resting on the fireplace mantel thunders in my head *ticktock ticktock*.

"Dr. Madeline?"

I shake my head. "Yeah, no, me either. Can't sleep."

The flames pop. A log falls, shatters apart. A dance of sparks and embers clamber up the walls.

"Won't you get in trouble with the headmistress if someone catches you?" My question hangs in the air. Violet tilts her head as if my voice was merely a whisper.

"I'm never *not* in trouble with the headmistress," Violet murmurs, eyes flickering toward the clock on the mantel. "I—I'm just—" She stops herself. "I had a bad dream," she says. "It woke me up. Then I came down here."

I had one, too, I want to say. But even now, I'm not sure it was a dream, if I imagined the scream or if it was real.

"Do you remember what it was about?" I ask.

Violet nods, curls her legs to her chest. "My mom."

"Was she okay?" I ask. She tilts her head, questioning. "In your dream?"

"Well—no. She's never okay. I don't know if you read my file…" She trails off, her emerald eyes peering at me inquisitively.

I try to remember. My mind is hazy, an avalanche of drowsiness overtaking me. I want to disintegrate into sleep.

"I did," I begin, staring into the flames. *Think. I read this.*

But all I can remember is darkness. Most of Violet's file was blacked out, as if it held government secrets. Classified. Erased.

"I…remember your file stating you loved painting." I push my glasses up my nose, hope it's enough to get her talking.

She grins her skeleton smile, proud I'd remembered.

"Yeah. Painting was my best friend when I was a kid," she says with a shrug. "My dad left when I was young and my mom, she'd—she'd leave me alone a lot. She'd do that. Leave me alone. Sometimes all day. But I was happier when she wasn't around."

She stops. I lean close, part my lips to speak. "How come?"

Violet shrugs. "My mom's strict. Most days I hate her for dragging me to this hideous, backwards school. I miss my old life," Violet confesses. "I miss my phone. My boyfriend."

"I understand," I offer.

Violet pinches her lips together, looks down at her lap. "Sometimes, I dream I'm still that little girl, alone in a giant house, painting. I paint the walls with faces and they look at me, laughing," Violet says, shaking her head, clearing away the cobwebbed memories. "Some good came out of it, I guess. One day, my mom felt guilty for leaving me alone. She always tried to buy my love with gifts. She bought me my first easel."

Over the past few days, I've learned Violet focuses on self-preservation. On survival. Adapting is imperative. Positive thinking enables the mind to survive.

"It's good that you see things with a silver lining," I say. "It says a lot about who you are as a person."

She glances down at her hands, a look of rapture fluttering over her face, as if it's the first compliment she's ever received.

"Thanks," she mumbles. "When I paint, it's like the world just stops, you know? Like I can do anything. I can paint anything I want. I can save my memories."

"What kinds of memories do you like to paint?"

She gives a wry smile, begins to braid her long black hair, ignores my question completely.

"I told you a story about *me*. Now you have to tell me a story about *you*."

Ticktock ticktock.

The scream I'd heard echoes in my head, now nothing more than a soft, ghostly residue. My body sings with weariness. What if Hannah had been right? What if, after she'd heard the scream, she went downstairs and—what if she did see blood that night in the hallway? The hallway right outside this very room...

Jeremy's words slam into my head.

Don't you get it? Yes, I called the police. But my footprints weren't the only ones in the snow.

What did he mean? Did he mean he saw Charley's bare footprints intermingled with his own? Or did he see someone else's footprints—a third person who was at the scene?

After Jeremy told me, Matt and Blake came upstairs. They interrupted us. I walked back to the school alone, much to Matt's protest. But I had to think. I had to be alone to think. My mind still buzzes with what Jeremy had said. The blood spots on the pink sweater I'd found—

"Dr. Madeline?"

"Yeah," I say, "oh, um, sure." I think back to what Violet had asked, force the hint of a smile, adjust the heavy blanket around my shoulders. "Uh, let's see."

Violet scoots around, sits to face me. She places her elbows on her knees, stares up at me like Izzi used to on our living room floor, her eyes wide with wonder, hanging on my every word. But I have no more stories left inside me. At least, none anyone else should know.

Mom, please just stop...

Violet glances at me suspiciously. "You okay?"

I nod, too eager. "Yeah, just thinking," I say quick, my eyelids heavy as mountains. "Okay, let's see. When I was fifteen—a little younger than you—I went to the beach. There was a fortune-teller on the boardwalk." Violet's lips curl into a smile.

"I'd gone with a friend from school. The woman had long, black hair, like you." Violet's smile widens, so light and buoyant she could float. "She took my hands and said I'd be coming into money in the future."

"And did you?"

The muscles around my mouth tense, a mask, wooden. "I did. Years later," I say softly. "But it wasn't money I wanted. It came only after I lost someone important."

Violet tilts her head. "What else did the fortune-teller say?"

Ticktock ticktock.

"She told me the secret to happiness."

Violet studies me a moment, lets out a taunting laugh. "Oh, come *on*."

"She did," I say and for once I feel a smile stretch across my face, too. "She said it was something simple. Something everyone could do, but something rarely done."

"Oh, now you *have* to tell me," she says, face beaming in the firelight.

"Before I leave the school, I'll tell you, I promise. Now go to sleep. I'll be right behind you."

Violet growls, stands up. "You play dirty." She walks toward the archway, stops, turns. "I always knew, you know," she whispers.

"Knew what?"

"That you played dirty."

Chills whip down my spine. "I—I don't know what you mean."

Violet rolls her eyes, seizes the bottom of her tee-shirt in her fists. Anger snaps into her expression. For a heartbeat, I fear she'll lunge at me.

"Yes, you do," she says flatly. "Stop lying. I know you're lying. But maybe you've convinced yourself," Violet says, arching a dark brow. "Like I've convinced myself."

Suddenly, I feel the need to catch my breath as she levels me with her eyes, the fireplace crackling between each of her words.

I inhale, slowly shake my head. "I'm—I'm not. Why would you say that?"

Her lips set in a sneer. "I already told you," Violet whispers. "I read your book, remember? *Dark Side: A Psychological Portrait of the Criminal Female Mind.* God, how apropos."

"Let me ask you this, Violet," I say, staring into the flames. "Why are you at this school? What happened?"

I know why the other girls enrolled: Hannah because her parents wanted her at a strict and holistic-minded school, far away, so she claims. Kiara because she hurt a bully at her previous school. Alice because she self-harms and needs specialized attention and rehabilitation. And Charley… Charley came to Shadow Hunt Hall allegedly because she was being bullied.

But Violet.

Violet is a mystery.

"Why would I tell you anything?" She breathes out a laugh, shakes her head. "I don't even know you…" She stares back at me. A flash of defiance, of anger, flickers across her face.

I watch her in the firelight, say nothing as she studies me. Finally, she shuts her eyes, as if in surrender.

"Two years ago," Violet begins, "I was—in a relationship. My mom said I was too young to date. I know she just didn't like him. He was…older. He had a kid my age. But that didn't matter to me…" She drifts off. "The point is, she took me away. From my home, my friends. *Everyone.* And she brought me here."

I focus on maintaining a poker face, expression deadlocked. Somehow, it doesn't seem to matter how I arrange my face. Violet has the ability to see right through people. As she looks at me, I wonder what she sees: A mother figure? An outsider?

Or someone who only wants what's best for her? But all are true, and however she sees me, my opinion will still be the same: I'd try to protect my daughter, as best I can, in any way I know how—just as Violet's mother had tried to protect her.

Violet's cries snap me back into focus. Though she moved away, sometimes heartache refuses to be left behind.

"How did that make you feel?" I ask, pass her a tissue.

She takes it, sniffles, nudges a strand of hair away from her face. "How would it make *you* feel?"

I gulp. "I'd feel…alone. Helpless. Isolated."

She nods, gazes into the fire. "I just wanted—someone to—" Violet stops herself, looks down. "Things only got worse," she says, "after I came here. I tried to escape, any way I could, at first. But then I knew there was nothing I could do to get myself out of here. I was trapped. I didn't know it… not right away. But I was—I was pregnant."

"Oh, Violet…" I slump over, rub a hand across my face. Violet claims she came to Shadow Hunt Hall two years ago. She's sixteen now. So that means…she was fourteen. Fourteen years old. Alone in a strange place. Pregnant with an older man's child. My heart sinks in my chest.

Violet sees my expression, shakes her head. "I lost it," she adds quickly, turning away from me. "It's better that way."

She stands from her spot in front of the fireplace, walks toward the archway, hovers near the hallway.

"Violet, I—" I blink, and before I open my eyes, she's slipped out of the library. This is what I was afraid of. One wrong move and she's gone, vanished, faded into the eerie darkness of the hall.

The fire softens, the room grows darker, the clock ticks louder. I lean back into the velvet sofa. And I think. And think. I think until the fire dies and nothing is left but smoldering embers.

I think of *Dark Side*. What's printed inside the pages. And I know Violet's right.

I think of the story I'd told her—about the boardwalk. The fortune-teller. I think of how I'd lied.

I am a liar. I lied.

About the story. About everything.

I wasn't fifteen when I went to the beach. It was just last summer. I went alone, not with a friend from school. The fortune-teller had told me the secret to happiness. And I'd run from the fortune shop in a storm of tears.

Sometimes, I don't even know who I am anymore.

THE YEAR BEFORE

FILE NAME: JPN00.012.00030923.mp3

[00:33:19]

INT: And what happened when you got home?

RES: Well…when I got home, no one was even there. [redacted] was gone, so I called—I tried calling her, maybe, ten times. I kept calling. And [redacted] phone was off. I figured he was at the doctor, so I didn't want to bother him there. So then I kept calling [redacted], and then I called her friend down the street to see if she was there.

INT: And was she?

RES: No, she hadn't seen her since the morning.

INT: Then what did you do?

RES: Well, I thought she was sick, so she'd be in bed, [inaudible] went upstairs and I see everything is still in her room, so I started freaking out.

INT: What was in her room?

RES: Her, uh, phone, her purse. I was—I was very afraid something had happened to her.

INT: So then what did you do?

RES: Well—I had to wait until [redacted] came home

from the doctor, so I went outside, tried to breathe. I let Oscar out—

INT: Oscar—that's your dog?

RES: Yeah, sorry. I let him out, that damn hole still wasn't fixed, but how could it be? My husband was sick—of course the hole was still there. I didn't want the dog to get out, so I brought him inside and tried calling [redacted] again.

INT: Did he answer this time?

RES: No.

INT: Then what?

RES: Well, I was panicking. My daughter was missing. I checked and rechecked my phone to see if I had a missed call or text but no one called me. So then I called someone I hoped could help.

INT: Who was that?

RES: I called [redacted].

INT: And…was he still at the hotel at this point?

RES: … I'm not sure—yes, maybe—he could've been. I remember he came right over.

INT: And you called him because of his—his profession as a police officer? You hoped he could help you locate your daughter?

RES: Well—I didn't really think of that. I just wanted—
I needed someone there to help me find her.

INT: And this was immediately after you left him at the
hotel and said that you wanted to break things off
with him? With your relationship—uh, with him?

[00:36:08]

RES: I know. I know, but I was panicking. I didn't know
if she'd run away. I didn't know what she knew
about me or her father. I didn't know if she knew
about her father—his cancer yet.

INT: So what happened when [redacted] showed up at
your house?

RES: Well, he was still angry, but he wanted to help. He,
really—he... I thought he was such a good person...
he was a good man—I...

INT: It's okay. Take your time.

RES: [inaudible]... I—after I called him, he came right
over. I tried to call him back... [redacted] had come
home.

INT: Your daughter had come home—just as your—just
as [redacted] was on his way to your house?

RES: ... Yes.

INT: And what did he say? When you called?

RES: I called to tell him to not come over, that my daughter was here, that she was safe and to not come over.

INT: Then did he anyway?

RES: He never answered. He came over, um, maybe, ten minutes later.

INT: And in that time, your daughter had already come home?

RES: Yeah, she came home. She'd gone down the street to get something from a friend for school.

INT: Then what happened?

RES: [redacted] came to the house when [redacted] was there. We were talking, and I kept trying to call him to tell him not to come over, but then his truck just pulls up in the driveway and he gets out…

INT: And your daughter is there?

RES: And [redacted] is there.

INT: Then what?

RES: Then…um, he gets out and he starts banging on the door. I ignored it, but [redacted] answered it.

INT: Your daughter answered the door?

RES: Yes.

[00:37:51]

INT: And how did she react?

RES: Well—she didn't know who he was. So I tried to, uh, I tried to just say he was a salesman, I think… I can't remember, really.

INT: Okay, it's okay. Do you remember what happened after?

RES: She's very smart. She knew. She figured it out… and [redacted] was mortified and he just stood there and I said nothing. Then he left.

INT: He left?

RES: Well, he tried to come in. I couldn't—I didn't let him. I had to go to [redacted]. She'd just—she started crying and I had to go to her. I remember… she said she hated me.

INT: She said she hated you?

RES: Yeah.

INT: How did that make you feel?

RES: Not good.

INT: Then what did you say to [redacted]?

RES: I tried to get him to leave. He wouldn't. So I said I was sorry I had called him to come over, that I wouldn't call him again, that it was a mistake. Then he said how I only use him when it's convenient for me, that I use him and he loves me and how I've helped him and how he can't lose me.

INT: And this is the same day you'd found out your husband had cancer?

RES: Yes.

INT: And the same day you told him your husband had cancer?

RES: Yes.

INT: And you had broken things off with him, but he still wouldn't take no for an answer?

RES: No. But I didn't help the situation. I'd broken things off with him and then I go right back and call him again, like two seconds later. And then he was at my house and he said he loved me. I just—I couldn't. It was too much.

INT: What did you do at that point?

RES: I slammed the door in his face.

INT: [inaudible] and how did he react?

RES: ... You saw how he reacted.

Tuesday, December 20

25

The curtains spanning the windows across from my bed are still open from last night, and I lift my head off the pillow to see a crushing black cloud slowly floating toward the school. Mist rolls in off the forest, dragging over the courtyard like a blanket. The sky looks dark. Too dark. Storm dark.

Last night, after I pulled myself back upstairs after talking to Violet in the library, I fell fast asleep. I'm not even sure what time it was. All I know is I haven't slept so heavy in weeks. Maybe all I need to sleep better is to be honest with myself. Maybe I can try a little each day.

Alice's viola echoes from down the hall as I check the weather on my phone. Emilia was right. The prediction is still twenty inches of snow in this region. Winds up to fifty miles per hour. Cold snaps stretching below zero. Just a few hours left before the snow begins to fall.

Alice's viola hits a quick succession of high notes.

If I can wrap this up by ten, maybe I can make it out in time. But still, there's so much to do, and if Emilia would just let me, I could stay, interview the girls again. I could help Matt sort through the evidence and dissect his research. I could piece together all of the sessions I'd saved on my voice recorder, make a transcript for each girl, one by one.

Half of me holds out hope. The forecast is never right. Is it? And would Emilia really have me dragged off school property by the police like she'd threatened to do yesterday?

I don't want to find out. But I do need to persuade Emilia to let me stay. But how? I look out of the window again. If only I can find a way to stay until the storm hits. Then I can't leave. Right? I'd be trapped here.

I wish I knew the right choice. Stay, help Matt a little longer. Find the truth about that night. Tell Charley's mother what really happened to her daughter the last day she was alive. Be trapped on a mountain in the middle of nowhere, Blake and Jeremy nearby, no place to escape…

Or, I can leave now.

The bloody sweater flashes in my head. Pale pink. Blotches of dried blood, dark and crusted, like mottled oil.

Please don't say anything. I—I had a nosebleed. That was all I could find.

Lies.

This school is filled with them.

Alice's viola falls softer, slower, soon going silent.

Getting out of bed, I cross the room, unzip my luggage, unfold the last clean shirt I'd packed: a silky black button-up. I pair it with a gray sweater and my usual black elastic-waist pants. I slip on my silver watch and wedding band and move toward the window, see the black clouds have grown darker, looming over the campus like a fist.

Grabbing my phone, I text Matt: Hi. Do you have time to come to the school today? We have to talk about last night.

Immediately, he replies: GM, OK I'll leave here soon.

I have to tell Matt about Jeremy. About what I'd learned last night in his bedroom. What I found. What I saw.

I think of Jeremy. The pink sweater. His face.

I think of his words.

Charley and I were friends. She was my best friend. I'd never hurt her.

Did the bloody sweater belong to Charley? Was it there before she died? Was Jeremy telling the truth and it really was the only thing he could find when he had a nosebleed? I don't know what to believe. Not anymore.

Jeremy was the one who'd found Charley in the woods. He was the one who'd called 911. What if the sweater *was* Charley's?

What if Jeremy stole it from the crime scene?

My hands go cold.

If Jeremy was Charley's best friend, why didn't anyone on campus seem to know? Why didn't any of the girls, besides Kiara, ever mention his existence? A handsome young man at an all-girls boarding school. Surely he couldn't have gone unnoticed. Either way, Charley was keeping her relationship with Jeremy a secret.

Best friends.

What if they weren't just best friends?

What if, somehow, they'd managed to keep their relationship a secret—from everyone—even Alice?

What if Jeremy and Charley were together?

That could mean Violet was telling the truth. She claims she wasn't the one who'd told Emilia about Charley and Alice's relationship. What if Jeremy did? What if he wanted to split them apart? Keep Charley for himself? They were best

KATIE GARNER

friends, allegedly. What if he wanted to be more? And what if Alice found out?

I'd wish Jeremy were dead.

Or worse—I'd want him framed for Charley's murder.

No no no. I can't go down this rabbit hole. Alice is innocent. She's done nothing wrong. She's hurt. Heartbroken. She would never hurt Charley...

There's only one way to know for sure. I have to find out if Alice knew Charley and Jeremy were friends. If she did...

I stop, realize I've been pacing my room back and forth. Run to the door. Grab the crystal glass off the doorknob, slam it on the table. Rip open the door. Run down the dark hall to Alice's room.

I don't knock. Don't pound the door down. I need answers. Reasons. Explanations. Not a fight. Not confrontation. I need to know what she knows. I need to know she's innocent. I need to ask Alice to her face. I need to know before Emilia forces me to leave.

Flinging the door open, I spot Alice hovering in the middle of her room. She spins around, yanks down the sleeve of her skintight sweater, covering her wrist.

"What are you doing? Get out!"

She crosses the room, her eyes on fire as she glares at me. For a heartbeat, I see Izzi's face. *Izzi in the bathroom. The doorknob turning in my palm. Thin, cross-hatched scars. Blood dripping down her arm, red lines, a road map.*

I look at Alice, feel my heart being ripped from my body all over again. She bolts away, tucks her war-torn wrist under an armpit, secret, safe. The familiar, sinking feeling of failure crashes over me. My cheeks go hot. I'd failed to protect Izzi. Now I'm failing Alice.

Mom, please just stop.

I gulp, step back, step away, the air expelled from my body.

244

Silence. I say nothing as I fight to steady my breath. Storm clouds move closer, throwing the room into shadows.

I decide to start fresh, act like nothing happened. "Alice," I begin, "we have to talk."

She shrugs, rips down an armful of clothes from the closet, plops them on her bed. From the pile, she extracts a purple cashmere sweater, slightly deeper than her lavender-tinted hair, tugs it on.

"Do you know Jeremy?" I ask. When she doesn't answer, I try again. "Did you ever meet the boy who lives on campus and works around the school? He was friends with Charley."

She stops, looks at me, eyes dead. "How can you even ask me that?"

"Just tell me—"

"No, okay?" She exhales, sits at the edge of her bed. "I—I never met him."

Alice wipes her nose dry. I can tell she's been crying. In the shadows from the clouds outside, her blue eyes have morphed into a bloodshot azure, brightened by an onslaught of tears.

I glance around her room. Her new roommate is gone for winter break, their half of the room empty, nothing save for a few postcards taped to the floral wallpaper beside her quilted bed.

Alice's side is a disaster. Expensive clothes explode across her bed, drip onto the floor. A mountain of sneakers and boots rest near the nightstand, the posts of her bed layered with a dozen dangling handbags.

"Why are you packing?" I ask, struggling to fill the silence. She's not kicking me out, yet, so I try to talk to her while I can.

"I don't know," Alice whispers. "I just know I have to leave." She looks down, presses her sweater against her wrist, winces. My eyes follow the movement, scan the fabric for blood.

"You don't have to—"

"I *do*."

My pulse quickens. I have to ask her. The time has come. I gulp, close the door behind me, make sure no one else can hear.

"You know what I have to ask you," I say quietly. "You know I have no choice."

Alice scoffs, turns away. She stares at the storm clouds, mutating and rolling off the mountains in the distance. "Of *course* you do," she says, keeping her eyes locked on the clouds. On anything but me.

"If I'm honest with you," I begin, taking the chance to sit down on her bed next to her, elbows on my knees. "Will you be honest with me?"

Alice's lips curl up at the corners with the promise of a spilled secret. She nods, looking at me without malice for the first time.

"I'll make a deal with you. I'll tell you my secret and you tell me yours. And we have to promise each other to never tell anyone else. Deal?" I say, holding out my hand for her to shake.

She narrows her eyes at me, thinks it's a trick.

But slowly, she places her tiny hand in mine.

26

"Okay," Alice mumbles, tucking a leg under the other.

"Okay." I steal another deep breath. "Well," I begin, "last year, I had a really bad year. I had anxiety. I had some moments where I just wanted to melt to the floor, like I couldn't even stand. I found out later they were panic attacks."

Alice gulps. "I get those, too."

I nod. "They're very common. But mine were especially bad, and I had to take some time off work. Then, when I went back to work, I felt I had to keep what happened to me secret. I didn't want people knowing. I didn't want people to think I couldn't do my job."

She shakes her head. "Then they're assholes," she blurts. "Of course you can do your job." A wrinkle of concern creases between her eyebrows.

"I knew I could," I agree. "But still, I kept it secret. And I haven't told anyone this—ever—just you."

"Seriously? Not even your daughter?"

I shake my head. "Not even my daughter. See? Everyone has something to hide. Everyone has a secret. I confessed mine to you, and you shook on it," I dutifully remind her.

Alice tuts. "Well..." she trails off. "I don't have any secrets." She looks up at me, face expressionless, blank.

I swallow, shake my head. "We shook hands—"

"*Fuck* your stupid handshake."

Alice stands from the bed, angrily walks to her closet, pulls down a large duffel bag, begins stuffing it with everything she'd laid out on her bed. I watch in silence as she shoves a final tee-shirt into the side compartment, zips it shut across the top.

"Alice," I say, my mind still in shock, feeling like she'd just punched me in the chest. "Where are you going?" Black clouds hover over the school, turning her bedroom dark. Soon they'll grow bright white, heavy, bursting with snow. "It's going to snow—you can't go outside."

Alice spins around, switches on a desk lamp. "I can go wherever I want."

As she turns, trails of tears glisten down her cheeks in the lamplight. She slings the duffel bag over a shoulder, the extra weight making her tiny body lopsided.

I stand from the bed, inch my way to the door to block it. "If you're leaving because of Jeremy—if he's threatening you—"

"No!"

"Then why?"

She stares at me, says nothing.

"Why? Tell me why."

Alice's face twists, filled with anger, with fear. She barrels toward me. I move closer to the door.

"No—no, you're *not* leaving."

She glares at me, teeth clenched. "Yes, I am!" she cries out, eyes wild. She lunges at me. I hold out an arm, stop her from moving forward.

"Will you just stop for a second?" I say. Alice looks away, adjusts the heavy bag on her shoulder. "I can't let you leave. Not when it's going to snow."

"Yes, you can—you don't have to say anything."

I look at her, really look at her. My heart skips a beat. It's as if Izzi is standing in front of me, her hair dyed pale purple, her shoulders narrower, her stature shorter. But it's Izzi. The same bright eyes. She has Dave's nose, a little button, slightly downturned and wide at the bottom, a tiny tulip. The same bandaged wrist, a pulsing symbol of her pain, my failure as her mother, her protector.

I love her. I can't watch her get hurt, can't let her leave my side, let her die… I shake my head. Still, Alice stares at me. I can feel the anger and hatred rippling off of her.

"I know you're hiding something," I say, force myself to say the words inside my head—*she's not Izzi, she's not Izzi.* "I know you're hiding something—about Charley." The words roll off my tongue like I'd wanted to let them free all along. Maybe I have.

Alice's mouth pops open, an exaggerated *how dare you!* "You don't know *what* you're talking about—I *loved* her!"

"I know you're lying. I don't know about what, and I don't know why, but you're lying about something," I repeat. I drill her, keep drilling her. I want to stop, feel myself trying to stop.

But I can't. Her eyes widen, like Izzi's, wide and open and staring. *She's not Izzi—she's not, she's not. Just stop.*

Mom, please just stop.

"What are you hiding? Tell me! I know what happened between you and Charley. I know she broke your heart. I know *I'd* want revenge—"

Alice freezes. I can't believe I just said it, but it came rocketing out, like a bullet. I couldn't stop it. I should know better. Maybe I should leave today. Maybe I never should've come.

Tears fill Alice's eyes as she slowly drags them up to meet mine. Eerily calm, she asks, "Have you ever felt so alone, like you're the smallest, most insignificant person imaginable?"

I bite my lip hard so I don't cry. "Yes…" The word comes out weary, road beaten and starved.

"Charley *never* loved me. I loved her and she always hated me, right from the start. And then—then it's like to prove it, to show me how little I ever meant to her—she starts hanging out with *him* over me. She *chose* being with him over me."

"Him?"

"*Jeremy!*" she screams, her chest rising and falling fast. "Charley made me feel like I was *nothing*—I meant nothing to her, and she was *everything* to me."

Her lip quivers. My heart begins to break.

"So you *did* know…"

Alice scoffs. "Of course I knew. It's what we fought about that day, outside. The last time I ever saw her and we were fighting. God, I loved her—*so much*. All I wanted was her."

That was the fight Kiara had overheard. It was about Jeremy all along.

"That night," Alice begins, "I went to meet her at our secret spot. There's a place by the willow trees behind the school. It's an old stone gazebo. We'd always meet there, every night. Charley hadn't gone there since we were ratted out by Violet to the headmistress, since she broke up with me. But that night, I wanted to see her. I had to. I had to apologize, say how sorry I was. But she wasn't there. She wasn't there, she— she was out *there*."

Alice stops, stares out of her window, toward the woods. A tear slips down her cheek, drops onto her purple sweater.

Hannah was right. She did see Alice outside in the woods

the night Charley disappeared. She wasn't lying. She wasn't making it up. Hannah was telling the truth. The night she'd heard a scream, went downstairs, saw blood in the hall—she'd seen Alice running toward the woods, toward Alice and Charley's secret meeting place.

Alice went out there to apologize. To talk to Charley, hoping and wishing she'd be there, too. But she wasn't. She never would be again.

"I understand," I whisper. "More than you know—if you only knew. I'll tell you. I'll tell you everything—if you just tell me. Tell me the truth and everything will be okay." Even I can't believe my words.

"I can't," she chokes, looking past my shoulder toward the door. "I found something out, and I can't tell you."

"Why can't you tell me? I'm trying to help—"

"You think I *killed* my *girlfriend*—how can you help me if you think I'm guilty?"

I look down, say nothing. Alice exhales. "I didn't do it," she says sharply. "I didn't do anything. I just have to get out of here. I can't be here."

"Alice, don't. There's a storm coming—"

She rushes past me, spins around. "I don't give a shit!" she chokes out. "You all think I'm this girl, this bad girl, right? Isn't that why I'm here? Isn't that what you all think when you look at me? That I'm just some giant fuckup?"

"That's not what I—"

"So fine," she says, resigned, tears overflowing. "I'll just make it true."

"No." I step forward, grab her by her wrist. "*No.* You're *not* going out there. Not in this. Not when it's freezing."

Alice winces. Blood trickles down her hand, out from underneath her sleeve. I flinch, realizing what I'd done.

She looks down at the stain of dark blood eking out through the soft, purple fabric, looks back up, eyes filled with fury.

"Alice—Alice, I'm sorry—"

"Don't you *fucking* touch me," Alice seethes, teeth gritting in pain.

"*Listen* to me—don't leave, please—"

Alice grabs my arm, as I'd done to her, twists it back with unexpected strength. My elbow pops. My wrist burns. I cry out, stumble back against the wall as she releases me. Pain shoots up my spine. I turn back toward her, suddenly aware that Matt was right. Anyone is capable of anything.

"If you leave now," I choke, grasping feebly at my twisted arm, "you'll freeze out there alone—just like Charley." I clasp a hand over my mouth. *What did I just say? What the fuck did I just say?*

Slowly, Alice inches backward toward the door, finds the doorknob, twists it open. Her mouth quivers as she struggles to battle back tears. In an instant, she disappears. I listen as her boots pound down the hallway, down the stairs. Too quickly, her footsteps fade.

I step into the hallway, shut Alice's door behind me. Drag my broken body back to my room. My hands find my bottles of pills. They knot, thick and dry, in my throat. Soon they'll lull me into the darkness of the room.

I could sit patient, wait until the shadows swallow me whole. *No.*

I won't. Not today. Not when I have the chance to save an innocent life. I won't fail. I won't let that happen.

Not again.

27

I clench my teeth together and force myself to stand. My hands find the doorknob and I twist, step out into the empty hall.

A thick and choking haze washes over me, a haze complete with an unsettling feeling of dread. All I want is to punish myself—for letting Alice leave, for so many things. If anything happens to her, anything at all, it will be my fault.

I had texted Matt earlier this morning, before I'd gone to Alice's room, asking him to please walk up to the school. I still need to tell him about last night, about Jeremy, the bloody sweater, how he knew Charley.

And now, I have to tell him so much more. How Alice ran away. How I don't know where she went. How she knew about Charley and Jeremy and how they fought about him before Charley's death.

I send Matt another text: Alice ran away. On your walk over, please keep an eye out.

More. I have to do more. I have to do something, say something. Even though I'm dreading seeing her, I also need to tell Emilia about Alice. As much as I want nothing more than to punish myself, to sit in the darkness of the room and sob, I can't. Not when Alice is out there.

My body is starting to feel heavy from the onslaught of sleeping pills I'd taken moments ago. On an empty stomach, against my own advice, they tend to work faster, edging out my consciousness, replacing it with a feeling of weight, of warmth, an invisible fist pounding me into the earth like a stake.

Teetering down the hall, I heave my heavy limbs up the spiral staircase to Emilia's office. Footsteps clatter in the distance and just as I reach the top of the stairwell, Emilia's shiny nude heels enter my view.

I look up. She's glowering down at me, arms crossed at her waist. To my surprise, she starts down the stairs to meet me, leans her back against the stone wall.

I don't say a word, just stare up at her until she speaks first.

"Good morning," she says quietly, studying me behind a fan of thick lashes. "I hope you haven't forgotten," she says, swooping a strand of golden hair behind an ear, "but I need you gone today—before the snow starts."

Shit.

I glimpse out of an arched stairwell window, see the black clouds have turned white, heavy and low across the courtyard.

I look back at her. "Okay. Fine. But I have to tell you something—and then maybe you'll change your mind," I add as she begins to step down the stairs past me. "Alice is gone."

Emilia stops, turns back to look at me. "What? Gone?"

I nod. She shuts her eyes, exhales.

"This is all your fault," she seethes.

"What?"

"You must have said something to her, done something to her that made her want to leave." Emilia's voice echoes through the stairwell, amplified. "What did you *do*?"

"I didn't *do* anything," I snap. "I'm only here to try to help *your* students. So stop trying to make everything seem like my fault when *you're* clearly the reason everyone here wants to leave."

She stops, lets out a little gasp of shock.

When she says nothing in response, I change the subject. "I already asked Matt to come to the school," I admit. "If it's going to be a storm like you say it is, Alice needs to be indoors."

Emilia stomps her fists on her hips. "He's coming here?" I nod, say nothing. "Fine. Come with me. We'll walk down to meet him."

As we make our way downstairs, heavy globs of snowy hail smack against the lead pane windows, like machine-gun fire. The storm has begun. The hallway stretches out in front of me, tilting like a funhouse mirror. The barrage of pills I'd taken are beginning to steep strong in my system.

I follow behind Emilia, clutching onto the wall to balance myself as Violet passes us.

Sweetly, she coos, "Hi, Dr. Madeline, how are you?" avoiding eye contact with Emilia.

One hand holds a heavy plastic art box, the other a fistful of paintbrushes. Tucked under an arm is the canvas of an incomplete portrait, still mostly just a pencil sketch.

"Good morning, Violet," I say, hoping she won't mention the night before, how we'd spoken in the library.

I try to remind myself that it doesn't matter if she's read *Dark Side*. It means nothing. She doesn't know the truth about me. No one does. And I intend to keep it that way. Still, I should've stolen that book when I'd had the chance—before she—

"Dr. Madeline," Violet begins, voice sickly sweet. "Are you staying much longer?"

I glance at Emilia. She turns away, stares out an arched window at the thick white sky.

"We'll see," I say in a wobbly voice when Emilia doesn't respond. "Busy day?" I ask Violet with a labored smile. "Painting going okay?"

She shrugs, adjusts the bulky canvas under her arm, taps her bedroom door open with the toe of a muddy boot. "Yeah. I was painting *plein air* this morning," she says out of breath, cheeks still flushed from the cold. "Until the snow." She places the heavy plastic art box on the floor, slides it beneath her bed, begins to shut the door.

"Violet," Emilia says, slapping a palm on the door to keep it open. "Have you seen Alice?"

"What?"

Emilia crosses her arms, awaits her reply.

Violet looks back and forth between us, confused. "Alice. Uh, no. Why?"

Emilia sighs in disappointment. "No reason. Continue on with your day. Do not leave the building again."

Violet sneers at Emilia before disappearing into her room. The door thuds closed. Emilia growls, marches faster down the hall toward the lobby. My head swirls. Every step feels like I could tilt over, slam to the floor.

My phone dings. I reach into my back pocket, dig it out, see it's an unknown number with a New York area code. I ignore it, follow Emilia down the staircase, careful not to fall.

"Is Detective Reyes taking you to the train?" Emilia asks as heavy wind hurls itself against the walls of the school.

"Um, yes. *After* we find Alice."

Emilia pauses in thought. Can she really turn me away when one of her students has gone missing? When a storm is coming? There's nowhere for Alice to go. She can't stay out-side. She has to be found. I hold my breath awaiting her an-swer.

She bristles in annoyance. "It's what has to happen now, isn't it?"

"Yes," I say sharply.

Emilia sighs. "The girls *must* remain inside during the storm," she says quietly to herself. "If Alice is really gone like you say, I can't have any of the students going outside look-ing for her in *this*."

"I agree," I say, glancing down at my hand. I didn't get a chance to change the bandage for the gash on my palm, so the healing wound, for now, remains exposed.

On the way to the lobby, Emilia stops, retreats down the hall toward the library. I follow, hearing voices from inside. We stand in the archway, peek inside to see Hannah and Kiara hunched over a table in the corner. Hannah's owlish glasses balance at the tip of her nose. Kiara keeps her eyes locked on the chessboard in concentration.

Hannah looks up, smiles. "Hello, Headmistress. Hey, Dr. Pine."

"Hi, girls," Emilia and I say in unison.

Kiara lifts her head, looks back down to the chessboard, long braids swinging around her face like a curtain.

"Girls," Emilia begins, "have either of you seen Alice?"

Hannah thinks for a heartbeat. "No. Something wrong?"

Emilia turns to Kiara. "Have you seen her?"

"Nope," she says, still not looking up. "Sorry."

My shoulders deflate.

Hannah watches me, her eyes focused behind her glasses. "I knew it. Something *is* wrong—"

Emilia tosses me a withering glare. "*Nothing* is wrong," she snaps, spinning on her heel to escape the library. She stops, turns back to the girls. "Just stay here. Stay inside. I will know if you don't," she warns.

We enter the lobby, snow beginning to dust along the edges of the windowpanes. Emilia's heels clack across the marble floor as we rush toward the main door. She unlocks the dead bolts, heaves it open.

Matt stands outside in the carriage tunnel, shivering, his black hair slick with melted snow.

My heart falls when I see he's alone. I'd been hoping Alice would be standing beside him.

Emilia rushes Matt inside.

"Has Alice b-been located?" he asks, teeth clattering.

I shake my head.

Emilia locks the main door behind him.

"Emilia," I say, "leave the door unlocked."

"Why?"

I sigh. "Alice is out there—what if she tries to get back in?"

Emilia purses her lips, unlocks the door. "Fine."

"You should come get warm by the fire," I tell Matt, placing a hand on his arm. I pull away. Even his wool coat is frozen.

Emilia leads the way back down the hall toward the library. Inside, Hannah and Kiara are still hunched over the table, eyes fixated on the chessboard.

Emilia approaches them, asks, "Can you both search the school? We need to find Alice."

Unflappable, they exchange quick glances before slowly turning back to the chessboard.

"Now."

Hannah stands, exaggerated concern etched across her face. "I'll take the third floor, Kiara will take the second. Right, Kiara?"

Kiara slowly scrapes her chair out from the table. "Yeah. Whatever," she groans, glaring at Matt as she passes.

"Be sure to stay inside the school. And find Violet," Emilia calls to them as they leave. "Have her help, too."

As soon as they leave, Matt rushes to the fireplace, pulls a chair close. Holding out his hands, red and stiff, he hovers them near the flames.

"One of us should put a call in to the police to have some officers on standby if Alice isn't found," he says, voice shivering.

I nod, glad there's some semblance of a plan.

"I'm going to tell Rosemarie about Alice. If Alice is inside the school, we'll find her," Emilia says. "Once the snow starts sticking, the police won't be able to drive up the mountain. I fear it may be up to us," she whispers, eyes landing on me. "And *you*. I want you both off my campus the moment Alice is found. You've caused enough trouble. You may stay in the guesthouse until the snow is cleared but then I want you gone." Emilia turns and flees into the hall.

The moment she's gone, Matt turns to me, lowers his voice. "None of this feels right," he confesses, running a hand through his hair. "How did Alice seem when you spoke to her?"

I shrug, collapse in an armchair. "She was packing. She was in a hurry."

"Did she say anything strange?" he asks, keeping his eyes trained on the stone mantel over the fireplace.

"She…" I trail off, replay the conversation in my head. "She said she'd found something out and had to pack. She said she had to leave."

"*Found something out…* What the hell is that supposed to mean? Are you sure it wasn't just some kind of veiled threat? Maybe she wanted attention or—"

"No. It wasn't like that," I say, adamant. "She looked worried, agitated. She was terrified."

Matt leans back. "Where could she have gone? She's either in the school or she's not."

The fireplace crackles. A log falls, swirling a cloud of embers. The golden clock on the mantel *ticktocks ticktocks*. The room grows brighter, the world outside the windows glowing a brilliant white.

Where would I go if I were Alice? If I wanted to run away, escape…

Why bother packing if I was just planning to hide in the school, in the attics perhaps, or some hidden, tucked-away wing closed off to the students. I wouldn't. Would I? I'd only pack if I'd planned on leaving for good, maybe hitchhiking or living somewhere else or camping—

"She's outside," I mutter.

Matt's dark eyes turn to me. "Is that what she said?"

I shake my head. "No. But it's the only thing that makes sense," I say. "Alice is heartbroken over Charley's death. What if she wants to die like her? What if she's going to the same spot?"

"There'd only be one way for us to find out."

I sigh, lean forward. "I know," I admit. "I never thought I'd say this but…let's go hiking in a blizzard."

"I'm shocked that I agree with you," Matt grumbles and kneels before the fireplace, feeding a log into the flames. "Hey, what happened last night?" he asks, a storm of sparkling embers raining against the ashen stone. "Last thing I know, you're upstairs and Jeremy runs after you. You were up there for a while. What happened?"

I glance over a shoulder, make sure we're still alone. Last thing we need is a student overhearing what I'm about to say. I tell Matt all about my conversation last night with Jeremy in his bedroom. How I'd found a pink sweater with dried blood on it. How he'd claimed he got a nosebleed. How he swears he saw someone else's footprints in the snow the morning he found Charley's body in the woods.

After hearing this, Matt reclaims his seat, lets out a deep breath. "Could've just been Charley's footprints. Or his own. After finding your friend's body, it's easy to lose track of what you think you see. The shock of it can—"

"Jeremy and Charley—they were more than just friends." The moment I say the words, Matt freezes, his body stilled.

"What? Wait, so first, Jeremy claimed he never even knew her and now—"

"He was lying. All this time, Jeremy's been lying. Now we know not only were they friends—they were more than friends."

"How do you know this?" Matt asks.

"Alice. Before she left, she told me. She said she and Charley fought about him…the night Charley disappeared."

"Jeremy's lying by omission. It doesn't mean he's guilty."

"No," I say. "But before Alice ran away, she was upset—*more* than upset. She said Charley chose *him* over *her*. To me, that can only mean one thing. They were—"

"Lovers," we say at the same time.

Matt stares at me in silence, in shock. "If Jeremy lied about knowing the victim and is now lying about the seriousness of their relationship," he says, "what else can he be lying about?"

"Victim?" I inquire. "So that's it? You're sure now Charley's death wasn't an accident?"

After a long pause, I turn away from the fireplace, glance at Matt. He gnaws callously on his thumbnail. "I don't know what to think, anymore," he whispers to himself, dropping his hand. "I should've known."

"Matt," I begin softly, "no one knew—"

"I should've seen it," he says bitterly. "And I didn't. What else am I missing? What else haven't I seen?" He stands, paces back and forth in front of the fireplace, his hands on his hips, eyes trained on the threadbare rug.

"It's no one's fault…"

Finally, he stops, looks at me.

I don't know why, but suddenly I feel like running, like I should run out of here, this room, this school, run away and never look back.

"I let this case get away from me. I only wanted to help her mother and—" Matt stops himself, slides his glasses up his forehead. "All I wanted was to give Charley's mom answers. She deserves the truth and now…"

"Now, what, Matt?" My skin begins to itch. I shouldn't have doubled up before, now I'll get nauseous if I don't have more, if I don't—

"Maybe Charley's death will always be a mystery," Matt says. "Alice is missing. All we have to go on is her word against Jeremy's. He can just lie again, unless we can prove his relationship with Charley. Aside from that, we have nothing. It's over." He spins, falls down on the sofa, lands in a pile of pillows. "It's over," he repeats. "I've failed. Failed Charley. Her mother. Myself. After the snowstorm, it's over. We have to go home…and not only because Emilia wants us to. But because my presence here has only made things worse."

I stand from the armchair, sit beside him, push away the sudden desire to smooth his dark hair out of his eyes. He takes his glasses off, rests them on the table. Without them, he looks younger and for a second, I can imagine him as a boy.

"You can't believe this," I whisper. "You can't—we have to keep going. I'll keep speaking with the girls. I'll—"

"When the storm is over, I'll tell Charley's mother the truth," he says. "I'll tell her the police report is correct and how the only thing I've managed to do here is allow another innocent girl to disappear."

"You can't do this."

"After I speak with her, I'll drive you to the train station."

I say nothing further as the same two words drum inside my head:

It's over. It's over.

But how can it be? If it was Izzi, I'd never stop fighting. I'd never quit trying to learn the truth. How can I stop now? But it's not my Izzi.

I stare ahead into nothingness, think about my daughter, about a dream I'd had of her. She was in the school's courtyard outside, floating above the snow, a single snowflake catapulted into the sky, swirling, lost. I watched as she danced in the gentle wind, caught on a breeze, invisible. I felt her presence. But nothing more.

As if she only ever lived inside my mind, like a thought.

Like I'd imagined her entire existence.

28

Matt may be defeated, but I'm not.

I refuse.

I left him in the library, told him to wait for me as I ran up to my room to change clothes. He may believe Charley's case is now a lost cause, but Alice isn't. She's still missing, out there somewhere. She could be alone, afraid—just like Charley. I won't leave her out there, in the woods, exposed to the elements, the frigid snow and ice and wind. I can't.

Scrambling around my room, I search for the warmest clothes I can find. I didn't pack much, as Matt had originally asked me to come to the school just for the weekend. I've now been here four days and have no clean clothes left, nothing but a gray sweater and pair of flannel pajama pants. I grab the sweater, shrug it on, when suddenly my recorder clicks on.

Voices unravel, muffled, distant. I freeze.

I didn't just imagine it.

Imagine it.

Imagine it.

The recorder seizes, replays the same words over and over. I jolt forward, paw it in my hand. It vibrates in my fingers, keeps repeating.

Hannah's voice:

I didn't just imagine it.

I didn't—

I turn it off. The red numbers die, fade away to black.

Snow whips against the windows. I look outside, see nothing but a world of white. It's beginning to stick, snowflakes blanketing the cobblestone courtyard. Sometimes, a rock peeks up through the snow, a pinprick of black in a white sea.

I toss the possessed voice recorder into my tote bag and check my phone. No new voice mails or texts. No emails. Nothing but spam. I am a ghost, invisible and unwelcome at the same time.

A knock at the door.

I fling it open, a thousand questions hurtling through my head: *Has Alice been found? Is she okay? Where was she?*

Matt stands in the hallway.

"Any news?"

He shakes his head, steps inside.

I let out a giant breath.

"You ready to go?"

"Almost."

My heart beats wildly as I spin around my bedroom, shrug on my coat, find my scarf, angle my back to Matt as I force my midday doses down my throat, feel the scraping pain as they travel to my stomach. No time for water. No time for anything but getting downstairs, getting outside, searching for Alice.

A lump crawls up my throat.

The voice recorder:

I didn't just imagine it.

Imagine it.

Though it's only late morning, the sky is dreadfully dark. Heavy clouds rumble overhead, painting the room in opaque shadows. Wind slams against the windows, threatening to break them open.

"You're sure you want to come?" Matt asks. "It's freezing out."

"I don't have a choice," I say, slinging my tote bag over a shoulder. "Alice could be out there. And if she is, it's because *I* didn't stop her."

"Don't blame yourself," he whispers, closing the door behind us.

Silently, Matt leads me down to the main floor. Secretly, I wonder if he's trying to think of something to make me change my mind. But I won't change my mind. I've been in worse situations.

I count the cameras tucked away in every corner as we head toward the lobby. Five, six, eight, counting the one in the hallway near my room, which I'd almost forgotten about. But all are turned off. All *smoke and mirrors*, Emilia had said. All pretend.

Too bad. If they'd worked, maybe Alice would've already been found.

When we reach the lobby, we're stopped by Emilia. She stands idly near a window, staring outside at the snow.

Hearing our footsteps, she crosses her arms, blocks our path. "If you're going to search the school grounds you need to leave now before it gets dark."

I exhale, listen as Emilia gripes to Matt about the snow, how ill-prepared he is, how he won't be able to see anything through a curtain of snow. A glance at my watch confirms it's already noon. Four hours left. Four hours until the sky turns dark, the air frigid, the school grounds coated with snow and below that, a layer of thick, slippery ice. Four hours to find Alice before our search has to stop for the night.

Matt turns to me, brows low and severe over his dark eyes, the skin around them puffy and sunken at the same time. He pops his collar up around his neck, checks his watch, looking like a villain tugged from a 1940s crime film.

"It'll be fine, Mrs. Hawke," he assures her. "Ready?" he asks, eyes scraping me up and down. I nod. "Are you sure you'll be warm enough?"

I look down at myself. I'm wearing the warmest clothes I'd packed: a heavy wool coat, cashmere scarf, gray sweater, black leather boots. I wish I'd packed more than just a single pair of socks, as I've been wearing the same pair since I'd arrived, but it's better than no socks at all.

Glancing back at Matt, I shrug. "We'll find out," I mutter, pull my scarf close around my cheeks.

"If it's too cold, we can turn around."

Emilia steps forward, grabs hold of my arm. I spin.

"You don't have to do this. You can leave now," she says. "Before it gets worse. You can get on the train, be home by dinner. Isn't that better than this?"

I scoff. "Of course I don't have to do this," I say, feeling anger rise inside me. "I *want* to. And you should be coming with us. It's another one of *your* students who's missing."

Emilia's face collapses.

I tear my arm from her grip, follow Matt through the main door, step into the protection of the carriage tunnel. Ahead, the courtyard glistens with freshly fallen snow. The wind blows, soundless, whipping snowflakes into little swirls that dance in the frozen air.

"You coming?" Matt asks, glancing over a shoulder at me, beckoning me to follow.

Slowly, I step out of the tunnel, the snow melting across my palm as I hold a hand up to the bulging white sky. We walk in silence into the woods, our bodies curling around the trees. Ugly thoughts caress my mind, cold and sick.

I think of Alice. What will happen if we never find her. Or worse—if we do—and we're already too late.

But still, I hold on to hope.

Hope.

I laugh softly to myself. Hope feels as delicate as the snowflakes that melt in my hand.

THE YEAR BEFORE

FILE NAME: JPN00.012.00030923.mp3

INT: Yes, I saw how he reacted. I saw how he—

RES: Please don't say it. I can't hear it anymore.

[00:39:42]

INT: Okay. I won't say it. So then what happened after he left?

RES: Well, nothing. Weeks went by. We all tried to take care of each other. I tried to take care of my husband. We were working things out.

INT: It was going well?

RES: Yeah, it was going better than I thought. [redacted] never told her father about the man at the door. I never brought up the fact that [redacted] told me he had cancer over the phone.

INT: [redacted]... I want you to walk me through everything you remember about yesterday, starting with when you woke up.

RES: It started—normal. We woke up, we went to breakfast. I cleaned the house a little. Just a normal day.

INT: A normal, typical Sunday?

RES: Yes.

INT: When did you realize—when…lead me up to the events that prompted the call to 911.

RES: [redacted] went out to go buy something. I think he was out getting some kind of lotion—with the chemo, it made his hands—his skin dry. I had offered to go, but he said he'd needed to get out of the house.

INT: And this was…what time?

RES: Maybe…this was just before dinner, around six.

INT: So your husband left the house.

RES: Yes. My daughter was upstairs. I'd told her to get a head start on her homework. But I went upstairs to ask her what she wanted for dinner. And when I knocked, she wasn't there.

INT: You went into her room and saw she wasn't there?

RES: No…she wasn't there. I went in and she was gone, her window was cracked. She has snuck out of her room in the past.

INT: And you believed she had snuck out again that night?

RES: Yes…so I called my husband and he came right home. We kept calling her phone and she never answered.

INT: Then what did you do?

RES: We called all her friends, left messages trying to find her. Then, finally, she answered her phone.

INT: Where was she?

[00:41:07]

RES: She said she'd told my husband she was going to a friend's house.

INT: Did she?

RES: He said he didn't remember.

INT: And, uh, that is, um, a side effect, I believe.

RES: Yes, memory loss. He's had it on and off the past couple weeks, from the chemo.

INT: So then did your daughter come home?

RES: No, I said it was okay that she stays at her friend's house until ten.

INT: So her curfew was ten?

RES: Yes.

INT: Then what did you do?

RES: I baked apple pie. It's their favorite. The whole house smells like it, and I wanted that—that comfort. And...[redacted] came up to me, and for the first time in a long time, he put his arms around me...and I wanted to say how sorry I was—all I wanted was to tell him how sorry I was for what I did. But it was…it felt, already, like it was so long ago, that it was in the past, and he's so sick, and I couldn't tell him that. I didn't want to bring it up and make him go through that pain.

INT: So you never told your husband about the affair?

RES: No. I—I'm afraid.

INT: What are you afraid of?

RES: I guess… I'm afraid of being alone.

29

We've been walking in the woods for hours.

No footprints.

No signs of life.

No Alice.

Matt hums beside me, hands shoved deep in his pockets, black boots crunching in the frozen snow. Beneath the forest canopy, the heavy snowfall has turned into the faintest breath of snow. My hair, fallen loose from my bun, gathers a lace of snowflakes.

Even though we have flashlights, the snow buries any evidence on the ground. I try to tell Matt we should keep pushing, keep going until we make it to the stone wall that marks the end of campus property. But his eyes are bone-weary, tired. Without him having to speak a word, I can tell he's already surrendered.

Maybe I should, too. The wind scours my cheeks, burns my

skin. My feet are frozen blocks of blood. Not even the layers of wool can stave off the inevitable—frostbite.

Each outbuilding we pass, we inspect. Alice could be inside. Hiding. Waiting. The white sky turns a deep, angry purple. It's cold. It's getting dark. Any minute, the sun will set. The flashlight is draining my phone's battery fast. I'm surprised it's even lasted this long.

Matt stops as we approach another small, forgotten outbuilding. It's crumbling, rickety, made of wooden planks that peel off like scraped paint. He checks inside, comes out a moment later.

"There's too many outbuildings and storage sheds to check," he says, rubbing his gloved hands together. "No way we can search all three hundred acres today. We should head back."

"We can't. We need to reach where Charley was found. That way, I think..." I drift off, pointing north.

He laughs.

"I'm serious."

"Oh, I know you are," he says, wipes his red, runny nose. "But because I listened to you an hour ago, now we're never going to make it back to the school before dark."

I cross my arms, try to keep in any remaining heat. "Am I the only one who wants to find her?"

He shakes his head. "Of course not, but you're no good to anyone when you die of hypothermia, either."

A twig snaps behind us. A whoosh of wind steals the hat Matt had let me borrow an hour ago. I run to catch it where it gets tangled in a dead knot of thicket. I stop, listen. Listen to the sound of crunching footsteps. The forest has remained quiet since we've been out here. No sounds save for the wind. But now, we're not alone.

Someone is following us.

My head pounds, heartbeat in my ears like thunder.

Matt stops as another crunch breaks through the sound of the wind. Hearing it too, slowly, he turns.

I hold up a hand. *Wait*, I mouth, but he can't see my face in the shadows.

He walks to me, whispers, "Did you say something?"

"*That*—did you hear that?" I ask when I hear the sound again.

He tilts his head, listening. "Yeah, I heard it, too."

"Stay here, I'll be right back," I say and walk toward a grove of evergreens, leaving him behind.

"Madeline!" he calls out. "We shouldn't split up!"

My phone slips from my frozen fingers, thuds quietly in the snow. I bend over, feebly attempt to wipe it dry on my coat. It's no use. Snow has begun to saturate my clothes, melting before hardening to ice. I shiver. My phone shakes in my trembling hands.

Matt's footsteps sound behind me. "You can't just walk away from me like that. Not now, not out here."

The world falls to darkness. Finally, the sun has set.

Cold overtakes me. My shoulders begin to shake so badly I'm nearly convulsing. My teeth clatter in my skull. There's no way to stop it once it starts.

Snap.

I turn toward the sound. What if it's Alice? What if she's out here, alone, freezing to death? I turn to him. "I'll be right back," I say, rushing past him.

"Madeline!"

I walk faster, soon breaking into a run, bending and looping between the thick pines. The sudden influx of cold air stings my lungs. I keep going. I'll see Matt's flashlight, hear his voice, be able to find my way back. Of course I'll be able to find my way back. Right? I have my phone, I remind myself. I can always call him, tell him what nondescript tree I'm standing near…

Shit.

I spin in a circle. Walls of snow-covered trees surround me, funhouse mirrors made of sap and wood. I'm alone. Matt has disappeared. I thought he would've followed me. Was he supposed to follow me? I stop, pause, try to ignore the sound of my racing heart pounding in my ears, force myself to listen to the sounds of the woods.

"Matt?" My voice shakes.

I bolt down an embankment into a tiny clearing, the snow melting in my hair, down my forehead. Snow saturates my clothes, turning clammy on the frozen skin beneath. I pull my scarf up around my head, tuck it down into my coat as I run.

Snap.

I turn, grind the inside of my cheek until my teeth hurt. Footsteps beat around me like drums.

"Matt!" I yell, lift my phone to ignite the yawning darkness.

It shines, a weak spotlight on tree trunks, fallen branches, snow-covered brush. The world is black and white, stark, yet murky, bleeding together. The light catches a wall of shadows in front of me. Finally, I've reached the stone wall.

The wall is made of fieldstones, stacked high over my head, taller than any person could climb in the slick snow. But what if there's an opening in the wall, even a tiny one, a spot where the stones have fallen, where someone could exit through? What if there's a way to enter the campus undetected? A way to come and go, secretly, silently. What if Alice is out there, somewhere beyond the campus perimeter? *An island in the woods…*

I turn off my flashlight, save the battery, press my hand against the cold stone wall. If only the stones could talk. They could tell me what they've seen. Or what they haven't seen.

Alice may not have even come this far. She may not even be out here, at all.

My mind races, thinks of all the possible places a person could be. If she's still in the main school building, she could be hiding in the attics, basements—the mechanical rooms. I shut my eyes, imagine a dark, cold, wet room, the burners churning and screaming. Why would she go there—why would she want to go anywhere?

I lean my head back, hope to see the white winter sky has somewhat remained after the sun had set. But there's nothing above me but darkness, the sky bulging, an angry shade of midnight purple. The heavy white clouds turned to nothing more than a blanket that blots out any trace of starlight.

I turn my flashlight back on—19 percent battery left— enough to get back to the school. Maybe I should get back. Maybe I should just quit, like Matt. Maybe—

The crunch of snow. Close. Too close. I gasp. Spin around. Hold the flashlight up.

A low growl.

Soft footsteps, close, closer.

No one is there. For now, I'm alone.

I relax, chastise myself for being so paranoid. And then, I hear it. A dog. I hear it *barking barking barking*. It won't stop, it won't—it's in the woods, all around me. For some reason, I feel it's trying to warn me. But why? It keeps going, I can't listen anymore, I can't!

And so, I run.

I run until I've escaped. I run until I don't hear anything anymore.

Not the dog. Not the wind bleating in my ears as I dash through the ice-slicked snow.

I just run.

I want Matt. I need Matt. I need warmth.

I scream, push my legs until my knees buckle.

Sweat crawls down my forehead, drips into my eyes.

The heat. The sweat. The cold. My glasses fog. I can't see.

I fall. Fall headfirst. Fall over a branch, a tree, a log, fall over everything and anything all at once.

My phone flies out of my hand, lands deep in the snow. The wind picks up. Snowdrifts form around my fallen body, blanketing me. Soon, I'll disappear.

Matt...

I crawl through the snow. It falls heavy. Blizzard. Blinding. My hands burn. My blood slows.

Matt...

I reach for my phone. I can't see it. I take off my foggy glasses, clasp them in my hand. I can't feel them, I can't feel anything but my heart slowly thumping. I look up, my eyes clear, free of haze, yet still I can't see.

I grab my phone from the snow, angle it down, squint against the barrage of snowflakes hurling into my face. The glow from the flashlight is all silver and haze. The wind howls. Cries. I slide my glasses back on my face. My vision goes grainy, like an old silent film. Cold clasps its claws around me, so tight the world spins. I feel death, I can see it, smell it, see the blood, thick, black—a lake. For once in my life, I wish I was hallucinating.

Forcing myself to stand, I hurl forward through the snow-flakes, snow so thick, it's blinding. My foot slips on something smooth, a rock, slick with ice. I fall, I'm falling, falling down a ravine, falling down a hill, just like Charley did. Was this what she felt? Was this how it ended?

Everything flashes inside my head. Charley's pretty face, sideways and staring and lifeless. Dave, in the beginning, when we were young. He comes home with flowers, purple, my favorite color, asks me to marry him. Izzi, a little girl, only six.

She still loved me then. Still needed me. I see her now, running toward me, arms outstretched, lopsided smile painted across her familiar face. I scoop her up, kiss her chubby cheek, swirl her around the kitchen.

It's the last thing I see before my world turns dark.

30

The snap of fingers.

I open my eyes. Matt leans over me, his hand in my face. *Snap snap snap.*

The air is dark save for tiny glowing fireflies. No, not fireflies. Candles. The scents of vanilla and lavender mix in my nose... *Alice*...her lavender hair... I can't think—I roll over on my side, vomit, not knowing or caring who sees.

"Oh, that's lovely." *Emilia.* "She needs to go to the hospital."

"I know..." *Matt.* His voice: quiet, hushed. Cold fingers tickle my cheeks as he brushes my hair away from my face.

I force my eyes open, hear the crackling of the fireplace, know where I am instantly. My vision is blurred. I feel my face for my glasses, but they're gone. Emilia holds a candle, leans to place it on the coffee table. The candlelight throws her face in a hazy dance of shadows and light.

I swallow down the pulsing panic sliding up my spine, try

to keep my composure. I look away from Emilia's delicate face, stare down at my hands folded in my lap. A ringing sounds in my ears as the room breathes in, contracts, like a lung.

I'm going to faint, right here, right in front of them all. Then they'll know I wasn't ready to do this job. That I've been failing all along.

I look back at Emilia. How can she be so composed? So professional? Star shapes appear around her head like a halo as she speaks, bright white and bursting like fireworks.

"Why so dark?" I whisper, feeling if I raise my voice any louder my throat will crack off and fall away into the sea.

"The power went out from the storm," Matt answers.

"Headmistress," Hannah calls. "We need more candles."

Emilia sighs, presses down on my shoulder to help her stand. I wince. She apologizes as she rushes from the room, but I hardly hear her as pain splits my head apart. I raise a hand to the top of my skull, feel it, make sure I'm not missing a piece of bone.

Matt moves up the sofa, sits at the edge near my stomach. He brushes another piece of hair out of my eyes, reaches toward the table, slides my glasses onto my face.

The girls speak in hushed voices on the far side of the library. I try to sit up to see them, count them, be sure they're all here. One, two—

Matt gently pushes me back down.

"Don't," he says. "You're hurt."

"Concussion?" I ask, staring at the blackness swimming above me.

"Possibly."

I pause, take it in. "Frostbite?"

He laughs darkly. "Oh," he groans, "you do know how to keep a man on his toes."

I think of the woods. The feeling of cold clasping around

me like a fist. How my fingers and toes felt like they'd disappeared, numbed, snapped off like dead twigs.

"I *must* have frostbite..."

He shakes his head. "No. No frostbite. But you should stay still. Try to get warm."

I glance at the girls awkwardly milling around by the bookshelves. "Why are the girls in here?"

"Emilia thought it was better to have everyone together, safe."

I attempt to swallow down the dryness in my throat. "Alice?" I gasp out. "Did you find her?"

Matt shakes his head.

"How did you find me?" I turn my head, look at him in the candlelight. "Out there, in the woods?"

His eyes fall. "I heard you screaming. I was looking for you, retracing your footsteps in the snow." He stops, drops his head down. "You fell. You must've fallen down a hill. Good thing you didn't get that far or you'd be—"

"I heard her..." I trail off.

"What?"

"I heard her. I heard someone out there. Someone else was out there."

Matt studies me, confused. "No...no one was out there."

I flip the blanket off my lap, the motion sending a rocket of pain shooting up my shoulder, singeing the nerves in my still-numb fingertips. I howl in pain, clench my teeth together to mute my cries.

"I should've stopped Alice from leaving. I could've tried harder, I could've known—"

"You *couldn't* have known."

A tear slips down my face. "What if she ends up like Charley? What if she wanted to—" I stop myself. I can't think this way. I turn away, lean my head on the back of the sofa, look into the darkness creeping over the library.

There's nothing but the gentle hum of little fires flickering, the sound of Matt's breathing, rising and falling, the scent of lavender and vanilla from the candles encompassing the room. Wind howls, the snowstorm showing no signs of stopping. I recoil, remembering the cold. The snow. I never want to feel it on my skin again.

"You know," Matt begins, "I've heard a lot of cases like Charley's over the years." He stops, looks at me. There's something sad in his eyes, something helpless. "Cops march onto a scene and immediately think it's an accident. And everything they do after that is based around that belief. Sometimes, the elements—rain or snow—have damaged any evidence, evidence that could've been present, but now was useless, unusable. It's what happened to Charley, too," he whispers. "The snow—it didn't matter what was found around her. A knife. A gun. It didn't matter. Not after the snowfall. Nothing could've been used. Not for DNA. Not fingerprints—"

"But nothing *was* found around her, right?" I ask. "Nothing. Not even her missing shoes."

"Her missing shoes..." He trails off, shakes his head, takes my hand in his, grips my fingers tight. "That's something I can't wrap my head around. How did she get out there, her feet, untouched? I—" He stops himself, covers his mouth with a hand. "I can't figure it out."

My face falls. "I thought you accepted the idea that the police were just never able to find Charley's shoes," I say. "Did you change your mind?"

He stares at me for a heartbeat, muscles flexing in his jaw. He lowers his head, says nothing, looks back at the girls clustered in the corner, far enough away where they can't hear. "I don't know," he finally says, expression serious. "All I know is—this is the first time I've ever made a case *worse* by putting more work into it," he says in a hushed tone.

"You didn't," I say and attempt to stand. A gush of wooziness overtakes me. "It's not too late. We can still find Alice. *Alive.*"

I swallow hard, lick my dry lips, pinch my eyes shut. I wince, feel another wave of nausea. I push it back, choke it down. I need to get out of here. I need to get to my room, to my bed, to my medications. I can't be without them, the headaches, the anxiety, I can't—

Emilia returns, arms bulging with candles. "Careful, don't place them on any wooden surfaces—or near any books," she warns sharply, passing them to Violet. "All I need now is an insurance claim." She sighs in exasperation, carefully sits on the coffee table beside me.

"How much snow?" I ask numbly, lift a hand to chew my fingernails, fight away the burning feeling at the back of my throat.

"Sixteen inches and counting. Just like I warned you. I bet you wished you left when you had the chance," Emilia says.

"I don't."

Emilia ignores me, turns toward Matt. "I called the police," she whispers, checking to see the girls can't hear. "They said the earliest they can make it up the mountain is first light."

Matt exhales in frustration. "So we're on our own." He looks away, shakes his head in anger. "God forbid someone had an actual fucking emergency," he vents. "Don't accidentally cut your hand off or anything like that when there's a goddamn snowstorm up here."

Emilia glares at him, knits her fingers together in her lap, her silver bracelets clinking together. "The hospital is an hour away," she says, voice dripping with derision. "So yes, if you cut your hand off, I hope you know how to cauterize it yourself."

Matt winces.

I shiver, pull the blanket up to my chin. "Please stop," I mumble. "You're going to make me puke."

"Here," Emilia says. "Drink some water." She passes me a crystal goblet, same as the one I use on the doorknob in my room. I take it, gulp the whole thing down.

Matt stands, bends over to tuck the blanket around me. "When we're done, please let me take you to the hospital."

I shake my head, saw off a fingernail with my teeth.

Matt sighs, leaves the room, leaves me alone with Emilia. I say nothing, keep my mouth shut. I have nothing to say. Not after she tried to kick me out. Not after what she said to me in my room. *You're sick... Delusional.* I wish I knew why she had such a grudge against me. I could ask her. But I won't.

Glancing over a shoulder, I see the girls are dressed in their pajamas, unrolling blankets, fluffing up pillows they'd pulled off their beds.

Rosemarie enters, falls into the chair beside me. I let out a sigh of relief knowing I don't have to be alone with Emilia. I offer her a wobbly smile as we gaze over toward the girls. They're whispering now, all bundled together on the floor, quiet as a pack of sheep.

I want to be here for them the rest of the night. I can leave tomorrow. I have to wait for the snow to be cleared, anyway. Matt has chosen to end his investigation. So I'm free to leave. My job here is over. I melt into the sofa, feeling free, feeling hollow. Feeling nothing but a thrash of pain pulsing in my skull, unsure now if it will ever go away.

"Stop lying!"

A sudden outburst from the girls. Emilia had been drifting off to sleep, and she snaps up, honey-colored hair tangled like a bird's nest.

"Girls! Quiet!"

Kiara yelps. "But Hannah won't shut up about some ridiculous story about how she saw blood all over the floor!"

My spine straightens.

"Girls, go to bed!" Emilia scolds, hoping her screams will keep them silent.

"But she's *lying*!" Violet shrieks. "Hannah's a *liar*!"

The power comes back on with a low whine of electricity. Hannah jumps, wraps her arms around herself, winces from the shock of bright light. Violet and Kiara roll their eyes at her reaction. I clamp my eyelids shut, a sudden flash of red overtaking my vision.

"You know, Hannah," Violet begins, twirling her long, black hair with a finger, "being caught in a lie trying to hide something makes you look *very* suspicious."

Emilia sighs. *"Violet."* Her voice is sharp. *"Shut—"* She stops herself, tries again. "Maturity is realizing how many things *don't* require your opinion. So keep them to yourself...until you know what you're talking about."

"But—"

"Enough!" Emilia's features contort in a way I've never seen. The entire room inches away. She stands up, hovers near the archway, slender fingers contorting into fists. "Rosemarie, can you watch them? I'm going to call the police station again to see if they can come up any earlier."

Rosemarie nods. Emilia storms out of the library, glaring at Violet as she passes. The girls let out lungfuls of air. I glance at Violet. Anger is etched across her face. If I didn't know any better, I'd think she was about to scream.

The rest of the girls fall back down on their pillows, heads lined up like little dolls. Violet. Hannah. Kiara. The three of them. Three musketeers. It's what me, Dave, and Izzi used to call ourselves. The three musketeers. Us against the world. But that was a long time ago. Now it's hard to remember the last time they didn't look at me with disappointment. Even so, if only I could see them now. If only I was looking at five girls instead of three. If only Charley and Alice—*if only, if only.*

Alice's voice echoes in my head. Some of the last words she'd ever spoken to me. Maybe some of the last words she'd ever said to anyone.

I found something out, and I can't tell you.

What did she find out? Something about Charley? Was there even something to find out? Matt said it was over...that Charley's death might always be a mystery.

It's over. We have to go home.

No.

Just because he gave up doesn't mean I have to. We have to find Alice. *I* have to find Alice. I can't let another girl die... I can't. Not Alice. Not her. Not another.

The news of her disappearance will leak soon enough. I imagine the headlines:

BOARDING SCHOOL STUNNED BY SECOND DISAPPEARANCE

SCHOOL HORROR: IN 2 WEEKS, 1 STUDENT DEAD, 1 MISSING

TEEN GIRL DISAPPEARS FROM SNOWY SCHOOL RETREAT

I look at the row of girls resting on the floor, at Hannah. The others don't believe her story about seeing blood on the floor in the hall. It's not the first time she's seen something no one else has. Hannah may be naïve and have a classic case of nosiness, but she wouldn't lie. Would she? It would go against her ingrained insecurity. She was the one who'd told me about how she'd seen Alice outside in the woods the night Charley died. And about the blood. She has no reason to lie. Nothing to gain from it.

Or does she?

I study her—slouched over, body curled inward. Her eyes are magnified behind her silver-rimmed glasses, so big and round they distort her entire face. An alien, I'd thought when I'd first seen her.

She removes her glasses and lifts her head, stares at me. Without her glasses on, her eyes are no longer comical. They're piercing, cutting, sharp, as if she can read my mind. My eyelid twitches. Heat floods my face. But I can't let it show. Not when she stares at me. I lower my head, try to slow my racing heart, wonder if she can hear it hammering in my chest.

I turn away.

Look back.

Still, she stares.

She stares as if she knows my deepest, darkest secret. What would she do if she knew? What would anyone do if they knew?

I will take it to my grave, this secret. My head spins. I fall back on the sofa, break my gaze from Hannah's.

What is truth, anyway...and what are lies?

I wouldn't know the difference. Not anymore.

Not when the truth has become the greatest lie I've ever told.

Wednesday, December 21

31

I wake in the morning, mouth dry, wishing everything was a dream. Outside the world is burning white—bright, reflective—the snow a mirror for the scalding sunrise, bending the brightness, burning my eyes.

I turn on my stomach, scream into the pillow. I'd failed. Failed miserably. Failed at being a psychiatrist. Failed Alice. Failed to find her. I should've worked faster, pushed the girls harder. Or maybe I pushed them *too* hard. All the things I should've done ricochet inside my brain.

After the library last night, Matt walked me to my room. I must've collapsed in bed. I don't remember the last time I'd slept that deeply, that dreamless. I don't remember if I'd taken anything to help guide me to sleep...

My head pounds. I get out of bed, rush for my medications. Cold air hits my skin as I kick off the blankets, wearing nothing but the bra and pants I'd had on the day before.

There's a fetid smell emitting from my hair and my skin is red and cracked across my cheeks from last night's cold trek in the woods.

I walk to the dresser to check my phone when a sharp pain shoots through my foot. I clench my jaw tight, lean against a bedpost. A glass shard is embedded in the thick meat near my toes.

Across the wooden floor is a constellation of broken glass.

I'd balanced the crystal goblet on the doorknob before falling asleep last night. And that can only mean one thing.

Someone had come into my room.

Quick, like ripping off a bandage, I tug out the shard of glass, toss it on top of the dresser. Blood pulses out. My throat tightens. I examine the wound, but can't hold back the swell of nausea. Blood trails down my foot, dripping perfect dots of red onto the wooden floor.

I limp toward the bathroom, slump to my knees, hover my head over the toilet, heave out my insides. Crawling to the bathtub, I run the hot water until the mirror steams with fog.

The water burns at first, then doesn't feel hot enough. I shut my eyes and sink beneath the surface, let the water envelop me, an embrace—my daughter's embrace—her heat, her body curled around mine. And I, for just a second, imagine I'm there, at home. In the water, I could be anywhere. I always choose home.

I come up for air. All traces of her disappear.

The placid water glows faint pink, blood strewing red ribbons across the bottom of the tub. I light up one of the few emergency cigarettes I have left, wash my hair twice. Polish off a new bar of soap I'd found nestled in the linen closet.

I limp back to bed, plop down naked and wet. The towel falls from my shoulders as I begin unrolling clean bandages

Rosemarie had given me, wrap them around my hand and foot. Soon I'll look like a mummy.

I sigh with relief. At least one thing is true.

Now I *know* I'm not imagining things.

Someone has been in here, lurking around while I was unconscious. How had I failed to hear glass shattering across the floor?

I'm not imagining things. The case files on Charley that Matt had given me had disappeared. My prescriptions were moved. My clothes were unfolded in my suitcase, moved around as if someone was searching for something.

But there were other things, too. The missing baseball bat. The brick beneath my pillow. The dog that keeps barking. The person I swore I'd heard following me in the woods last night. If I shut my eyes, I can still hear the snow crunching, the twigs snapping. I breathe a sigh of relief. I'm not imagining things. This isn't all in my head.

Hannah's voice on the recorder: *I didn't just imagine it.*

No. I didn't.

I grab my phone off the dresser, see it's been turned off. I never turn it off. I press the power button and slowly, the screen ignites. It's already past noon. How? How is that possible? No new calls. I don't know what I was expecting. I replay the message from Dave from earlier, pressing the phone to my ear, desperate for comfort, for home:

Hey, just wanted to call and say hi. I hope things are going okay at work. Izzi is fine. She's upstairs now. She told me she wants to talk to you about something, so maybe when you come home, keep that in mind. Okay, talk to you soon... Love you.

Clicking off my phone, I toss it on the bed, hop across the room, reach to grab the school's copy of *Dark Side* I'd stolen from the library last night after the girls fell asleep, hope to find some consolation within the pages. But it's gone. I hobble back to the bathroom, check inside my luggage. Check the dresser. Check under my pillow.

I tear everything apart, open my luggage, flip my tote bag upside down on the bed, let the contents tumble out, fall to the floor, slide into the broken glass. When I stop to catch my breath, the room is a disaster, destroyed, every drawer pulled out, every item in the room touched and re-touched and checked.

My phone rings. I jump, subconsciously look to the door, think someone's coming in. I want to run to it, press my back against it, slide down to the floor, know for sure the door won't open, that no one will come in. But an ocean of sharp glass separates us, a minefield.

Anxiety attack. I feel it happening. I've been off schedule with my prescriptions. I forgot to take them last night. I was too exhausted to remember. No one ever told me how long I'd been in the woods, freezing, alone in the snow. One hour? Two?

I stretch out a hand, reach for the orange bottles stashed inside my luggage. I can't find them. My book is gone. And my medications are gone. I grab my wet hair in both fists, cry out in frustration. Frustration with what I've done to myself. With who I've let myself become.

I snatch my phone, swipe it open, see the same unknown number has called again. Once. Twice. I ignore it, throw the phone on the bed, stop myself from screaming. Then, I see them, back on that same damn shelf, just like before.

I grab the bottles, wobble to the bathroom, tuck one, two, four beneath my tongue, slide my head under the faucet, the metal clicking against my teeth. I gulp them down, stare at myself in the foggy mirror.

I'm losing it. This is how it started last time—I'm confusing what's real, what isn't. I'm terrified, making the panic thicken, clasp tighter around my neck. My eyes have turned dark, hollow—rings around them like I've never had before.

I gulp, tongue swelling, choke, feel like someone has shoved their fist deep down inside my throat. I turn away from the sight of me, hop back into the bedroom, collapse into bed. My heart hammers in my chest. I need to calm down. I try to deep breathe. I try to think of good things, of Dave, of Izzi.

I think of her sixteenth birthday party. How friends and family came over, brought her little gifts tied to balloon strings. The adults got drunk and cried how their kids were growing tall, too tall, towering over them. I think about Izzi's face when she opened the gift we'd given her. Dave and I bought her a couple of lessons on how to fly a plane.

They were expensive. It was ridiculous. But Dave dreamed of mimicking a picture his father took of him when he was her age, one where he was shown how to fly a little single-engine plane, the sunset glowing his face gold as he flew over the farmlands and neighborhoods of his small town.

Izzi opened the gift. She didn't know what to make of it, at first. Dave explained to her what it meant, how she gets to go up in a plane with an instructor to help pilot it on her own. She panicked. Said she hated heights, that she couldn't do it, could never do it, how could she?

Why didn't her parents know she was afraid?

Dave looked at me, devastated, as Izzi fled to her room, slammed the door so hard the pictures shook.

Mom, please just stop.

The party ended after that.

Knock knock.

I bolt up, look at the glass on the floor, look at myself, my wet hair, my naked body beneath the blankets.

Knock knock.

I hop to the bathroom, sling on a robe, call out, "Who is it?"

No one answers. I jump around the broken glass, slide to the door, wrench it open, step into the hallway.

"Hello?" My voice, wobbly. My knees, unsteady.

I'm alone in the hall.

I step back inside, slam the door shut. Picking up my phone to call Matt, I stop, think, think of what I could possibly tell him. The screen fades to black. I click it on again, stare at the picture of Izzi I use as my wallpaper. She smiles in the kitchen. So beautiful. So amazing. My mind tumbles down an endless hole, imagining getting a phone call, answering to hear the chief of police's voice on the other side.

Feeling queasy, I dig my last protein bar out of my tote bag and pop open a bottle of antianxiety pills, hoping the combination will settle my stomach. I bite off a chunk and cup my hands under the faucet, tuck the pill into the side of my mouth, the flavor unusually tangy. I wince, the sour taste staining my tongue, drown it down with lukewarm water.

Reaching for a towel, I knock the plastic bottle into the sink, pills clattering around the porcelain, stopped by holes in the metal drain. I rush to pick them up, wipe them dry on my robe. Sliding my glasses up my forehead, I hold a pill close, read the tiny stamped name on the chalky white side. It's unfamiliar. A flush of coldness leaches up my spine.

This isn't one of my pills.

I snatch the bottle off the sink, read the label. This pill doesn't belong inside this bottle. This pill doesn't belong to me, at all. I've never even heard of it. *Me.*

My pulse quickens. I'm not sure what it will do once it hits my bloodstream. Immediately, I try to heave it out of me. Bending over the sink, I force myself to try to bring it up, but no matter how much I try, I can't get it out.

My cheeks grow hot. My mind swirls. *What the fuck did I just ingest?* I run to my phone, search the name of the pill, hands shaking. Reading the top result, I see it's a generic version of a brand of antipsychotic medication used to treat schizophrenia. Even *I* have never taken anything this intense. It was 500mg—the maximum dose.

My head starts to pound as I read the side effects: dizziness, hallucinations, nausea, headaches, tremors... I stare out of the window, think back to how long I've been tasting the strange tangy bitterness of these pills, how long I've felt them dance down my throat. Have I been swallowing them for days now?

My heart rate speeds up, mind buzzing with the possibilities of drug interactions, of how these pills may be the culprit behind how I've been feeling. The nausea. The shaking hands. The fogginess, dizziness, hallucinations...

Then, the obvious hits me, a pulse too late.

Who would switch out my pills?

And why?

I look over my shoulder, suddenly feeling like I'm not alone. Maybe I never was.

The smashed crystal goblet, fallen from the doorknob. Someone has been in here. Someone has been coming in here, all along. I've only ever been able to leave the goblet on the doorknob when I'm *inside* the room. Not when I'm outside. The goblet would've fallen to the floor, smashed, when I twisted the doorknob open coming back into the room.

And now...who knows who's been in here. Who knows who's been able to come in during the day, when I'm gone. All I know is I can't stay in this room another minute, another night. How can I? I feel myself hyperventilating. I ignore it, try to focus, slow my uneven breaths.

I don't want another nervous breakdown—yes, they told me not to call it that anymore, but that's what I always called it in my head. I call it what it is, thinking somehow if I faced the truth, it would help me. It never did.

A whoosh of dizziness hits me. I tip over, stop myself from falling, latch onto the bathroom doorway, my nails digging into the wood. I try to read more search results, see if I can find any drug interactions, feeling like my skin is on fire, unsure now if it's only in my head or if this is real, too real.

My eyes grow fuzzy as I read. I whip off my glasses, toss them onto the bed, pull the phone close to my bleary eyes. Try to read as best I can.

Drug interactions: do not mix with…hallucinations…paranoia. Memory loss.

I feel faint. The room spins.

Why would someone do this to me?

Why?

I've done nothing wrong to anyone.

Lie…

I've been a good mom.

Lie…

A good wife.

Lie…

A good doctor.

Lie.

I fall into bed, stretch my arm out to the table on the other side. The school's copy of *Dark Side* rests near the lamp. But when I was looking for the book before I couldn't find it anywhere—I swear on my life it was not in this room!

But it's here now. I flip it open, get a paper cut. The sudden drop of blood turns my stomach inside out, connecting it mentally with the gash on my foot. I feel it throb when just a moment ago, I'd nearly forgotten my foot altogether.

Flip flip flip to the part about medications, not even sure what I'm trying to find. My mind feels like it's fading, like I'm a smaller, cut down shadow of the person I used to be. Like I don't really exist.

I flip to the back, not finding anything I need, finding nothing to help calm me down. Flip to the acknowledgments, to the index, to the footnotes. Flip to the back dust jacket.

To the author photo.

A black-and-white airbrushed face. A woman, younger than me. Shoulder-length dark hair, perfectly undone waves. Sleek silver glasses.

Pearl studs on ears that aren't mine.

Silk shirt, unbuttoned, just above her cleavage, just enough so you know what's there.

The same. Different.

Better.

I drop the book. It falls off the bed, bounces off the mattress, lands on the floor with a thud.

I glance up, around, as if I'm surrounded by white coats. They gawk at me, notepads held up, nodding as they take shorthand notes in sloppy handwriting not even they can decipher. They examine me, stare at me, look at me like I'm a caged animal to be studied.

My lip quivers. My hands shake. It's not real. It can't be real. All of this. None of this. How could it be when the woman in the picture isn't me.

THE YEAR BEFORE

FILE NAME: JPN00.012.00030923.mp3

INT: So you're baking apple pie, your husband is slowly coming back to you—what happened next?

RES: I—finally, I asked him why he felt like he couldn't tell me about his diagnosis. He said he'd read online how you shouldn't tell people who could possibly react negatively that you have cancer, because you should cut out negative people in your life. He said he thought I was being negative, and he was hoping to deal with it on his own, on his own terms.

INT: Do you believe you were being negative?

RES: Of course not. I mean, I reacted the same way any wife would react when their husband tells them something like that.

[00:43:14]

INT: And how is that?

RES: Concerned! Sad! Heartbroken... I would've done anything for him. I would've stayed with him and we would've beat it together, as a family. But he didn't give me that chance.

INT: Did you tell him this?

RES: Yes, I told him. He said he was sorry, he said when he was told the news, he couldn't bear to bring himself to tell me, that he was sorry for telling me over the phone. That I deserved better than that. Then he said I seemed to be doing so great—he... I'm sorry.

INT: It's okay.

RES: ... He, uh, said I was doing so great, he didn't want to bring me down with him. And—and how could I tell him that I was doing great because I was cheating on him? I couldn't! I couldn't tell him that!

INT: I can't imagine...

RES: So then, you know, we talk, we reminisce. We have some apple pie, some drinks...

INT: How many drinks would you say?

RES: ... I don't know...maybe he had two and I had... maybe, three, four.

INT: Three or four?

RES: Yes.

INT: What kind of alcohol?

RES: Wine.

INT: Red, white?

RES: [inaudible] red.

INT: So then what happened?

RES: We heard a bang upstairs. And I checked the time and saw it was way past ten.

INT: So you assumed it was your daughter coming home?

RES: No—I mean, no...why would she come through her window?

INT: Well, if she was way past curfew.

RES: Yeah, I know what you're saying. It's just, I—I don't think she would...it didn't cross my mind that it could've been her at the time.

INT: Even though you say she often came and went through her bedroom window?

[00:45:22]

RES: Well, yeah...yes—she did. But I don't know, the bang shattered the glass.

INT: And you heard it—the glass shattering.

RES: Right, we were downstairs in the kitchen and heard it from upstairs.

INT: Then what did you do?

RES: My husband went up to see what had happened.

INT: Now, at this point, when the window broke, was the home alarm system set?

RES: No—we never really remembered to use it.

INT: Okay…so the alarm system was not activated last night?

RES: No. No, I don't think so.

INT: Then what happened, when your husband went upstairs?

RES: He came back down and he had a rock.

INT: What kind of rock?

RES: A—like a brick.

INT: And someone had thrown it through your window? Which window?

RES: Just through one of the windows in the hallway upstairs.

INT: Tell me about the brick.

RES: Nothing. It was just a brick.

INT: Tell me what your husband said about the brick, who did he think it was?

RES: We didn't know what to think.

INT: Uh-huh. But you knew who it was.

RES: I had an idea.

INT: Why would you have an idea of who would throw the brick through your window?

RES: … Because he'd grown increasingly violent the past two weeks.

INT: [inaudible] you're referring to [redacted]?

RES: Yes.

[00:48:05]

INT: The man you had an affair with?

RES: Yes.

INT: Did you have any contact with him since that day you called him to come to your house when your daughter was missing? The day you broke it off with him at the hotel?

RES: No. None.

INT: You're positive?

RES: Yes. Yes, I'm positive.

INT: How did you know he had been becoming increasingly violent if you say you had no contact with him?

RES: Because of the messages—he'd leave me voice mails, texts.

INT: How often?

RES: Every day.

INT: Every day?

RES: Yes.

INT: And how did your husband react to the broken glass, the brick?

RES: ... He, uh, he didn't handle it well.

32

My vision crawls sideways.

I fall to my knees, pick up the book, flip to the back dust jacket. Look at the author photo. She stares back at me, her arms crossed. I rip the glossy paper, tearing across the photo, leaving torn white lines over her face, like claw marks.

I'm not imagining things. I'm not. I bite back a scream, flip backward in the book, rip out a page. Then another. It feels good. I shut my eyes, flip to another page. Hear the tearing sound of paper, so soothing, like falling asleep to the sound of ocean waves.

Flip tear flip tear, listen to the *rip* of each paper, so beautiful it's nearly orgasmic. Too soon, I reach the front cover, open my eyes, see I'm kneeling in a sea of white paper. The empty shell of a book slips from my fingers, plunges to the floor.

I am fully aware of what's happening. I know. But I can't stop it. It's reaching the point where it feels like a game, like

I'm on a hidden camera show. Any moment someone will pop out, say *Surprise!*

I pull myself upright, the wound on my foot pulsating with stinging pain. On a chair across the bed is a pink sweater. It's draped across the back, purposefully done, like it's been taken from a magazine photo shoot.

I know this sweater. I'd seen it before. A plain pink sweater, mohair and polyester, size small. The same sweater I'd seen half-hidden in a box in Jeremy's room. Who'd put it in my room? I glance around, unsure if I'd asked the question aloud.

I can't help but laugh—an inebriated, maniacal laugh, a throw my head back and cackle kind of laugh—when I pick up the sweater and remember it's smeared with dark red blood. I'm so sick of blood, of seeing it, of smelling it. This could be Charley's blood. She could have been wearing this sweater when she died. It could be one of the articles of clothing she'd allegedly stripped off in the woods. Maybe Charley didn't go out into the woods wearing only her pajamas. Maybe she was wearing clothes. She just removed them herself.

There can only be one explanation why this sweater was planted in my bedroom. Someone is trying to set me up. Someone is trying to frame me.

For Charley's death.

But only one other person knows I know about the sweater—Jeremy. He was in my bedroom. It was him...it had to be him...

I grimace, soft laughs bubbling out of me, feeling resolved to protect myself, to concentrate. I test myself, see how straight I can walk to the bathroom. The room wobbles sideways, like the world has fallen over. My eyes start to tear as I carry the sweater in my arms like a baby and rest it gently in the bathtub, as if it were a crib.

I grab a match from my well-worn pack of matches, snap a flame alive, and set the pretty blood-splattered sweater on fire.

And then, I collapse.

When I wake, the air around me has shifted, filling the space with gloom. The walls spin as I stare up at the ceiling, welcoming the feeling like I've been pushed from a plane, left to free fall back to earth.

I know what's happening. I'm fully aware. Drug interaction. It's never happened to me before, but I've read about it. There's nothing I can do except have my stomach pumped or wait for my body to absorb the medication, let it leach out of my system.

I shake my head back and forth on the floor, *no no no*. Denial. Denying any of this is real. Unsure if it is. Is it? I have no idea… I only know I'm not imagining it. I couldn't have made this up. I couldn't have. I wouldn't. But there's only one way to find out.

I have to see what I'd burned in the bathtub. I have to see if the book has a picture of my face on the back. I try to stand, wobbly, like I just grew a fresh new pair of legs. Slowly, I peel myself off the tiled floor, grab the edge of the tub, hurl myself upright.

At the bottom of the bathtub, there's nothing but ashes; the faint trace of smoke haunts the cold air. I'd burned something. Maybe it was nothing. Maybe it was my favorite shirt. Maybe it was a pale pink sweater with dried bloodstains on it. There's no lock on my door, I remind myself. Anyone could come in here. Anyone, at all.

There's no reason for me to be here, not anymore. Just like that, I'm done. I stand, walk to the dresser, fill my luggage, zip it tight. Wobbly wheel my bag down the hallway, slip, pinball against the walls. I follow signs pointing toward the headmistress's office. Unattached, my hand floats up, taps Emilia's office door.

I'll stay the night inside her office, leave early tomorrow morning. Hopefully Alice is found by then. I can't see the girls now. I can't see anyone. Not like this. Not when my head spins and every muscle feels like it's vibrating, humming like a plucked guitar string. It's over. I resign.

I stand outside Emilia's office door, pull my hair back into a low bun knotted at the nape of my neck. I straighten my glasses, smooth my shirt, adjust the tote bag on my shoulder.

I'm fine. Nothing happened. I'm just done and need to go home. I won't blame anyone. I won't be angry at anyone for doing what they've done to me. I just need to leave.

Pressing my ear to the wood, I listen closely, hear nothing, hear no one. I check my watch again, glance behind me. No one is there, only a long stretch of shadows, ending in the hollow blackness of the stairwell.

Slowly, I creak the door open and step inside.

33

The sun sets as I wait alone in Emilia's dim office, watching dust motes float in the faint light seeping in through the stained-glass windows. Dozens of hanging plants drop from the ceiling near a wall of windows, potted blooms propped up on iron stands, palm trees eight feet high. A humidifier puffs out white clouds of steam, fogging the glass.

A winter cactus blooms red flowers in a pot on the windowsill. I pinch a little waxy piece, knowing I'd never be able to keep it alive. Every birthday, Dave would buy me a plant. *Try again*, he said. *This one will survive.* But by every winter, it had died.

The room is quiet and still. I listen for footsteps echoing from down the hall, but no one comes. Emilia, like the rest of us, must be trapped somewhere inside the school. One glance at the blizzard outside confirms it. It looks as if someone taped white paper to the glass, shielding my view of the outside world, permitting me to see nothing but an opaque world of infinite white.

But it doesn't matter where Emilia is hiding. I am not returning to my room. I drop my heavy tote bag onto her desk, onto her keyboard, the computer scolding me with an error-fueled *beep boop boop*.

I'm determined to stay here, hidden in her office, far away from my bedroom, far away from the ripped bits of paper, the ashes of the blood-splattered sweater, the half-filled bottles of mystery pills—pills that aren't mine.

I think of the side effects. Think of the possible outcomes of drug interactions, of too many chemicals mixing together in my blood.

Dizziness, hallucinations, nausea, headaches, tremors...

Outside, a dog barks. Faint at first, then louder, louder. It's relentless, so relentless I gaze out of the window, peer down below. Maybe I can see it through the endless snowflakes, see it standing in the middle of the snow-covered courtyard, *barking barking barking*.

But there's nothing. No dog. Nothing but a world of white, the limbs of evergreens sagging, drowning in snow.

I exhale, step away from the drafty window, flick on a desk lamp. The murky room glows faint gold, lighting up dark corners. Emilia's forest of hanging plants casts shadows on the walls like sea creatures.

Something glints in the newfound light. Something familiar. I edge closer, cross the room, take it in my hand, feel the wrapped leather grip, twist it until warmth melts into my palm.

The metal baseball bat feels light in my hand, like a feather, like a shadow. I whip it through the air, hear the little slicing sound. I do it again, *whip whip whip*, feel the air subtly shift around me. The dog outside keeps barking. And then, it falls silent. I lean the bat back against the wall, crumple into Emilia's chair.

The room looks different from behind her desk. The door is directly in front of me, the windows on one side cluttered with a tangle of vines and dripping plants. The windows on the other are topped with a stained-glass arch, leading down to the courtyard. The world falls silent. The dog is most likely far away by now, long gone deep into the snow-drowned woods.

I spin in the chair, go until I'm dizzy, go until I can't see shapes. A portrait of a girl hanging behind Emilia's desk whips away, comes back, whips away. The girl in the painting laughs at me, her thick black hair swinging like ropes around her face, her red mouth open and giggling.

I stop spinning, feel my brain pirouette inside my skull. The room goes sideways. I drag my fingertip across the top of Emilia's perfect, mirrored desk, watch as my touch leaves a trail of sludge in its wake.

Alone in the silence, I lurch forward, grab the recorder from my tote bag, switch it on. Alice's voice fills the room. It feels nice to pretend I'm not alone. I listen to Alice's words, feel tears tickle my eyes.

Are you sure you're okay? she'd asked.

Oh. Yeah, sorry. My voice. Brusque with embarrassment.

You don't have to be nervous. I'm nervous, too.

I exhale, switch the recorder off, tuck it under my thigh.

Emilia's desk has six drawers, three on each side. I open the first one, poke around, my hands trembling like a tightrope. Inside are pens, all the same, all blue. Little bags of tissues, golden-capped lipstick. I pull it out, swivel it up, smear the soft wax across my dry lips.

I close it, open the next drawer. Look, look again. Right on top, there they are. My missing case files. I curse under my breath, feel my cheeks enflame with heat. Something swells inside me—relief, satisfaction—because I wasn't lying—at least not about this. I knew someone had come inside my room. And now I know who it was. *Emilia.*

But why?

Footsteps.

Footsteps, tapping.

Quickly, I tug out the stack of files, shove them into my bag, slam the drawer shut.

I sit straight up, act natural, stare ahead. But the door fails to open.

Shuffling.

Voices.

That's it. I guess this is my life now. Dogs barking in the middle of a blizzard. Strange, ghostly footsteps and muffled voices dancing in the air, sounding like they're all around me. Now I have no choice. I have to accept it. Maybe the mystery pills I've been taking are not at fault. Maybe it's *me. I'm* the common denominator. There's no going back now. Voices, footsteps—they're a part of my life now, a part of me.

Words—someone's speaking. I furrow my brows, listen closely. The walls? Am I hearing someone through the walls? Through the old radiator pipes? Or maybe my phone has called someone accidentally? I lift my bag off Emilia's desk, off her keyboard. Her computer lights up. Dropping the tote bag on the floor, I listen closely.

A voice—I know this voice. It's Kiara. I tap on Emilia's mouse. Her desktop is a picture of an English garden, a sea of primrose and lavender nestled beside sculpted topiaries. Kiara's voice stops. On the keyboard is a volume button. I turn it up.

Static.

There's a program running in the background. I maximize it, bring it to the front. It's a video. No, not a video. A live feed.

A *camera* feed.

My stomach sinks.

It's not just a camera. It's the camera in the hallway right outside my bedroom door.

In the distance is a tall, slender girl tossing a ball into the air, catching it as she walks. Kiara. Slowly, her silhouette fades down the hallway before she turns a corner, disappears. I search the program, see if there are any other working cameras. Maybe one had caught where Alice went, maybe one in a hallway shows where she might be hiding inside the school—but this is the only camera working. It's the only camera working on the entire campus.

Smoke and mirrors.

Lie.

Not only has Emilia lied about the missing case files, but she's lied about the cameras not working. And…she's been watching me.

She's been lying all along. Lying to me. Lying to Matt. But why? My heart races as I dig through Emilia's saved video files. Not all of the audio has been saved, but I don't care. I'm only interested in finding footage from one day.

The day Charley disappeared.

I check the dates. Recheck them. The cameras had been filming since the beginning of the school year, the footage saved in the cloud linked to Emilia's account. I find the day Charley died. Blink. Check again.

It's gone. Erased. The dates for the saved files don't start again until Friday—last Friday. The day I'd arrived at the school.

Did Emilia just so happen to shut off all of the cameras the day Charley died, never to turn them back on again until I'd arrived? Is it a coincidence? Maybe something happened that day—maybe the police came and took the footage and

Emilia had forgotten to turn the cameras on again. But then why would she lie? Why would she tell me that the cameras never worked?

I stare at the dates of the files, try to piece it together in my head. I stare until my vision blurs. I reach down to my tote bag, feel around inside for my phone. I need to call Matt. He has to know. He has to know *now*. I stand from the desk. Aim my feet toward the door. The world starts to spin again. I fall back into the chair, palms sweating, heart hammering.

Down the hall—footsteps.

I lower the volume on the computer to be sure what I'm hearing is real.

Slowly, the door creaks open.

Emilia steps inside, closing it shut behind her.

34

Emilia flicks on a light switch. My eyes adjust to the sudden throb of light. I wince away like a vampire.

"What are you doing in here?"

She stares at me, her pale eyes unlocking from my face as she walks toward me, toward her computer, the light from the screen glowing across my panic-stricken face.

"Madeline—why are you here?"

I say nothing as she stalks closer. I don't know what I *should* say. All I can think about is the missing footage from the day Charley disappeared, erased from the rest of the files. I think of the camera outside my door, staring down at me from the ceiling, think of how many times I'd felt I wasn't alone.

"Answer me," Emilia demands. "Answer me *right now.*"

"What did you do?" It's all I can think of to say. My mind races, bouncing from thought to thought, failing to land on anything solid, on anything real.

"What?"

"You lied, Emilia," I say, breathless. "About the cameras. About my missing case files. What else have you been lying about? Have you been lying about Charley?" Emilia's cheeks flush. She turns away, attempts to hide it. "You know what happened," I whisper. "You know what *really* happened to her, don't you?"

Right before me, I witness a woman become undone.

Emilia's knees buckle. She clutches the wall, her purse slipping through her fingertips. She catches herself, reverses her reaction, adjusts her face to appear hard as stone.

"How did you find out?" she mutters, voice as soft as baby's breath.

I freeze, the air punched from my lungs.

"What?"

Emilia edges closer.

I snatch the recorder from beneath my thigh and stand from the chair, nearly knock the computer off her desk. "Stay away from me," I warn, fight to keep my voice steady, even though my insides hum and the side effects of the mystery pills catapult me into oblivion.

Emilia backs away, her shoulder knocking into a bookcase. "I want you to leave," she seethes.

"No." My vision whirls. The gash on my foot burns. I need to sleep, need to run. I need to know what Emilia did. What she knows. What else she is lying about. "Charley is dead," I say, the words falling out of my mouth. "One of your students is dead. Another is missing. Doesn't that matter to you? Don't you want to start telling the truth?"

Emilia sneers at me, calmly sits at her desk, folds her hands together. I circle around the other side, keeping the desk between us, a barricade, safety, protection.

She shakes her head, lifts her gaze to me. "I would never

harm Charley," she says, expression twisting. "I would never harm anyone—"

"You're *lying*."

I inch closer toward the door, prepare to run from the room, down the hall, run outside. Run right to Matt's guesthouse, run right to him, to safety. I have to tell him. He has to know. I have to get away from here—away from her.

"No, I'm not!" Emilia shouts. My bleary eyes snap back into focus. She cries out, looks up at me, trembling. "Everything I do is for these girls. And I can't—I can't *do it anymore*."

"So don't."

Emilia inhales, temples her fingers together. "That night, I—I went outside to clear my head. I went for a walk. I walk the same path, no one else is ever out there…" She trails off.

I switch on the record button. My fingers tingle. I can't see straight—I can't see—*Dizziness, hallucinations, nausea…*

"What are you saying?" I ask, my voice wavering.

Emilia's eyes go dead. "Charley wasn't supposed to die."

I back away. Before I can reach the door, Emilia has stood from her chair, rushed across the room. I blink, and she's standing right in front of me. I press my back against the wall. Still, she steps closer.

"Don't you understand?" Emilia asks, her expression twisting with desperation. "It was *me. I* did it. *I* killed Charley."

Emilia's bottom lip begins to shake. Her eyes are bloodshot, wild, glazed with tears. I freeze, study her, study to see if she's filled with sadness or anger. I can't read her. I can't clear my head to figure her out.

Something nags at me, deep inside. Something is wrong here. Something isn't right. Either way, I need to get out of here. I need to get away from her.

"Why?" I croak, fingers itching toward the doorknob. "Why would you?"

"Please," Emilia says. A tear falls down her soft cheek. "Please—before you do anything, please try to understand."

I exhale, feel myself crumble as I stitch her story together. "You want me to understand what? That you went for a walk outside in the woods and saw Charley?" I say, trying to rearrange her words together inside my head.

"Yes."

"And you killed her? Just like that?"

"No. She was angry. She pushed *me* first." Emilia looks down to the floor in thought. "Her mother was threatening to withdraw her next semester and Charley blamed me. But I have a responsibility to these girls. I had no choice but to call her and tell her about Charley's relationship with Alice. And she blamed *me*," Emilia says softly to herself. "I had no choice."

A swelling knot hovers in my throat. "What exactly did you do?" I whisper, backing away. "What did you do to her?"

"I pushed Charley off me. I had no idea she would fall. I never meant to hurt her…"

"And you left her alone out there—an innocent teenage girl—to die." The knot in my throat grows.

"She was *already* dead. It didn't make any difference," Emilia says brusquely. "I thought I could protect the school, protect the rest of the girls…" She shrivels away, turns her head to stare out of the windows.

"Bullshit. You were only protecting yourself. You could've told me, you could've told anyone a thousand times over. Instead, you let Charley's mother suffer. You let the *girls* suffer."

"No—"

"And now Charley is dead. And Alice is missing—probably also dead at this point."

"What I—"

"Because of *you!*"

"No!"

Silence.

Nothing but breathing.

"Alice was *not* my fault," Emilia says. "I didn't know this would get so out of control. I did a lot of things, but I—" She backs away, leans against the stained-glass window, the light glowing her face red, her features twisting, wretched and possessed. "I never knew this would happen. I never knew any of this would go this far."

Emilia had cut the cameras. She had erased the footage. Emilia knew the recordings would show her walking into the woods that day. She knew she'd be implicated. And so, she destroyed the evidence.

The knot in my throat burns. The entire thing makes me sick. I reach for my tote bag, sling it over my shoulder, wrench open the door.

"Where are you going?"

"I'm leaving. It's over, Emilia."

She grabs hold of my arm. I shrug away, try to push her off me. Her fingers clamp into my skin. She holds me tight. Our eyes lock.

"Haven't you ever lied?" she asks, eyes smoldering with rage. "Haven't you ever done something you know is wrong, but you do it anyway? And your self-preservation—just for a second—overwhelms you. And you'd do anything to protect what you love. *Anything.*"

I turn away, ignore her, know in my gut she's right. I know the best way to tell a lie is to mix it with truth. But I clearly can't trust her. How much of her story is real? How much is a lie? Or maybe she did confess it all to me, no more lies, nothing but truth?

What is truth, anyway?

Truth is whatever we believe it to be.

I can't bring myself to look at her. "I'm calling Matt," I say quietly, looking at the floor. "I'm telling him everything. And you'll face the consequences."

Emilia unlatches her grip on my arm, stumbles back, expressionless.

I step into the hall. For a moment I wonder if Emilia will try to stop me. If she'll grab the strap of my bag, strangle me with it, hide my body beneath the floorboards. But she doesn't. She stands there, silent, unmoving, her thin arms crossed, face emotionless.

Stepping into the hall, I close the door, and slide out the voice recorder from my back pocket. Switching it off, I slip it into my tote bag beside my case files. The hard plastic case dings against my phone at the bottom, like an anchor in the sea.

Emilia can't escape this. She won't.

Because I have her confession. I have it all.

35

No one is going anywhere tonight.

No one except me.

The storm rages. In the glow from the bulging purple clouds overhead, snow ravages the school, hurling winds that blow the main door open the moment I twist the handle.

I've texted Matt again and again:

Where are you?
We have to talk.
It's URGENT.

But none of the texts go through. I've tried calling but get a busy signal over and over and over. There's no phone service or internet, thanks to the storm. And now, I can't wait any longer. All three girls are safely stowed away inside the library with Rosemarie. For now, they're safe. It's risky to make the trek to Matt's cabin, but it may be even riskier to wait…

My mind spins. Only three things are clear to me now:

1) Emilia *killed* Charley.

2) I recorded her confession.

3) Nobody else knows but me.

The police can't make it up the mountain to question Emilia until the blizzard stops. Maybe Emilia never even called them, and now the lines are out. But that doesn't mean I can't do something, anything, to help Charley's case.

No matter what Matt said, it's not over. There's no way it can be over, not when I have Emilia's confession saved on the voice recorder safely tucked inside my pocket.

I use the weight of my body to close the main door behind me and step into the carriage tunnel. Up ahead, the entire campus is drenched in white, the world shrunken, eaten by snow. Snow hangs down over the roof of the school, like a new appendage, threatening to fall any moment, crush anyone beneath.

I pull my coat around my cheeks, secure my scarf around my head. Beneath my arm is my tote bag, and I stow the voice recorder away inside. I hold a deep breath and exit the carriage tunnel. Wind immediately whips into my face, stinging cold, stinging until it burns.

My glasses thankfully keep the snow out of my eyes, but the thick flakes freeze on the lenses, making it impossible to see. I push forward, arms wrapped around myself, eyes squinting as the freezing winds lash against my cheeks.

I cry out, the muscles in my legs burning as I trudge through the deep snow. Heaps of it fall into my boots, gathering around my feet, freezing my socks, turning my toes to ice.

I keep going. I have to speak to Matt. He'll know what to do with Emilia. It's the only option we have until the police can come. *I can do it*, I tell myself, over and over. *I can do it*. His cottage is just ahead, and soon I'll be out of the open courtyard and into the safety of the woods. The snow will be buffered, diffused, the winds softer, and I'll be safe.

As I push myself forward, my knees buckle. I collapse into the snow, hands stinging, and soon I feel nothing at all. My entire body is numb. The woods are ahead, and I claw myself out of the snow. The scarf has fallen off my head, exposing my hair, freezing my brain. A headache sprouts. Soon it will be too much. Soon I'll collapse for good.

And then, I make it to the edge of the woods. The winds still reach me, but the snow isn't as deep. My muscles relax, and I'm able to trudge forward at a faster pace. Matt's cottage is in the distance, so close I can taste it. I shut my eyes, walk forward, hope I can make it there before the cold claims me.

A door opens, thuds closed in the distance. The wind howls in my ears. It's loud, angry it hasn't taken me. Warm arms wrap around me. I crack my eyes open when the world around me goes quiet. No more wind hurtling itself in my ears. No more crunching of the snow beneath my boots. Silence.

"Madeline—what the hell were you thinking?"

Finally, I'm safe.

Matt shuffles me inside, rushes me in front of the fireplace, tells me to sit. I obey, shut my eyes, feel the weight of a hundred blankets fall across my shoulders.

"I'll be right back," he says with an exasperated sigh.

Thawing in front of the fire, Matt at my side, I'm finally able to pry off my damp clothes. Leaning back into the chair, I peel off my boots, take a peek at the gash in the sole of my foot. A dark purple stain has erupted beneath my skin.

"It's still bleeding," Matt says, examining my foot in the firelight.

He scrubs a hand through stubble on his cheek. I feel an

odd pull to reach for him, to hug him, needing some kind of human contact. Needing to feel him, someone, close to me, telling me things will be okay. The past few days, I've been surrounded by people, surrounded by more people than I've seen in the past year. But still, I've never felt more alone.

"Matt…" I whisper. He turns, eyes wide and innocent, filled with a strange sort of hope that makes my stomach sink.

I bend down, pull my tote bag onto my lap, reach inside, pull out the voice recorder. I switch it on. Emilia's voice spills into the tiny room: *Haven't you ever lied? Haven't you ever done something you know is wrong, but you do it anyway?*

Matt stares at me. "Is that Emilia?"

I nod, inhale a deep breath. And I tell him everything. I tell him about Emilia. How she erased the camera footage on her computer. How she stole the case files from my room, all in an attempt to cover up what she did to Charley. I tug them out of my tote bag, rest them on the coffee table.

"My god…" He trails off, staring past me, deep in thought. He shakes his head in disappointment.

"Matt…" I look down. Blood from my wounded foot begins to saturate the pale carpet. I'm cold, so cold. Sleep fights to overtake me. "Matt," I begin again. "We have to go back to the school. The girls—what if she kills again—Violet, Hannah, Kiara. What if something bad happens to them? What if—"

Matt exhales, drops his head down. "It's too dangerous for you to go back outside." Quickly, he stands, rushes to toss on his coat.

"I'm going with you," I say, attempting to stand. Heat explodes through my foot so forcefully it sends a shockwave of blistering pain up my leg. I fall back onto the chair, whimper, grip my calf.

Matt looks at me. "I think it's getting infected," he says. "Please, stay here. Try to relax. I promise—I'll be back soon."

He turns back to look at me as he opens the door. Freezing air immediately swallows the faint warmth from the fireplace. "Madeline...promise me you won't let *anyone* in."

My eyebrows furrow. I nod. The door closes. My phone vibrates in my tote bag. I pull it out. Another call from the same unknown number. I ignore it.

I sit alone in the shadows and wait, thoughts of what happened to Charley flashing in my head. Emilia claims she went for a walk in the woods, saw Charley, and killed her. Tears prick my eyes. I imagine someone doing that to Izzi. It's too hard to even think about.

Anyone who takes a life, whoever they are, deserves to feel the bite of cold metal handcuffs, hear the snick of locks clicking closed around their wrists...

Izzi's face wanders into my mind again. I think of all the hours, days, weeks I'd spent looking at her. In the hospital. In her crib. Her little body curled into mine as we sat in front of the fireplace. I'd make us hot chocolate this time of year. Until the water boiled, we'd watch the snow fall through the window above the kitchen sink.

That was when things were good. Before Dave became consumed with his work. His cases. His clients. Before he preferred the office to us. Before he preferred *her* to us.

Izzi grew up, and I forgot how to light the fireplace. I tried again, once, last fall, when the first fallen leaf kissed the lawn and the smell of winter crept out at night. I'd asked if she wanted to sit and watch a movie together, like we always used to.

I knew a day would come when she'd rather be with friends or a boyfriend or girlfriend over her mom. But I didn't prepare for it. When she looked at me on the way upstairs to her room, I could see the woman she'd grow up to be. And I wondered if she would be happy. If she'd remember all the good days we'd shared. If, as time went on, she'd ever know how much her mom loved her. How her mom would kill to keep her safe.

She turned down movie night. I tried again the next weekend. I practiced how to start a fire. I made hot chocolate. I even picked a bloody horror movie, hoping she'd at least be intrigued. But still, she ran upstairs, and I listened as her door closed, locked, and her music was turned up, and I sat in the quiet of the living room alone, knowing day by day, hour by hour, my little girl was growing further and further away from me.

Mom, please just stop.

I check my phone again. The background is a picture of Izzi. She stands in the kitchen, the sunlight glowing her brown hair gold.

I wish my daughter didn't hate me. If I had three wishes, that would be one of them. But what I did... I deserve it. I deserve it all. I never wanted to harm my family. I never meant for my actions—my careless, impulsive actions—to have such a lasting effect on our lives.

But they did.

Izzi hates me. She'll hate me forever. There's no going back to the way we were. Not anymore. There's no more chances for me to make things right. Not when I put her in that position. Not when I cheated on her father.

Yes, I cheated.

I cheated on Dave. I knew—I always had a feeling—*he* was cheating on *me*. Everything has become so foggy in my head now. Looking back through the lens of time, I can't help but question everything. I only cheated on him because I was in pain. I thought I could get back at him—do to him what he had done to me. A revenge, of sorts. A retaliation. *You cheat on me and I'll cheat on you.*

Izzi found out. She knew. She's smart. She knew I was having an affair and she kept my secret. And it ripped her apart. I never asked for this. I never meant to hurt her…

I never meant to hurt her…

Emilia had said the same thing about Charley.

I glance out of the window. A huge part of me is hoping to see Matt trudging back toward the cabin. The outside world glows dark with the sharp gray light of a storm. Wind whips snow through the bare branched trees. But no Matt. I'm alone.

Desperate for sleep, I feel my eyelids grow heavy, closing on my lonely view of the outside world. My head lolls to the side. My foot aches, burns, as do my fingertips, still half-frozen from the cold.

I never meant to hurt her…

If Charley's death really was an accident as Emilia claims, why remove her clothes? Her shoes? A million questions fill my head. But still, one question floats above all others, one that never fails to engulf me with regret every time it resurfaces inside my head: *Why did I make all the wrong choices?*

I don't know why I always have to be so damn impulsive. They will never forgive me. But can I ever forgive myself?

Either way, I don't deserve peace. And so I let my thoughts consume me, the firelight dancing in the shadows until I slowly fall asleep.

THE YEAR BEFORE

FILE NAME: JPN00.012.00030923.mp3

INT: Now, when you say your husband didn't handle it well, what do you mean? Did he yell? Call the police?

RES: No—yes…well, after the brick, my phone rang.

INT: And who was it?

RES: [redacted].

INT: And what did he say?

RES: I don't know. I never answered. He called all the time.

INT: But you saw his number, knew it was him.

RES: Yes.

INT: And what happened?

RES: He kept calling. He called and called and left a dozen voice mails. It got to the point where I wanted to shut off my phone, but I couldn't because [redacted] still hadn't come home.

INT: And how late was your daughter at this time? Her curfew was at ten, you said.

RES: And now it was…maybe around…midnight. I don't

know, I'm not sure about the time. I had… I'd been drinking.

INT: How are you feeling now—with the, with the wine? Have you been drinking today?

RES: I'm fine. Are you serious?

INT: I need to clarify your state of mind at this time.

RES: How the fuck do you think my state of mind is at this fucking time?

INT: I didn't mean it like—

RES: Are you kidding me? I'm—I'm trying my… I'm trying. I'm calm. [inaudible]

INT: You're handling this incredibly well. So, um… getting back, how did your husband react to the phone calls from [redacted]? I'm assuming he was unaware who was calling you?

RES: He didn't know. I'd never told him about the affair. He only found out when…he took my phone.

[00:50:00]

INT: He took your phone?

RES: Yes. He didn't believe me when I said I didn't know who was calling so late. I was in the kitchen and I didn't know he'd taken my phone into the bathroom.

INT: And what did he do with your phone?

RES: When he came out, his face—his face was bright red. He'd listened to [redacted] voice messages.

INT: So now, your husband knew of the affair…

RES: … Yes.

INT: How did he react?

RES: How do you think he reacted?

INT: I just need an answer. Do you feel like taking a break?

RES: No. No—it's fine. Well, to answer your question— he didn't handle it well, why would he? I wouldn't have handled it well, either. And when he started screaming, I told him how he was the one who'd said we should see other people. He said he didn't think I'd actually do it…especially not so soon. So then—the phone rang again.

INT: And what happened?

RES: [redacted] answered it.

INT: Your husband answered your phone?

RES: Yes.

INT: What did he say?

RES: "Who's this? Why are you calling my wife? Are you fucking her? Are you the one fucking my wife?"

INT: Then what?

RES: Nothing. [redacted] didn't respond, he just hung up on my husband.

INT: Do you know why [redacted] kept contacting you a month after ending it with him?

RES: No, I have no idea.

INT: His voice mails...all his voice mails, texts...none of them suggested the reason why he'd wanted to contact you?

RES: They were what you'd expect—"I miss you. Please give me another chance. You made me a better man." I just, I couldn't. I couldn't do it again. Not to myself, not to my family.

INT: Okay. So what did you do then? Your husband knows of your affair. Your daughter is late returning from her curfew. A brick has been thrown through your window.

RES: I went upstairs, went to wait for her to come home.

INT: And your husband?

[00:52:16]

RES: He said he was going to go lie down in the guest bedroom. He didn't want to look at me at this point.

INT: So your husband went to sleep in the guest bedroom?

RES: Yeah…he wasn't going to sleep with me in the same bed, there was no way. I wouldn't, if I were him.

INT: And your daughter, did you ever see her come home?

RES: Just briefly. She came into the bedroom. I told her how worried I was, that she needs to be home on time. She told me to please just stop worrying so much about her. Then I fell back asleep.

INT: And what woke you?

RES: Her scream.

Thursday, December 22

36

Wake up.

The voice is unmistakable. I roll over on my side, almost topple off the edge.

Wake up, Mom.

I don't want to move. My body is heavy. My muscles are stiff. A little hand presses on my shoulder, shakes gently.

Mom, wake up. I want you to see.

My eyes yawn open, see the outline of a girl dressed in white.

"Izzi?" My lips curl around her name like a warm wind.

Mom, don't you see?

I wake with a jolt.

Her name hovers on my lips. *Izzi.* I want to call out to her, to see if she's here. The dream felt so real. Too real.

It's dark. I'm in Matt's cottage on the sofa. The fire has died, leaving nothing but embers in the ashes. Matt still hasn't returned. I hope that means he has things under control with Emilia at the school and the girls are safe.

I stretch my body awake, glance out of the window to see the sky is still dark, the air settled from sharp gray to a soft milky hue. It's still snowing, but much less than last night. The blizzard has died down, the snow now a faint trickle of fat snowflakes lazily drifting through the icy air.

I drink an old glass of water resting on the fireplace mantel, check my pack of cigarettes. Matt told me not to let anyone in before he left last night, but I desperately need some fresh air. Plus, maybe I can make the trek back to the school to help him.

With one cigarette left, I sling on my coat, slip on my boots, unlock the door, and head outside, wrapping an arm around myself in an attempt to keep warm in the early morning frost. A bare hint of sunrise bleeds from above the forest, deep purple and smudged, like a bruise. Snow blankets the courtyard, the naked trees standing black as coal, stark and ghostlike against the white winter snow.

The world is silent and peaceful as I walk through the woods, the smoke mixing with the cold as it floats away in a cloud. I let my mind wander to my dream. How I saw Izzi. How she hovered over me, trying to tell me something. What was she saying? I focus, push away all other thoughts, try to stitch the dream back together.

Izzi came to me. She was in the cottage, standing near the fireplace. I saw her. I swear she was real. She was wearing white. A man's white tee-shirt, long and baggy, falling past her hips. The dream is fading fast. I try to hold on to it, try to remember. But I can't.

Snowflakes lace in my hair, melting in the strands. Shivering, I turn around, head back to Matt's cottage, boots crunching in the snow with each step. Another sound intermingles with my footsteps. I stop walking, listen close.

The sound of someone shoveling snow stops me cold. Through the trees, a shadowy smudge lingers in the darkness. The shoveling continues, the hollow sound echoing *scoop scoop scoop* across the courtyard. I squint to better see in the dim light.

I see a man—tall, black hair, black beard encroaching across his sharp, bitter face. His back is bended, lowered down as he shovels scoops of snow, heaves it over his shoulder.

Blake.

Turning on a heel, I head back toward the cottage. I don't want to walk past Blake. I can't face him. Not now. Not after everything that's happened.

"Who's there?"

Shit.

I stop. Turn around. Rearrange a frozen smile on my face, hope he can't see the fear lingering beneath.

He heads toward me now, drops the shovel in the snow.

"Hey," he says, sauntering over like a seesaw. "You got a spare?"

I look to the extinguished cigarette in my fingertips. I'd forgotten it was even there. "No, sorry. My last one."

"*Tsk*, damn."

"Sorry..." *Sorry sorry sorry.*

"I'm just trying to catch up on shoveling," he explains, though I never asked. "The trick is to keep it up all night, even if it's still snowing, you know?"

I nod warily, step away.

"You know," Blake says, pounding a fist on his hip. "I can't sleep. Haven't been since...since it all happened."

"No," I offer, feeling the need to turn back to him, to be

polite, to show I'm listening, even after I accused his innocent son of murder. "Right, of course not."

"Figure I'd come out here, do some work. Work off some anger with the snow."

"Yeah, I get it."

Heavy silence.

"I'm—I'm trying to keep my mind off things," he says, rubbing his black-bearded neck.

I shouldn't feel this way, feel so uncomfortable around him, so tense, my entire body a clenched fist. I know that. Blake didn't kill Charley. Emilia did. But still, I can't help but feel this way. With the thought, the tension returns. Ever so slightly, I begin to recede back toward the cottage, to safety. Blake notices, edges closer.

He glances to the ground, kicks at the snow. When he looks up at me, his eyes fall from my face, lips pursed. "You look like you've seen a ghost. Why are you out here, anyway?"

I stop breathing. "I—I don't know. I should go." My words sound like a gasp.

"Why, when we just got to talking?"

I say nothing, try to come up with an excuse to leave. The moment I'm about to bolt away and disappear, Blake inhales a deep breath. "I've been wanting to talk to you…" He trails off. "I've been wanting to ask you if you and the private eye were taking off, now the storm's almost over."

"We—we are, yeah."

Awkward, I glance around, look for someone else out here who can whisk me away. I reach a hand behind me, feel my phone in my back pocket. I could call Matt. He would be here in minutes. My back stiffens. I wouldn't have minutes.

"I can't believe it," Blake says. "Rich family gets to hire a private eye to check into their kid's death. If it was my kid, hell, you think anyone would give a shit? You think anyone would even care?"

"Of course," I say, strained and stiff, no longer able to mask my fear.

I fine-tune my hearing, listen for any police sirens. Even though it's still snowing, maybe they can make it up to the school. *No*, I think to myself. *They can't. The snow may be calming but the roads are still impassable. We're trapped here. Stuck here...*

A heartbeat later, the snow begins to fall heavier, the lazy, fat snowflakes drifting sideways from incoming wind.

"Yeah, sure," he says. "That's what all of your kind say. Always so polite."

I hold my breath, look away, step away, keep my sights on Matt's cottage up ahead.

"Hey—"

I freeze, slowly turn back to face him.

"You know," Blake says. "Jeremy is my son. You may think I'm a coldhearted bastard, but I do what I have to do to protect my son. That is *my* job." He looks at me, features contorting into a look of sheer pain. "But I—I let myself get caught up... I should've told the truth. But I didn't. I was a coward. Now that's something *I* have to live with."

My heart does a little flip. Suddenly, I feel light-headed. "Told the truth about what?" I ask. *Play dumb. Walk away.*

"Never mind. Just go," Blake chokes out. To my shock, tears run down his stubbled cheeks, their tracks shiny in the soft lantern light. Wiping his eyes dry with the back of a hand, he adds, "Go. Forget you ever saw me."

37

The snow grows heavier as I trudge through the woods back to Matt's cottage. In the distance beneath the starry night sky is a small outbuilding I've never noticed. Light oozes through the windows, a soft orange glow cascading through the bare trees. A shadow flickers past a window.

Someone is inside.

Alice?

Could it be? Could she have been inside all this time? I have to see. I have to know. Escaping the woods, I limp down the hill into a clearing toward the building, footsteps crunching in the virgin snow, hoping every second Alice is inside—*alive*.

In the darkness, the building looks like a converted greenhouse, wide windows like mirrors beneath the fading stars. Skeletons of ivy vines cling to the glass walls like a kraken pulling a ship into the sea. Icy wind hits me as I enter a tiny vestibule, the cold air sucking into a vortex.

I tug the door open. "Alice? Hello?"

No one responds.

I step inside. The room is open and bright, a vast and empty space, the only object a single easel perched in the center. The piercing scent of turpentine singes my nose. An artist's studio.

I pass a wall of shelves, little cubbyholes, each one labeled with a girl's name. There are dozens of them all rowed together. Some are empty, some bulge with crumpled papers and dirty aprons. Some have sketch pads curled to fit inside.

I near the easel in the center of the room. Taped to the side of the pencil-sketched canvas is a photograph. It's two women—two women I know well. They stand outside on a hot summer day, hands held near their foreheads to blot out the sun.

One is Emilia. She looks younger than she is now. Happy. Blond hair cascades down her shoulders, pink smile pinching faint dimples in her blushed cheeks. She stands with a girl, around fourteen, rag-doll thin with long, raven-black hair.

Violet.

They look happy. They look normal. There's only one problem: their eyes have been scratched out.

I back away from the easel, unable to look away from the photograph. I inch backward until I tap into the wall of cubbyholes, until I've neared the door.

Izzi's words from my dream finally reach me.

Mom, don't you see?

The realization hits me hard.

Then, beside me, movement.

"Dr. Madeline?"

My heart thumps in my chest. I turn around. "*Shit*—you scared me," I cry out. "What are you doing here?" I assumed all the girls would still be asleep this early in the morning.

Violet laughs lightly, walks toward me. "I'm sorry," she

says. "I just *had* to get out of there. Too much talk of—I don't know—of Alice, you know? Like, I get it, she's missing, can we please move onto something else?" She rolls her eyes, meets my gaze. She looks dead tired, exhausted, dark circles beneath darker eyes.

Words escape me. I offer a weak smile.

"Do you like my latest painting?" she asks, eyes nudging over my shoulder.

I turn around. Next to the wall of cubbies, an incomplete painting leans against the wall.

"It's beautiful," I say, and I mean it. It's a portrait of a girl, beautiful wide eyes filling the breadth of the canvas. She has freckles trailing across her hint of a nose, the pencil sketch of future hair swirling around full cheeks.

The background is still empty, the details incomplete. But still, it's stunning, though the more I stare at it, the more something sits uneasily with me. Something about it feels off. Her mouth is set in a grimace. Her eyes are too wide, frightened, shocked. Afraid.

"Who is it?" I ask.

"Um…it's Charley."

"Charley?"

"Yeah. My mom has been trying to get me to do something nice for her family."

I wander back toward the easel standing in the center of the room, pretend I've never noticed it before, think of a question I can use to prompt her to speak.

I turn. Violet stands directly behind me now. Too close. Staring. Unblinking. The scent of her patchouli perfume burns my nose, more burning and painful than the turpentine. She sniffles, her slick black hair waving around her face like tentacles. I'm afraid to move, afraid to even breathe. I wonder if she can see my pulse leaping through the skin at my throat.

I inch away until my back presses against the wall. "Do you have anything you want to tell me?" I ask, throat closing up, tears burning my eyes, turning her into nothing more than a hazy dark outline, a shadow.

Coiled silence.

Emilia's voice: *Your self-preservation—just for a second—overwhelms you. And you'd do anything to protect what you love. Anything.*

Not what—*who*.

Could Emilia give a false confession to save someone she loved?

Could she do it to save her *daughter*?

A million buzzing thoughts slam inside my head. Everything collides at once. Fireworks.

Emilia didn't delete the footage from the day Charley disappeared to save herself. She did it to save her daughter. To save *Violet*. I imagine Emilia, hunched over her desk, eyes staring at the screen, images floating in the glaze of her eyes.

What did she see? There are no cameras in the woods or outside around campus. So it had to have been something that happened inside the school that no one else was supposed to see. What was on that deleted footage?

"Emilia—your mother. She was protecting you, wasn't she?" I say flatly, realization slamming into my head.

Violet's eyes widen.

There *was* something about Emilia's confession in her office yesterday that felt wrong. She claimed she'd pushed Charley, that Charley had lunged at her, angry Emilia had called her mom to tell her about her relationship with Alice. But if Emilia had pushed Charley to her death, when would she have had the chance to remove her jacket and her shoes?

No. Emilia didn't kill Charley, no matter how much she claimed she did. Emilia was taking the blame, confessing to the murder in order to save someone else.

And there's only one person in the world I would do that for. Only one person in the world I would sacrifice my life for. My daughter. If I were given the chance, I'd do it in a heartbeat.

"Your mother confessed, you know," I admit, studying Violet's pretty face. "She confessed to save you." Violet's bottom lip begins to tremble. "I'll only ask you this once," I whisper. "Why did you kill Charley?"

The sun rises higher over the trees, setting the studio on fire with a fuzzy golden glow. A nebula of dust motes float in the air between us.

Violet says nothing.

"Why!" I slam a fist against the wall, stinging pain gushing up my arm. "What did Charley ever do to you?"

Rage builds inside me as Violet slyly looks me up and down. Thick, fat tears slide down her cheeks. Even now I can't tell if they're real.

She stays silent.

"Let me tell you what I think really happened," I begin, hoping what I'm doing is right.

If I can bait her, if she lands in my trap, tries to correct my story, I may get out of here without any trouble. My hand itches toward the phone in my back pocket. If I could just record it, record her confession, I could end this, once and for all.

My head spins a hundred miles an hour. I try to find a soft place to land.

"I think Charley did something to hurt you," I say, voice shaking. "I don't know what, exactly. But you killed her. You brought her out to the woods and you left her for dead."

Violet's green eyes jolt awake, stare directly through me, straight through the back of my head.

"No—"

I go. Keep going. Go until she snaps.

"You lost control. Somehow, you lost it. You killed Charley. You killed her in the hallway outside of the library. Hannah saw blood on the floor. You carried her, brought her body out to the ravine," I say, my voice losing its shakiness, its hesitation. Anger swells inside me. "You rolled her body down the hill, thought no one would ever find her, removed her clothes and shoes to try to hide any evidence, maybe *your* DNA. Maybe *your* blood mixed with hers. And Alice—Alice figured out what you did to Charley, didn't she? It took her a week, but she figured it out. She was scared. When she left the school, she was terrified, she—"

"That's not true!"

"Say you did it!"

"*Okay!*" Violet's screams bounce off the glass walls, ricochet back like a bullet. "Okay..." she whispers, wipes her nose with the back of a hand. "But—you've *always* been wrong about one thing. I didn't kill Charley for just no reason. I would *never* just 'lose it' for no good reason. I did it for someone I *love*. I did it for Blake."

38

I grab hold of the wall, steady myself, feel the earth spin.

Violet looks up at me. Guilt oozes from her face.

"Blake?"

Violet sobs, horrible sounding sobs, choking on her own tears.

"What does any of this have to do with him?" I ask after a heartbeat, giving me time to steady myself. I have to default to professional mode, try to get what I can out of her. Who knows if this moment will ever come again.

A flash from the day Alice disappeared ambushes me. Standing in the hallway. Violet. The heavy plastic art box. Her muddy boots. *I've been painting plein air this morning.*

"It—it's okay. You can tell me." I gulp down the giant knot in my throat, calmly adjust my glasses, struggle to take a breath.

"It wasn't an accident," she whispers. "I did it."

"Don't lie—"

"I'm *not*! That night, I was in the library with Blake." I nod for her to continue, keep my mouth shut, nearly bite my lip off. "We were...*you know*." She raises an eyebrow, gives her shoulder a little lift. "Charley came in. She saw us. She said she'd tell Emilia—she'd tell my mom. I had *just* ratted out her relationship with Alice. My mom split them apart, called their parents. They were humiliated. Of *course* Charley would pounce on the opportunity to tell my mom about Blake!"

"You killed Charley because you thought she'd tattle on you?"

Violet scoffs. "I told you why I was forced to come here. I told you everything—that night in the library. If you were even *listening*, you'd know!"

I remember that night. How the firelight danced across her face. How she looked at me, checking my reaction when she confessed she had gotten pregnant by an older man. How her mother took her away from him, from the situation. It's something I would have done, too, with Izzi. I'd take her, force her, to come with me, far, far away. Emilia did nothing wrong in *that* situation. But then neither did Violet.

Blake did.

The man who got Violet pregnant did.

If Izzi dated an older man, I don't know what I'd do. Try to break them apart? Ground her? Chase him with an axe? Lock her in her room? There is no good choice. There is no good ending. All we can do is hope we raised our daughters right—to be strong, smart, courageous, fierce.

Wise.

But that's the thing about wisdom. It doesn't just rub off of you, onto your child. If it did, everything would be different. Wisdom has to be earned. People have to make their own choices. Learn from their own mistakes. As much as we hate it. As much as we hate seeing our babies suffer. As much as I hated seeing Izzi...

I shake my head clear.

All around, it's a horrible situation to be in—for Violet—and for Emilia.

"My mom got this job, and she dragged me with her," Violet cries. "Before we moved, I asked her to promise one thing—that no one here would find out she was my mother. She was *always* ashamed of me. I wanted her to know I was ashamed of her, too."

"Emilia kept your secret," I say. "No one knew. Not even me."

A look of pride fills Violet's face. She gulps it down. "She made me suffer all this time—alone—with no one to talk to." She stops. Tears storm in the rims of her eyes. "She knew I was pregnant. She knew, and she took me away. The only place I was allowed to be was a place for girls only. I know what she thinks of me. I know what she sees when she looks at me. She only got this stupid job because of *me*—to punish *me*!"

"So when Charley saw you with Blake—another older man..."

"What do you mean *another* older man?"

I tilt my head, study her. "But I thought—"

"Blake is the only boyfriend I've ever had," Violet says. "He left everything to come and be with me. It took him months before the job opened, but I made sure it was open. And we were together, no matter what my mom said or did, we were going to be together."

"*Blake*—he was," I breathe out, eyes dropping subconsciously to her tiny belly. "He was the father."

Violet pouts, gives a single, sharp nod. "My mom was the one who hired him. She had no idea who he was. And she could never know. If she ever found out, if *anyone* ever found out, I'd be—*he'd* be—he'd lose his job, his son, he'd lose everything. He knows I'm only sixteen." She sniffles, shoulders shaking up and down with ugly sobs. "I *had* to stop Charley from saying anything. We got into a fight. I grabbed her, pushed her. I grabbed Charley's head—"

"Oh *god*—"

"She *tripped*! She hit her head on the fireplace." Violet lifts a hand, touches a spot on her skull. "She fell. We didn't know what to do, I—we panicked!"

"Charley fell?" I ask incredulously.

Violet nods, eyes wide and innocent.

I think of Hannah. How Violet had called her a liar. Hannah had told me she'd seen blood in the hallway the night Charley disappeared—in the hallway outside the library. The next morning, it was gone. I didn't believe her. Not really. But she'd been telling the truth.

That night, Hannah had seen Charley's blood.

"I know you're not who you say you are..." Violet mutters. "So I won't say anything—if *you* don't say anything."

"That's not going to work," I snap.

Violet's lips quiver. *"Fine!"* she explodes. "I smashed her head on the fireplace, does that make you feel better? She saw us and I—I did it." She looks at me, frantic, wild-eyed, boiling with rage from the inside out.

I'd seen that fireplace mantel. It was solid stone, thick and heavy.

That night I couldn't sleep. I'd followed a scream downstairs into the library. It was her scream, Violet's scream, I realize now. And then, I saw her. She'd asked me to tell her a story. I told her about the fortune-teller.

"What happened after you—killed her?"

I press my back firmer against the wall, my body suddenly too heavy for my bones to hold. I imagine my notepad in one hand, pen in the other. I slide my glasses down my nose, peer at her from over the tops of the rims, waiting. We're sitting in the library together, just the two of us. Imagine the ticking clock. The crackling flames.

The fireplace mantel where Violet cracked Charley's skull open.

Ticktock ticktock.

"We did what we had to."

"Oh, god…" I whisper under my breath. My stomach twists. "And you tried to blame it all on sleepwalking."

Violet shrugs. "That was my mom's idea." She stops, catches herself, looks up, her emerald eyes wide.

Nausea stings the back of my throat.

"Emilia helped you…"

"She saw the camera footage in the library," Violet explains. "She saw me and Blake and Charley. What else was she supposed to do?"

That's why Emilia always seemed to hate the mere idea of Matt and I staying on campus. She was afraid. Afraid we'd learn the truth. It's why she'd stolen my case files on Charley. What else had she done to make me want to leave? To make me go away?

How far would she go? How far would *any* of them go?

Far, a little voice inside me says. *As far as humanly possible.*

To save my daughter, to save Izzi… I'd do anything.

"Violet." I have to know, I have to. "Did you swap out my pills? Put ones that weren't mine into the bottle?"

Her lips twitch. "Yes," she says smugly.

"And the brick?" I ask, frantic, my body buzzing with tension. "How could you? Why?"

"Brick?" she asks. I study her face. She's motionless, no memory of the brick traipsing across her expression.

"Yes, a brick. Someone put a brick under my pillow," I

urge, frantic. "Someone—I need to know who. I need to know *why*."

Violet chuckles. "I don't know." Peering at me with disgust, she steps back, crosses her arms. "I don't even know where I'd *find* a brick."

My head spins.

No no no, she's lying, she has to be—

Violet takes another step back.

"And Alice," I say flatly. "She learned the truth—and you killed her."

Violet watches me, calm, still. She says nothing more, just glances down, picks lint off her sweater, holds the fuzzies out in her fingertips, lets them float lazily down to the floor.

"What did you do to Alice?" I beg, tears sliding down my cheeks. My lips tremble. I don't even bother trying to hide it. "Please tell me. I'll do anything—just tell me where she is."

"Alice," Violet begins, "needed to mind her own business."

I found something out, and I can't tell you.

Alice had learned the truth. She knew what Violet had done to Charley. Somehow, she knew. And she was terrified. So terrified she left the school, ran away, vanished. But why not tell someone? Why not tell *me*? I would've helped her, I would've—

"You know," Violet says softly. "It's all I can ever paint." Her gaze flickers toward the portrait of Charley leaning against the wall. "It's all I ever see. Every time I close my eyes. I see her eyes, wide open and staring."

Violet looks back at me, eyes dead.

Footsteps.

I twist. Too late.

My head explodes with shooting pain. My limbs contort. I fall, hands slapping the concrete floor. My glasses shoot off my face, slide across the room like a hockey puck. A foot nudges at my spine, flips me sideways.

Blake's panic-filled eyes dance with rage.

It's the last thing I see before the world collapses.

39

"Blake—Blake, please—"

Violet grapples with Blake's arms. He holds me, cradles me, my legs dangling in the air, my head snapped backward. I open my eyes, peer up at the blurry sunrise. I turn my head, see Violet marching beside us in the woods, her hands balled into fists, entire body shaking.

I look to Blake. He steps deeper and deeper into the woods, his hands curled around my waist, my thighs, as he carries me in his arms. He sees I'm awake, his dark eyes darting back and forth between us, calculating, thinking, plotting.

I look behind us. The light from the art studio looms farther and farther away.

"Violet—" My throat creaks.

Her face is bleary, the forest around me a haze without my glasses. I wriggle and writhe, try to find my strength. A hot pulse of fear bolts down my spine. The woods. Charley. Alice.

Violet and Blake left them for dead, right here, right in these woods. The realization hits me hard, floods me all at once. I'm surrounded by killers.

I try again, kick, pull, fight. He holds me tight, so tight my ribs pop. Everything I have inside me wilts.

"You know," Blake begins, "I'd be arrested for having sex with a minor. You know it and I know it. I'd be fired," he says. "If I lose my job, I lose my home. I'd have nothing. *Nothing.*" He cranes his head to Violet who walks silently beside us, biting back tears. "I had no choice. I had to. And now—her *mom* knows, and *you* know, and now that's too many people, you see? Too many people."

I look up at Blake. His eyes are sharp, unblinking. A muscle pops out from his jaw, face going red, slicked with sweat. Suddenly, he stops, lets me roll out of his arms. I thump onto the ground, my forehead connecting with a stone buried beneath the snow. I wince, grab my head, feel the slick warmth of blood.

Blake straightens his back, glances down at me, moves in my direction. I scramble away, hide behind a tree, my back against the cold, biting snow, stinging raw against my skin.

He stomps around the tree trunk, eyes flashing with rage. He stares down at me, straightens his back, a whip of silver growing from his fist.

He lunges for me, knife held high over his head.

My mouth stretches wide, open in a silent scream.

I pivot away, scramble to my feet, limp into the woods. I can't see—I can't see anything but shadows and flashes of orange sunlight escaping through the bare trees. Violet screams my name. I push myself until my lungs burst.

Izzi's voice: *Mom—run.*

I lurch into the forest.

I follow the direction of the sun, stagger toward Matt's

cottage, Blake and Violet close behind. The wind howls in my ears as I run, the cold clasping tight around my throat, plunging icy fingers deep into my lungs. I follow the flicker of lantern light ahead in the woods. Blake's footsteps pound behind me.

Twilight splashes the air a dark, angry red, too dark to see. My feet give out just as my lungs do. I crumple to the forest floor, the snow seeping through my flimsy pants, my foot pulsing with stinging pain. My body shudders with cold.

I silence my sobs, watch as Blake stops nearby, catches his breath, the knife glinting a perfect slice of silver from a flash of rising sun.

I could let him kill me. I could die, right here in these woods. Would Matt be the one to find me? Would Hannah? Or Kiara? Bitterness thickens inside me. I can't. Not here. Not like this. I dart behind a tree, scramble away, like a mouse.

Mom—hide.

My breath spurts out in quick little gasps, exhaustion sinking into my bones, the chill of the winter air biting every part of me.

Hide!

No, I can't hide. Not anymore.

Not again.

Then I see it. Just ahead, a tiny shack, snow piled high all around it, the wood siding nearly hidden by snow-laden pines.

The door catches in a snowdrift. I grab the metal handle, pull it open as I kick away the snow. Soon the door cracks open just enough for me to slide inside. I shut the door, press my back to it, slump to the floor. My chest heaves, gasping for breath in the icy air.

Stay silent. I have to stay silent. The only way they'll be able to find me is if they see my footprints in the snow. I open my eyes. It's dark inside, the faint breath of sunrise barely creeping in through cracks in the wooden slats. The shack is filled with junk, tools, all sorts of storage boxes and forgotten things, cobwebs creeping like connective tissue. Snow drifts in through holes in the roof, plunging to the dirt floor like waterfalls.

"Help me."

My spine goes straight.

"Please—help me."

I scramble off the floor toward the voice, pull away wooden crates, old tractor tires, piles of used, empty oil cans. And there she is.

Alice.

Her mouth is duct-taped, halfway peeled away on one side. Her wrists are bound, tied tight with zip ties that have cut deep into her skin. Red, angry lashes weep with caked blood, oozing down the sleeve of her pale gray coat.

"Oh, god, Alice," I whisper. "I'm here, it's okay, it'll be okay."

I grab her, pull her upward, peel the duct tape off her lips. Her body is frozen stiff and sore, and she whimpers.

"We have to be quiet, okay? We have to be quiet. I promise— I'll save you."

Alice nods. Tears fill her eyes. She's tired. So tired. Her body falls limp at my side. I lasso her arms around my neck, her wrists still bound, and slowly nudge open the wooden door.

No one is outside. The woods are still. If I can make it to the school, or even to Matt's cottage, we'll be safe. We'll survive. It's what I have to tell myself. It's all I have.

"Alice, try to stay quiet, okay? You're safe now. You'll be okay."

Alice nods again. Her head lolls to the side, drifts away on her shoulder.

In the distance, Blake crashes through the woods.

"Why are you making me do this?" he roars. *"Why?"*

Mom—run.

I can't. Not without Alice.

Run!

I run.

I drag Alice along, her legs barely moving. Her arms slung around my neck begin to choke the air from my lungs, so I use all the strength left in me to heave her onto my back, carry her like I used to carry Izzi, carry her like a child. She holds on, her arms still digging into my throat, but I have no choice.

I run.

Run until my legs disintegrate beneath me, become nothing but an itch of muscle and skin. Run until my back is close to snapping in two.

A flash of Blake's tan coat through the trees.

A twig snaps. I barrel over, fall in the snow, hands burning with cold. My lungs shrink. I gasp for air, pull my hands out of the snow, skin red and raw and bleeding.

Alice cries, slides off my back. She removes her arms from around my neck, detaching herself from me. I inhale a deep breath, cough—*shit*. Alice's blue eyes widen. I grit my teeth, grab her arm, pull her to her feet. If it ever comes down to saving her life or mine, I choose hers.

We run as fast as we can through the woods, toward the faint light glowing through the trees, toward Matt's cottage. My hands sting, my foot burns, every part of me pulses with pain. Alice cries every time her body moves. We charge toward the cottage, my hand a vise around Alice's tiny arm, as I scream for help, scream Matt's name, scream for anyone who can hear me.

I trip, foot ensnared, land on my belly, the air punched out of me. Alice falls sideways, slips into a snowbank, disappears from my sight.

Mom—run!

KATIE GARNER

I can't.

I flip onto my back. Stare at the blurry branches knitting together beneath the morning sky. In an instant, Blake stands over me, blocking out the fading stars. He licks sweat from his lips, lurches backward, forward. Kicks me in my lungs. The air stirs. An ocean of breath spurts from my lungs.

Mom—

Izzi, I love you.

The blade rushes toward my heart.

Thwack.

The sound of metal hitting bone. Blake crumbles into the snow, a heap of blood and cloth.

Violet screams.

Jeremy rushes to my side.

"Dr. Pine," he says, shaking me. "Dr. Pine!"

He pulls me up, holds my shoulders to keep me steady. Blake is sprawled on the ground on his chest, his face turned toward us, eyes open in final shock. Beside him rests his metal shovel, tossed into the snow, a smudge of blood where Jeremy had connected it with his skull.

"Oh my god, is he dead?" Violet falls to her knees, crawls to him, reaches out a hand, feels for a pulse. She flinches, yanks her hand away, her expression blank, her body trembling. She begins to sob.

Jeremy helps me to my feet. I gasp in pain, grip my arm. Blood clots through my sweater, drying to a jet-black stain.

We stand in silence, gulp down air.

"Alice—Alice!" I shout. "Are you okay?"

Slowly, she pokes her head over the mound of snow. I run to her, wrap my arms around her. The world spins. The stark white of freshly fallen snow. Black tree trunks, lines of darkest ink on white paper. The forest falls into an eerie calmness.

Violet's sobs grow quiet as she gently rocks herself back and forth over Blake's body. Then I remember. My phone is in my back pocket. With a bloodied hand, I pull it out. Violet's gaze is glued on Blake as I cross the small space between us, hold out the phone to her.

"It's over," I whisper. My hand shakes. I don't try to hide it.

She peers up at the phone, afraid, her body going rigid. I hold it closer. She keeps her eyes on it, studies it in my trembling hand. Her lips relax, tension slowly draining from her shoulders as she slumps, lifts a hand, reaches to take it from my grasp.

Violet examines the screen before tapping it on. She turns to look at Alice, dark brows creeping into thin lines of worry. She looks up at Jeremy, then slides her eyes to me.

"What's going to happen to me?" Violet asks softly. Her lips crack open as she cries, her skeletal smile stretching into a frown.

I inch away, lift a hand to my mouth, speak into the shell of my palm. "I don't know."

She breathes out deeply, glares at the screen, taps in 911.

"Hello," she whispers. "I'd like to confess to a murder."

40

Matt runs toward us through the forest. Jeremy helps Alice walk, slinging her arm over his shoulder. Matt and I drag Violet back to the school, holding her hands behind her back. Hopefully the police will arrive any moment.

We hover in the shadows beneath the carriage tunnel in silence. It may be my nerves about what Violet had confessed to me, but the time we spend waiting for the police strings on forever in numb silence. Every so often I glance at Matt, see him staring down at the top of Violet's head, watching and waiting for if she attempts to slip free.

Clutching my arm, I focus on the sunrise over the tops of the trees, watch the sky paint itself into tangles of wispy blues and pinks, suffused with deep gold. A leaf breaks loose from a snowbank, flutters across the top of the ice-slicked snow. I focus on anything to stop myself from yelling at her, from strangling her. I'm not sure what I'm capable of anymore, so

I keep my arms crossed tight over my chest, teeth biting my tongue.

I glance at my arm. Blood has saturated the sleeve of my sweater, but the wound has stopped bleeding. Luckily, Blake only managed to slash my skin. If he'd stabbed me, gone deeper, it would be a different story. Once the police arrive with first aid, I'll be okay. But I can't say the same for him.

We left Blake's body in the snow. It was Jeremy's idea to leave him. He may still be alive, his heartbeat too weak for us to hear. If he's alive, he may die of hypothermia. It was a chance we were willing to take.

Jeremy sits on the cold, icy ground beneath the carriage tunnel, arm wrapped around Alice beside him. She shivers, even with Jeremy's and Matt's coats wrapped tightly around her shoulders. Her skin has grown translucent and pale, as pale as the newborn snow. Every time I glance at her, her gaze is deadlocked on the back of Violet's skull.

Jeremy stands, moves away from Alice, comes to hover beside me. His shoulders are up near his ears, his hands shoved under his armpits to try to stay warm. He's spoken little since the woods, since he'd saved my life. I turn to see he's shifted his gaze up from the ground for the first time, onto me.

He gulps, screws his eyes shut. "I'm sorry," he whispers. When he opens his eyes, the sunlight glistens a glaze of tears over his brown eyes.

I choke back a sob, feel my throat begin to close. My muscles tremble from the cold, from the shock. It feels like the weight of a thousand winters all at once.

"You have nothing to be sorry for, Jeremy," I tell him. "You saved my life."

He nods, turns away, sits back down next to Alice. Finally, the distant sound of police sirens echoes up the long mountain drive.

Violet's entire body goes stiff as the sirens grow closer. "I'm scared," she mutters, taps her toes in the snow.

"You should've thought about that before." My voice is biting, harsh. I don't look at her. I can't.

"You know...you never told me," she croaks.

I peer at her. "Told you what?"

"What the fortune-teller told you. What was the secret to happiness?"

My shoulders slump. I focus on a dirty mound of snow. I can't bring myself to look at her, can't bring myself to look at anything as I whisper, "Never live in the past. Nothing can be changed."

Violet begins to cry. Matt steps behind me, keeps his grip on Violet's wrists tight. His warm breath hits my neck when he speaks. "Madeline, they should be here any second."

"Madeline," Violet mocks. Looking up at me, she coughs wetly. *"Madeline,"* she repeats eerily. Glancing at Matt, she ropes his eyes with hers as she speaks to me. "What do you think your detective would say if he knew about *your* past?"

Matt's head whips in my direction as the school's main door bursts open. Emilia runs toward us, slippers slapping the icy ground, worry etched across her face. She glances at Jeremy and Alice huddled together on the cobblestones, then up at Matt, whose hands hold her daughter's fragile wrists tight.

"What happened?" Emilia asks, eyes seized with stress. "What happened?"

I drag my gaze to her, drop my head down. Violet stares straight ahead, chin up, bottom lip trembling. A tear falls down her cheek as the sirens grow louder, the sun rising faster, blinding orange light flashing across the courtyard.

Emilia holds up a hand to block the sun from her eyes as a dark SUV trudges up the snowy drive, tires skidding in the snow.

Matt releases Violet's wrists as police open the doors and

storm out. Violet stands alone, looks over at her mother, petrified. An officer grabs hold of her shoulders, spins her around, clicks handcuffs around her wrists. Violet's gaze is glued on me, so afraid, her mouth open, twisted, emerald eyes flashing with fear, with pure undiluted panic.

Emilia gasps in shock, knees buckling, hand clenched over her mouth. Tears streak down her face. They'll come for her next—when Matt releases the voice recording I'd given him, however false her confession may have been. Even though she was lying, she still worked with Violet and Blake to cover up the murder of one of her own students.

It didn't matter if she did it to save her own daughter. It didn't matter how she'd turned her life upside down to take Violet out of a bad situation. How she'd left her home, uprooted her entire life in order to give her daughter a fresh start. She could have sacrificed the entire world. Emilia was still guilty, all the same. And she'll have to live with that guilt every day, as I have done with mine.

Flashes of movement catch my eye. I tilt my head back, see a line of faces pressed against a window upstairs. Rosemarie, Kiara, and Hannah watch as the officer places his hand on top of Violet's head, guttural sobs ripping through her as she bends her body into the back of the SUV, staring straight at me one final time.

I don't look away until the door slams shut behind her.

THE YEAR BEFORE

FILE NAME: JPN00.012.00030923.mp3

INT: So, you say your daughter's scream woke you?

RES: Yes.

INT: And…at this point in time, you were unaware any-one had entered your home?

RES: No—I was sleeping.

INT: When you were woken by your daughter's scream, where in the house would you say her scream was originating from?

RES: You mean, where was she?

INT: Yes—was she downstairs? In her bedroom?

RES: [inaudible] no—she was downstairs.

INT: Did you hear anything else—after you'd woken?

RES: Yes… I heard a gunshot.

INT: Just one?

RES: Yes. One. Then, I got out of bed, and I heard voices but at first I wasn't sure what I heard.

INT: What do you mean?

RES: ... I heard—I heard my husband. I could tell he wasn't alone.

INT: What made you come to that conclusion?

RES: I heard him run down the stairs. I heard a struggle, banging.

INT: So you were awoken by your daughter screaming, then a gunshot. Then your husband proceeded to go downstairs, where you say you heard him have a struggle with an intruder.

RES: Yes.

INT: And what did you do at this time?

RES: ... I—I wasn't sure, I didn't know what was happening.

INT: Because you were still drunk?

[00:54:02]

RES: I wasn't drunk. I had just woken up. I didn't know what was going on. I went into a panic, I guess.

INT: Did you call 911?

RES: No.

INT: Did you go downstairs?

RES: ... No.

INT: So what did you do at this time? Your daughter screamed. You heard a gunshot. You know someone is inside your home late at night. You don't call 911, and you don't go downstairs?

RES: No. I stayed in the bedroom.

INT: What did you do in the bedroom?

RES: ... I hid.

INT: You hid. Where did you hide?

RES: I hid in the closet.

INT: You hid in the closet.

RES: Yes, oh god... I didn't know what to do. I didn't know what I was thinking...

INT: Then what happened? Did you hear anything else?

RES: Yes...the dog—I hid in the closet...through the heating vent all I could hear was the dog.

INT: What did you hear?

RES: The dog—he kept barking barking barking. He wouldn't stop.

INT: Then what do you hear?

RES: Nothing. The dog kept barking. Then... I heard another gunshot.

INT: And what did you do when you heard a second gunshot?

RES: I stayed in the closet.

INT: You stayed—hiding in the closet?

RES: Yes.

INT: Did you have your phone with you?

RES: No. I think I'd left it with [redacted] in the kitchen after our fight. I think he still had it.

INT: So you're hiding in your bedroom closet upstairs [inaudible] no cell phone. You hear two gunshots. Your daughter screamed, your husband has a struggle with someone who had broken into your house. What do you do at this point?

[00:56:28]

RES: At that point, all I could think was if someone was going to come upstairs and find me.

INT: So what did you do?

RES: I couldn't move. I stayed in the closet until the dog stopped barking.

INT: And then?

RES: Then, um, I don't know, I quietly came out, saw no one was there. Then I went downstairs.

INT: You went downstairs. And now, you still had no access to a phone.

RES: No.

INT: And what did you hear?

RES: I didn't hear anything.

INT: No more gunshots, no barking?

RES: No. It was quiet.

INT: So you go downstairs. What do you see?

RES: At first, I see nothing. The lights are out. Then… I—I went to the kitchen and…

INT: Take your time.

RES: And in the kitchen I see [redacted] and [redacted]. And oh god…they were—there was blood— everywhere. I peek around a corner into the kitchen and—I—they're there. I know what happened.

INT: What do you think happened?

RES: They were shot.

INT: Did you check for a pulse?

RES: No—no, I didn't think about that. I knew they were… I could tell they were dead.

INT: What did you see?

RES: Please. Please don't make me…

[00:59:46]

INT: [redacted], I just need to hear your side of what happened. That's all.

RES: I—I saw my baby… I saw my daughter, [redacted], she was lying there, on the floor. She was wearing her father's white tee-shirt and there was—it was…god I'm [inaudible] to be sick.

PAUSE—BREAK IN AUDIO

41

The sun sets as we drive to the train station.

Matt and I ride in disjointed silence. I stare out of the window, watch as the world blurs into streaks of white and brown. And I'm grateful. Grateful I was able to save someone in the end, someone I'd once thought was lost to me. Alice will get the chance to grow up, to grow old. She'll have a life, something too often stolen from other girls just as young and innocent as she is.

Matt's eyes flicker to me, turn back toward the road. He shakes his head, tightens his grip around the steering wheel. "I've been meaning to tell you," he says. I turn to glance at him. His eyes are trained straight ahead, unwavering from the endless highway in front of us.

"Tell me what?"

Without turning, he says, "The final autopsy report came in." Finally, he drags his gaze to meet mine.

My heart climbs up my throat. "What did it say?"

Matt gulps, licks his lips. "Charley died of hypothermia," he whispers. "After everything she'd suffered. After everything they did to her. She still could've survived. In the end, she always could've been saved." He swipes beneath his eye, wipes the stray tear across the breast of his peacoat. "How the fuck do I tell her mother that?" He cries, and I cry with him, side by side, the only sound the muffled road noise surrounding us.

Charley froze to death, outside, alone, just as we feared. A choking sadness overwhelms me. I say nothing. There's nothing to say. Not anymore. I chew the inside of my cheek. Looking at Matt, at his sudden sadness, I want to fall apart.

"What are the odds? Charley's mother put her in a private school thinking it would be safer," he says, staring straight ahead. "But she lost her anyway."

"I know," I whisper. But he doesn't hear.

Somewhere, deep inside, I think we knew. I think we both knew. Just as somewhere inside her, I think Violet wanted me to know the truth. Maybe, underneath it all, we weren't that different. We were both hiding secrets. Both composed of mostly gray parts.

Witnessing Violet confess her guilt to me in the art studio had unlocked something inside me. Violet could've been free. She could've walked away. She'd barely been a suspect. She could've denied everything. Emilia made sure all evidence was erased. It was over. But still, she told the truth.

It's my turn now.

I'm going home, whatever that means. And no matter what awaits me there, I'll face it. I have no other choice. I lean my head against the cold window, close my eyes until we reach the train station, never speaking a word.

Soon, the station comes into view. The bell rings as I step out of Matt's SUV. He wheels my luggage out from the trunk.

We stop. Face each other. I blow warm air into my hands, rub them together, careful not to disturb the bandage on my palm.

He takes a step closer, stops when his arm touches mine. "You know," he begins, head angled down, "you don't give yourself enough credit."

"Credit?"

Matt nods. "Yeah. You were my Hail Mary, Dr. Madeline Pine. Without you, *nothing* would've been solved. And who knows if Alice would've ever been found. This whole thing could've ended up being just as awful as that case you had last year, the one I'd heard about. The, um…" He stops, snaps his fingers. "The Strum case."

I shiver. All thoughts I had inside my head vanish. "I—I don't deserve any credit," I say numbly.

He licks his lips, moves closer. His face is serious now, his jaw set. "We both know the truth," he says, eyes aimed on my lips. "We both know it was *you* who saved her life. But I have to ask you—just one question."

"I think you've earned that."

He smiles, but for once, it doesn't reach his eyes. "Standing outside of the school before the police came, what did Violet mean when she asked what I would think if I knew about your past?"

I let out a strangled laugh. "I have no idea," I whisper. "Maybe it was her final attempt at trying to shift attention off herself."

"That's what I thought, too," he says, wrapping an arm around my shoulders. His sudden touch takes me by surprise. The train roars forward, brakes squealing in the cold.

Slowly, we detach.

I turn away. Thank him. Wish him goodbye.

Another life, maybe. Another life, and he might've been mine.

Adjusting my tote bag on my shoulder, I walk toward the train when he calls out to me.

Turning, I drink in the sight of him one last time. He smiles at me, fondly, satiated, as if he'd seen the future and was simply content. He clasps his hands in front of him, speaks loudly above the roar of the engine.

"What will you do now?"

I mirror his contented smile, step up the steep staircase.

"I'm going home to my family."

THE YEAR BEFORE

FILE NAME: JPN00.012.00030923.mp3

INT: Okay, we're back in the room. [redacted] had to use the ladies' room. Are you feeling better? Here's some water, tissues.

RES: [inaudible] thanks. I'm fine. I'll be fine.

INT: Now, we left off with you—walking into the kitchen. What did you see when you entered the kitchen?

RES: I saw my daughter.

INT: And what else did you see?

RES: I saw my husband.

INT: What else?

RES: I saw them on the floor. They'd been shot. There was…their blood was everywhere. It was a lake— so much—too much blood.

INT: You're assuming they've been shot, or do you know they've been shot?

RES: I'm—I'm assuming they'd been shot. I heard the gunshots.

INT: And what do you do at this time? You said you didn't check for a pulse?

RES: No. They were both dead.

INT: Who else was in your house?

RES: ...[redacted].

INT: [redacted], your lover—your ex-lover, correct?

RES: Correct.

INT: And where was he?

RES: He was on the floor near my husband.

INT: And did you check his pulse?

RES: No.

[01:07:43]

INT: What did you do? Did you call 911?

RES: No.

INT: What did you do at this time? You come downstairs, you see both your husband and your daughter have been shot. You don't check for their pulse. You don't call 911.

RES: No.

INT: So what did you do, [redacted]? Tell me.

RES: I—I looked at my husband.

INT: And what did you see?

RES: I saw… I saw he was looking up at me.

INT: Was he alive or dead?

RES: … He was dead.

INT: He was dead. Okay. And what did you do?

RES: He was just looking at me. H-his eyes were open. I knew what happened—I saw the bat…it had…it was still in his hand.

INT: You saw your husband was still holding a baseball bat?

RES: Yeah.

INT: Was it metal? Wood?

RES: Metal. Silver.

INT: And what did you do with that bat?

RES: … I took it.

INT: You took it.

RES: Yeah.

INT: Then what did you do?

RES: I took it and I saw [redacted] on the floor. He had a gun next to him.

INT: You see the man who you had broken up with, the man you were having an affair with, in your home, on your floor, a gun next to him?

RES: Yes.

INT: So what did you believe had happened at this point?

RES: I knew he'd broken in.

INT: And [inaudible] what else?

[01:10:51]

RES: I knew he'd come in and shot my family.

INT: And your husband defended himself with a metal baseball bat?

RES: Yeah. He kept it in the linen closet upstairs.

INT: So your husband, who'd been sleeping in the guest bedroom, hears your daughter scream, gets the metal baseball bat he kept in the closet upstairs, and goes into the kitchen to see a man in his home.

RES: I assume, um, yes...

INT: And your husband fought with this man, a man he'd never seen before?

RES: No—not to my knowledge, he'd never seen him.

INT: So your husband believed it to be a home intruder who'd just shot his daughter in your home?

RES: Yeah.

INT: And you come down to see your husband and your daughter shot dead in your kitchen, the man who you'd been having an affair with holding the gun that shot them?

RES: Yes. The gun had fallen from his hand but it was right next to him.

INT: Are you sure? Look at me, [redacted]. Are you sure the gun was not in his hand? [inaudible]

RES: I… [inaudible] I… Yeah, uh, yes. The gun was in his hand.

INT: Okay. Good. The gun was in [redacted] hand. And what did you do at this point?

RES: I—I didn't know what to do.

INT: Did you check his pulse?

RES: No.

INT: Did you believe him to be alive or dead at this point?

RES: Alive.

INT: And how did you know your ex-lover was still alive, after struggling with your husband and shooting your husband?

RES: Because…he looked at me.

INT: He looked at you?

RES: Yeah.

INT: But you knew he had entered your home illegally and shot your husband and your daughter?

RES: Yeah.

INT: Did you see any blood on or near [redacted], your ex-lover.

RES: Yes.

INT: Where?

RES: His head.

[01:13:49]

INT: Why do you believe he had blood on his head?

RES: There was blood on the bat. I assumed my husband had hit him with it.

INT: Your husband hit the intruder, your ex-lover, in the head with a metal baseball bat, in self-defense?

RES: Yeah.

INT: And then [redacted] shot your husband?

RES: Yes. That's what I assumed, yeah. He was on the floor and he looked up at me.

INT: And did he say anything?

RES: No.

INT: Did you say anything to him?

RES: ... No.

INT: Are you sure?

RES: Yes.

INT: What did you do with that metal baseball bat?

RES: ... I knew what he'd done.

INT: Tell me, [redacted]. It's okay. I'm here [inaudible] you. Tell me, what did you do with that metal baseball bat?

RES: I killed him.

42

I close my eyes, see *His* face.

Look at what I've done. Look at what you made me do.

The mind is amazing. How it can blur what is truth and what isn't. How it can make things disappear until you call it out of your memory and whisper to it, *you're real.*

I remember everything.

I just don't want to.

Violet's words echo back to me: *I know you're not who you say you are.*

You're right, Violet.

I'm not.

Saturday, December 31

43

Two hours until the ball drops.

I sit propped up in bed, sipping hot chocolate, hot water running for a bath. Candles light every inch of my bedroom like I'm about to have a séance. The TV is muted, the light tossing flickers of gold across the walls.

Charley's murder investigation has blown up the past few days, and Matt refuses to take credit for catching her killers. Sometimes, when he's on the nightly news, I pause the TV on his face.

Shadow Hunt Hall has declared bankruptcy. Emilia is gone, her trial scheduled the same time as Violet's. Matt helped build an entire case against her, thanks to what I'd taped on the voice recorder. Sometimes, I daydream of visiting Emilia in prison. But I always decide against it.

I listen until water reaches the top of the tub, run to turn off the faucet. I lean my head over to feel the steam on my skin, open my eyes, see fog has clouded my glasses.

Slinking off my robe, I walk back to toss it on my bed and grab my phone. I click it on, see the wallpaper—Izzi's picture, alive and brilliant and smiling—standing in our kitchen on her first day of high school. Lifting the phone to my ear, I listen to Dave's voice mail to me. The last one he'd ever left.

Hey, just wanted to call and say hi. I hope things are going okay at work. Izzi is fine. She's upstairs now. She told me she wants to talk to you about something, so maybe when you come home, keep that in mind. Okay, talk to you soon… Love you.

I never found out what she'd wanted to talk about.

I toss my phone on the bed, grab a book to read in the bath. I've patched together the pages of *Dark Side*—the same copy I had destroyed at the school. The one I'd ripped all the pages out of, convinced it wasn't mine. One by one, I'd pieced them back together, a Frankenstein edition. Some days, when I look at it resting on my nightstand, I think of how I should burn it in the fireplace. But I never do.

I'm not even sure why I stole it from the library. I should've thrown it away. It was ruined, anyway. But I did. I stole it, even though I already own a copy. I like to think of it as a memento, I guess. Something small to have, something that reminds me of the week I'd spent at Shadow Hunt Hall, the week that'd opened my eyes so I could see myself clearly.

I pick up the book, walk into the bathroom, flip to the back cover, see the author photo. Such a beautiful picture.

My phone rings. No one calls me, not anymore. Only the same unknown number, again and again. I sigh, wanting to go enjoy my bath before the water goes cold. But I've put this off long enough.

I answer the call, press the phone to my ear.

"Hello?"

A long sigh of annoyance. "Hello, this is Detective Wis-niewski with the Suffern Police Department."

"Hi, how are you?"

"Good, fine. I have to advise you that this call is on a re-corded line."

"Okay."

"May I ask where you were on Friday, December 16?"

Suddenly, I realize I'm standing naked in my bathroom. I turn off the lights and slide into the tub, my skin rubbing the bottom of the porcelain.

"I was... I was out of town," I say, water splashing onto the phone. "That morning I took a train to upstate New York."

"Are there any witnesses who can attest to that?"

"I have the ticket. I can prove it to you." I pause. Exhale. "What is this about? Am I in some kind of trouble?"

Silence.

But the man on the other end doesn't have to say a word. I know all too well what this is about.

"I'm afraid we have some bad news regarding a person you may have been in contact with recently—a Dr. Madeline Pine. We understand tomorrow is a holiday, but if you would be willing to come down to the station to answer a few ques-tions, we can provide you with more information than we can offer you over the phone."

"You want to question me?"

"If you're unable to get here on your own, we'll send a cruiser to pick you up, ma'am."

"Yes," I whisper. "Fine, I'll come by."

"We'll expect you at seven. Ask for Detective Morrow when you arrive."

"Yeah, I will. Good night."

"Thank you for your cooperation, Mrs. Strum. See you tomorrow to further discuss."

I hang up, drop my phone onto the bath mat, slide down into the water to wet my hair. I'd propped the book up on the windowsill dangerously close to a vanilla-scented candle. Maybe it will catch on fire.

Maybe if a million things were different, it could've been my face on the back of a book.

THE YEAR BEFORE

FILE NAME: JPN00.012.00030923.mp3

INT: You killed him. And at this point, you saw he had killed your husband and your daughter and still held the gun he'd used to kill them—the gun was still in his hand, correct?

RES: Yes. Correct.

INT: And you feared he would use the gun to kill you, correct?

RES: Um, uh—yes, that's correct.

INT: So before he had the chance to discharge his weapon on you, you subdued him with a metal baseball bat?

RES: [inaudible] did, yes.

INT: Do you believe you acted in self-defense?

RES: Yes...

INT: Can you please describe how you killed him?

RES: I—I hit him in the head.

INT: In self-defense?

RES: ... Yes.

INT: How many times did you hit him?

RES: I don't know.

INT: How many would you say? Once, twice?

RES: I—maybe, um, four or five times.

INT: You hit him in the head until you felt confident he was dead?

RES: Yes.

INT: And then what did you do?

RES: I don't remember.

INT: Did you call 911?

RES: No.

INT: Did you stay in the kitchen?

RES: Yes.

INT: And what did you do?

RES: I—I sat with them.

INT: You sat with them?

RES: Yes. I stayed with them.

INT: And you still did not call 911 at this point?

RES: No.

INT: Why didn't you call 911 at this point?

RES: I—I was in shock. I didn't know what to do.

INT: And, uh, did you ever call 911?

[01:16:07]

RES: No.

INT: What do you remember happened next?

RES: The police came.

INT: Yes, the police came. A neighbor heard the gunshots and called 911.

RES: Okay.

INT: Did you ever plan on calling the police yourself?

RES: I—I don't know.

INT: When the police came, they found your back door open. He had entered through there, presumably. Do you remember locking the back door? Do you remember turning on your home's security system?

RES: I don't know. I don't think so.

INT: What do you remember happened next?

RES: The police came, and I was in the ambulance.

INT: What do you remember seeing?

RES: … Oscar. I saw him running. He was running away, down the street. I couldn't get him. I—I couldn't.

He was running so fast. They wouldn't let me go get him.

INT: Oscar, your dog.

RES: Yes.

INT: The...the police report never mentions seeing a dog in the house... I'm sorry, [redacted]. He must have been startled. Maybe he escaped out of the back door...

RES: That fucking hole in the fence.

INT: Or that hole in the fence. What did they do with you when you went to the hospital?

RES: They handcuffed me.

INT: Do you understand why they handcuffed you?

RES: Yes. Now I know. When it was happening, I didn't care. I, um, I guess I just accepted it.

INT: You accepted it... Okay. I understand. Now can you—

RES: Why did he do it?

INT: You're asking why did [redacted] enter your house at night and commit homicide?

RES: Yes.

INT: ... I'm not sure I can answer that.

RES: Please. I need to know. I need to know why…

INT: [inaudible]…if I had to guess, I would assume he'd planned to kill your husband.

RES: And [redacted]?

INT: … I believe your daughter came downstairs first. I believe [redacted] thought she was your husband.

RES: It's my fault.

INT: What's your fault?

RES: All of it.

INT: [redacted], it wasn't your fault. You may be guilty of some things, but you are innocent in the deaths of your husband and your daughter.

RES: I'm not innocent. I allowed that man into my life. Into their lives…

INT: Well, I don't think you're going to prison, let alone stand trial, if you want to know my professional opinion.

RES: Why not?

INT: Well… [inaudible] you were acting in self-defense. That is my opinion.

RES: But… I—[inaudible]

[01:18:52]

INT: [inaudible] yes. You were. Listen, your husband was a great man. I know he will be sorely, sorely missed. He was...very much loved. But between you and me, you aren't guilty of this. [redacted] is. Maybe even the police. They let a man like that work on the force for years. They gave him that gun. They ignored his past experience with his ex-wife, his violence toward her. They may be just as guilty. But you are innocent, do you hear me? You didn't do things how they should be done, but you did not kill your family. Okay?

RES: ... Okay.

INT: Now, um, is there anything else you want to say? We've gone over our allotted time.

RES: Please just know I'm—I'm sorry.

INT: ... This is [redacted]. The time is now 0-5-2-4—p.m. This concludes my first session with [redacted].

[01:20:45]

44

I'd been seeing Dr. Madeline Pine for a year when I decided to become her.

I'll admit it. I'll admit everything, right now, just as Violet had done with me.

Friday the sixteenth. The roads were icy. I drove to her office, my car skidding around each turn, tires bald, useless.

No. Back up. Rewind.

It had taken a year, but finally, *finally*, I was getting well. The loss of my family had devastated me to the point where I hardly even knew the woman looking back at me in the mirror. But she had tried to build me back up. After the investigation was closed, Dr. Pine stayed with me. Helped me. And I had told her everything. *Everything.* Every minute, embarrassing little detail of the life the three of us had shared together. Every tear, every smile. Because she said it would help me *heal*. It would help my mind *forgive* itself. Make me *whole again*.

I'd sat across from her, across from Dr. Madeline Pine, week after week. For one year. And that day, I realized something I'd never thought of before. My eyes glazed over as she spoke, faded out across her face, blending together in a haze with her pink silk shirt.

And I thought: we're the same, she and I. We could be sisters. She's the million-dollar version of me. We had the same face shape—oval with a rounded chin and rounded eyes. Same shade of brown hair and brown eyes. Only she dazzled. She was dazzling. Beloved by her husband, her daughter. And it showed.

If the last year had never happened, if my marriage was stable, if my daughter never hated me, then, *maybe*, I might possibly look as glowing as the woman opposite me. She had no dark circles blooming beneath her eyes. No bloat aching around her belly. She wasn't alone, day after day, night after night. Standing in the same kitchen where her family had been killed, staring at the spot on the floor where her daughter's blood had soaked the linoleum, thick, black, a lake.

No.

But still, I wasn't jealous. Even though she was condescending, I didn't hate her. I didn't even dislike her. I admired her. She had a family. A loving husband. A beautiful daughter around Izzi's age. She was everything I wanted to be again. And I loved her, in a way.

So at first, I wasn't sure I'd heard her correctly.

I snapped out of my daydream, her pink silk shirt coming back into focus. I blinked, moistened my eyes, gone dry as I'd spaced out across her beautiful face.

"What?" I'd asked.

Madeline's shoulders tensed, ever so slightly, as if someone had poured a glass of cold water down her back.

"What did you say?" I repeated, and in my head, I begged—
Please say you misspoke, please say you misspoke.

She cleared her throat, stood, fled the room, never speaking a word.

The door clicked shut behind her.

Alone, at first, I didn't know what to do. Should I go? Was she coming back? Did I do something wrong?

No, I did nothing wrong.

Did I really hear what I thought I'd heard?

Yes—you did.

I replay the conversation inside my head as I watch my dark hair float beneath the bathwater like seaweed.

Madeline: Try to imagine your regret as a fish, Anabel. And I'd like you to really focus here, okay? Let's walk through this exercise together.

Me: Okay.

Madeline: Think of your regret as a fish. You try to hold it tight in your hand. You hold it, yet the fish does what?

Me: It wiggles.

Madeline: It wiggles. And no matter how hard you squeeze the fish, it wants to escape, it wants to be in the water. Your regret is the fish. Let it free. Let it return to the water. It doesn't belong in your hand. It doesn't wish to be on land. Now imagine the fish returning to the water. Focus on pushing away the regret, focus on all of your regret disappearing into the water.

Me: I don't know if I can.

Madeline: You can. Focus. Let's take things step by step. Your greatest regret is what?

Me: My daughter hating me—her dying hating me.

Madeline: Your regret stems from your belief Izzi died hating you. That she took her hatred of you to her grave.

Me: Yes.

Madeline: But she kept your secret. She wouldn't have done so if she didn't love you.

Me: She felt if she told Dave about my affair it would only make him sicker. And she was probably right. She always was.

Madeline: And you believe because your daughter harbored this secret, that is why she became depressed.

Me: Yes.

Madeline: You know, I tried to help her.

Me: What?

Madeline: Dave asked me. He thought I could help—

She stopped herself then. Cut herself off.

Me: What did you say?

She didn't have to say anything.

She already knew.

And I knew.

On the worst days, I'd let myself imagine. Imagine what I'd do if I ever came face-to-face with the woman having an affair with my husband. I'd ask her why. I'd ask if she knew he was married, positive the answer would irrevocably be *yes*.

I'd ask her for her forgiveness.

Because for the past year, I blamed her. I blamed her for my marriage falling apart. For my daughter's eventual hatred of me. For the confusion and anger she had felt at the end of her life. But most of all, I blame her for their deaths. Yes, I blame *Him*. For coming into our home and murdering my family. But I blame her, too.

Without her, I never would have cheated. I never would've brought *Him* into our lives. If I never knew Dave was cheating on me, I never would've cheated back, tried to get revenge on him, my naive, silly, disastrous revenge. Because of her existence, they don't have one.

Because of her, my family is dead.

Yes, I'd ask for her forgiveness.

Because I knew what would happen if I met her. If I ever got the chance.

It would not end well.

A million thoughts sped through my mind as I sat, alone, in Dr. Madeline Pine's wretchedly hot office, beads of sweat collecting at the back of my neck.

Then, finally, the door clicked open.

I turned, saw her standing behind me.

The moment our eyes met, Madeline's tiny office shrunk even smaller. I couldn't stop it, even if I wanted to. It was too big, bigger than me, bigger than all of us.

And it felt like destiny.

45

Madeline swayed in the doorway as she looked at me. Her expression softened, an attempt to placate me, a method she'd deployed all too often in our early sessions, when I was ripe with rage and bitter with hate. Maybe nothing had changed.

It felt like an hour had passed as we stared at one another, but in reality, it couldn't have been longer than a heartbeat. And then, finally, she spoke.

"Please, Anabel, try to understand," Madeline whispered. "I came to you that horrible day because *I* wanted to be the person to question you. All I've *ever* wanted was to help you and Izzi and...Dave."

"Don't—"

"I—I only met him by chance, when I needed an attorney. He was the only one who helped me. You have to understand... *I* lost him, too." Her voice shriveled away until nothing but a gasp escaped her lips.

And then—

Silence.

At first, I was unsure how this was even possible. But then I thought. I thought about how every time her name ruptured through our home Dave looked so...happy. Not Madeline.

But *Lynn*.

Not even her full name. No. That was how close they must've been. *Dave*. And *Lynn*. And my husband would smile. A wide grin stretching open across his freshly shaven face.

He and *Lynn*, his "client," going to lunch together.

Meeting for coffee.

Staying late at the office for a meeting.

Going bike riding together.

Only to build a rapport.

I should've known right then. Dave hated riding bikes.

I guess that was all a lie, too.

Madeline had known *exactly* who I was, all that time. For an entire year, she knew. I think that was what sent me over the edge. The fact that she knew—*everything*—for an entire year.

And said nothing.

I stepped closer. She held out an unsteady hand in the air between us, slowly backed away. She knew. Right then, she knew.

"Don't say anything you'll regret, Anabel," Madeline breathed. "Stop. Think. Don't you wonder why you never went to prison? Why you never even went to *trial*?" she said, voice cutting, sharp. "We both know what you did in that kitchen. I can go back to the judge like *that*," she said, snapping her fingers. "Just remember—there is no statute of limitations for murder."

Still, I stepped closer. And I whispered, "I know."

I lunged. Grabbed her. Her head fell back, fell hard. I felt her neck crack in my palms. One minute and it was over. And I felt nothing. No rush of relief. No release of pent-up rage.

I dropped her body to the floor. Her skull connected with a glass coffee table. It shattered instantly, hurling tiny shards throughout the room. Blood expanded beneath her head, thick and red, as her eyes flickered, confused.

I sat in her armchair until her body stilled. I thought and I thought. And when I stood, I saw her giant tote bag resting behind her desk, on her expensive executive chair. And my decision was formed.

I just had to escape.

Who would've thought she'd kept everything in that giant tote bag? Her wallet, phone, files. Everything. I grabbed the handles, fled the office. When I was driving home, her phone rang. I pulled over on the side of the road.

It was Matt.

I was always afraid of being alone. And for the past year, alone was all I was. Me and my memories. Slowly, they were killing me. And I was tired of it. I wanted to escape. I wanted to escape what life had become for me.

I wanted to stop being Anabel Strum.

I wasn't sure I could do it. But it worked. At least, it worked most of the time. Besides, what did Dr. Madeline Pine have that I didn't have? What had my husband seen in her that *I* couldn't also possess?

I'd studied her, how she sat with her notepad and pen. How she tilted her head and listened and prompted me with mundane follow-up questions that she probably used on every one of her patients.

I'd never be perfect, like she was. But I tried. Like hell, I tried.

Plus, I'd read Madeline's book, *Dark Side: A Psychological Portrait of the Criminal Female Mind*, a hundred times. She is—

was—a criminal psychiatrist. Her specialty was interviewing and evaluating female killers.

And I was a killer, long before that day.

I was a killer the moment I took *His* life. But that's the past. I don't want to think about him, anymore. I should focus on good things now, positive things. I'd saved Alice's life. In the end, I think that's an accomplishment. I couldn't save my daughter—but I'd saved someone else's daughter, so maybe it can almost be like Izzi didn't really die, right?

Fireworks snap in the distance outside my bathroom window, lighting up the glass in flashes of red and gold. For a heartbeat, I wonder if they're sirens. And it would be okay.

I'd promised myself I'd give the police until New Year's Eve. If they'd found out what I'd done, well, that would be fine. If they didn't, that would be fine, too. I'd accepted things, either way, a long time ago. All I want now is to be with my family.

I sink deeper into the tub, water kissing my cheeks. Holding my breath, I shut my eyes, slip under the water. And hold on to the image of Izzi laughing in the kitchen, the sun shining in her hair.

★ ★ ★ ★ ★

Acknowledgments

There aren't enough thank-yous in the entire world for my amazing literary agent, Melissa Danaczko, and the team at Stuart Krichevsky. Thank you for your (literally endless) patience and all of the hard work and wisdom you've poured into these pages. This book wouldn't exist without you.

To my wonderful editor, Dina Davis, who deserves the world's most enormous thank-you for taking a chance on me. You are a genius and a superstar all rolled into one. Thank you for all of the invaluable advice and immense talent you've put into this book. It's better because of you.

Thank you so much to the entire team at MIRA and HarperCollins: Nancy Fischer for your keen eye; Ana Luxton for loving this book from the start; Nicole Brebner; Leah Morse; Evan Yeong; Tamara Shifman; Gina Macdonald; Ashley MacDonald; Puja Lad; Randy Chan; Pamela Osti; Lindsey Reeder; Brianna Wodabek; Riffat Ali;

Hodan Ismail; and Ciara Loader. A big thank-you to Erin Craig, Sean Kapitain, and Denise Thomson for your brilliant cover design. Thank you to Reka Rubin, Christine Tsai, Nora Rawn, Whitney Bruno, Loriana Sacilotto, Amy Jones, Margaret Marbury, and Heather Connor. And last but certainly not least, Katie-Lynn Golakovich, Janet Chow, Heather Foy, Colleen Simpson, and Prerna Singh. Thank you to Xe Sands for lending your amazing voice to narrate the audiobook. Also thank you to anyone else I may have missed who has helped along the way. I'm beyond grateful for your hard work and for every second of your time you have spent working to bring this book into existence.

I've been beyond fortunate to have some of the most thoughtful, admirable, and talented women read this book and write some delicious, honest, beautiful early reviews and blurbs, and to you, I owe so much. A massive bottom-of-my-heart thank-you to Amanda Jayatissa, Ashley Winstead, Hannah Mary McKinnon, Amber Garza, Hank Phillippi Ryan, and Halley Sutton. I am so proud and honored you offered your time to give the most precious gift a debut author can receive.

Thank you to my TV/film agent, Orly Greenberg, for taking the time to read—I love your passion and am so fortunate to have you on my side as a champion for this book.

Thank you to my little buddy, Henry, for always wanting to sit by my feet and for being my fluffy partner in crime while I wrote this book. I owe you a thousand good-boy cookies.

Thank you, Mom, for doing it all on your own. I think we turned out okay-ish. For my big sister, whose thriller addiction rubbed off on me when I was a kid. For my big brother, who always made me laugh and has the best taste in movies.

Thank you to my husband, who's been on this journey with me from the start. Thank you for always being there, for never saying I couldn't, and for always being positive when I wasn't. For knowing how my brain works and still sleeping next to me in the dark. Here's to many more late-night conversations beginning with "So...you wanna hear my new idea?"

And while he has this book's dedication, I still have to thank Graham for being the reason why I keep going. You'll grow up surrounded by books, and the very thought brings tears to my eyes. I love you beyond a million words can say. As I write this, you're being rocked to sleep by Daddy, bottle empty at your side. When this book is published, you'll be a toddler. Time will go by so fast, but I'm trying my best to enjoy every second of you.

And thank *you*, reader, for reading even this sentence. You're amazing.